Grave Dealings

A Case File From:
The Grave Report

R.R. Virdi

Grave Dealings
A Case File From: The Grave Report
R.R. Virdi

Dedication

To Tribe, for always having my back and helping me overcome the hardest things in life.

Acknowledgements

Thank you to my wonderful editing team: Michelle Dunbar, Cayleigh Stickler, and Aaron Fernandez. You all really helped shape this novel up. Much love and thanks to Abby for the final polish on this.

Also by R.R. Virdi

<u>The Grave Report</u>

GRAVE BEGINNINGS

GRAVE MEASURES

<u>The Books Of Winter</u>

DANGEROUS WAYS

<u>Short Stories</u>

"CHANCE FORTUNES"—THE LONGEST NIGHT
WATCH ANTHOLOGY

"A BAG FULL OF STARS"—ALWAYS STARDUST
ANTHOLOGY

"CHANCE DEALINGS" & "CHEATERS AND
FORTUNES" "—THE LONGEST NIGHT WATCH
ANTHOLOGY, VOL. 2

What reviewers are saying about The Grave Report:

"I believe R.R. Virdi belongs with other Urban Fantasy greats like Jim Butcher. The Grave Report is sure to go far and only pick up more fans with each successful novel. I can't wait to see where R.R. Virdi will take us next."
—A Drop Of Ink Reviews

"Fast paced, humorous, with action and drama on every page and paragraph, this paranormal thriller is reminiscent of one of my all-time favorite authors. This is like Jim Butcher's The Dresden Files but with a flavor all its own. RR Virdi is fame-bound with this series. If you like Jim Butcher, you'll enjoy this one. Highly Recommend."
—CD Coffelt—Author of The Wilder Mage

"A fast paced story with great characters, I loved the story and fell even more in love with the future possibilities… Virdi maintains both the suspense of the case at hand, and the character's past and current transformation, making us feel both for the victim and the investigator. He excels at action scenes - I have rarely read books with such well-described yet fluid action scenes."—Shadow and Clay Reviews

Chapter One

Waking up in someone else's dead body isn't for chumps.

I exhaled water. Bubbles formed in front of me, and the world blurred like my eyes were smeared with dark jelly. My heart beat a drum solo. It took me a moment to realize what was happening. Panic set in, and I couldn't draw breath. I thrashed on instinct, but the binding around my wrists and ankles kept me from moving any direction but down.

Drowning sucks.

I shut my eyes and ignored my body's desperate urges. My lungs felt like balloons close to bursting, and a huff of air filtered out of my nostrils as the pressure in my chest built.

Thinking is hard when you're low on oxygen. My mind raced, dredging up any useful information from my prior cases. Clarity came seconds later followed by a solution. I needed to resituate my body.

My hands were bound behind my back, so I tucked my knees to my chest. Another plume of bubbles left my nostrils. My arms came under and upwards as I brought them in front of me. I cupped my hands together, facing them downwards. My legs kicked like pistons. My hands followed. The act propelled me up. It wasn't enough. I repeated the action.

A murky film of water swayed above me. It was like looking at plastic wrap splashed in motor oil. I pumped my legs and paddled like a dog. There was a moment of resistance as I reached the surface. The water fought to pull me under. I exhaled fully and kicked one last time.

I broke the surface. Air rushed to fill the vacuum in my lungs, but relief was short-lived. An invisible cord tugged around my waist and legs. I leaned back and took another breath. Staying afloat was easy. Finding and getting to shore was another matter.

I shut my eyes, giving thanks I'd once inhabited the body of a Navy Seal. Drownproofing came with the skill set I managed to retain in my memories. I shifted my torso and pulled with my shoulders. My body rolled. I opened my eyes and was rewarded with a pier hemmed in sapphire lights. A shore, more rock than sand, hugged its right.

Good enough for me.

I inhaled again before lowering my head. My body sank below the surface and I scrunched like an inchworm. The tugging returned, threatening to pull me below. I kicked behind me and undulated like a dolphin. Several yards had passed before I broke through the surface again. I repeated the process. My body rolled, and the water slipped below my back as I drifted.

The sky greeted me as an unmarred canvas of black. I didn't have time to stargaze. With another twist, I was back underwater. I undulated and swam as best as my predicament allowed. A fire built in my body and my muscles felt like they were lined with lead. I ignored it.

The depth decreased. I struggled to find balance as my feet skidded against a floor of loose sand. Wading through the shallow water was a chore with my ankles fastened together.

A flash of color at the edge of my vision prompted me to look up.

A young woman came to a stop twenty feet from the shoreline. She was a walking advertisement for a jogging catalog, from her athletic apparel to her appearance. Her eyes widened, and her mouth moved without words.

I doubled over, placing my palms on my knees. "Nice night for a swim."

She stared at my wrists.

"Oh, these?" I held up my hands. The silver tape took on an eerie blue tinge under the nearby pier lights. "It was a really kinky swim?"

Her head shook before she turned and ran off in the opposite direction.

"Oh, good. Now I can collapse in peace." I lowered myself to the rocky bed and rested my head on a large stone. It was nice.

I stared at the sky. If there were any stars, they were

drowned out by swatches of warm gold and cool silvery lights coming from the concrete monoliths behind the poor excuse of a beach. A laser-like red light blazed in the corner of my vision, and I turned to the source.

A neon sign looped over a section of the pier. I recognized it and smiled. New York had a heck of a way of welcoming me back. My smile slipped as I thought of my recent cases in the state.

Cases. Right, work. The train of thought galvanized me. Stones prodded and scraped against my clothes as I rolled over. A breeze wafted by. My muscles tightened and shuddered. I gave silent thanks for the agreeable temperature. Hypothermia isn't fun.

My fingers brushed over small rocks, and I hissed as my thumb trailed over a sharp edge. It was a task, fumbling with the rock and my quivering muscles, but I managed to get a grip on it. I thumbed the stone over and lined its edge against the bindings.

The thing with duct tape is the more you apply, the more it acts like a single piece. It's strong. It's also easier to break than several loose layers of the stuff. My shoulders strained as I pulled my hands away from each other. The tape resisted but stretched a bit. I pulled again. A breath of exertion left my lungs. Satisfied that I had stretched it as much as I could, I brought the sharp rock to it and filed. The tape's edge bowed and flitted away from the rock, but it refused to tear.

I released a string of obscenities and kept at it. A millimeter-long notch appeared on one side. It wasn't much to work with. I scored another incision on the side closest to my body. The edge cut deeper until it only served to bend and twist the tape rather than tear it. I discarded the rock and pulled my knees to my chest. My arms went around them, and I jerked my wrists towards my center. The tape impacted my knees, refusing to let my hands come any closer. The compromised bindings gave and tore free. I peeled the scraps from my skin, wincing as the adhesives pulled at me.

Freeing my legs was easier. I took the point of the rock and jabbed like a savage until the tape was peppered with holes. The stone cut through shredded restraints.

"Okay, that sucked." I rubbed the side of my head and shut my eyes. "Focus. Find a church. Find Church. Punch him in the nose." I nodded and pushed myself to my feet. Stone shifted beneath me as I stepped towards the sandy portion of the shore. The grains, coupled with my wet weight, didn't make things easy. I shambled towards the boardwalk, ignoring the odd stares from passersby. Water splotched and darkened the wooden planks beneath me. I debated stripping on the pier to wring out my clothes but pushed the idea from my mind.

Public stripping is frowned upon.

Instead, I put my hands to my chest and brushed my body. Feeling yourself up is slightly less offensive. I patted down my pants.

Nothing in my clothes.

I spat over a railing. "Shit." No clues to work with. His clothing wasn't much good. A simple shirt and jeans never are. The shoes were low-grade sneakers that seemed more for show than use. I leaned against the guardrail and sighed.

All I had to work with was that he had drowned. I ruled out aquatic monsters. He wasn't out for a routine swim. Not at night. Not with his limbs bound. Something brought him to the water. Pressure built simultaneously within my chest and skull. I concentrated the feeling in the base of my fist as I slammed my hand against the railing.

I turned and marched towards the street. Unseen fingers trailed against the back of my neck. The skin around my shoulders prickled like waves of static coursed over them. People get an odd sensation when they're being watched. You just know. And there's an art to spotting who's got their eye on you.

My pace quickened. I crossed the street and homed in on a path that ran between a pair of buildings. It was narrow and out of sight. A good start. My brisk walk turned into a light jog, and I cut through another street.

A car horn sounded, followed by colorful profanity. If I had the time to stop, I would've given him a one-finger salute for his creativity.

Old brick walls surrounded me as I slipped into the alley. The buildings on either side had definitely seen better days. Much of the masonry was pitted, with the occasional fist-sized chunk missing. My pace slowed and I winced. A second later, I released a raucous noise, more through my nose than my mouth. I looked over my shoulder through the feigned sneeze.

It wasn't the subtlest thing.

A single figure stood out. He waited at the end of the last street I had crossed before making my way into the alley. The lonesome figure was the walking embodiment of a motorcycle fetish with an armored black jacket and matching gloves. I wish the hardened apparel ended there.

For whatever reason, he decided to keep the dark helmet on. Most people would feel it was a stretch to assume someone in a helmet was staring at them. It's not that much of a leap when the street was empty save for us. I picked up my pace and headed for the corner.

I rounded it, coming into a parking lot with enough room for a dozen cars. One of those weak, sheet metal garage doors filled most of the wall to my right. I flattened myself against the wall and waited.

Seconds passed.

Nothing.

I was tempted to chalk it up to paranoia. But in my world, paranoia is a survival trait.

The sound of boots on concrete filled my ears. A thin smile spread across my lips. Graves wins again. Although I wished I were wrong. My muscles felt like quivering strings waiting to go taut.

An armored glove broke past the corner. I surged forwards, grabbing him by the collar. The surprise and my momentum made it easy to drive him into the opposite wall. There was a plastic crack from the back of his helmet as it ricocheted off the brick.

"Why are you following me?" My fists balled around the collar of his coat.

There was no sluggishness in his movements. He was completely unfazed after having his noggin thrust against a wall. His hands blurred faster than I could keep up with. With a series of quick, coordinated movements, he broke my grip and seized the front of my shirt. The material squelched, releasing a spurt of water on his clothing.

I gave him a weak smile. "You're not here for the wet t-shirt contest, are you?" I gave the shirt a gentle tug. "I think I win." My smile slipped as he pivoted, putting his hips against mine. The world looked like I was on an amusement park ride. It tilted sideways and inverted. The helmeted freak grew farther away as I sailed through the air.

My ride was cut short by Newton's law. The opposite force came in the way of groaning metal. The broad of my back felt like I'd volunteered to be a piñata. The flimsy garage door warped behind me. My shoulders took most of the impact as I crumbled to the ground.

Fuck you, Newton.

The assailant was atop me in a second. I shifted my body, scissored my legs around his, and twisted sharply. He wobbled and I pulled my legs towards me to upset his balance. The asshole crashed into the damaged door. I used the momentary lull to scramble to my feet.

He was faster on the recovery, snapping out with the back of his fist. The blow caught me on the underside of my chin. My vision flared and everything seesawed. One of these days I'm going to learn to stay down.

"Do I owe you money?"

His fist lashed out against a section of nearby brick, which shattered like it was cheap clay.

I blinked. At least I knew I wasn't dealing with a vanilla mortal. Having my ass kicked might as well have been an enlightening experience. I arched a brow and took a cautionary step back. "You got a name, pal?"

He snarled.

"How do you spell that?"

My mystery attacker hunched, bringing his arms in tight. Great, he knew how to keep his body protected. This wasn't his first rodeo.

It wasn't mine either.

I turned to my side, narrowing my profile. "Bring it, asshole!"

He did. Helmet Head closed the distance between us in a fraction of a second. His shoulder turned towards me, and I knew what would follow. A fist arced towards the center of my face.

I stepped towards him and threw an arm over his collar. My fingers dug into the leather jacket as his blow missed.

With my free hand, I clenched his belt line. All it took was a sharp twist of my torso and a bit of effort. His feet left the ground, and I took him down. I landed atop him, working to straddle his arms. The leverage of my position was an added boon, and I used it.

My palm crashed into his visor. Plastic vibrated and flexed, but remained intact. The second strike sent a series of hairline cracks running through a corner. I followed up with a third blow. The visor shattered. My fingers hooked around the opening, and I wrenched. The helmet slipped off. I understood why he had chosen to keep it on.

The freak squirmed beneath me and bared his teeth. Four fangs stood out. Shoulder-length hair spilled onto the concrete. The locks were strands of polished pearls caught in the nearby flickering streetlight, seeming to glow. A Night Runner. Ashen Elves.

The bastard younger brothers of the Svartals, a race of dark elves.

My hand slid against the side of his face, past his tapered ears. I seized a fistful of his hair and pulled.

The elf's citrine eyes narrowed. Heat built within them.

I grabbed him with my other hand and hauled him up. "Why are you following me?"

"Stay out of affairs that don't concern you." He bared his fangs at me.

"You followed me." I released my hold and snapped a fist towards his face. His lips folded back against his teeth and split. Blood welled at the edge of his mouth. It took on an odd sheen atop his ashen gray skin. "Give me a straight answer." I twisted and used my position to drive a second blow to his skull. My fist tightened for a third strike when the elf pulled away from me.

His knees rocketed into my back. He shimmied until he was free of my pin. The Night Runner's knees pulled back to his chest. They fired like pistons, driving his heels into my chest.

The world rolled and my eyes followed suit. They fixed on the sight of concrete. I got a better look at it than I wanted a second later. It felt like I'd taken a sledgehammer to my torso and skull. I shook my head and placed my palms on the ground. The world teetered as I got to my feet.

"Round...whatever we're on?"

The Night Runner cocked his head to the side.

I scowled. "Just come here so I can kick your ass."

He smirked. "Is that what is happening?"

Wise ass.

"Can you, for one second, not be a total tool and give me a straight answer?"

He blinked and looked away for a second. "I was sent to warn you not to become embroiled in your mistress's entanglements."

"Whoziwhat? Mistress?" I held up my hands in a gesture of placation. "Look, I think you've got the wrong guy. Hell, so do I. I'm just borrowing this body for a while. A short while, I hope. I don't have a mistress, I think?"

He spat and looked at me like I was an idiot. "You are a fool."

Way to make it personal. "Yeah? And you're a dick-bottle."

His face lost all expression. It took him several moments to recover. "Relinquish your position as her emissary, and you will live."

I didn't know how to respond to that. It's hard when you have no clue what the freak is referring to. "Yeah, sure. Now beat it before I beat you."

His lips spread into a thin smile.

Uh oh.

He blurred into motion faster than before.

I hunched close and threw a blind punch, hoping to connect.

His shoulder buried itself in my gut. He didn't slow his momentum and drove me back.

Metal crunched. So did I, leaving a Vincent Graves-sized indent in the garage door. It was taking "making an impact" to a literal level.

The elf pulled himself away and dusted his hands. "Stay out of the matter. Next time I won't go so easy on you, and it won't just be a warning." He turned and raced out of sight.

I pressed a hand to my chest. A series of coughs racked my body. "Good...talk." My head thunked against the door, and I shut my eyes. "And I just got this body. Church is going to be ticked." My rest could wait. I had a case to start.

It felt like firecrackers went off inside my chest and back as I got to my feet. I pushed the strange encounter from my mind. It was a problem for another time. I shoved my hands into my pockets and left the alley. Finding the nearest place of worship wouldn't take long.

The static buzz over my neck and shoulders returned. Someone was watching me—still. I cast a glance over my shoulder but saw nothing. I ruled the Night Runner out. He had made his point—painfully. I guess I had attracted another party's interest.

This was going to be a long walk.

Chapter Two

Moving through the streets of Queens isn't difficult on its own, but when you're forced to rubberneck and take odd paths, it adds up. I veered down an ill-maintained sidewalk. The cracked concrete looked like a dumping ground for adolescent trash. Torn pages from adult magazines and fast food wrappers whisked down the street with the breeze.

Nobody followed me, but the feeling I was being stalked lingered, refusing to let go.

Whoever was trailing me was good.

I sped up and rounded the corner, doubling my pace until it became a jog. A cathedral came into view. It was a simple thing of brick, capped with a white tower. Much of the color had faded with age and the elements. I paused at the double doors and glanced over my shoulder one last time.

Nothing.

The pressure in my jaw built as my teeth ground. I cupped a hand to the side of my face. "You suck salty moose wang!"

There was no reply.

Figures.

I scowled and pushed my way inside. The interior was the opposite of its outside. Beautifully crafted pews of dark cherry filled the floor. Columns of white wrapped with intricate filigrees of brass. The ceiling was painted to resemble a velvet sky strung with stars. It could've been pulled from a night in the African savannah.

I moved towards the front, keeping my eyes open for anyone else. The place seemed deserted. I whistled. "Candygram for blonde and geekily handsome!"

Someone cleared their throat, prompting me to turn.

He sat several pews back with his legs crossed. The man was a dead ringer of what I'd called out for. Church's looks were the definition of geek chic. He eyed me and arched a brow.

"Uh, I woke up underwater—with my hands tied, by the way. Thanks for that."

"I don't choose the circumstances, Vincent. You know this."

"I have the feeling you have a lot more control than you're letting on, Blondilocks." I eyed him hard.

He sighed and pulled his designer glasses from his face. The dark frames stood out against his wavy, shoulder-length hair. Church pulled a cloth from his pocket and polished the lens without taking his eyes off me. It was like gazing into frozen azure waters. A heck of a stare.

I fought not to blink.

The edges of his mouth quirked like he was fighting not to smile. "Have you changed your mind about punching me?"

I blinked. "The feeling's coming back." My fingers dug into my palm as my fist tightened.

Church took note and eyed me. "Violence isn't always the answer."

I snorted. "Tell that to the freak who jumped me on my way over here."

He thumbed shut the journal on his lap and clasped his hands over it. "I'm not surprised."

"Really? I am. I just got this meat suit." I hooked a thumb to my chest. "How am I already pissing people off?"

Church folded his lips and stood. "Vincent, I am always surprised by your ability to irritate others. In that regard, you have no equal. I'm sure you found a way." His eyes shone with amusement.

"Thanks. I'll take that as a compliment."

"Please don't. I'm not trying to encourage you."

I rubbed the back of my neck and looked past Church. Two journals sat on the pew; a rich burgundy atop a saddle brown. They belonged to me. One helped me keep my memories straight between all the body bouncing I do. The other was a compendium of every bit of mythological lore I'd come across over my cases. It was the only real tool I had. I nodded at them.

Church inclined his head and fetched both. He

presented them to me like they were a gift. "Wait here." He moved towards the altar.

"Um, okay." I stood rooted to the spot and blinked. That was new.

Church vanished from sight and returned just as quickly. He carried a set of folded clothing atop his hands.

"Aw, shucks, you shouldn't have. I'm only drenched." I placed my journals on a nearby pew.

He raised a brow. "Technically, you are damp. Most of the water dried during your trek here." Church placed the clothing on a pew next to me.

I scowled and snatched up what looked like a perfect replica of the clothes I wore. Well, they were dry at least. I hooked my index finger within the collar of my shirt and pulled. Fabric stretched. Strings tore the next second sending buttons bouncing onto the floor. I tossed the shirt aside with a callous flick of my wrist. My pants fell to my feet after I kicked off my shoes.

Church's eyes went wide, and he turned away. "Vincent, I don't think it's wholly appropriate to strip in a place..." He gestured to our surroundings.

I waved a dismissive hand. "Whatever. It's not my body. Don't suppose you can tell me what killed this stiff and save me some time?"

Church's back was fully to me now. "You know I can't."

I pulled off the guy's briefs and slipped into the new clothes mechanically. My muscles loosened in response to the first touch of the shirt around my chest. It was like it had come out of the dryer. The pants were the same. "Toasty. Thanks."

"Of course." Church tilted his head.

"You can look, dude. I'm dressed enough." I pulled on the socks and slid into the replacement sneakers.

He turned and faced me. "You have questions on your mind."

"Yeah, I do. I've got a feelin' you know what I'm going to ask."

Church nodded. "Ask anyway."

"I'll ask the ones that matter, how's that? I know how you'll answer the others."

He gave me a paper-thin smile.

"How is Lizzie?"

"She is doing well in the care of her grandmother. Elizabeth still thinks about you, Vincent. You had quite the effect on her."

I shrugged.

"You saved her and her sister. She's at home with someone who cares about her because of you."

I grinned. It was good to hear. Lizzie was a little girl I'd met on one of my cases. Pretty normal, except for the fact she had the peculiar ability to see and speak to ghosts. Kids, right? They're weird.

Church cleared his throat. "That's not the only question on your mind."

I shook my head. My throat seemed too tight, refusing to let me voice my question. "How's Ortiz?"

He brushed a lock of hair away from his eyes.

"Church?"

He remained silent and looked away.

"How's Ortiz?" My heart felt like I'd gone another round with the Night Runner.

"I can't answer that." His voice sounded like he had swallowed a handful of sawdust. I could hear the desire mixed in with restraint. He wanted to tell me.

I arched a brow. "Let me guess: These weird rules—the ones you can't tell me about—are keeping you from answering?"

He nodded.

"Your boss is an ass, no offense."

Church blinked, and his face twisted like he was caught between wanting to laugh and remaining poised. "Vincent"—his lips twitched—"I don't think you can say that and mean it without offense."

I smiled.

He held out his hand. "We've spent enough time talking. You have work to do."

I sighed. "Thanks, Mom." I pulled on the cuff of my shirt, rolling the sleeve back to my elbow.

Church grabbed my forearm. The man had a hydraulic grip. Heat radiated over the inner part of my arm and intensified. It felt like I had touched my skin to a stove.

I shut my eyes. My teeth slid over each other as I grimaced through the pain. It went quickly. "Ow."

Church removed his hand.

There was a patch of reddened skin. A black number fifty-seven sat in the middle. The magical tattoo would decrease in number by the hour until I found the thing responsible for murdering the previous owner of the body I inhabited. I glanced at it, then Church. "Feeling generous?"

"You'll need the time." He paused, and his mouth pulled to one corner. "And luck."

The desire to bury my fist in his face returned. But I'm a mature adult. I reined it in and gave him the finger.

He sighed.

I gave him a look. "Don't suppose you could give me something to go on here? Not even a teensy clue?"

Silence.

"Give me something work with, Church."

"I did." He pointed to the journals, then my tattoo. "And time is passing."

I bent at my waist and looked down as I recovered my journals. "Fine." When I looked up, Church had vanished. I exhaled through my nose. "Yeah, you're a regular Harry Blackstone, congrats." The smaller burgundy journal slipped from atop the stack. Its corner struck my palm as I fumbled for it. The collection of memories hit the ground at an angle. A plastic card slipped out.

I bent and scooped up the journal and card. A picture of a man that could have been used on a Korean travel brochure stared back at me. Cognac eyes and tousled black hair with a hint of a tan. Good lookin' guy. I smiled at the driver's license and held it towards the ceiling. "Smartass." I had a feeling Church heard me wherever he was. The man always seemed to know.

I tucked the journals under an arm and turned my attention to the piece of plastic. My index finger bounced off the card as my fingernail struck the section with his information. I burned the name and address into the back of my mind. "Let's go find out who you really are, Mr. Kim. And...what the hell offed you."

Chapter Three

The walk to Daniel Kim's apartment complex took longer than I'd have liked. I had taken the longest route I could. I couldn't shake the feeling that my unseen tail nipped at my heels the entire trip. It felt like a pair of screws had drilled their way through the back of my skull. Whoever was keeping tabs on me was good, and annoying. Their presence had cost me.

I'd lost an hour. Fifty-six left.

The apartment complex was unremarkable. Three stories of brick with windows trimmed in white paneling. Sturdy and, by the looks of things, affordable. I walked up three concrete steps and stopped at the door. The glass was clean enough to offer me a hint of a reflection. It wasn't much, but with the street lamps behind me, it gave me a decent view over my shoulder.

Nobody sensible would roam the streets this time of night. The only thing that passed by was a 90s sedan with dimmed headlights that barely illuminated ten feet before it. Still, the unshakable feeling someone was watching didn't subside.

Dull pressure radiated around my gums as my teeth ground. My fingers dug into the meat of my palm. I balled my fist tighter before releasing the tension. A series of gentle breaths through my nose and I was calm. I raised a fist over my head, hoping my stalker would see it. A smile spread across my face as I extended a single finger.

They got the message.

I pulled the door open and stepped inside. The white tile was in serious need of polishing. I crossed over to the carpeted staircase and stopped. A burgundy plaque, with tenant names and apartment numbers, hung on the wall. My finger trailed across the list horizontally until I found what I was looking for. I stayed an extra minute to commit the names of his neighbors to memory. It's hard working a case when you're stumbling over who's who.

Nodding to myself, I grabbed the railing and hurtled up the stairs to the second floor. I passed doors the color of rustic oak as I searched for Daniel's apartment. I found it halfway down the hall. My lips folded under my teeth as a realization hit me.

"Urfle, murfle, gruhl." The base of my fist ricocheted off the wooden door. It vibrated where I had struck it. It did little good to open it. I nursed the temptation to drive my heel into the spot just above the doorknob. If I did it right, I could force the sucker open. I resisted the urge. It didn't seem like a good idea starting off my case by damaging the victim's home and pissing off the building's superintendent.

A click sounded behind me. I turned to the source. The door opposite pulled back, and a young, dark-skinned male blinked at me, then at the door.

"Locked out, Daniel?" He scratched the side of his head and offered me a lopsided smile.

I growled.

The scrawny kid recoiled. He looked like he was in his mid-twenties and the definition of an information technology geek. The guy had a shaved head, and his rectangular glasses sat askew on the bridge of his nose. The only thing he had going for him was his height, standing a little over six feet.

I raised a hand as a way of apology. "Yeah, sorry, rough night."

He looked me over and nodded. "Sounds like it if you're coming in this late. Working overtime at the gallery?" He arched a brow.

I nodded. It was a nice bit of information I wouldn't need to fish for, and it made sense. Long Island City was home to a fair bunch of artists. I didn't know how it was useful, yet. At least I had another stop after I checked out his place. As soon as I figured out how to get into it. I let one of my hands rest on the knob.

A disorienting wave rolled through my brain. It was like syrup crashed down and congealed within my skull.

Daniel's foot bounced off the door and he swore. He jostled the knob in frustration. His hands burrowed into his pockets, fishing for a key he didn't have. He placed his back against the door and crossed his legs. The man shut his eyes and thought for a moment.

The vision snapped out of clarity only to be replaced by another. I watched Daniel cross over the concrete roof to an ill-maintained looking ventilation system. His fingers closed around the poorly fastened grate, and he pried it loose. Daniel ran a hand over the side. Something rippled against his fingertips and clung to the skin. It felt like tape. One of his fingers came across a sliver of metal that was cool to the touch. He closed his hand around it and pulled.

The memory faded, and I blinked several times as I readjusted.

My neighbor eyed me sideways. "You...okay, Daniel? You look like you've had a four-oh-four error in your head."

I blinked again.

"You know, error, broken page?"

I stared.

"Like your mind went blank—crashed."

"Oh." I nodded. "Yeah, sorry. I've got a lot on my mind."

He nodded to himself. "Fair enough. You want me to call the super and see if he can get you into your place?"

I shook my head. "No, thanks. I've got it. I know where I left my key." I took a step towards the stairs.

"Wait. You coming to movie night tomorrow, or, um, I guess tonight—shit. What time is it?"

I stopped. "Movie night?"

"Yeah, you know, at Ashton's place?" He pointed to a door several apartments down from mine. "The gang gets together, and we watch a movie...like the name suggests."

I bowed my head. "Sure, yeah, um, count me in."

He looked at me like I was strange then yawned. "Cool, cool."

"Sorry for waking you." I turned to move towards the staircase.

"No worries, was already up troubleshooting stuff for clients. Perks of the home IT gig."

I ignored him and raced forwards. My legs hammered over the stairs as I made my way to the roof. I flung open the door and rushed to the grate. My journals came to rest near the ventilation shaft as I placed them down. I closed my fingers around the edges like Daniel had, and pulled. The grate resisted. Rolling my shoulders, I placed my heels against on framework and leaned back. The metal pulled free. My hand slid against the inside.

The same coolness filled the tips of my fingers as I brushed the key. I gripped and wrenched it free. Ribbons of clear tape tagged along.

Daniel may have been absentminded if he needed a spare, but he was clever enough to hide it well. I pursed my lips and hoped he wasn't too clever. It could have been a contributing factor to his death.

I discarded the tape and stuffed the key into my pocket. The grate fought me as I tried to realign it on its brackets. I managed to get it to stay in place, albeit a bit crooked. A quick look around reassured me no one was nearby. My foot lashed out. Weak metal groaned as the grate warped and fell into alignment. It'd be a pain to remove in the future, but it wasn't like Daniel was going to use it again.

The thought sent a numbing cement through my gut that solidified behind my navel. It's something that never fails to get you. The idea that I'm running around in what used to be someone else's body. Someone who had a life, one taken by the paranormal. Like mine had been. All I could do was gank whatever killed them and offer that person some semblance of justice. Or vengeance.

My fingernails dug deep into my palm. The feeling pulled me from my train of thought. I recovered my journals and moved towards the door, shutting it without looking as I headed down the stairs.

I approached his door and unlocked it. My hand closed around the knob, and I took a breath before opening it. The muscles along my spine tensed.

Daniel's body may have ended up in the water, but when it comes to the paranormal, nothing is that simple.

I pushed the door open and surged inside. I expected a fight. Instead, I walked into what looked like the aftermath of one.

Daniel's apartment looked like he'd left his windows open during a tornado. A bleak, gray velour sofa lay on its back in the middle of the room. A cheap lamp sat next to it, the cord ripped from a nearby socket. Its shade lay flattened under a small stand. A variety of art-related books littered the place.

I let out a low whistle as I flung the door shut. The television was barely hanging on the wall from its mount; only one of the brackets remained intact at a corner. I stepped over various utensils, art supplies, and a broken laptop.

Something had definitely targeted Daniel here before deciding he needed to work on his breaststroke.

I moved around with caution, partly out of respect. As I stepped further inside, I shut my eyes and nearly pinched my nose shut. Someone had gone overboard with the pine freshener. It was thick enough to gag a person. I could almost taste it.

I pulled the shirt collar over my nose as I moved towards the open kitchen in the far corner. Nothing stood out enough to jog my knowledge of the paranormal. The disarray looked like a burglary gone wrong rather than anything involving a monster. I scanned the room one last time before moving on.

The small bathroom on the other side appeared untouched. Two doors remained. One ahead, and one to my right. Both were shut.

If anything was lurking around his place, those would be the last places for them to hide. Opening the wrong door would signal them and lead me into a world of trouble.

Everything you do leads to trouble. I frowned. It was true however.

I held my breath and placed a hand on the doorknob to my right. Please let room number one be free of nasties. In one swift movement, I turned the knob, leaned in with my shoulder and barreled through. I stopped as suddenly as I'd started. My arms went to my side, spinning like pinwheels to help keep me from tumbling over.

The room was fashioned into an artist's workspace. Supplies littered the floor in groupings that made no sense to me. An easel to the far right boasted an unfinished drawing done in charcoal pencil. Streetlights filtered through the window and cast an eerie amber glow over the work. My fingers trailed over the webbing of a short hammock strung across the left wall.

A closed portfolio, larger than any suitcase I'd ever seen, sat under the hammock. A simple table stood crammed against the far wall. Countless other supplies littered its surface, ranging from pencils to brushes and pastels. Despite the mess, the room seemed like nobody but Daniel had ransacked it.

I ignored the mess and approached the easel. The closer I looked at it, the stranger the image appeared. It was a disorienting blur of shapes. An unfinished man tightly held a woman of fierce beauty. Hair fell past her shoulders, and she had full lips. Like the man, the rest of her detail was lacking. A figure hung around the corner of a street that vaguely resembled the road outside. The stranger had a shock of frizzy, thick hair that stood out as the most prominent detail.

My eyes trailed over the piece, fixating on the image above the people. It dominated the remaining space. A pair of orbs—the only color on the canvas—contrasted the monochromatic work. Violent red anything is never a good sign. There was no face to frame what looked like eyes, and a series of lines spread out from them. They connected at the edges and littered the inside of the odd, jagged shapes on either end. It looked like spines and a membrane.

I blinked and bit my lip. I couldn't recall any creature with those traits. My heart sped up as I stepped closer. It was probably taboo, but I reached for the corner and tugged on the piece. It fought back, flexing and folding as I pulled on it. I gave it another yank, and the sound of tearing paper filled my ears. The drawing pad was blank underneath.

I flipped open the journal containing my collection of mythological lore and folded the piece of art into it. This likely wasn't the only piece of art on the pad. I followed the hunch and slipped an index finger under the paper folded over the top of the easel. With a simple flick, I sent the next work tumbling towards me.

"Well, damn." Something was clearly nipping at Daniel's heels before he passed. It was detailed work of something that looked like an old-fashioned drawing of a devil crossed with a bat. I blinked, not knowing what to make of it. The next page left me just as clueless. A work of all black streaked with gray lines. It looked like massive wings. A pair of white eyes hovered between them. It was a stylized piece, whatever it was.

Great, looks like Daniel was haunted by freakin' Batman.

"Third time's the charm." I reached out and flipped over the next sheet. Hideous was an understatement. The thing looked like a cross between a gibbon and a bat. A claw-like hand covered in fur reached out from the page to give the illusion it would grab me. I shook my head then paused. Something caught my eye within the work. There were lines—faint—within the monster.

Another face. One with a shock of thick, frizzy hair. I squinted and leaned closer, making out a speckle of dots on either side. The rest of drawing was difficult to make out.

None of this made any sense. I tore the other sheets free and stuffed them into my journal. I'd go over them later.

I backpedaled until I reached the door, turning and giving the room one last look. There wasn't anything else to take away from it. No one said my cases were easy. I sighed and shut the door. Only Daniel's bedroom remained.

I covered the distance in a couple of long strides. The door was cracked open just enough for me to slip my pinky into the space. I gave it a gentle push. Daniel's bedroom was a stark contrast to the rest of his home. Simple, orderly, and clean. Every mother's dream.

My eyes trailed over the room from left to right. The dresser and small television were coated in a thin layer of dust. More artwork dotted the walls. They were professional and held within slender, black frames. A warm heat, like fresh-out-of-the-laundry clothes, flared in my chest. Daniel favored those pieces. One caught my eye.

It was rough in comparison, but not bad by any means. A man and woman with their backs turned to the viewer. They held hands over what looked like the roof of Daniel's apartment. The scenery seemed a tad too fantastical, from the pink and vermilion-tinged sky, to the white clouds that seemed to carry a hint of turquoise. It was almost too colorful.

A lance of pain shot through my skull. A streak of light followed, and my vision blurred. Something tugged at my heart at seeing that piece, like it was strung with invisible weights threatening to pull it to the floor. The back of my throat dried. Whoever it belonged to must have been close to Daniel. I felt like I'd been hit by an emotional freight truck. I shook my head clear and separated Daniel's thoughts and feelings from my own.

Focusing on the case was my best bet to keep my borrowed head in check. I shut my eyes and inhaled. Something tickled my nostrils. I blinked and took a step back. The smell was of burnt oranges. I looked at the floor and a hint of Daniel's face stared back at me in reflection. It was some wood polish to give off that shine and odor. I cleared my throat and pushed the smell from my mind. My attention turned to the bed.

It was the only thing out of order. The sheets looked like he had suffered through one hell of a nightmare under them. I stepped closer and gravitated towards sections of the sheets that were darker than the others. Burnt citrus wasn't the only odor in the room. Sweat—barely noticeable, but it was there. I shut my eyes tight and balled my fists. Things weren't adding up.

The drawings pointed to a slew of different figures; some looked like combinations of animals. Daniel's home had been ransacked. That was a clear sign of...something. He ended up in a fatal underwater routine. Something kept him from his eight hours of beauty sleep. And he had poor taste in floor polish.

My fist tightened until my knuckles ached. I took another series of breaths. "Calm down. Take it slow. Take it all in." I repeated the mantra until the muscles in my hand loosened. My gaze fell over the nightstand.

I made my way over to it and fumbled under the lampshade for the switch. Weak light flickered into life and gave me a better view. I pulled open the first drawer. It was like looking inside a recycling bin filled with paper. Various letters and envelopes lay atop one another without any organization. I sifted through them. A few of them smelled like cheap perfume, the sort that was more of a chemical assault than anything pleasing. I ignored them.

Most of the papers were notices of late payments. I thumbed through them until they were replaced by utility bills and statements. His art gallery's income had taken a sudden turn-around to do well.

I had seen shifts of fortune like this before. Someone's luck and finances going from dismal to successful, like a wish come true. Only, that wish had a price.

They always do.

I rummaged through the letters until I found one with the information I needed. The address was another long walk away. I frowned. If this kept up, my timeline would dwindle to nothing simply from walking.

Note to self: Ask Church for a car. If Daddy doesn't buy you one for your birthday, steal one.

I blinked.

Keys, you idiot!

I pressed my hips against the drawer and shoved it shut. The act of thinking about Daniel's belongings triggered another flash. A painless one, thankfully.

I followed the vision and sank to my knees. My index finger hooked around the handle, and I pulled on the lowest drawer. It opened. I found a wallet made from black faux leather and one of those overly expensive smartphones. A ring of keys sat next to the wallet. Bright colors caught my eye. Each of the keys had a thumbnail-sized strip of electrical tape stuck to it. A stack of art-related magazines served as a bed for the items on top.

I pursed my lips as I snatched the items. The tape was a good way to keep track of what key did what. I flipped the wallet open, sliding his license into a flap. The cell phone was a good place to dig.

I gave it a sideways look. Technology and I don't always get along. I pressed my thumb to the only visible button. The screen flared to life and prompted me for a password.

"Fuck." Somehow, I didn't think Daniel's phone would unlock from profanity. I shut my eyes and tried to clear my mind.

The subconscious is an amazing thing. Sometimes you simply need to turn everything off and just trust yourself. If only it were that easy.

I tapped the screen without thought, hoping Daniel's body memorized the repetitive action of keying it in. No luck. My grip tightened, and I felt the plastic and aluminum shell threaten to warp. I sighed and loosened my hold. One last try couldn't hurt. My index finger bounced over the screen.

A warning message appeared, alerting me that if I kept it up, I'd be locked out.

I glared at the phone and wondered if it would unlock after impacting a brick wall. A growl escaped my throat, and I stuffed the phone into one of my pockets. The wallet followed along with the keys.

"Man, I hope one of these is to a car." I clung to them and headed to leave, pausing near the door. A thin coat-rack stood there; a lone windbreaker hung from it. I snatched it up, slipping into it. It had mesh pockets large enough to stow my journals. I did so and left the room.

There was no point in cleaning up Daniel's home on the way out. The dead don't care much for how their place looks. I lowered my head, giving the apartment a final look. "I dunno if you can hear me where you are, Daniel, but I'm going to gank this sucker." I looked up to the ceiling, hoping my words reached him and stepped out of his apartment. The door thudded shut.

I headed down the hall and the stairs. The keys jingled as I bounced them in my palm. As I neared the exit of the complex, I grumbled to myself. No memory passed through my noggin of Daniel owning a car. My teeth ground. I opened the door and scanned the street. None of the vehicles lining the curb triggered a thought in my host body.

"Figures." My shoulders sank as I sighed. "Guess I'm hoofing it."

I recalled the address to his studio. An electric charge went through the muscles in my back causing me to shake. The last time I had visited someone's workplace in New York, I had ended up in a fight with one heck of a monster.

I hit the street hard. A single thought crossed my mind as my feet pounded against concrete.

I really hope there's no monster lurking around your studio, pal.

Chapter Four

The darkness persisted. I had hoped things would brighten up as I trekked to Mr. Kim's art studio. Monsters have a fondness for skulking around at night. Go figure.

There was no point in keeping a lookout for my mystery stalker. I knew they were out there. And they knew I knew. I got the feeling they wanted me to know I was being watched.

I hate being the mouse.

Instinct is a wonderful thing. We all have it and need to trust it more. Mine has sharpened to something uncanny over my cases. The muscles in my body contracted like I had been dumped in ice water. I let impulse take hold and spun.

A hand pressed against my chest. The attacker drove me into a wall. The streets of Queens blurred and shook. I tried to clear my shaky vision but was cut short as fingers dug into the meat of my neck.

"Hurgkh!" My feet left the ground, and my eyesight worsened. I batted at the arm. It was like being suspended from machinery. Nothing budged.

"I warned you, mortal."

It took me a moment to pin the voice. Goody. The douche-trumpet from earlier. "Gleckh?" The grip loosened, and I sucked in as many ragged breaths as I could. I glared into the Night Runner's yellow eyes. "And I told you, what the fuck, man?"

The creature blinked. "There only one place to represent her interests. Step down. That place belongs to me." A dangerous light gleamed in his eyes. He shifted his grip. His hand cupped my lower jaw, sending a fire through my bones and teeth. The vertebrae in my neck screamed as he lifted me higher.

I sputtered something incoherent.

He squinted and lowered me. His grip moved to the

front of my clothing, rumpling the shirt. "What did you say?"

I grinned and looked down at Daniel's ruined shirt collar. "I just put this on."

The Night Runner's eyes widened.

My head snapped forwards. There was a wet crunch like someone striking a piece of fruit with a baseball bat.

The Night Runner recoiled. He blinked several times, and his hand hovered a fraction from his nose. He didn't seem keen on touching it. Blood trickled and congealed with mucus along his upper lip. His hand shook.

I couldn't tell if it was with anger or the pain. Hopefully both.

The Night Runner's eyes ballooned. "You broke my nose?"

My grin widened. "Keep it up, and I'll break more than..." I trailed off as the creature reached to its side.

Something scraped like glass against stone. A curved blade fashioned from a clear, crystalline material came into view. It was the length of the average man's hand. The weapon didn't give him much of a reach advantage. It wouldn't need to. The blade looked sharp enough to serve up a side of Fillet-O-Graves.

I wasn't keen on that dish. I gulped and raised my hands in an effort to calm him down. "Okay, things seem to have escalated. You jumped me from behind in the dark. You wrapped your hands around my throat. I broke your nose. It got really kinky-violent fast. Maybe we need a safe word? Or, we could film this next time and send it out—make some dough?"

The Night Runner's eyes flattened into slits. "You are the most infuriating being I have ever come across."

I blinked and gave him an oblique stare. "Are you...coming onto me?"

The Ashen Elf threw his head back and let out a roar that was sure to rouse people in the nearby buildings. He charged, sending the blade through a dizzying flourish.

I bristled as cold adrenaline wracked my heart. My back was up against a wall—literally. The tip of the blade hurtled towards my left eye. I dropped to my knees and reached out with my arms. Brick crumbled as the blade passed through without any signs of the weapon weakening.

Holy shit. I made a mental note not to let that thing nick any part of me.

My arms closed around the back of the Night Runner's legs. I pulled.

His momentum, coupled with my maneuver, drove him into the wall. He released a pained cry over a familiar sounding squelch.

Kissing a wall like that couldn't have been good for his damaged nose. I didn't get a second to enjoy it. My muscles tensed and I pushed off my heels. I tumbled to the side as the elf's knee struck the wall. Another shower of bricks rained to the ground. I blinked and rubbed a hand to the side of my head. That could have been my skull.

The Night Runner wasted no time. He pulled his leg back and stormed over to me.

I need to stop fighting out of my weight class. I don't have many advantages against the supernatural. I'm stronger than the average person, and I don't tire as easily. That doesn't count for much against things that can bench press a Smart car. Other than that, all I have is my supernatural ability to recover from injuries within a frighteningly short time. I'm a paranormal punching bag. One that can fight back, courtesy of the skills I've remembered from all the bodies I've inhabited.

My feet kicked against the ground as I scuttled my ass away from the elf. I placed my palms on the sidewalk and pushed. The action sent me halfway to my feet as I fought to balance myself.

The Night Runner double-stepped forwards and twisted. His left hand arced out. The knife carried a glint of the streetlamp's light along its edge.

I stepped into the blow and bent my arms up at a ninety-degree angle. The inside of his forearm crashed against both of mine. I winced as the force shot through my arms. My muscles quivered as I held the block. I held my ground and gritted through the pain.

The Night Runner snarled and reached out with his other hand.

I spread my arms wide, twisting to snake them around the one he'd used to strike me. My right forearm buried itself in the crook of his elbow. I used my other hand to grab the base of his wrist and wrench.

The Night Runner's free hand clenched the waistline of my pants. He tugged.

My body shifted, but I used his mass against him. I pulled back against his arm, angling him towards me. It became a contest of strength and experience. The freak had the strength. I hoped he didn't have the experience.

He released his grip on my beltline and reeled his hand back.

I tensed and leaned away as much as I could.

His fist rocketed out at a sharp angle.

A dull throb filled my side just below the ribs. The force caused the soles of my shoes to grate against the ground. I hadn't pulled away from the blow as much as I would've liked. At least he didn't hit my ribs. The force could have cracked a few.

I grimaced and maintained my grip on his arm. Letting go wasn't an option. Not unless I wanted to be sliced into lunch meat. I leaned in, using my weight to bend his arm towards him. "Don't you think things have gotten a bit personal now?"

The Night Runner's lips peeled back. He flashed me a smile that was more fang than tooth. The freak pulled his free hand back.

I knew what would follow and capitalized on the brief moment between. The muscles in my legs tensed as I took a step forwards. My momentum drove the elf back a step.

He winced and refused to give ground. Instead, he arched back, bending in a manner reserved for acrobats.

I pushed harder, hoping his back had a limit. The elf's upper body was near horizontal. That took freakish strength and flexibility that I could never hope for. So, I decided to fight dirty. I balled my hand and snapped my arm out, connecting with the creature's throat.

His eyes widened before they shut tight. He pawed at his throat, gagging from the strike.

I pulled away and jabbed again. The blow rocked the elf's head back. I smiled as he let loose another scream. There's only so many times you can strike a broken nose before the pain overwhelms the person—or, in this case, elf.

The back of my hand dragged against his clothing. Streaks of blood trailed behind. Elf blood is icky.

The Night Runner reached out to touch his nose again, stopping short of making contact. Moisture welled at the corners of his eyes.

I seized the moment and bore down on his other arm. The tip of the knife slipped through the jacket like it was made of wet paper. I twisted my hips and turned the knife. It sank into the meat of his shoulder.

The cry he let out would definitely have people dialing the cops. I needed to finish this—fast.

There's a certain point where pain galvanizes someone into levels of amazing strength and reactions. This was that point. The Night Runner's uninjured arm hooked around my side. His hand gripped a part of my shirt and he wrenched.

My hands broke free of the blade and my feet left the ground. The world slid sideways until it stopped with an impact that I'm sure my future bodies would feel. I spun to face the Night Runner more from instinct than anything else. The back of his fist blurred into view. My vision flared. It felt like I had caught a fastball with my mouth. The taste of salt and iron brushed over the tip of my tongue. My vision cleared in time for me to witness the Night Runner ripping the blade from his shoulder.

There was a wild look in his eyes. Something past anger; he looked deranged. The elf's mouth spread into a macabre smile.

Shit. I'm going to be killed by a Legolas reject.

He dove.

Something primal triggered in the back of my mind. Ah, hell. I charged. My shoulder crashed into his chest. The edge of the blade dragged against the side of my shirt. It felt like a blowtorch as fine as a scalpel had raked my bicep. My impact drove the Night Runner to the ground and I followed him down. I used my position to drive my forearm into the crown of his skull.

His eyes lost focus for a moment.

The side of my torso felt like it couldn't twist any further. I shifted and sent my fist into the side of his skull.

The Night Runner bucked.

I leaned in, pressing down to pin him.

He lashed out with a fist.

The lower half of my jaw felt like it had dislocated. I reeled enough for the elf to shove me to the ground.

"Why...won't you...die?" His chest heaved, and he looked like he was reaching his limit.

I blinked to clear the stars as my head lolled. "I'm not allowed to yet!"

The elf's face lost all expression. He pressed a hand to his bleeding shoulder and grimaced a second later. "This isn't over, fool."

He had to take a dig at me, even after having his ass kicked. Some people just can't be professional.

The Night Runner slashed the air with his first two fingers extended. A thread of light the color of candle smoke parted the air. It was like watching a stopper being pulled from a bathtub. The surrounding colors bent and warped, siphoning into the funnel.

It was a Way. A link to the world of the paranormal.

The Night Runner gave me one last look and spat at the ground. Guess he didn't think much of me. He turned and dove through the opening. It snapped shut with a plume of smoke shooting out from both sides.

I let my head fall against the wall behind me. "Yeah, you better run." My brain felt like it was tumbling. So did my eyes. I rolled my tongue around the inside of my cheeks. Saliva mixed with blood. I turned and spat.

Lights radiated from some of the windows atop the buildings nearby. Our fight had drawn some attention.

I sighed and clawed at the wall to haul myself up. A tongue of grease chilled to arctic temperatures made its way down my back. I shuddered and broke into a brisk walk, hoping it would push the feeling from my mind. It didn't.

I crossed the next street as fast I could, putting the block behind me. Rounding the corner didn't do much to get rid of the chilling sensation. I felt like I was in a paranormal game show. My other tail had watched that throwdown. Someone was sizing me up. I just wish I knew what for.

My pace doubled as I tried to put distance between the fight scene and myself. The next streetlight offered me a place for a much-needed stop. I turned my forearm and took a peek.

Another hour lost. Fifty-five wasn't a lot of time. More than I've had on some, but this case was particularly irritating. Outside parties were involved and kept me from making progress. My jaw ached as I clenched my teeth. Getting frustrated wasn't going to do me any good. I cast a look over my shoulder to let my tail know I hadn't forgotten about them.

Nothing stood out, but I'd expected that. I turned and broke into a run. Even with all the energy I had expended during the fight, I could push on. My bodies recover fast. I pushed the stinging cut from my mind and did the same for the split corner of my lip. The throbbing jaw was harder, but I buried its pain as well. They would all heal in a short time.

Running absorbed more than my energy. It swallowed my errant thoughts. I needed the clarity it offered as the streets passed by. The muscles along my torso and hips ached occasionally. I shut my eyes during those fleeting moments until the pain dissipated. It was a tedious process. I focused through it until a gentle tug pulled at my heart and the pit of my stomach.

My pace slowed to a crawl. The side of the building was draped in a massive banner that covered all three stories. Gray and black lettering made things clear. It was Daniel's gallery. I smiled and rushed towards the front.

It was the same unassuming brick that comprised so many of the buildings in Queens. The only difference was that the gallery seemed to have gotten a touch-up on the surface. A rich burgundy tinged each of the bricks. Arched stained glass windows ran along the floors above the ground level.

"Fancy." I moved to the door and fumbled through the ring of keys. The first key refused to fit. I thumbed through to the next. No memory from Daniel triggered. Guess struggling with keys isn't important enough to warrant help. The next key clicked to the base. I exhaled and made a silent prayer. I turned it and was rewarded with the sound of a bolt unlocking.

I pulled the door open and slipped inside. The second the door shut, I paused and turned around. My lips folded back as I frowned. I'd been getting jumped far too often on this case. And, notably, by the same ashy-skinned asshole. I locked the door and gave it a tug to confirm that it was shut. It wouldn't do much. Not when windows, just as large as the door, ran along the side of the ground floor.

I figured there would be an alarm system that would trigger in the event something broke its way in. I could hope.

My vision struggled to adjust to the darkness. Flickering streetlights threw staccato bursts of weak light into my face. It wasn't helping. I moved away from the front of the gallery and into the dark.

If ever there were a time and place for a nasty to ambush you...

Shut up.

I blinked at the realization that I was arguing with myself. It was that, or admit that I was unsettled. My heart lurched for an instant.

A piece of Daniel came to the rescue. The vision snapped through my mind. I placed my back against the nearest wall and stretched a hand out. My palm brushed along the smooth surface until something cold and hard stopped me. I inched across it with a finger until the surface changed. The feel of plastic is almost second nature to most people.

I grinned and ran my index finger against the rectangular switch. One corner rocked back. A row of panels illuminated the far side of the room; a bright light tinged with a hint of blue. My vision adjusted, and I thumbed the rest of the switches. The room came to life.

I let out a long whistle. The walls were a stark white, clearly chosen to make any piece stand out. Paintings raced along the wall. Each had a level of appeal that would catch someone's eye. And their wallet.

An intricate piece of metalwork seemed to pull all of the light and attention to itself. It dominated the center of the room. Copper rods arced and balanced atop one another in gravity-defying positions. I couldn't tell if it was art or an engineering feat.

Everything stood undisturbed, unlike Daniel's apartment. I turned to scan the remainder of the room. A particular piece caught my eye, forcing me to stop. I blinked and leaned forwards.

It was a canvas of all white. I wouldn't have noticed it if it weren't for the black-trimmed edges. Most of it was the same shade as the wall. A beige tag hung from the corner. My eyes grew twice as large after I read the figure listed on it. I blinked twice. It didn't help me understand the piece, but it made sure I wasn't hallucinating.

I walked away from it realizing that art is confusing. So is its price.

Another fixture of metal pipe work sat in the far corner, fashioned from solid steel. A layer of rust—fake from appearance—splotched the surface of some of the piping.

The new hall was as dark as the previous room had been. Something like carpet resisted as my fingers trailed against the wall. I flipped the only switch available. Amethyst light flooded the room. It brought to life streaks of neon-like paint that danced across black boards on both sides of the hall. I took a moment to squint at the squiggles. My bones felt like they shifted on their own.

The squiggly art conjured up a series of bad memories. They weren't from Daniel. I shut my eyes and buried that last case I had in New York. My shoulders tightened before relaxing. I shook my head and made my way out of the hall.

Repeating the process for the lights was tedious. You'd think modern buildings would have a more convenient setup. The new room was as untouched as the last. None of the art stood out. I gave it a detailed look-over anyway. Missing a possible clue was not an option.

I rotated in place, taking everything in. Though I was an art novice, it was easy to spot the changes in the styles of art hanging from the walls. Every artist has their unique touch and preferences. Daniel's pieces stood out at the beginning of the first wall. They transitioned into pieces from another artist with a flair for monochromatic schemes. I blinked when the art simply stopped.

A twelve-foot section of the wall lay bare. I moved towards the wall, noting the supporting screws and brackets remained. Someone had their pieces taken down. I eyed the end of the wall. More artwork ran along from that point. I pursed my lips.

It looked like an individual's work that had been removed. Someone might take that personally. And it was a good motive to want some payback. But if this were simply about human vengeance, I wouldn't be involved.

Nobody said the paranormal made sense.

I made a mental note of the missing art and moved on to the next hall.

The sound of footsteps over tile is distinctive. Nearly everyone's familiar with it. It's ingrained in so many of us from years of field trips, visiting museums as children, as well as hospitals. Especially when it's someone who's on the hefty side.

I raced down the hall towards the source without bothering to flip the lights. The newcomer had done me the courtesy of turning them on in the next room.

My eyes reached owlish proportions when I saw him.

He turned to face me. His face could have been pulled from the catalogs of Thugs-R-Us. The man's thickset head could have been used for demolishing buildings. He made professional strongmen look tiny. Both his beady eyes and his dark bowler cap seemed too small for his head. And someone needed to help him shop for new clothes. They looked like they were lifted from the 1920s, only that era didn't cater to men of his size. The buttons of the tweed coat strained against his belly.

He opened his mouth and snarled.

I shuddered. He needed to visit his dentist—fast. Or star as a warning for gingivitis. Well, for the teeth that remained.

He jabbed a thick finger at me. "Who you?"

How do you respond to that? "Uh, your grammar tutor as well as your stylist. I do in-person consultations, and your outfit needs work." I waggled my finger from his hat down to his shoes.

Kong the Giant blinked and squinted like he hadn't understood a word I said. "What?"

He wasn't a bright guy. I hooked a thumb to my chest. "I'm the owner of this here gallery."

His eyes widened.

"So, wanna tell me what you're doing here—scratch that." I waved a hand. "How'd you get in?" Heck, I had to work my ass off just to find the place and get here in one piece. Not to mention fumbling through keys and finding all the lights.

His flabby face split into a wide, toothy grin. "I opened the back door. Secret door."

My face lost all expression. "You mean like a fire escape? An emergency door? Something...that has a silent alarm?"

His face mirrored mine.

Well, shit. The genius ruined my plan to skulk around for clues. I couldn't walk away from this empty-handed though. "Who are you? What are you doing here?"

"Looking for Little Spirit. Going to smash him. Prove I'm best." His grin grew as he folded a massive fist within his other. The sound of his knuckles cracking was like listening to splintering wood.

I swallowed a gulp. Little Spirit? Smash him? That's me! I gave him a weak smile and backpedaled. "Uh...good luck with the whole smash thing. Promise not to break anything, and I won't have you arrested. I'm going to go now." I gestured over my shoulder and turned.

"Wait!"

Oh crap.

He sniffed the air several times. His eyes narrowed and shone like he had just won a prize. "You smell wrong." Lips peeled back like the smile a wolf gives before it jumps its prey. "Smell like wrong spirit—wrong body."

I gulped louder.

"Little Spirit I'm here to smoosh."

My brain turned to frozen pudding, and surge of cold electricity rolled down my spine to my toes. "You're not human...are you?"

His grin widened into something grotesque. The air shimmered like there was a curtain of light and faint traces of particulate glitter. It fell a second later.

I sucked in a breath. Glamour. The magic used by the Fair Folk—faeries—to mask their true appearances. Not-so-fair in his case.

His mass doubled, which was saying something. The clothing vanished and was replaced by the sort of skin you'd find on a pachyderm. I wish his outfit stayed. It was outdated, but at least it covered the freak. He wore a mess of mismatched fabric tied together in a horrible loincloth.

Layers of freakish muscle were roped atop each other in his arms. It was just wrong. His eyes were larger and the sort of yellow that accompanies nail fungus.

I rubbernecked to take in my surroundings as fast as possible.

The monster gave me a smile that made it clear I was on the menu.

I remembered specifically asking for Daniel's studio to be monster-free.

"Oh, I hate trolls."

Chapter Five

The beast lumbered forwards. His arms went out like he planned on giving me a hug. The last hug I'd ever need.

"Nope!" I skirted to the side, turning the corner to race down the hall. "Screw this!"

The troll snuffled behind me like he was nursing a horrible case of congestion. The sound that followed implied he had just cleared up that issue.

I fought the urge to retch. That was all manner of disgusting. I pushed it from my mind and pumped my legs harder. Getting into a physical tussle with a troll is never a good idea. Anyone that does so is an idiot.

I barreled into the next room and reeled as my foot caught on something. My body lurched to the side. I reached out and flailed my arms, hoping my hand would catch something. My fingers hooked on the edge of a painting. A grunt left my throat as one of its corners bounced off the front of my ribs. I winced and scrambled to my feet. I wasn't fast enough.

The troll shambled into the room and spotted me immediately.

My job is horrible. Stay in school. Don't die. Otherwise, you'll end up like me.

I smacked my hands against my thighs, dusting off my pants, and gave the troll a weary smile. "You're not going to let me go, are you, big guy?"

The troll shook his head. "No." He touched a thumb to his chest. "Shum going to break you. Then Shum eat you."

"Oh, wow. And if I said I disagree with that plan?" I took a cautionary step back.

He chortled. It sounded like a diesel truck backfiring. "Shum break you."

"Yeah, I got that. Say it in a Russian accent, huh, Drago?"

The troll's face tightened as he squinted.

Not all monsters are intelligent. But for what they don't have in brains, someone saw fit to make up for in bulk and freakish strength.

Whoopee.

I raised a hand in the hope it would give the troll pause. My fingers brushed against the fallen piece of art. It was the canvas of pure and confusing white. I smiled. "Hey, answer a question will ya?"

The troll's brows furrowed.

"Do you get art?" I snatched up the piece and twisted. It sailed through the air and impacted the troll's forehead. The frame shattered like glass on concrete.

The troll blinked and brushed a hand against his Neanderthal-like skull. The smile he gave me was reserved for sharks.

"Uh oh. Guess you're not big on art, huh?"

"Shum fan of abstract expressionism—Pollock. Gonna paint walls with yer blood. Splatter red and bone marrow."

There's a first time for everything. Like meeting a troll who can make a better highbrow art joke than you can. I found that unacceptable.

"I don't suppose you can answer why you want to pancake me?"

"Shum the best. Only one for job. No want you interfering. Leave."

His spiel sounded like the Night Runner's. Something was going on that had me wrapped up in the center, and seemed like a contest. One I wanted no part of. I made that clear. "Hey, your elf buddy found out I'm not involved the hard way." I put a hand over my heart.

Mentioning the Night Runner wasn't the best idea.

The troll shook his head, sending spittle everywhere. A cavernous roar reverberated through the room. He charged.

Ooooh boy. I leapt to the side, pressing myself flat against the wall as he steamrolled by. Paintings wobbled and shook on the walls. The freak must have weighed over a ton. And he didn't stop.

The sound of drywall and wood turning into dust is something else. It was like a car had crashed into the far wall.

Daniel was dead, but I felt a bit of obligation on his part to decry the action. "The dead dude's gallery! You ass crumb!"

An oversized hand popped from the gaping hole and gripped the destroyed edges of the wall. The rest of the troll followed. His eyes settled on me and flattened.

I licked my lips. "Uh, the ass crumb thing, nothing personal." I let out a weak laugh.

The troll palmed a painting that had managed to remain hanging. He grinned and hurled it like a discus, and I had no intention of catching it.

I fell to the ground and crawled towards the next hall. I didn't make it far.

Shum covered ground quickly. His fingers clenched around the back of my shirt, and my body left the ground. An amused light hung in his eyes.

I knew what was going to happen.

He sniffed me, and his face twisted in disgust.

I found that unfair, considering that he was the one that smelled like he had spritzed himself in Eau de Garbage. "So, while you've got me all warm and tender in your grasp, mind telling me how you figured out who I was?"

"Can smell you, Little Spirit. Smell wrong in wrong body."

That was new. I wasn't aware I carried an odor trolls could pick up. Church needed to know about that and fix it.

"Heh, look who's talking. You smell like shit."

Wrong words to say.

The troll pulled me close then swung his arm wide. He did so with no visible effort.

There was one benefit though. His ugly mug grew further away from me. So did the far wall as I soared through the air. I shut my eyes and tightened in preparation of the inevitable. The entire backside of my body felt like I'd been whipped and stoned at the same time. Every inch throbbed as the surface of my skin endured bursts of heated shocks. I shook my head and reached out to grab both sides of the crumbling drywall.

Thank God the only stud that got hit was me. I didn't think my borrowed body would be able to take going through one of those wooden beams without my spine being atomized. My abilities ensure I can take a heckuva lot more punishment than any normal person. They didn't make me invulnerable—sadly. A low groan was the only sound I could make. I lay corrected when my chest tightened and a dry wheeze passed through my lips.

Shum came towards me.

Lying around on the job wasn't professional. Nor was it safe when a troll was headed my way. I groaned and stifled the internal screaming throughout my body. My arms tensed as I pulled against the deteriorating wall to haul myself up.

The troll angled his shoulder towards me and picked up speed. Shum aimed to be a battering ram. If he hit me, I would have my own line of jelly.

There's always one fail-proof technique to rely on when fighting something laughably out of your weight class. I pushed away from the wall and ran. My feet skidded atop the floor as the room juddered from Shum's impact against the wall. He passed through like a freaking semi.

Debris spewed across the room.

I gawked at the scene. Running wasn't an option. If I kept it up, Thomas the Troll Engine would steamroll my ass, and the gallery, into dust. There was one option left. I hate last resorts. I balled my fists and raised them.

He eyed me obliquely. "What doing?"

I sighed. "Proving I'm an idiot. Let's go!"

He released a series of amused huffs through his nostrils. Shum seemed pleased by the prospect of getting into a fistfight. He raised a hand that could have easily engulfed my head. His fingers curled into a fist and he lashed out to his side. The troll's hand crashed into an intricately carved obelisk. The stone shattered like it was made from cheap clay.

I gulped.

Shum smiled. He took a single step towards me. His face broke into an expression saying he looked forward to this.

I didn't. I looked around the room, trying to find something to give me an edge. My chest shook, and I couldn't hold back the laughter.

Shum stopped and eyed me like I was a lunatic. "Why laughing? You crazy?"

"A bit." I waved a hand to the pair of metal sculptures in the room.

The troll's eyes fixated on the copper piece. They filled with a hungry light and seemed to swell.

"That's a lot of copper. I know how much you folk love that. Think about it; you could walk away from this a rich troll. I own this place. How about we calm down, you explain things—maybe try not to squish me—and you can take all the copper you can carry, huh?"

Shum's eyes narrowed and his lips pursed. He scratched the underside of his chin before turning to me. The look he flashed me made my stomach feel like it was churning cement. "Why not Shum kill you and take copper anyway?" He grinned like a kid who found out they could eat their cake and have it too.

Great. I had to end up fighting the one troll who had taken weekend entrepreneurship classes.

"Well, sucks we couldn't come to an agreement, big fella. I'm going to have to hurt you now."

He snorted.

I leaned towards him, prompting him to rush me. The plan wasn't to get in a grappling session with him. I leapt to the right and sped towards the other sculpture. My feet left the ground as I hurtled and tumbled over it. I reached out and grabbed a steel pipe, using my body to lean back and wrench. Metal groaned as one of the pipes relinquished its hold on the others. It popped free.

The piece was the same length as my forearm and as thick as my thumb. Solid enough for what I needed. I gave it a quick flourish.

Shum didn't seem perturbed by the blunt weapon.

Ignorance hurts most.

I beckoned him with a wave of my hand.

His face twisted as he made an abhorrent gurgling noise. A globule of spittle struck the floor. Shum stepped towards me, rolling his shoulders like he was loosening them.

A series of short breaths left through my nose as I tried to calm myself. My plan would work. In theory. Okay, I hoped it would work. My grip tightened on the steel rod, and I rushed the troll.

He snarled and swatted a hand at me like I was nothing

more than a fly.

I took offense to that. My knees bent, and I twisted my torso, avoiding the hand as it sailed overhead. I reversed the pipe, ensuring the sharper edge pointed out. With a snap of my arm, I sent the piece plunging towards the troll. It bit into the side of his forearm. There was a flare like the first light of a firework.

Purple light strobed, and the troll's skin sizzled like meat hitting a skillet. The pipe parted flesh with ease. It skewered the arm and shot through the other side.

Faeries cannot abide the touch of iron and steel. Man's metal is like a poisoned scalpel on their flesh. He should have paid more attention to what I had grabbed.

I twisted and wrenched the pipe free. Another twist and snap sent the piece dragging across his belly.

The skin split and seared.

I winced and recoiled. Burning flesh has a smell that clings to the hairs in your nostrils. It stings and makes your nose feel like you've snorted sand.

Red, hair-thin lines streaked through Shum's eyes. Moisture lined his lids and a few drops fell down his cheeks. He pressed a hand to his belly, staring at the wound in disbelief. He blinked several times as if it would clear his vision and he'd find the injury was an illusion.

Too bad.

Shum turned his watery eyes to me. "You cut Shum...with steel?"

I shrugged and twirled the rod in my hand. "Shum wrecked my gallery, tossed me through a wall, and wanted to turn me into a spread for toast. Shum can go fuck himself." You know your life has taken a wrong turn when you're talking to the monster you're fighting in third person.

The troll glanced at the rod. It was coated in a viscous ichor the color of boysenberry. Troll blood wasn't a pretty sight. Shum got that much. He also knew if he kept it up, there would be a lot more spilling over the place.

"Go again?" I twirled the pipe in a flourish. It got the point across.

Shum eyed the weapon, then me. The hungry look from earlier returned.

That's never a good sign. My heart felt like a row of

firecrackers going off. Liquid nitrogen flowed through my veins.

Shum confirmed my fear the next second. He squinted, looking like he was using all his brain-power to accomplish the task.

The air hissed behind me. I turned.

A streak of poppy-colored light rolled through the air, splitting open like a blossoming flower. Another Way.

I turned back to Shum. I should have done it sooner.

The troll closed his fingers around my left arm and shoved.

I spun, trying to keep my balance. There was only one way to go—backward. The orange light enveloped me, and I passed through the Way.

I had a bad feeling Shum would follow.

* * *

My back cried out for the hundredth time since starting my case. The skies were streaked with colors pulled from a neon sign. A shock ran through my body from my heels to the base of my skull.

Shum had landed.

Wonderful. The Neravene. A world of infinite domains belonging to everything out of mythology that called it home. That included the crude, business-savvy troll keen on killing me.

I propped myself up on my elbows and glared at him. "So, now that you've dragged me back to your place for a night of drinks and gossip, care to tell me what's going on?"

Shum squinted. "You making fun of me?"

I sighed. "No, just tell me what the hell is happening. And be clear." I smacked the pipe against the ground to accentuate my point.

His eyes traced the pipe's movements. He whipped his head around like he was worried about being seen. Shum leaned forwards and put a hand to the side of his mouth. "It safe here. Alone. Quiet."

I bristled. Those weren't the words I wanted to hear after being tossed through a magical doorway. Not from a troll, and definitely not in that order. "Uh, thanks?"

He nodded. "No more hurt Shum?" The troll arched a brow and stared.

"You started the fight. I was just finishing it. I'm totally fine with moving on. Just answer my questions."

The troll twiddled his thumbs before tapping the points of his index fingers together. It was like watching an anxious child—a kid that weighed tons and had a hankering for eating people—work up the courage to say something that should be kept secret. "Shum fighting for job."

I didn't know what to make of that. "Yeah, I hear the job market is shit these days. How does that involve me?"

His body went rigid, and his eyes widened. "You don't know?"

"No! That's what I've been saying."

He pursed his flabby lips and put a finger to them. "Um, Shum don't know word."

That wasn't a surprise.

"Powerful being looking for help. Many rewards." He mimed a large circle with his hands. "Big ones. Do job. Lots of favors." His mouth spread into a leer. "Much power."

Trolls coveted that more than they did copper. They were competitive to the point of being barbaric. Strength and power were the way to the top. You fought. Weak trolls were torn apart by the strong. It's not pretty what happens to those that can't cut it.

It's a troll-eat-troll world—literally.

"Okay." I nodded. "I think I've got a bit of it. Someone's putting a call out for what, muscle?"

He bowed his head and winced. The bleeding hadn't stopped. They weren't fatal injuries, but they weren't paper cuts either. Shum was hurting. Good. It'd serve as a reminder to keep him from trying anything.

"What do they need this muscle for?"

Shum shook his head. "Dunno. Only know rewards."

I bit my lip. This seemed less to do with my case and more to do with something stirring in the paranormal world. Something that had managed to drag me into it. "Do you know anything else?"

"Nobody want competition."

My mouth opened, but nothing came out for a moment.

"Are you saying I'm part of the competition?"

He nodded.

"But I didn't even know about this!" I've built a bit of a reputation for causing trouble and starting problems in the paranormal world, but this was ridiculous.

"You were named, Little Spirit."

Someone called me out by name. That meant someone wanted me dead. Another thought crossed my mind. This was starting to look like tryouts. Someone was watching me to see if I was recruitment material.

Yeah, but for what?

"And you know nothing else about the job, right, Shum?"

He shook his head again.

"Okay, fair enough. So, a supernatural draft is going on, and I'm in the running."

Shum's eyes lost focus as he fumbled to make sense of the string of words. "Uh huh."

I eyed the troll and crawled a foot away. "Does this mean you're going to jump me again? You're not still raring to take out the competition, are you?"

He raised a hand and waved it at me. "No. Shum no want more pain."

Wow. I'm not one to push my luck. I inclined my head as a way of thanks. "I don't suppose you can open a Way and let me get out?"

He shook his head.

My stomach knotted. "What?"

"Shum open only two Ways." He jabbed a finger to the ground below. "Home." He arched his arms over his head, interlocking his fingers to form an arch. "And safe place there."

His place of holding. Every creature out of the Neravene had one. A place they could home in on that established a connection with them. Navigating and opening Ways was complex. It's like driving across the world with a road map, except the routes are always changing. And if you don't have that map, you're not going far. Most beings struggle to discover more than a handful of Ways. Two is commonplace.

My stomach wound tighter. I had an idea where the

troll's Way would lead. "Is the bridge in Queens? Better yet, how 'bout Long Island City?"

Shum's brows knitted together. "Not bridge. Shum not..." He looked away before turning his gaze to the ground. "Shum not big troll. No have bridge of own."

I resisted the urge to snicker. That would have been rude. I was starting to feel sorry for Shum. A fist-sized spasm in my lower back caused me to reconsider my sympathy. The jerk had battered me good. I arched a brow and waited for him to clarify.

"Alley."

Oh. That would work just fine. "Okay, so how's about you pop open the magical express and let me hop on through?"

He nodded and repeated the action of opening his Way.

The air parted, and I stared at a mirror image of the opening from before. A vice-like grip ensconced my ankle. My eyes widened.

Oh no.

Shum wasn't a bright guy.

I shut my eyes and tensed as my body left the ground. Air rushed by as I flew through the Way.

I hate trolls.

My body tingled as the magical opening swallowed me. Tingling turned to feeling like I had been body slammed by a bus. I opened my eyes.

The alley was dark, but I could see morning light filtering through the opening.

I lay against the wall. My brain was still doing an acrobatic routine inside my skull. Passing out seemed like a good idea.

So I did.

The alley's darkness enveloped me.

Chapter Six

My lids felt like they were sewn shut. I buried the heels of my palms against my eyes in the hopes they'd open. "Hsst." I winced and recoiled from the mouth of the alley. My eyes shut on reflex from the morning light.

My nap must've lasted a while.

A jolt of electricity coursed through my mind and nestled in my heart. The thought galvanized me to check my forearm.

Six hours had passed. I had forty-nine left and not much of a clue where to go. Never mind the fact I didn't know where I was.

Everything the troll had given me pointed to a power outside my case. It was too much of a leap to assume my search and the strange interruptions were related. All that train of thought would do is taint my investigation with a bias it didn't need.

The facts I did have weren't adding up to much. There was only one thing to do: gather more.

My body had healed during the siesta, but phantom aches plagued my lower back as I braced myself against the wall. I pushed off the back of my heels as I shimmied to stand. A series of cracks rang out from the base of my neck and I turned towards the alley's mouth.

Daniel's gallery gave me a bit of insight into the man's life and work, but nothing stood out as a reason for killing the fella. If I was right about the state of security in the gallery, some form of alarm had been tripped by the troll. The cops had likely paid a visit after we'd tumbled through the Neravene.

They'd be looking for Daniel. And I'd been napping the morning away after a break-in.

Oh crap!

I pushed off the wall, racing down the alley. Returning

to the gallery wasn't an option. I had to get back to his place and fast. The police had likely tried to get a hold of him somehow.

I maintained my frantic pace as a notion crossed my mind. My hand went into my pocket and closed around Daniel's phone. I plucked it free and held it before my face. The screen was a spider-web of cracks. It was a small miracle the phone hadn't shattered completely given the beaten I'd taken. My thumb pressed against one of the buttons. The screen flashed. I squinted to make out a symbol informing me that Daniel had indeed missed several calls.

Great. Moving around with the discretion and autonomy I needed was going to be a chore now the cops were involved.

I crossed a busy intersection, giving no regard to passersby or the traffic signs. Street signs blurred, but a distant part of my brain managed to recognize them. I sorted out where I was and asked more from my legs as I hammered along.

Scenery and thoughts melded together to become a blur I had to bury. I focused on breathing. Even I'm susceptible to fatigue after a certain point. I didn't have the option of caving into it.

Thankfully, Shum wasn't the complete trolly tool I'd made him out to be. The alley he'd dumped my spirity keister in wasn't too far from Daniel's apartment.

I rounded the corner of a block, and it came into view. My pace slowed to a crawl, allowing me a moment to double over and place my palms on my knees. It'd been a hell of a run.

There weren't any police cars parked along the block. That was a good sign. If they had visited Daniel's place, they were long gone. I swallowed. But if they did check it out, they could have found and collected something I might have needed. My stomach felt like a bundle of rope balled into knots.

I cast a wary eye to both sides of the street before crossing. Nothing stood out. But then, nothing stood out before I had been assaulted by two creatures from the Fair Lands.

"Fucking faeries." I opened the door as my grumbling morphed into incoherent muttering. People passed by, and I paid them no mind. I fixated on what to do in the event an officer had remained behind to check out Daniel's pad.

It would be an interesting predicament having to explain to a cop what was going on. An explanation I wasn't keen on giving. I crossed my fingers as I passed the doors leading to Daniel's. My hand fell onto the knob, and I froze.

Using the outside of my palm, I rolled it, giving the knob a light jostle. There was no click of resistance. It was unlocked. Someone, or something, was inside. I took a breath and turned the knob. The door opened just enough for me to slip a credit card through. I pushed a bit more, easing it as I peered through the crack.

I blinked several times as I examined what I could see of the apartment. It didn't look like the police had stopped by at all. Hell, it looked like a cleaning crew had come through. I released my hold on the knob, letting the door drift open. My jaw hung slack as I scanned the place.

It was perfect. The apartment could have been used in magazines featuring cleanliness. You hear about places that are tidied up to the point they nearly sparkle. I looked to his countertops and the windows. They fit the description.

"What in the..." I trailed off and stepped further into his place, brushing my hand against the door. It shut as I moved to the center of the room.

"Ackh!" My throat tightened and the insides of my nose followed. The scent of pine freshener barraged my senses. It was overpowering, like someone had snuck in and doubled up on it.

Someone had definitely come through here.

A sound like someone letting air out of a balloon came from the bathroom. It lasted a split second.

Or...someone's still here, Graves.

I took another whiff and thought about the cleanup. Things clicked into place. The stench of pine intensified as I drew closer to the bathroom. It was thick enough to taste when I leaned against the door. I grasped the handle and twisted. The second it unlocked, I stepped back and pulled a knee to my chest. My leg snapped out sending my heel crashing into the door.

The bathroom was empty. I brought a hand up to mask my mouth and nose as the stink threatened to choke me. The mirror shone like it'd just been cleaned. White tiles glistened under the light in a manner that homeowners wished was possible. The tub and metal framing were the same. It took more than expensive cleaning supplies and elbow grease to make this kind of clean happen.

I stopped and homed in on the potted plant sitting at the outside corner of the tub. A simple thing of clay nursing a slender stalk of green. It was devoid of flowers. Green, pointed leaves like oak sprouted from its sides. It was nice.

Except Daniel didn't have a plant the last time I checked his bathroom. I thought back to the door and smiled. The tip of my right shoe ground against the tiles. I pulled it back, dragging a bit of street dust and grime against the clean tiles. My eyes remained fixed on the plant.

One of the leaves twitched. Any sane person would have attributed it to a stir of the wind. Great theory if we were outside or the air conditioning was blowing.

My smile widened. I lashed out with my foot. The front of my shoe struck the pot, sinking into it like it was a pillow.

A high-pitched scream tore through the bathroom. I fell to my knees and pressed a hand to the creature's mouth. "Jesus, shut it!"

The little freak struggled. He was about three feet—tops.

"Ow!" I yanked my hand back, shaking it as a row of crimson droplets formed over my index finger. It felt like I had brushed it against a cactus. The little shit bit me.

I glared at him, giving him a look to settle down, otherwise my foot would lodge itself firmly up his faerie ass. I rolled up the sleeves of my jacket to make the point.

He stared back at me. His eyes were a shade of green that could only be found in nature and were tinged with hints of white. It was like looking at pine needles. They stood out against his sun-bronzed skin. "What was that for?" He puffed up his bare chest.

I shook my head. I didn't know what it was with some faeries and their aversion to clothing. At least he was wearing a pair of leather breeches. "You're in my home, and you're asking me why I kicked you?"

The creature deflated, running a hand through his comical hairdo. It was styled like a paintbrush. His hair was the same shade of brown as you'd find in the bristles, and it stood up nearly a foot. It was ridiculous.

I reminded myself I was dealing with a supernatural creature. Ridiculous was part of the job.

He jabbed a slender finger at me. "You kicked me after I cleaned this filth. Was a chore too, I'll say that much, ungrateful, lousy...."

I tuned out as the little monster rambled on.

He vibrated and shook his head. "Wait a tick, mortal, why aren't you surprised to see me here? You should be terrified! I am of the fae." He raised his arms above his head, spreading his fingers out like they were menacing claws.

They weren't. But it was a cute act.

I fell back against the door, pressing a hand to my stomach. The rolling laugh filled the bathroom and caused him to shrink. "Creature of the fae? You're a puck. You're a paranormal maid sans the outfit and cleaning supplies. Come on, you..." I blanked out for a moment. "Wait a second. Why are you cleaning my place?"

He snorted. "Your place? You're not the owner. He died."

What?

It's always a possibility that I could run into someone or something that knows the person I'm wearing is dead. The amount of times it's happened, though—well, that's something else. It makes things easy.

My hand snaked out, fingers digging into the puck's throat. I grunted and heaved. The creature's feet dangled near my waist as I pressed him against the wall. "How do you know that?" I bared my teeth.

There's something lodged in the back of every living creature's brain when it comes to flashing your teeth like that. Be it a wolf, a man, a monster—there's a silent message that comes across. It's a threat. I didn't have impressive fangs or a handful of chipped and stained troll's teeth. I didn't need to. My action accentuated the point, and the puck got it.

I felt his throat harden against my fingers as he

swallowed. I shook him. "Speak!"

He didn't.

I sighed. Pucks are a far cry from trolls and the scarier creatures out of Faerie. They're honestly nothing more than neurotic neat freaks. Torturing one for information wasn't something I wanted to do, but I needed answers. I grimaced and pulled my fist back.

The puck's body tensed. He winced and raised his hands to cover his face.

I turned and swung my arm behind me. The back of my fist struck a glass container of liquid soap. It flew through the air, shattering as it struck the wall. Gel trailed along the bathroom as it slid to the floor.

The woodland spirit's eyes bulged. "What are you doing?" He squirmed and batted my arm.

I gave silent thanks that he didn't have supernatural strength. I flashed him a feral grin. "I'm redecorating." The sole of my shoe sank into the puddle of soap and I pulled my foot back. Liquid cleanser dragged with it, leaving a thin, translucent layer of the slippery substance over the polished tiles.

The puck bucked harder. His throat burbled with sounds like those of an upset stomach.

It was working. My grin widened as my fingers fumbled with the latch on the medicine cabinet. I flung it open, stifling a laugh as I spotted all manner of goodies. The confines of the room made it easy for me to lean over without relinquishing my hold on the little fae. I plucked a can of shaving cream free from a shelf. It was too hard to resist. A maniacal smile stretched across my face. I made sure the puck noticed it.

His eyebrows rose to the point where it looked like they'd touch his hairline. "You...monster!"

I snorted. "Monster? That's rich considering you're involved with this guy's death." I lowered my head, touching my chin to my chest to make the point.

The puck sputtered and shook his head.

"Save it. I know you didn't kill him."

He froze, managing to turn his head just enough to shoot me an oblique stare.

I had his attention. "Come on, murder isn't the MO for

a puck. Having a fit because someone did this..." My grin widened, and I thumbed the cap off the can and depressed the nozzle. A white torrent of cream looped and squirted through the air. It struck the tub's frosted glass screen, trickling down. I shook the can and pointed the nozzle at the floor.

The puck sucked in a breath. His lip curled, and his breath escaped as a whimper.

I pressed down again. Cream collected into a small pile over a section of the tile. First soap, now this. Fireworks must have been going off in his brain. The little fella would short circuit if I kept it up. I was sorely tempted.

"Stop!" The puck shimmied and beat the back of his heels against the wall. "Stop, stop, just stop!" Tears formed along his eyelids. A few beads dribbled down his face.

Wow. I had really struck a nerve. A fist-sized pang went through my heart and gut. I felt a hint of guilt for hurting the little guy. It could have been worse. I could've pummeled him. I buried the guilt. "You ready to talk?"

He bobbed his head so fast I was afraid he'd damage his spine. "Yes. Yes-yes-yes. Just...." He whimpered again and nodded to the can.

I bowed my head and released my hold. The can struck the floor, bouncing before coming to rest. "Talk."

The puck glanced down to my hand then to me.

I sighed and released my grip.

He crashed to the floor, wobbling as he fought to stand straight. "What do you want to know, you sociopath?"

I blinked. Sociopath? Me? The hell I am! I glared and reached for the zipper on Daniel's pants. "Keep talking crap and I'll take a leak all over the just-scrubbed floor."

His face went blank for a microsecond before his jaw dropped. He looked like I'd threatened to burn down an entire forest. Pucks are among the biggest tree-huggers you'll find, literally.

Maybe my threat was a bit over-the-top. That didn't make me a sociopath, did it? I shook my head and cleared away those thoughts. "How do you know the owner of this place died? Why were you here at all? I smelled your scent twice. Once before when this place was a mess, and now."

His eyes looked like they were going to spin any second

under the barrage of questions. They settled a moment later. He cleared his throat and looked around the room as if searching for an escape. His shoulders sank when he realized there was none. "I was asked—no—compelled to be here." The puck's brows touched at the center of his forehead as it crinkled. His eyes narrowed, jaw tightening as well.

Something pushed him to this, and it didn't sit well with the forest fae. Many supernatural creatures have their own nature. It's something beyond a personality. Older, deeper things take root inside them and compel them to be the way they are. Little to large, many creatures don't like being forced or tricked into doing something outside their nature. That anger was something I could use.

I motioned with a lazy roll of my hand for him to continue.

He took a deep, calming breath and nodded more to himself than me. "Yes. I was enticed to come here and..." The words froze in his throat. He swallowed the lump with a shudder. "Forced to make a mess." His hands pressed to his biceps as he squeezed and rubbed them in a reassuring self-hug.

I tried not to smile. It would be an asinine thing to do. The little guy was distraught over the disarray in Daniel's apartment earlier. It was sort of pathetic and adorable at the same time. I smiled.

I'm an ass.

I bit my lower lip, breaking the smile until I could look like I was serious. It took me a moment. "Okay, something made you do this. I get that. Sorry about that by the way. I know it's hard going against your nature like that. It must've hurt." The sympathy card is hard to play with some members of the supernatural. With others, it's easier.

The puck looked me in the eyes with an expression of mild relief.

There isn't much to relate humans to magical creatures, but all of us have feelings. Whether we're in control of them or not. Whether we're in good states of mind and mood or not. Whether we act on them or not. Just because there's a world of differences in our looks doesn't mean we're without our similarities. Sometimes all that separates a man from being a monster, and a monster from being a man, is what they're willing to do and act on. It's a thin line and a rather fragile thread. A connecting thread that's useful. Tugging on it for information is a delicate art.

Too much pull, and something breaks. Not enough and no info. If I went heavy on the act, he'd lock up and leave me with squat.

I held up a hand, gesturing that it was okay for him to take a moment.

He sniffed and nodded.

So far, so good.

The puck cleared his throat again. "I didn't want to, of course."

I nodded. "Of course."

"It didn't give me a choice."

"What didn't? It threatened you?"

"Yes. Don't ask me what it was. All I know is that it's pulled from mortal nightmares."

I swallowed, hoping it wasn't audible. That wasn't good news. Something straight out of our nightmares. Those are bad enough to endure when they're just figments of your imagination. Not counting the actual bad memories. Trust me. I've lived through enough to have my fair share of those.

My thoughts flashed to an asylum where shadows skulked across the walls. I smacked my palm against the side of my head. It brought me back to reality. That wasn't a case I wanted to think about.

Here. Now, Graves. Focus.

I sank to my haunches, getting eye level with the little faerie. "Can you tell me anything more?"

His eyes darted from side-to-side like he was worried someone was nearby and would reprimand him for speaking. "It's not anything from the Fair Lands. It's old and one of your devils, not ours. When it passed into my woods, the air stank of a burning orchard." He shuddered.

I filed that away for future reference. "Did you see it?"

He shook his head. "It was wrapped in a cloak of darkness, and it was smart."

I arched a brow. "What do you mean? It conjured something? Glamour—no—you said it wasn't fae. An illusion? Myrk?"

The puck blinked rapidly as I rattled off more questions. "I don't know. Quite possibly. No, not glamour. Possibly? Possibly?"

I stared at him, debating whether to call him out on being a smartass or not. Instead, I exhaled and shut my eyes as I thought. "Fine. Fair enough. You couldn't see much of it. How exactly was it smart?"

"The fiend plucked me from unclaimed land."

I eyed him. "You're neutral? No affiliation to any of the courts?"

He shook his head and grinned. "Wild, free, and proud."

I frowned and wriggled my nose. Being a free fae had its advantages. It also had its downfalls. "That means you can't go to a queen or anyone with a measure of power with your grievances."

He sulked. "Most true. But freedom has its boons, and it has its costs."

He had a point.

"Are the lords and ladies of the Neravene not an option?"

The puck paled, an odd look for his golden complexion. "Root and bark, no! It would be a slight to queens. One they couldn't—wouldn't—forget, much less forgive."

That was true. Nobody held onto a grudge like a Faerie Queen. You didn't get involved with them unless you were monumentally stupid.

"Good point. But why'd you come back?"

His cheeks flushed, making his skin look like rose gold. "Well, I couldn't leave a place—one that I had a rather large hand in mucking up—a mess now, could I?" His face twisted in disgust. "I had to right it."

My chest shook, and something built in the pit of my belly. I couldn't contain it. It spread through my body and the laughter filled the apartment. "You...you came back because you couldn't stand a messy room?" Tears formed and I had to brush my eyes with the back of my hand. My legs felt like wet string, ready to collapse. "I can't..." Air refused to fill my lungs as fast I forced it to leave. My laughter intensified.

"Yes-yes, very funny, mortal. Make light of my

suffering. Do you know what it's like?"

I fell against the door and laughed harder. "You poor little neat freak!"

He scowled and crossed his arms. "I was made to do this. Have you any idea what that is like?" The puck quivered like he was going to lose it any second now.

Boy, do I. That's all I know, bouncing from one body and case to the next. The puck had normalcy in his life. He had a home, a place he could return to. I had a notebook with thoughts and memories jotted down as I remembered them. Fragments of my life in a journal, nothing more than scratches of ink.

"I think I can imagine." Something in my voice must have clued the puck to what I was thinking.

He folded his lips and adopted silence.

I ran my tongue against the inside of my cheeks. "Okay, here's the big question—why?"

The puck arched a brow. "Why, what?"

"Why make you come all this way to mess up Daniel's apartment? What's the benefit, to you or the freak that set this up?" I propped my chin on my fist and pursed my lips. Something didn't add up.

He shrugged. "I was told to make it look like a mortal altercation. Something that would..." He stopped and squinted like he was searching for a word. "Something to confuse your constabulary."

That was something. My mind raced with possibilities. This was supposed to look like a robbery, perhaps. One gone wrong? That wouldn't have explained Daniel's absence though. There was no evidence of violence. A place being torn up isn't enough to leap to a conclusion.

But, then, what was I doing? My job revolved around jumping from one hunch to the next, sometimes without solid clues. Evidence is a wonderful thing. Never let it discount your gut feelings and training though. Everything adds up in the end. Refusing one piece in favor of something else keeps you from seeing the big picture.

I flexed my fingers and made a fist several times to help me release my frustration. The questions piled up. The leads...not so much.

When in doubt, ask more questions.

"Alright, so this was supposed to look like a tussle gone wrong to throw off the cops. Why? What good does that do? Make them think it was a burglary? All that means is his home was trashed and he wasn't home. Robbery gone wrong means he was here and things took a nasty turn. There's no blood. No other signs either. Hair fibers, old, if the cops get any at all. Besides, if things got that out of hand to go in concert with that level of mess, the neighbors would have heard. Something would've been filed. No."

The puck stared at me as I rattled through the possibilities. He held up an index finger. "Are you okay, human? Words are dribbling out of you." He flashed me a sideways look and took a step back.

"Yeah. Fine. Thinking." I held up a hand to silence him. All the wrecked apartment served to do was throw me off whatever trail was there. This was better calculated than some of the monsters I've dealt with. But there's no such thing as a perfect plan. I just needed to find the hole. And if there wasn't one, I'd make my own.

The puck blurred past me, grabbing the edge of the toilet paper. He yanked the sheet. The roll unwound, somehow folding upon itself and into his hands.

A touch of magic.

He took the wad, ignoring me, and fell to his knees. The little fae scrubbed the soap and shaving cream from the tiles. His hands and arms moved with a fervor found in industrial-level equipment.

"Was it bothering you that much?"

He shot me a feral look. "Yes."

I raised my hands in a gesture of placation. "Clean on. I've got more questions to ask."

He grunted and scrubbed harder. "I can hardly wait."

I bit back a retort and sighed. The question on my mind was more important than being witty. It was a tough call. I rubbed my brow and shut my eyes for a second. "Okay, were you made to do this"—I broke off and waved a hand to the door—"making a mess out of anyone else's place?" Reiterating what's been said can help process facts.

His arms locked, and he convulsed for a microsecond. "No."

I stared at him, hoping he'd give me more than that.

"That's it—no?"

"Not entirely."

I narrowed my eyes and kept up the stare. "What's that mean?"

"It means, mortal, that no, I was not asked to ruin another human's home. But...I was asked to do something just as horrible."

"Oh?" I leaned back and crossed my arms, waiting.

"I can't tell you."

I blinked. "Uh, why not?"

He gulped and reached towards his throat, stopping as he became aware of what he was doing.

"Why not?"

"It doesn't involve the owner of this place. Whatever happens outside here is not for your ears."

"I'm going to call bullshit there. You're not bound by a code of honor or fae laws. You're Free Folk. You don't want to tell me, or...you can't?"

He swallowed again.

"The monster you can't tell me anything about?"

The puck nodded.

I pressed a hand to my forehead and massaged. "Right, you were threatened."

He nodded.

Of course. The paranormal world was complex and shifting in balance. Not much remained static. What did shift was power. And power could be traded, built through favors. It was a heck of a currency. But, as with any system, sometimes you don't need to pay to play. There are other avenues you can take. Like throwing around any measure of physical and magical power you might have. Sometimes threats work.

But the thing about that is, it gets you what you want in the short term. Threats aren't great for building a working relationship. They get you put on the shit list. If I was right about my brush-headed friend, he had an axe to grind. He was just too weak to do it himself. He needed muscle.

"You're worried, I get that. What if I told you I'm out to put a hurtin' on this freak? I'll kick its ass, square things out for me and for you. Willing to talk now?"

He shook his head. "No chance. I don't know much

about you, mortal, but I know enough. And I know you cannot win. You will die, just like the true owner of this place did. If I help you, and it comes to that, then I am next."

He had a fair point. I mean, it was wrong, but you can't blame a guy for self-preservation. Go, go Gadget charming. I flashed him a smile. "This is the part where you say, 'But I like you, human, so I'll help anyway.'"

The puck snorted so hard that I thought mucus would've shot out. "I hate you. Look at what you did!" He gestured to the remaining soap and shaving cream.

"Yeah, and I'm real broken up about it; I am." I placed a hand over my heart in mock sympathy.

He scowled.

"Give me something work with, please. Look, this thing strong-armed you, and I know that doesn't sit well with any fae. You can't tell me that you're not itching for some measure of payback?"

His nose twitched, and his mouth followed. He was mulling it over. The puck looked away, his gaze peering through the walls almost. A long sigh left his nostrils. "Yes, I want that."

Never underestimate faeries. They've made an art out of getting everything they want. They don't just get mad; they get even.

"So, fess up. Whatchya got?"

He shook his head. "I can't answer that—"

I lowered my head.

"Not for free."

"Huh?" I raised a brow and waited. When he didn't go on, I shrugged and offered a hand. "Like what? You want collateral? A bribe?"

He smiled. "Something like that."

Like I said, never underestimate a fae. They're tricky, conniving little shits that will fleece you for whatever they can. They can be grade-A opportunists.

"Fine." Two could play that game. "I'll give you something of my choosing."

The little fae crossed his arms and fixed me with a sullen look. "You don't get to decide its value to me."

"You're right. I don't." But if I was right about this, it

was invaluable to any fae. He didn't know how little good it'd do him, but he didn't need to know that. It had perceived value. Sometimes the perception of worth is good enough. "My name."

A hunger built in his eyes as they widened.

Names have power. They're linked to our identity, who we are. And there's another level of power in that. One that stretches back as far as the spoken word. Faeries know that. There's not much more they love than being able to pull on mortal strings and make us dance like puppets. Even lowly fae like a puck get off on that.

I had him. "That's got to be worth something, right?"

His face morphed into a mask of stone, but he couldn't hide the light in his eyes. Good poker face. Just not good enough. "It's worth something, mortal."

I grinned. Names can be used to track or summon something, if you had the skill. Worse, you could compel someone to act in a horrible manner. One contingency though. Your name needs to be bound to more than just an identity. It needs a body.

We're all more than our body. It's part of us, and rightfully so. In my case, it's a different story. Add to that my fractured memories and all the borrowed ones tagging along, my identity is unstable. I clung to it, but it wasn't as concrete as a normal person's. Which meant the faerie wasn't going to be able to do much with my name.

I've dealt with enough fae to know how to game 'em.

"So, mortal, are you going to tell me?"

My grin widened. I told him.

"Thank you." He bowed his head low.

About time I got some respect from the paranormal.

He dropped the clump of toilet paper and leapt past me. His hands clawed at the door and he wrenched, flinging it open. The puck hurtled into the living room before I processed what had happened.

Sometimes the supernatural are just cheating assholes.

"You little turd." I got to my feet and spun, tearing after him. The door handle slammed into the drywall and left an imprint.

The puck bolted towards the front door.

I wasn't going to let that happen.

The door opened, and it wasn't the puck's doing.

She was striking. Beige skin complected with a hint of gold. Chestnut hair that fell past her shoulders. Her brows were the same color but carried a hint of smokiness in them. She had full, wide lips that defined her mouth. They were spread wide in shock.

That happens when you walk in on a guy chasing a faerie.

Camilla Ortiz. An agent of the FBI. A one-time resident of a mental asylum that had gone through the Hollywood horror treatment. And...my friend. Though she didn't know it.

She brushed the side of her slim-fitting, burgundy leather jacket. Her hand blurred to her holster. She pulled and drew a handgun, tucking it to her chest before extending her arms. It happened in a second. It was smooth and practiced.

I froze.

The puck didn't. He threw back his head, letting out a shrill cry. The fae scampered towards the back of the apartment.

Ortiz bristled, but to her credit, and training, she didn't fire. Gold on a field of black caught my eye. The FBI badge hung from a silver chain that stood out against her black shirt. I noticed how nicely her jeans clung to her as well. I'm a detective. We pick up stuff like that.

The puck swiped his hand through the air. The simple gesture was tinged with unseen magic. Daniel's back window seemed to open of its own accord. The puck bent and leapt through it.

My mouth mirrored the woman's, widening at his course of action.

Light flashed, and the screaming ceased.

The creature had opened a Way and skedaddled back to his home.

I turned and offered a hapless shrug and a matching smile. "Huh, that was weird."

She blinked twice before kicking the door shut with the back of her heel. Ortiz moved into the room, keeping the gun leveled at me. Her hands were steady, and her molasses eyes carried a fire I'd seen before. It was like looking at molten steel.

I swallowed. There had been a supernatural creature in the room, and she still had her gun trained on me. Most people would've gone after the creature.

She wasn't most people.

"Um, hi." I waved. It was a dumb thing to do.

She homed in on my forearm. Her eyes ballooned, and I saw her jaw harden. She nodded to my tattoo with a slight thrust of her chin. "What's that?" Ortiz arched a brow and fixed me with a stare I was all too familiar with.

Shit.

"It's a tattoo." I tapped my index and middle finger against it. "You know, ink; it's cool—fashionable."

Her jaw tightened further. "You think that's funny?"

Not anymore. I remained silent.

She took another step closer. The gun was pointed just below my sternum. "Does this tattoo change by the hour?"

I exhaled then nodded. There was no point lying. Camilla Ortiz possessed an uncanny ability to separate fact from fiction. I'd seen her call out a supernatural creature— an expert on falsehoods—on their bullshit. "Yeah."

She tilted her head to look away for a second. The gun remained steady.

...Yay.

"You know, I've met two guys with tattoos like that."

I opened my mouth but stopped when she flashed me a glare that told me it wasn't a good idea.

"But you already know that, don't you?"

What could I say? Open my mouth and lie—I'd be called on it. Tell the truth, and I'd likely be shot. I'm allergic to bullets. And if I kept my trap shut, was it just as good as saying yes?

I kept quiet.

"I'm going to ask you another question, and you're going to answer it." She licked her lips, and her hands shook for a microsecond that I almost missed.

I nodded.

"Who are you, really?"

God. If ever there was a question I wished I could answer. I've been wondering that for a long time myself, Ortiz. "My name is Daniel—"

"Don't—" She broke off and shook her head. "Don't do that. Don't lie to me. Not again. Not while you look like—" Ortiz lowered the gun to my beltline before raising it again. "Not while you look like him."

A hand coated in ice gripped my heart. "What do you mean?"

"You're not Daniel Kim."

My heart lurched inside the frozen grip.

A bead of moisture formed at the corner of her left eye. It was mirrored a second later by her right eye. Her hands shook again, but she brought them under control. "Daniel Kim is my friend, and you're not him."

Oh, God. The invisible hand squeezed tighter, and my chest felt like it'd cave in on itself. It's one thing to tell someone the truth. It's another to do it when you're wearing their friend's body. How do you tell someone the person they cared for is dead?

There is no easy answer. Not that the right answers are ever easy. But she deserved to know. Hell, for everything she'd gone through at my side, I should've come clean long ago. But, because of everything she'd gone through with me, her life had taken some nasty turns. Where's the line where it's okay to hide something from a person to protect them?

It's a blurry line. And maybe somewhere along the way, I'd crossed it. The question was: which side did I go over to? And where did that put Ortiz? Someone I used when I needed help? Or a friend?

Friends deserve straight answers.

And they deserve to live.

My mind felt like a swarm of bees on amphetamines.

"Who are you? I'm not going to ask again."

I eyed her then the gun. She wouldn't kill me. I knew Camilla Ortiz. She was honest, played by the law, and most of all, she was a good person. But...that didn't mean she wouldn't cap my ass and drag me to the nearest station. She'd get her answers one way or another; I'd learned that much. So maybe it was best they came from me. Maybe it was time she knew me the way I knew her.

"My name is Vincent Graves, and I'm a soul."

Chapter Seven

Whatever had gone through my mind must have paled in comparison to what was going on in hers. I could almost visualize wires being undone within her noggin. Sparks were crackling about, and there was a processing error.

She may have had a built-in polygraph, but I think my little truth had just broken it.

Her mouth moved several times without sound. The tip of the gun lowered a fraction. "You're...telling the truth."

I nodded.

She shook her head and shut her eyes for a second. "Or you believe you are."

I shrugged. "That's possible too, but it's the truth, Ortiz."

Her spine went rigid. "What did you say?"

I repeated myself.

Ortiz let out a low, almost unheard breath. "It's Daniel's voice, but you sound like..." She trailed off.

My hands came to my side. I hoped it wasn't enough of an action to prompt her to shoot. "Charles? Norman?"

She shivered and licked her bottom lip before folding it under her teeth. She did that when she was deep in thought.

I shut my mouth and let her process. The break was nice. My heart rate didn't settle to a calm pace, but it was getting there. The tips of my fingers and the surface of my skin felt like a cold static charge crackled over them.

No biggie. No pressure. You just told Ortiz the big secret you've been keeping from her since you first met. She wouldn't hold a grudge. I shut off my inner thoughts and stared at the gun. I changed my belief on the grudge thing and took a step to the left. Better for Daniel to have a hole in his wall than his solar plexus.

"Ortiz?"

She shook her head and came back to earth. "Yeah?

Yes—no—you don't get to call me that."

I nodded. It was fair enough. After everything we'd gone through together, and I had kept something like this from her. She had every right to distrust me. That didn't make it feel any easier. My gut felt hollow and lined with lead at the same time. It was like an empty shell threatened to drag me through the floor with no stopping. I didn't know what to say.

"Norman. Charles." She didn't look at me. Ortiz was trapped in a mental circus trying to figure it all out. When she did look up, the steel was gone from her eyes. They looked softer. "Tell me about them."

"Yeah, sure. You already know most of it."

She nodded.

"I...borrowed their bodies when I met you."

Her face lost focus. She didn't say anything but motioned with her hand for me to continue.

"Like I said, I'm a soul. Do you remember what I said over a year ago when we were riding in your car to see Marsha?" An invisible fist struck my chest and stomach in quick succession. That name brought back an unpleasant memory, and I have no shortage of those.

Ortiz pursed her lips before nodding. "You said something about not remembering who you are—were—and how you're stuck in this life."

I bowed my head. "Yeah. Here I am." I gestured to Daniel's chest with a hand. "I don't have a body of my own. I don't know what happened to it. All I know is that I was murdered, and that I got stuck in limbo. Since that moment, I've been tasked with inhabiting the bodies of those murdered by the paranormal. I use their bodies, skills, and memories to figure out what killed them, and stop it." I tapped the tattoo. "And I've only got so long to do it."

Her brows rose and her eyes widened. "Norman. Charles. You inhabited the bodies of those who died."

I tried to look away, but I watched from the corner of my eyes.

Her hands shook. They didn't stop this time. "Daniel...."

I didn't say another word.

"My friend is dead. And you're wearing his body like a

suit?"

It was the truth—a hard one, and I didn't know how I could make it bearable.

The beads of moisture at the edges of her eyes became thin streams. An invisible sickle cut the strength out of her legs and she collapsed to a cross legged position. The gun came to rest on the inside of her thigh as she folded her arms.

"I'm sorry."

She looked at me. Seeing her like that banded my chest with heated iron.

I looked to the ground. "I'm sorry."

"For my friend dying?"

I looked back at her and flinched. Some of the heat had returned to her eyes.

"Or for lying?"

"Yes." I nodded.

"You really are the same guy?"

I nodded again. "One and only."

She lowered her arm, thumbing the safety on her pistol before stowing it.

I exhaled as quietly as I could.

She placed her hands on the floor and pushed, using the momentum to help spring to her feet. Ortiz closed the distance between us in a matter of seconds.

I offered her a weak smile. I should've clenched my jaw and leaned away.

Her collar shifted. Leather tightened as she took another step, twisting at the waist. I could see the muscles in her legs flex against the tight jeans as she pushed off her back leg.

My jaw felt like I'd been kicked by a horse. Pain rippled into the rest of my face. I hadn't seen her fist move. My vision became a pixilated blur of color. Everything snapped into clarity as fast as it had left. I moved my lower jaw side-to-side, wincing as it throbbed. "Uh, ow."

Ortiz's eyes froze, giving me a look that spoke volumes. "You deserve more than that."

I couldn't argue. I sure as hell did deserve it. I counted my blessings in getting off so easy.

She bristled, and her hand twitched.

"You going to punch me again?" I tilted my head and

arched a brow.

"I'm seriously considering it. It won't do anything but make me feel better."

Life's complicated. We're told so many things throughout it. What to do. What not to do. How to behave at certain times and in select people's presence. In all of that, one of the things we've been taught is to not cave into our temptations. Don't pull the trigger on impulses. That's not always the best thing. Sometimes, it's okay to indulge. It's a fine line, and you have to take precautions to make sure you don't go too far over it. But sometimes you need to give in to what you want in the moment. It can help in the long run.

I gave Ortiz a goofy grin. "Sometimes you need to do what makes you feel better."

My ribs felt like someone had dropped a bowling ball on them when the second punch landed. I doubled over, pressing a hand to the area in hope of dulling the pain. It didn't work. "Jesus! You can indulge without being so hostile about it."

She blew a breath out through her nose.

"Feel better?" I winced and rubbed the spot again.

"A bit."

That worked for me. I wasn't keen on letting her use me for kickboxing practice.

She didn't back away from me, but she didn't bring the gun back out either.

Mixed blessings.

Ortiz placed a hand on my shoulder and shoved, driving my back against the wall. She held me there. "Explain."

"What? One-word commands are rather ambiguous."

She blinked twice. "God, you're still a smartass."

I pressed my lips together and gave her a coy look before turning my gaze to the ground in mock embarrassment. "Aw, you're just saying that." An acute row of pressure filled the meat above my collarbone. I twisted and tried to shrink away from her fingers. "Okay, okay."

She released her hold.

I shook my head. "Jeez, Ortiz. I know there are some issues between us, and that they're mostly my fault."

She arched a brow. "Mostly?"

I held up a hand, motioning for her to give me a chance

to explain. "Yeah, mostly. Look. Everything else aside, we've worked together to stop monsters—twice now. We've helped people—"

"You lied to me." There was an edge to her voice that could have cut through stone, but there was something else too. That sharpness carried an undertone of brittleness. There was a part of her that still had a level of feelings towards me.

I didn't know what they were, only that they were powerful, and causing her some measure of conflict. But she was right. I'd lied to her. I had my reasons. It didn't change anything, except maybe how we'd move on from this. I cleared my throat and rubbed a hand against it. "So, what's left to tell? You know my story as well as I do."

"I want to know why." The last word rang like a silver bell, and it carried a ton of weight behind it.

"Suppose that's the question that really matters, isn't it?" I met her stare for a fraction of a second before breaking the hold. "What do you want me to say?"

She licked her lips and swallowed. "Anything."

"I can do that." I shut my eyes, thinking about what I could say. Nothing would fix the damage. But maybe there was a way to move forwards—together. We'd kicked some serious paranormal butt side-by-side. It wasn't worth losing her, as a partner and a friend. "Alright, but it's the same reason I've given you before."

Ortiz fixed me with an oblique stare. "And they've all been bullshit."

If words could bite, those would have left marks like a rottweiler on a mailman's ass.

"To you, maybe. And yeah, some of them weren't great; that doesn't mean they were untrue. You know that. Remember when I was in Norman's body?" She opened her mouth, but I waved her off. "No, seriously. What happened to you?"

Her color paled just enough to mute the hints of gold in her complexion. Ortiz brought a hand halfway up to her left breast before she realized what she was doing. She stopped before her fingers touched her coat over the spot. Her hand shook, but she reined it in.

That had an effect. Good. I was making my point. "I

can't imagine what that was like for you, Ortiz. But you know what?"

"What?" Her voice had lost the hardened edge. Only the brittleness remained.

"I had to watch that. I saw you fall, and guess whose fault it was? No—before you say anything—don't give me the crap about your choices and decisions. Yeah, you're right; you get to make those calls. But I could have turned you away at any time. You know that. You made your choices, and I made mine. I dragged you into this, no matter how you want to argue it. Remind me where I found you next? What happened to your life after—" The light of the world dulled before flashing across my eyes like lightning. My right cheek felt like I'd been slapped with a hot iron.

Ortiz's chest heaved, and her breathing followed in sync. Her right hand twitched, and the skin of her palm reddened. "Keep going. I'd love another reason to hit you."

I rubbed my cheek, blinking until I could think again. "Uh...no, no, it's cool. Your turn to talk, I guess?"

She balled her fists, planting them on her hips. "You're damn right that was my call." Ortiz's index finger bounced off my chest as she made her point. "I never once blamed you, did I?"

She didn't.

"Every decision I made, I've lived with the consequences, including the six-month break from my job. Yes, I was in a horrible place in my head and in the world. You didn't drag me into that."

That didn't do much to alleviate the guilt.

"What you did, Vincent Graves, was worse."

I swallowed and cold lumps of iron formed in my stomach.

"You lied to me. Do you think that's what I needed? Protection? What I needed was for you to trust me the way I had you."

Had. Three letters. A simple word. And in the context, made me feel like a piece of frozen glass. One that just shattered. Trust is a fragile, living thing. It changes and evolves over time. You can nurture it, help it grow. You can let it wither, slowly, until the inevitable. And you can do what I did—break it completely.

"I didn't want you to hide things from me. I needed you to tell me, share them. That's how you should have protected me if that was your goal. I needed to know. You blinded me, kept things in the dark. How is anyone supposed to help like that? You weren't protecting me. You were protecting yourself."

And that was the sound of a hammer hitting the bits of broken glass that made up yours truly.

Ouch.

She was right though. Dammit, she was right. Everything I'd done was for me, and it didn't matter how I tried to paint it. I could have brought her in, told her the truth. I didn't. What I did was worse. I kept her at arm's length. Close enough to ask her for a hand when I needed her. Far enough to push her out of the way—away from me. I thought if she wasn't too close, she'd be safe. My misguided sense of heroism broke whatever it was we had.

My voice lodged itself deep in my chest, refusing to surface. The muscles in my throat felt like frozen steel cables. Nothing moved. That entire section of my body locked down. I worked down what little saliva I could and cleared my throat.

Ortiz watched me the whole time. She didn't say a thing, just stared at me, and it was terrifying. There was no heated glare. No icy daggers. Ortiz's face was a stone mask. I'd never seen that before. It hurt.

"Yeah, you're right. About all of it, and I'm sorry. I kept you in the dark because I was scared. Hell, Ortiz, look at it from my point of view."

A hint of fire kindled in her eyes, but she remained silent.

"I'm not saying I'm right. I'm looking for understanding. I'm a soul without a body. Let that sink in. Do you know have any idea what that's like?"

The fire in her eyes dulled.

I didn't give her a chance to respond. "Do you want to know something really terrifying?" I didn't stop to see if she wanted to hear it. She asked for answers, and here we were. She was going to get them. All of them. "I don't remember."

She blinked. "Remember what?"

"Any of it. Honestly. Not just my past, or who I really was. When you go to bed each night, how do you do it? As Camilla Ortiz. You know how I do it? I don't. I don't know. It's like the lights go out for a split second and I'm not awake to register it. It's like blacking out and waking up in someone else; God knows who or where. My life—lives— whatever they are, go by in flashes. I live by the hour." I held up my forearm and slapped the tattoo. "With all of the unexplainable stuff we've gone through together, tell me this: how do you explain that to someone?"

I wasn't aware of it at first. The thin muscles in my eyelids quivered, and something wet slipped across them. I shut my eyes and cut the tears off. Something fell on my shoulder, and I tightened in response.

Ortiz gave me a gentle squeeze. "You tell that someone just like that, Vincent. What did you think—that after everything, I wouldn't believe you? Or worse, did you think I'd hate you? Maybe be afraid?"

"Honestly, Ortiz?"

"Honestly."

"I don't know." I gave her a smile of brittle glass. "That's what's scary. I didn't know how you'd react. I wanted to tell you. God, I did. When I took you to that church in Norman's body, I had every intention of talking things out." I thought of Church and turned away.

He warned me not to tell her. That Ortiz wasn't ready yet. It didn't matter much now. I sighed and clenched a fist. But Church didn't deserve my anger. So long as I was being honest with myself, the truth was...Church never physically stopped me. I don't know if he could have. I likely could have told Ortiz anytime I wanted. But I didn't. I made that choice. And every choice has a consequence.

Ortiz tilted her head, regarding me. She gave me a gentle shake. "But?"

"But...I don't know." I felt that sword point again. It dug deep into my gut. "And here we are."

She made a sound like she had swallowed what little moisture remained in her throat.

I knew the feeling.

"Yeah, not the best place to be." She rubbed her index and middle fingers against her temples. "Who you are. The lies. Daniel's gone."

I said nothing.

"Jesus, it's insane."

"The summary of my life, Ortiz. That's what it is."

"God, your life sucks."

I snorted so hard it felt like the inside of my nose had been stripped by sandpaper. "You're telling me."

We laughed. That was something we both needed. It was like the entire room had been blanketed in magic that instant. Everything felt lighter—fresher. Something clean took the place of something foul. Things weren't better. Not that quickly, but maybe there was a chance they would be. I'd take it. Sometimes all you need is a chance, one you're willing to take and follow through on. You just have to decide if it's worth taking.

I gave Ortiz a look. Yeah. Definitely a chance worth taking. "So, where's this leave us, Ortiz?"

She looked away, eyeing the apartment door, before returning my gaze. "I don't know. Work in progress, maybe?"

Aren't we all?

"Yeah, yeah, I can get behind that." I exhaled and peeked at my tattoo. Between everything that had gone on with getting back, the puck, and Ortiz's impromptu interrogation, I'd lost another hour. Forty-eight left. I blew out through my nose again. Two days to solve an investigation that had me feeling like I hadn't even started.

"Something's going through your head. I can see it."

I shook my noggin clear and raised my forearm.

Ortiz spotted the tattoo and put it together. "Right. Daniel's death. You're on a case, in my friend's body." She let out a heavy breath.

"Yeah, that's not something you're going to get used to."

She gave me a grim laugh that made horror novels seem cheery. "No, it's not." Ortiz's neck pulsed visibly as the muscles in her throat contorted. She was choking on something.

I had an idea what. It's never an easy question to ask, but if I knew her as well as I thought I did, she had the guts to ask it anyway.

"So, how did he die?" Something flashed in her eyes. It was like a quick spark of static, lasting a second before fading.

I told her what I knew.

"That's not much to go on, Vincent."

"You're telling me. I've been running back and forth trying to piece together his life and..." A thought struck me. I eyed her and turned away from her slightly. "You mind if I ask you some things now?"

She rolled her shoulders in what amounted to a half shrug. "Sure. Seems fair." There was an edge to how she said it.

She wasn't going to let this go. But then, would I?

"How'd you figure this"—I waved at my borrowed body—"out?" Something didn't add up. Ortiz was damn smart, but putting together enough to come after me took a lot of time and resources. Not to mention an uncanny ability to put things together. It's not as if someone's first thought upon meeting me in a new body is going to be, You must be a soul jumping from meat suit to meat suit.

I may have given her the answer, but Ortiz had come close to the ballpark. Call me curious, but I had to know how.

"Things weren't adding up." She folded her lips and chewed on them before continuing. "Norman. You left your—his...ugh." Ortiz shook her head and shut her eyes tight.

I got the feeling. It's never easy referring to your borrowed bodies. It's worse for others.

"When I woke up at the end of our first case together, I found a body."

I shrugged but said nothing.

"There was a problem though. Norman's body didn't look the same it did in his license, the way he should have looked."

I didn't think about that. It must have reverted after I'd left it. But why didn't it revert after killing the Ifrit? Or after I'd woken up at the beginning of the case? The deal was done by then. My brain felt like a dry sponge being torn to pieces.

"That wasn't all."

Her words pulled me back to reality, and my curiosity deepened.

"Norman's body looked like it'd been dead for days, but that wasn't the weirdest bit."

Maybe Ortiz needed to reconsider that. It sounded pretty weird to me.

"When the mortician got her hands on the body, things got unexplainable."

I laughed, passing it off as a cough when she glared at me. "Um, after all you'd been through at that point..." I trailed off when her stare intensified.

"The mortician ruled it a heart attack, except it had happened earlier. It was like something had kept Norman's body together." Her eyes narrowed on me. "Something kept him young. Something kept him from falling to pieces when everything inside him said he had done that long ago."

I gulped. "Yeah, that's weird." The false smile I forced across my face didn't do much. I'd hoped for a little quirk of her lips. A small smile perhaps. Nope.

"You know what happened next?"

I did, but remained silent.

"It was the same story with Charles. You were acting weird, almost like Norman had. I didn't say anything though. I mean, the only thread connecting the two of you was that." She bowed her head, shooting a look at my tattoo. "It was how you acted, how competent you were, and then, the moments where you weren't." A hint of a smile touched her lips.

It suited her.

"Charles was never like that. Functional, yes, but the way you operated through the whole case was the way Norman had."

My gut roiled like living ropes twining over one another and stretching taut. Even through all of that, she thought I was competent. Another form of trust. Another one I'd broken. I kept the thoughts to myself, motioning for her to continue.

"Imagine my surprise, Vincent, when I found your— Charles'—body on the floor of the chapel."

I didn't want to think about it. I never gave it much thought before. When I end a case, I'm pulled from the

body and the process repeats. That happens with no regard
for anyone who comes across the dead body. It hits people
hard, especially loved ones and friends.

"When I turned the body over—" She winced and took
a moment to regain her composure. Ortiz's chest rose with
every deep breath. Her fingers curled and folded into a fist
several times.

I gave her the time she needed. It was the least I could
do, and I'd done enough. That was for sure.

"He looked like the rest of the victims, Vincent." She
sounded like her throat was lined with sawdust. Hoarse and
strained.

It hurt to hear her like that.

"The insides of his face were just wrong." She
suppressed a visible shiver. "It looked like the phage had
gotten him too." Ortiz gave me a look. "But it couldn't have
because you stopped it."

I tilted my head to the side and waggled a hand in a so-
so gesture. "Technically, we killed it." I grinned.

She returned it, a bit weaker than I had hoped, but I'd
take it. "Thanks, but when his body was examined, it was
the same thing. His insides were filled with the same gunk
we found in the other bodies. It was a mess, again. But you
know what else was the same?"

I didn't answer, but boy did I have an idea.

"The mortician told me that body had been dead for a
while. The only thing that made sense was that Charles had
been attacked before our case." She gave me a knowing
look. "That's a lot of similar situations, too similar for
coincidence, and I don't believe in those. Some sort of
magical glue held him together until the end. And now that
glue's holding my friend's body together."

I lowered my head. "Yeah, I know. Trust me when I say
it, Ortiz: I didn't ask for this."

"I know, Vincent." She rubbed the back of her hand
against her eyes. There weren't any tears that I could see, but
I knew how she felt. And I knew Ortiz wouldn't want me to
see any.

I looked away out of respect, just in case some rogue
tears appeared. "That's a lot of circumstantial stuff. It
doesn't add up to you figuring it all out."

"No, but it didn't sit right. I've always had good intuition. I just had to dig. The second I left the asylum, that's what I did, and I didn't stop."

Never discount intuition. You can have all the tools and knowledge in a field, but there's something intangible that comes with intuition. You can't buy it, and it can't be given. It's formed and honed over years of dedication. Your mind knows a lot of things and buries them. It takes in more than we realize and shapes them, follows and connects threads. It's a powerful thing. We process a great deal more than we realize. We're smarter and cleverer than we give ourselves credit for.

We may not have powers like the supernatural, but don't think for a second that we're powerless. We're not. We've got knowledge, and in my world, that's about the best form of power you can have.

All Ortiz needed was a thread to pull on, and to keep tugging until she got close enough. She'd succeeded.

"That's great and all, but that's still not enough to bring you here."

Her mouth spread into a lopsided smile, and she looked rather pleased with herself. "You're right; it's not." She waggled her fingers in a gesture I'd given her before. "Secrets."

I blinked. There's an unspoken rule—that I might've made up on the spot—that you do not steal someone's thing. I glared at her.

Her grin grew. "I had help."

"Uh, what?"

Ortiz pulled a phone from her pocket, and tapped her fingers to the screen. I heard a faint ringing until she lifted it to her mouth. "Can you swing by?" Ortiz gave Daniel's address to the person on the other end of the line.

I arched a brow and eyed her sideways, waiting for an explanation.

She fixed me with a look that would have been unreadable but for a slight quirk of her mouth. "Just wait for about thirty minutes."

"It'd better be worth it."

She smiled. "It will be."

So we did.

Thirty minutes passed.
The door opened.

Chapter Eight

She was a mousy thing. A young woman in her early twenties with a willowy build. Her outfit was picked from one of those hip urban apparel stores that sell popular nerd culture clothing. She wore periwinkle sneakers that clearly weren't made for running. Her pants were tight-fitting jeans torn for fashion's sake. She wore a t-shirt that caught my attention off the bat. It was black with bold white lettering that read: I Want To Believe.

I resisted the urge to snort. The kid had taste. A bunch of them, it seemed like.

Swirls of ink raced over the fair skin of her left arm in a tattoo sleeve. I couldn't make out the design. Her hair was a coppery brown and worn in a pixie cut with a heaping of hair product. It had been textured and pulled to resemble something like a cockatoo.

An olive-colored canvas laptop bag hung from her shoulders. It looked filled to the brim and like it should've been causing her discomfort. She flashed Ortiz a smile that made its way to her eyes. It looked like they were made from chips of cobalt mixed with gunmetal. Her smile widened in a way that brought out the dimple in her cheeks and made the small dusting of freckles stand out.

Ortiz returned the smile before turning to me. She waved a hand to the woman in the doorway. "This is Kelly Page."

Kelly tapped two fingers to the crown of her head and tipped them in a salute.

I extended a hand. "Nice to meet you."

Kelly looked at my hand then turned to Ortiz, tilting her head as she waited for a cue.

Ortiz inclined her head.

Kelly took my hand.

We shook, and I flashed her a reassuring smile. "I'm—"

"The alien." Kelly's face lit up in self-satisfaction.

My mind buzzed and tingled like a limb that had fallen asleep. I'm pretty sure it sent that signal to the rest of my body as well. I don't know how long ticked by before I was able to respond. "Say, what?"

She fixed me with a quizzical stare, tilting her head like a dog hearing a new sound. "The alien."

That's what I thought she said. As if my life wasn't weird enough already. I turned to face Ortiz, eyeing her and arching a brow.

"It's—she's complicated."

Kelly shook her head, moving to the sofa where she plopped down. "Not really." She unfastened the metal clasps of her bag, pulling a thin laptop out of it. "I'm the one who helped her put all this together."

I couldn't see how. The kid was clearly a bit off-kilter. I eyed Ortiz.

She blew out a breath, looking away for a moment. "It's a long story."

Kelly snorted. "Not really." Her fingers danced over the keyboard, eliciting a staccato of mechanical clicks. "I've been following your work. We all have."

My eyes spun, and I think something short-circuited in my skull. I looked at Ortiz and mouthed the word we.

Ortiz said nothing.

Kelly turned the laptop around, tilting the screen back so I had a clearer view. She pointed at a web page, smiling as she did. "People talk. They keep track of this stuff. People all over the world with tattoos just like that one." She inclined her head towards mine. "I've kept track of all the sightings and compiled them onto my blog."

This wasn't happening. I shook my head and winced. "Did you hear that, Ortiz? She has a blog." I hoped Kelly wasn't the sensitive type. My tone could have sanded wood to dust.

Kelly ignored me, scrolling down so I could see images blur by.

They were the sort of pictures reserved for Bigfoot sightings and the like. Each was a mess. But I recognized them. Mostly because I was there. My eyes felt like saucers. Each of the bodies that scrolled by...was one of mine. Case after case. Someone, somehow, managed to get a snippet here or there.

She scrolled until a familiar street in Manhattan came to view. A lens flare obscured part of the photo. The body of a large beast, golden in color, was partially visible. It was chasing a blonde-haired man in a suit.

The case I'd gone through in New York around a year and a half ago. The case where I'd met Ortiz. I remembered that bit, and the people snapping photos as it happened.

Kelly turned the computer around and tapped away as she spoke. "There's tons of these over the web. Lots of people think it's a group or a cult. A few of us got smart and started putting things together. It took a lot of file-sharing and chat sessions."

My mind numbed. If there was enough evidence lying around, other people with Kelly's skill and dedication could put this together. They could figure me out and—worse— the world in which I operate. It's hard enough for me to safely navigate it. Someone stumbling into this with a little bit of knowledge was going to get into trouble.

Knowledge is power in my world, but a little bit of knowledge is the worst. It's just enough to chase things, and when you chase something, you normally follow it to the end. That end in my world is normally danger. A little bit of knowledge gives you just enough rope to hang yourself with.

Acid seared my muscles, making its way to the lining of my throat. This is what I was afraid of.

I backpedaled, not taking my eyes off Kelly. My hands fumbled as I reached out blindly. I got my fingers around Ortiz's arm and tugged.

She gave me an oblique stare. "What?"

I hooked a thumb to the corner of the room, signaling her to follow me. I wanted to be out of earshot from Kelly, but close enough to keep an eye on her. It's not that I didn't trust her. It's just that I'd been attacked more frequently than ever on this case. If it happened again, Kelly would be in the crossfire. I couldn't accept that. And I couldn't risk being in a position not to help should the worst happen.

She followed me to the far corner while Kelly remained engrossed in her computer. Ortiz arched a brow and folded her arms under her breasts. "What?"

I gestured with a subtle tilt of my head to Kelly.

Ortiz followed the nod. "What about her?"

"You getting involved in this—fine. I can't do anything about that. We established that a while back. You're too curious for your own good, and you've been through hell with me. You've earned your spot here, no matter how much I worry."

Ortiz gave me a knowing look. "I'm sensing a but."

"But, her? Ortiz, come on; she's a kid. Older than Lizzie—sure—but Lizzie didn't ask to be part of this world. She was without a damn choice. Kelly's snooped too far already. God knows how she figured this much out." I swallowed and lowered my voice. "Besides...alien?"

Ortiz's lips pressed tight. Her eyes shone in amusement, and her mouth twitched like she was trying to fight the urge to laugh. "Give her a chance to explain why."

I didn't think I wanted to hear the answer.

"So, what's the real issue here, Vincent?"

"The real issue? How about everything we've been through? Do you really want to involve another person? Someone with enough curiosity and knowledge to know there are things going bump in the night, but without enough sense to leave it all alone?"

"You can't make that call for her, Vincent, just like you couldn't for me."

I could feel the heat building in my face. Any more and I'd be a living tea kettle spitting steam out of my ears. "But you can? You made the decision to rope her in."

Her face paled. "What?"

"You heard me. She's, what, in her twenties? How'd you find her anyhow?"

Ortiz looked to the floor for a moment.

Now she knew how I felt. It's not always about the choices of others. Guilt's a chain fashioned from barbed wire. It wraps around you and anyone who gets too close. They can come of their own volition, but it doesn't keep you from feeling guilty if things go wrong. It makes the barbs sink deeper and drag you down. Every mistake is like a tear in your body. And I know something about tearing up your body.

"Like I said, I started digging. I came across her blog,

her theories, and photos."

"And you called her up because the alien theory made sense."

Ortiz snickered before swallowing it. "No, but she was close on a lot of it. Enough for me to connect the dots and run with the idea that there wasn't a group of people running around. There was just one. Somehow he—you—managed to look like..." She stopped and rubbed the side of her head. "God, you're a frustrating man, thing, soul."

I blinked, unsure how or what part of that to take offense to. So, I settled for all three. "I'm not a frustrating man-thing-soul. I'm an adorably witty soul-man-thing."

Ortiz's lips quirked. "I really want to punch you again."

I raised a hand. "Sorry, I can't pay for any more of the whole dominatrix thing. I'm broke."

Ortiz rolled her eyes.

"But seriously, Ortiz, we can't keep dragging people into this. Do you have any idea how horrible I felt for what happened to you?" I waved her off before she could argue. She had a point, and it was probably a good one. I didn't need that right now. I needed her to know what it was like to be on the other end. The supernatural world did not care for mortals. It wasn't nice. And more often than not, it left them in pieces. "You handled everything thrown at you, fine. You're tough—no arguing that. But what do you know about her? She's curious. She's a blogger. Great. Can she fight? Is she ready for this?"

Ortiz's skin flushed.

"What happens if she's not? What happens if she gets hurt or worse? Now tell me it's her call, and how you'd feel if she died?"

Ortiz failed to meet my stare.

"I know I lied to you. You're mad about that. Fine. But do you understand why?"

"Yes, I do." Ortiz rubbed her arms and gave me a look that let me know I might have gone too far.

Great job, Graves. Way to bully your friend.

I sighed and rubbed my eyes. "I'm sorry. Let's just—" I broke off to wave a hand towards Kelly. I didn't wait for Ortiz's response before I moved near the blogger.

Kelly looked up, scanning me with eerie attentiveness.

I felt like I was under a microscope. Changing the subject seemed like a good way to break up the creepy stare. I got enough of those from Church. "So, uh, you never finished explaining how you figured all of this out."

Kelly stopped typing and gave me a blank look. "Easy. I did a lot of sleuthing, putting things together, and reading up on reports."

I wanted to point out that browsing the internet did not count as sleuthing. What I did—trailing monsters, following clues, and more—counted as sleuthing. It took a second for something to register. "Reports?"

Ortiz groaned behind me. "That's how I really found out about Kelly."

An impish grin spread across the young woman's face. "I broke into a bunch of confidential stuff here and there. No biggie."

I eyed Ortiz then Kelly, who was clearly more than just an internet surfer. "You...broke into?"

"She's a hacker"—Ortiz sighed, pressing a hand to her head—"with a record."

My mouth parted, but I couldn't find the words.

Kelly beamed. She didn't seem the least bit upset or embarrassed by the fact. "People have a right to know about this stuff. This information affects us all. I mean...aliens!"

I glared at her. "Stop that. I'm not an alien. What makes you think that?"

"The reports, consistent actions, your attitude, the tattoos. It's all indicative of a single personality. It's too consistent. You can't ignore the signs. The dead bodies at the end of a case. You're an alien, using corpses as a host."

I lost it and told her everything.

She shook her head in denial. "No, that doesn't add up. There's no scientific evidence for monsters, magic, the metaphysical, or any proof of a soul. We're chemicals and electrical signals." She looked me up and down. "Some more advanced than others."

My head throbbed, and I had to put my hands to my temple. I winced, trying to recall the signs of an aneurysm. This girl was going to kill me.

This was getting out of hand, and fast. Ortiz knew my secret and had no intention of leaving this world alone.

She'd also dragged another person into it now.

Don't forget what the Night Runner and troll said. Someone was testing me, and it had nothing to do with the case at hand. Speaking of which, I had very little in the way of information. My only real lead was a puck that managed to escape. Daniel's gallery was likely a crime scene by now, so that was out.

I shut my eyes until the muscles around them ached and quivered. My palms ground against the sockets in an effort to dull the throbbing in my skull. This case was a nightmare. I needed more answers, and the best way to get them was to ask.

"Ortiz."

She looked at me. "Hmm?"

"How'd you and Ancient Aliens over here find me? Not the me-me. How did you know that something was going on in Daniel's life?"

Ortiz's cheeks flushed and a light touched her eyes. They faded quickly, but I made note of them.

Was she embarrassed?

"I called his cell the day before. He didn't answer. It's not the first time. He's usually busy with his gallery, the clients—he's got a busy life." She spoke rapid fire, rambling. I'd never seen Camilla Ortiz be anything but concise and to the point. "I tried again a few times over the day and into the night. When I didn't even get a text reply, I got worried." She shrugged.

"And that's when you got to work. It wasn't about me. You were worried about Daniel."

She inclined her head. "Yeah. He's—he was—a scatterbrain, but he always made time for his friends." There was a certain inflection that filled that word. She didn't mean it to, but the way she said it left me wondering.

They were more than friends. I felt like a cheap aluminum can, one that had just been stepped on. Ortiz cared a helluva lot more for Daniel than was obvious. As good as she was at masking it, this hurt. And I was about to hurt her some more.

I sighed and took a deep breath, not wanting to continue the conversation. "I think I can put the rest together. You got a tip-off about his gallery?"

"Yeah. The alarm went off, sent out a distress to local PD. I was keeping an eye out for obvious reasons. After that, I came back here."

Back? I didn't know anyone else had been here at all. "You were in his place, how?"

Ortiz looked away.

"Oh my God. Do you have a key?"

"No, no, I took a page from your book. Your horrible, above-the-law book."

It was my turn to look away. I don't always have the option of getting into places with just a knock or a key. Breaking in is sometimes the way of things. Especially if there's a lot at stake. I flashed a weak smile.

"I picked the lock and checked out the place."

I arched a brow. "And?"

She shook her head. "Nothing. It was his usual mess."

That was something. It'd been a disaster when I'd first come in. So sometime between her visit and mine, the puck had sabotaged the scene. Not much of a timeframe. I couldn't do much with it either, not until I found that freak. I needed something though.

"How well did you know Daniel's life, Ortiz?"

"Pretty well. Why, you know something?" She gave me a look.

I sunk my head. "No, I don't. That's the problem. I wish I did. I'm lost here." I fished out his phone, holding the damaged piece up. "I was going to comb through this, see what I could find but—" I waggled the device to make my point.

Kelly leapt to her feet like she was a coiled spring. In a smooth move, she snatched the phone, plunked down on the couch, and stuffed her hand into her bag.

It took me a ten count to register what had happened. "Uh, what are you doing?"

She ignored me. Kelly retrieved a slender cable and inserted one end into the phone. The other end plugged into her laptop. Her fingers clicked away. "The phone's fine." She didn't look at us, remaining fixed on her screen. "It works. Screen's damaged. Keep quiet while I work."

Ortiz and I exchanged puzzled glances. Kelly's tone and movements were robotic as she did whatever the hell she was doing. I pointed to the hall where Daniel's bedroom and art studio were. Ortiz eyed me as I moved towards it. I didn't look back, but I heard her footsteps as she followed behind. I stopped outside the studio door, pushing it open and gesturing with a hand.

Ortiz passed me, stepping into it.

I followed her in and kicked the door shut.

"What's going on, Vincent?"

My fingers brushed against the side of my neck until I reached my hair. I dug in and scratched, unsure of what to say. "How are you—really?"

She froze.

"I know you. I know the badass parts of you, and I've seen the cracks, Ortiz. How are you? You're shaken, but you're not upset. You're not in tears. I know what Daniel meant to you." I turned my back to her and exhaled as I reached into the windbreaker and pulled my journal free.

Ortiz watched in silence.

I opened the journal and flipped through the pages with my index finger. I stopped when thick, quality paper brushed against my fingertip. I plucked the first piece of artwork free and unfolded it.

Ortiz's gaze went over it like a trained investigator. She took it all in and raised an eyebrow. "And?"

I pointed to the couple on the street, particularly the woman who possessed a fierce beauty. "Look at the woman." I tapped the sheet. "Long hair, full lips, enough detail to be compared to someone." I fixed her with a knowing look. "Someone we know."

Ortiz's eyes widened.

"So, you and Daniel were close." I tapped the tips of my index fingers together.

Her eyes grew larger than before. "Oh my God, no, nothing like that!"

Oops. "Oh, so close, but not that close."

She inclined her head. "Our jobs got in the way. He was struggling to get his gallery off of the ground for a while. I had a rough year." She stared at me.

Heh. Yeah, we both did.

"Things got in the way. We had something but..." She inhaled, licking her lips. "I'm not good. I'm not, Vincent.

But I'm going to have to be until this is over. I can't grieve until the thing that killed Daniel is dust. I'm not upset. I'm angry, and I'm scared of what will happen if I don't have somewhere to point that." Her hands balled into fists and shook.

I grabbed her wrists until the shaking stopped. I looked her in the eyes. "I know. And you know for damned sure that we will find this freak and gank it. We've done it before. We have a bit of a record now." I smiled.

She returned it. "Yeah, we do."

I folded the piece back into my journal, stowing the book. "Ortiz, I'm lost here. I'm clutching at straws, and I don't know where to go. You know anything that might help?"

She shook her head. "I didn't even have a chance to talk to his neighbors. I was going to ask Ashton—"

"Ashton?"

Ortiz paused. "Yes, that's what I said. Why?"

"Someone else mentioned him. The guy opposite here." I pointed straight ahead, gesturing to where the apartment across from Daniel's would be.

"Ashton is the oldest of the newer tenants."

I quirked a brow. "New?"

"Daniel's lived here for years. The rent's cheap, and the place is friendly to artists. More of them moved in recently. Ashton was the only one I ever met. I think he moved in about two weeks ago. Nice kid, works at the hospital ten blocks down."

And now I had someone to talk to. I'd have to dig up what I could on his neighbors. Anyone new was suspect to me. But Ashton might have lived here long enough to recognize anything strange in Daniel's life. He was the best bet to finding out what was happening.

"You got an address for this hospital?"

Ortiz told me then stared hard at me. "You planning on going alone?"

I nodded.

"Every time you go out looking for something, something usually finds you first." She tilted her head and kept up the stare.

Ortiz had a point, but I had to make mine. "I know

what you're going to say, and no."

She glared.

"Look." I nodded towards the living room. "Something's already after me. I need to hit the hospital—alone. You need to get Kelly to a safe place. She knows a fair bit, so let's keep it there, nothing more." I gave her a knowing nod.

She returned it.

There was a knock at the door before it was pushed open. Kelly stood there, leaning against the doorframe. She waggled the cracked phone. "Pulled a lot off this. Contacts list, text messages, but it's not useful. I can compile a list for your quest."

I blinked. "Quest?"

She nodded. "Whatever it is you aliens are really here for."

I took three breaths before I could to think clearly. "Yeah, sure. Thanks, kid."

Kelly jiggled the phone again. "I'll see what else I can recover, but I dug up the profiles of your neighbors."

Ortiz and I glanced at each other.

"Uh, can she do that?"

Ortiz's jaw tightened. "You mean, should she?"

"Yeah, sure that, and what I asked."

"No." Ortiz glared at Kelly. "She shouldn't be pulling up people's personal information. But, yes, apparently, she can."

Kelly wasn't the least bit perturbed by Ortiz's chastisement.

I threw my hands in the air. "Okay, Ortiz, get her somewhere safe."

Miss Conspiracy Theory did a double take between Ortiz and I. "Wait, where are you going? Can I come? I've never been with an—"

I waved her off as I headed to leave the room. "I've got a hospital to visit." And hopefully a solid lead. But first, I had to swing by a church. There were an awful lot of coincidences happening on this case.

That's fine, except I don't believe in those.

Church had some explaining to do.

Chapter Nine

I hit the streets, pulling the windbreaker around me for no other reason than comfort. I normally had something on a case by now. All I had at the moment were a dozen unconnected strings. I could only hope the one I was going to pull would lead me to something larger.

But, first, I needed to pull on a nagging suspicion involving Church. If I was right, he had a larger hand in everything going on. Something he'd likely deny. I didn't need the truth from him. I just needed an answer, any answer. Even a lie. So long as I could spot it for what it was. One way or another, I was going to figure this out.

I doubled my pace and almost broke into a run. The cathedral was far enough away to be an axe to my timeline. I hoped it wouldn't be too much of one.

Unless you get ambushed again.

I squinted and imagined my evil inner voice. "Quiet, you." That shut it up. There was enough going on. I didn't need extra distractions.

That's the thing about doubts and fears. They're webs ready to ensnare your mind in dozens of clinging strands. You tug and tear yourself free of some only to have the rest wrap tightly around you, but that doesn't mean you don't fight—you do. And sometimes you needed to know when to run from them. So I did.

I broke into a full sprint, maintaining the speed until I reached the cathedral. It came into view not long after, and I slowed. My pace morphed into a jog that shifted to a brisk walk as I made my way to the door. I didn't stop, extending my arms and ramming them into the doors. The place was empty.

Another coincidence.

"Church!" Echoes greeted me, but nothing else. "Church, get your manipulative, scheming Blondielocks butt down here right—"

"Vincent."

A lance of electricity shot up my body. I leapt, spinning around to face the source of the voice. "Holy-shits-of-whoziwhatsit?" My fists came up in defense, and I took a breath to calm myself. I let my hands fall to my sides as I composed myself. "Church, could you for once be normal and—I don't know—knock?"

He stared at me, unblinking, like I was speaking a foreign language.

Guess not.

"You have something on your mind, Vincent?" He gave me a look that made it clear he knew the answer.

"Yeah, lots of somethings. You already knew that though, didn't you? You seem to know and set up a lot, Church."

He moved to the closest pew and put a hand against the wooden back, gesturing to me. "Sit?"

I nodded and waved a hand. "After you." I followed him and sat down as he lowered himself to sit a foot away from me.

"I sense a great deal going on within you, Vincent. I'm worried."

Worried? That was new. Church was never the hug-it-out, feely type. With everything he's thrown me into over the years, it never seemed like he was ever worried. I frowned and thought it over for a moment and reconsidered. He had saved my ass many times and pointed me in the right direction when I needed it. I crossed a pair of mental fingers in my head, hoping he was willing to do it again. "Yeah, there's a lot going on."

He clasped his hands, resting them atop his knees, and stared. Church was the definition of a patient listener. Sometimes I wish he wasn't.

I ran a hand through my hair, pumping a fist several times. "I don't know. How about with this. We've established that you pick my cases, right?"

He said nothing. Not that he needed to.

"So why this one?" I held up a hand the instant he opened his mouth. "Not done. I need to say it. I know you know what I'm going to say, but I need to say it."

Church closed his mouth and inclined his head.

"Ortiz." I let her name hang in the air.

"I suppose this was going to happen." Church seemed to be talking more to himself than me. He turned his head a fraction and stared over the top of his glasses. "I once said that I hoped for you two to meet."

I remembered that. I took it on faith that's all he meant.

"I did, Vincent. I know you believe I'm manipulating your life—"

"And reading my mind." I flashed him a scowl.

He sighed. "I am not. It's complicated." Church waved a dismissive hand. A sign to bury that part of the conversation for the moment. "Yes, I choose your cases. Yes, Vincent, I need your help on this particular one. And yes, it is no coincidence this case has you possessing the body of someone close to Camilla Ortiz."

My eyes were like a high-speed camera shutter. Everything flickered for uncountable seconds. Church had been straight with me. No riddles. It wasn't the first time, but it was rare. "Um, okay. Thanks."

He bowed his head. "Of course. You deserve as much, Vincent."

I narrowed my eyes. "Who are you, and what have you done with the real Church?"

A light huff of air left his mouth in what I assumed was the most minor of laughs. As far as expressions from Church went, I counted it as a laugh. "You have more questions, Vincent."

"Why?"

He pursed his lips. "I suppose that is the one that matters most, isn't it?"

"It's one of the ones, but not the only one that's important." I gave him a long, hard stare. There was still the matter of my missing body and my real name. But I've learned to stop pressing that. I wouldn't forget, but there was something out there killing people. My identity was further down on the list of priorities for the moment.

"I know. As to the why, why do you think?"

It was like an invisible hand had slapped me. "What? Aren't you supposed to answer the question? What's with giving me one back?"

"The best way to get an answer, Vincent, is by asking a question."

My eyes narrowed. "Did you just quote Gnosis to me?"

Church's face was carved from stone. An inner light radiated within his eyes, making them more blue than gray. He made no comment on what he'd said.

I stared him down, hoping to make him budge. No luck. Church gave statues lessons on how to be stone-cold and unmoving. I cradled my forehead in my hand and sighed. "Alright, fine, I'll play along."

He moved a tad as he repositioned himself. Church hooked a finger around the frame of his glasses and pulled them free. His fingers slipped into the pocket in his shirt, plucking a thin cloth from it. He watched me out of the corners of his eyes as he cleaned the lenses. For a guy who kept his trap shut, he sure had a way of saying a lot.

I brushed a hand against my lips and cheeks, thinking. "You want Ortiz involved." It was rather a simple statement. It was right though. Don't discount something simply because it isn't complicated. Sometimes the simple stuff's the right stuff.

Church gave me a look that said I could do better.

And sometimes the simple answers don't placate everyone. I sighed. "You feel she's important—to the case—or something else that I don't know about."

The left edge of his mouth twitched.

"I'll take that as warmer."

Church said nothing.

"Okay, she's really important to things, maybe even beyond this case. I mean, she's certainly showing up in a lot of them." I stopped as a cold wave rocketed from one side of my skull to the other. "Not a lot." I blinked. "She's showed up every time I've had a case in New York since I was in Norman's body."

Church's mouth spread into a thin smile.

As far as I was concerned, that was Yahtzee. "This has to do with all the weirdness going down here, right?" I pointed both index fingers towards the ground.

Church inclined his head. "Yes, Vincent. And you're going to need help. More than I give. Camilla Ortiz has proven herself time and time again—especially now."

It hit me. I scooted an inch away from Church and eyed him. "Proven herself like figuring out the oh-so-puzzling mystery of me." I hooked a thumb to my chest.

"Yes."

Oh, you shit turnip.

Church winced. He pushed aside a rogue lock of curly blonde hair with a finger. "Vincent, I don't believe it is any more appropriate to swear in your head than it is aloud in this place."

He had a point. Better to be open and honest about it. I looked him in the eyes. "Shit turnip."

Church sighed. "Petulance doesn't get anything accomplished, Vincent."

Pfft. Maybe not, but it helps. Sometimes you don't need a win; you just need something to help you deal with things until you can win.

"I don't have long, Vincent, and neither do you." He nodded to my tattoo.

I looked. Crap. Another hour had passed. Forty-seven left. What was going on with this case? Time was slipping faster than normal. And I still didn't have a decent lead.

"You have Ashton Campbell, I believe." Church gave me a genuine smile. Hell, it almost sparkled.

I frowned before my mouth slipped open. "How did you know his last name? I didn't even get that bit."

Church held the smile and patted me on the shoulder. "Finish the important questions, and never question good blessings."

I squinted at him. "Is that a proverb, or are you just trying to get me to drop it."

He smiled. "Yes."

Wiseass.

"Fine, you're right. Time's slippin' and I ain't got much. You wanted Ortiz to figure it out on her own, didn't you? You were testing her." It wasn't a question.

Church nodded. "I told you to leave it alone, and that she would come to her own conclusion."

He did.

"Lizzie. Kelly." I stared at him, watching for a reaction.

He gave none.

I kept the look up regardless. If he blinked, I wanted to

take note of it. "First, Ortiz pops into my life. Next, a girl who can see ghosts, and now some college kid who thinks my life's an X-Files episode."

"It's a good show, but I don't hear a question." Church matched my unblinking stare.

It always creeped me out when he did that. I exhaled. "Ortiz wasn't the only person you 'hoped' I bumped into, was she?"

His mouth twitched. As much a sign as I'd ever get from him.

"That's a yes, isn't it?"

He stared.

"Don't suppose you can tell me why?"

"Can you tell me why you harbor such an aversion to having people enter your life?"

"You're putting people in harm's way, Church." My teeth ground, and my fingernails dug deep into my palm as I tightened my fists. "You don't have that right."

I don't know how he kept his voice calm. It was something out of meditation videos. "None of us have the right to decide for another person, Vincent, including you. You'd do well to remember that. And yet there are times when perhaps it would be better if others chose for us. Every choice has consequences. Sometimes it's better to have friends to help us make the right ones, hmm?"

I didn't know what to make of that. "Uh, word."

He gave me a thin smile as he tapped his forearm.

I waved a hand. "I know. Time. Slipping. Yeah. Got it."

"More than you know, and more will as well."

Say what? My heart felt like it was beating in concert to a samba routine. I looked down out of fear. The tattoo hadn't changed. I looked up and sighed. "I can't believe I fell for that."

Church had vanished.

I licked my lips and rose from the pew. Polished nickel caught my eye. I gazed to the spot where Church had sat. A few folded bills rested in place, held there by several nickels. I snatched the money up and paused when I found a small note folded into the bills.

It read: You're welcome. Take a cab.

I smiled and held the note up. "Okay, you're not a

complete ass." I rushed out of the cathedral, hoping I'd be able to flag a cab down and reach Ashton. I muttered a quick prayer that he'd have the answers I was looking for.

Chapter Ten

My head rattled against the seat of the cab. It smelled of too much leather polish, apparently used to bury the underlying smell of last night's vomit. Guess the cabbie had a night nearly as exciting as mine. I was grateful for the rest, no matter how short. Shutting my eyes gave me time to think, and filter through the information I did have.

Daniel ran an art gallery—one that had turned his crumbling future into success. I'd heard a story somewhat like that before. I frowned and considered the notion. It was too early to assume there was any foul play involved with his career success. That didn't mean I could rule it out either.

The one person I'd met in his apartment complex didn't seem surprised or disturbed by Daniel's appearance. Monsters usually stumble or do a double take when someone they've drowned comes back to life.

And there was the little bit the puck had left me with. A creature not of faerie. That didn't narrow it down, but maybe I could call on someone else—another creature of faerie.

I pressed my lips tightly together and reconsidered. Every time I'd called in a favor of late, they had a nasty way of coming back to bite me in the ass. I wasn't a fan of that.

A screech filled my ears as the cab slowed to a halt. The cabbie apologized for the brakes and muttered about maintenance. I drowned out most of it, catching the total sum out of the corners of my eyes. I forked over the fare without looking and swung the door open. My hips brushed against the door as I shut it with a gentle bump. I buried the change in my pants, just enough for a return to Daniel's pad.

I stared at the hospital and scowled when I noticed where I was. I whirled around to face the cab. "Hey—"

The driver had made it to the end of the block.

I exhaled and stowed my hands into the windbreaker's

pockets. The guy had dropped me in front of the ER. I shook my head and skirted along the building's edge. A few minutes later, I was rewarded with the entrance for general admission. Finding Ashton wouldn't be difficult since I had his full name.

I turned to the side, narrowing my profile to let someone in a wheelchair pass, as I slipped through the sliding doors. My body spasmed like my bones were trying to shift under my skin. I rubbed my arms for a second. I can't put my finger on it, but hospitals have an eerie vibe. It's like having a cold blanket thrown over you, sapping your heat and making you go numb. Don't get me started on how they all look the same. At least to me.

I swallowed and banished the throng of people bustling by. Thankfully, hospitals are well laid out. I spotted a curved desk of brushed wood and approached. Here goes nothing.

The woman behind it had an expression that said she worked the job because it was easy and boring. She was a bit on the plump side and looked to be in her twenties. She was as memorable as a face on a bus. Unremarkable and dressed for her position.

I flashed her a smile. "Hi." I propped my elbows on the counter and leaned forwards.

She scowled.

I let out a weak cough and pulled myself back. Wow. I was only into the hellos and this was already going badly. "Um, I'm a friend of an employee here. I wondered if you could tell me where to find him? I think he's on schedule right now."

She seemed mollified and leaned back in her chair. The seat creaked in protest. She crossed her arms, fixing me with a haughty look.

So much for mollified.

"What's their name?"

I told her.

Her eyes grew to owlish proportions and her cheeks colored. "Oh, Ashton?" She pulled herself to the computer and got to work searching. "I saw him earlier. He's on the third floor—patient care attendance."

I drummed my fingers against the desk and thanked her before moving off.

"Uh-uh, hold up."

I stopped.

"He's working. I can't page him for ya, and you can't bother him. You want to see him, you can go up there, but you'll have to wait." She fixed me with a look that suggested if I didn't do exactly that, she'd give me hell.

I had enough to worry about. I didn't need a pissed off college kid with a soul-crushing job to give me trouble. There were elevators nearby. A small relief. I hustled over to them, motioning with a hand in the hopes I'd get lucky.

A slender hand snapped out from within the elevator to hold the doors open.

I leapt in and exhaled. "Thanks."

"No problem." I winced as her perfume hit me. It was like citrus and wood. A rather earthy scent for a woman.

She was dressed in scrubs—a nurse—slim built and with a bit of bounce in her step.

I glimpsed at her ID. "This is going to be terribly forward of me, Anna, being that I'm a stranger and all—"

"You want my number." She smiled and ran a finger through her auburn hair. "I get that a lot."

I could see why. She was attractive by any standard. I almost felt bad for clarifying the mix-up. "Uh, no, sorry. I'm looking for someone I'm supposed to meet."

She stared at me, her lips quirking as she waited for me to explain. Her eyes held my stare. They were a shade of burnt sienna, a rich brown tinged with warm orange.

I'd never seen anything like it.

She arched a brow and leaned against the elevator wall. "So, this person have a name?"

I shook my head. "Yeah, Ashton..." I stopped and realized I had no idea what he looked like. My best bet would be to have someone point him out. That's not normal when you're already friends with them though. "I think that's his name. Never met him before."

"We work on the same floor. He expecting you?"

I nodded.

"At work? During his shift?"

Right. The hole in my plan. One I needed to plug, fast. "It can't wait; it's an emergency."

Anna's brow creased, and she looked at me like I was

unhinged. "You said he was expecting you? Aren't emergencies sudden?"

Why did I have to get trapped with the nurse who moonlighted as the captain of a debate team? I sighed. "Yes, they are. The emergency already happened. A mutual friend is in trouble, he's expecting someone. I'm that someone." I tapped a finger to my chin. "He doesn't know that he's waiting for me. Got it? Good." It wasn't completely a lie.

Technically, I wasn't Daniel. I was just wearing him. As far as I was concerned, that made me a mutual friend. And I sure as hell was in trouble. I was still fishing for clues. Ignorance is one of the worst problems a man can have.

She blinked and sniffed the air like I was displeasing. "So, you need me to introduce you?"

"It'd be awfully nice of you. Maybe I'll pick you up a tuna melt from the cafeteria." I gave her my best smile.

Anna gave me a look like I'd offered her a roadkill sandwich. "You need to work on your lunch bribes."

I needed to work on my best smile, apparently. The elevator sounded and I flourished with my hands. "After you."

She huffed, but a smile touched her lips. "You're relentless."

"You have no idea."

Anna tugged on the end of her ponytail and chewed her lip. "Alright, fine, you win."

I didn't smirk. That would be rude. Besides, I'm a good winner. I pumped a fist in the air and slapped on the widest grin I could.

She snorted and laughed. "Yes, you wore me down. Congratulations." Anna plucked a handheld mirror from her pocket, unfolding the disc in her palm. She gazed into it until a voice blared over the intercom, draining the humor and color from her face. "Code blue, I have to go." Anna raced out of the elevator and barreled past people.

"But, Ashton—yeah, okay." I clucked my tongue against my cheek and got out of the lift. My foot hadn't touched the tiles before the screaming started. The world slowed as adrenaline and thoughts flooded me. I homed in on the source, breaking into motion.

"Hey!" A male nurse spun to glare at me as he

stumbled.

I ignored him, bustling past. Maybe I was overreacting. I'd rather that than be right and not do anything about it. The screaming intensified. It became a race between me and the staff trailing behind. I pushed harder.

My fingers gripped the side of the doorframe as I swung around and into the room. Red vapor, like blood turned to fog, trailed through the room. It flitted into a doorway on the right. I chased after it and came to a dead end in the form of a bathroom. The bloody mist coalesced, plunging into the mirror. I raced over to it.

Not the brightest thing to do.

I held my face an inch from it, staring.

Twin orbs, like burning coals, stared back.

"Holy shit!" I pushed myself away from the mirror. The room smelled of the same stench that filled Daniel's bedroom. I didn't think killer wood polish was the cause of death. I had something to work with now.

The screaming slowed.

I left the bathroom and saw the visitor in the chair beside the bed had slumped over. She was in her later years and could've been on senior care commercials. Her thick glasses sat askew on her face. Her skin paled before my eyes. She wore a crocheted shawl, thrown over comfortable clothing that you'd expect grandmothers to wear. Her eyes clouded, looking like foggy glass. Blood poured from her nose like an unending tap of red water.

That wasn't normal.

A choking sound stole my attention. I turned to face the sobbing patient.

Acne riddled his forehead, the oils giving his face a slight sheen. The kid had the look of someone who spent a lot of time out in the sun. He was probably an athlete on a middle school team. His eyes were as wide as saucers. Sweat plastered his greasy, black hair to his head. He gawked at me.

I returned the awkward expression. It's not like I was supposed to be there. That was affirmed the next second.

A trio of staffers surged into the room, eyeing the scene, me, and back to the old lady.

Things didn't look good or in my favor. They never do.

I threw my hands into the air. "I can explain." Well, I hoped I could. "I heard screaming, and I ran to see if I could help." It was the truth.

The kid's teeth chattered, and he looked around the room like he was still in danger.

A middle-aged doctor, whose hair had gone prematurely gray, eyed the kid like he was seeing a ghost. "Timothy, you're...conscious." He sounded surprised.

I took note of that.

The kid's chest heaved like he was running a marathon and showed no sign of slowing. He ignored the doctor, focusing on me. "You saw it. You saw it!" It wasn't a question.

I felt everyone's eyes boring holes into my skull. My stomach churned, and the back of my throat felt like someone had slathered grease over it. What I was about to do was horrible. "Is the kid okay? I've got no clue what he's talking about."

The doctor bustled past me, giving me an understanding, but strained, smile. "He'll be fine. We appreciate your help, but you need to leave." He tilted his head and looked to someone behind me. The doctor moved to the grandmother, placing two fingers on the side of her throat and leaning in. He fumbled for his stethoscope and did a more thorough check. His face turned to stone. I didn't need to hear what he said to know her condition.

A pair of hands gripped my biceps and pulled. I turned to face a reedy man in his late twenties. A rubber band-like twang snapped through my mind, followed by a bright streak. A carousel of images flooded through me, and I worked to dissect them. I wish they weren't accompanied by just as many feelings.

Something swelled in my heart and made its way to my stomach. Laughter seized me, wanting to burst free. It gave way to cold anticipation like I was watching a horror movie about to hit the climax. Frenzied excitement. My body shook again.

I blinked several times, trying to clear it all.

The assistant gave me a gentle shake. "Daniel, are you okay? What are you doing here?"

I exhaled slower than normal, working to draw the

breath out and buy some time. It took a three-count before I was able to put it together. I trundled through the images in my mind. I may have snuck a peek at his badge. That helped the most.

Ashton was an inch shy of six foot, built like a plank. His hair was greasy black and pushed back in a poor imitation of James Dean. He could have been a stunt double for the actor back in the day. He was close enough in appearance to pull it off. Except for the eyes. They were brown and nursed a bright cherry glow that reminded me of Anna's. His cologne smelled of woody notes and citrus.

"Daniel?" Ashton whistled as he pulled me out of the room. He snapped his fingers in front of my face. "You there?"

I snapped to reality. "Yeah. Sorry. Here. Freaked out by...that. What happened?"

Ashton's eyes were close to resembling pinwheels after my rapid succession of answers. He put two fingers to his temple and shook his head. "I'm going to pretend I understood most of that. As to what happened, you tell me—you were there."

My neck felt hot, and I rubbed a hand against the back of it. A breath left through my clenched teeth as I thought it over. This wasn't one of those times where you tell the truth. I'd likely have the cops called on me if I told him what I really saw. "I ran into the room and saw the old lady bleeding out of her nose. The kid was shrieking. Makes sense. He woke up to find—who was that lady exactly?"

Ashton's head sank. He took several steps away, beckoning me with a motion of his hand. "Come on." He gave the room one last look.

I followed him, stepping beside him, waiting for an answer.

"That was Timothy's grandmother and legal guardian."

That hit me hard. There was a reason the grandmother was his guardian, whatever it may have been, and she was gone now. The kid had no one. And he saw what I had—a monster doing God knows what to his grandma. I needed to get back in there and search the place. I didn't think the staff would be keen on letting that happen.

"She's been watching over him for days now. He's lucky

to have her, especially after the stunt he pulled." Ashton shook his head.

I stared, making it clear I had no clue what he was talking about.

"Timothy took his grandmother's car for a joy ride. He didn't even have his permit yet. It went...south."

I didn't need him to tell me that bit.

"Timothy tried to avoid someone, panicked, and gunned it, veering off the road towards a building." Ashton gave me a level look. "The building won."

Yeah. Cars and concrete don't go well together.

"He was unconscious when they brought him in. Miracle he survived. The trauma to his body was insane. His grandmother was waiting until..." Ashton inhaled.

"Wait? You're telling me the kid wasn't expected to pull through?"

Ashton shook his head.

I tilted my head in the direction of his room. "So, what was that back there?"

He rolled his shoulders. "A miracle."

I tried to keep my face neutral. I didn't believe in those. In my experience, miracles came at a cost—terrible ones. "A lot of those happening around here—miracles?"

Ashton pursed his lips as he thought. "It's a hospital; people are saved all the time. Some consider it a miracle when the odds are slim. Depends on who you ask." His expression darkened. "Ask the wrong person, and trust me, man, miracle isn't the word they'd use." He put a hand on my shoulder and squeezed.

He had a point. For every life saved, there's always one that slips away. It was a bit of cruel balance in the world.

"You're coming to my place when I get off tonight, right?"

I stared, unsure of what he meant.

"Movie night?"

"Everyone else is going to be there?"

Ashton nodded.

This was my chance to meet Daniel's friends, and, hopefully, pin down what was going on.

He reached into his pockets and plucked a phone, not unlike Daniel's, free. It was wrapped in a leather case that nursed a small mirror on the back. Ashton spread his mouth, holding the mirror before his teeth. He ran his tongue over them.

"Uh, I'm pretty sure your teeth are fine. You can still do mouthwash commercials."

He snorted. "Sorry, finished a quick meal before that fiasco in Tim's room. Don't get a lot of time to eat. Sneak food when I can."

"When's your next break? We could catch a meal and hang out." I hoped my eagerness didn't seep into my voice, or that he'd take it the wrong way. I needed to question him and figure things out. If he was the oldest of the leasing tenants neighboring Daniel, he might know something. He could have heard or seen the monster. People don't just end up miles from their home and drowned. There's some noise to be made.

Unless Daniel was killed at home and tossed to hide the evidence. Why tie his hands though? Dead bodies float. I raced through the points, trying to narrow something down that would give me a better direction. I ended up with imaginary arrows pointing everywhere.

Ashton clapped me on the shoulder, giving me an apologetic look. "Sorry, gotta run." He pointed a finger at me. "Remember, movie night, my place."

I nodded and waved him off. So far, my trip hadn't gotten me any closer. Well, that wasn't true. I'd caught a fleeting glimpse of the freak. If red mist and passing through mirrors were worth anything. They didn't conjure any name of a creature I knew. I needed more, and a chance to hit my journal—hard. But first things first.

I needed to pay little Timmy a visit.

I ambled by, waiting outside the room until it looked clear. It took a while. An imaginary hook tugged at the base of my brain, prompting me to gander at my forearm. I pulled on the sleeve of the windbreaker, frowning at the result. Church could have given me more time. Forty-six hours wasn't a whole lot. Not with what little I had to go on. I yanked the sleeve down to my wrist and grimaced.

"Screw it." I took a breath and relaxed my posture, strolling towards Timothy's room like I was supposed to be there. I stepped inside and eyed the bathroom. The mirror shone like a mirage under the bright lighting. I stared hard at it. Anything that could pass through a mirror like that warranted keeping my guard up.

There were a handful of paranormal nasties that could move through mirrors. I didn't know them all off the top of my head, but if I did things right, I'd soon know what I was dealing with.

After a long stare, I concluded the mirror wasn't harboring any magical bullshittery. I made my way to Timmy's bedside and crossed my fingers that the kid was in a mood to talk. My hand slid over the cool metal bed frame as I neared him. He was out cold. They'd either sedated him after the panic, or the sudden exertion of energy had tired him out. He wasn't in great shape to begin with. I made a fist and rapped my knuckles on the wall above the kid's head.

He groaned and rolled to face me. His eyes opened to slits before snapping open. "You!"

I grinned. "Me."

He stammered, fighting to find the words. Thankfully he didn't break out screaming again. Timothy swallowed and looked around the room.

I held my hands up in a calming gesture. "Easy, kid. It's just me. Ain't nothing else here, okay?"

He leaned over, looking past me and rubbernecked for half a minute. "Are you sure?"

"Positive. I came to check up on you, remember? You think I'd let something follow me?"

He leaned back, placated. "I thought I was having a nightmare."

I gave him a weak smile. In my work, nightmares were a common staple of reality. No need to share that with the kid though. Sometimes ignorance is bliss, and it's best to let someone keep theirs. I didn't see the harm in letting the kid continue his life without knowing about the paranormal. "That's what I'm here to talk to you about. You've been through a lot, Timmy—can I call you Timmy?"

He nodded.

"With everything concerning your accident, you got rattled pretty good. I'm a psychologist here to help check you out." I was so going to hell. So long as it was after my case, I could live with that. Church needed to get me a series of fake credentials one of these days.

Timmy waited in silence.

"What do you remember seeing?"

He pursed his lips. "It was real. It felt like a nightmare, but it was real." His eyes steadied, and the look he gave me made cold steel look soft. "My grandmother's dead, isn't she?"

I sucked in a breath through my teeth. Children are perceptive, more so than we give them credit for. Even so, perceptive and capable of dealing with harsh truths are two different things. The latter is something adults still haven't gotten the hang of. How do you answer a question like that?

Truthfully, Graves. I had a point. I released the breath through my nose and scrubbed my face with a palm. "Yes, I'm sorry."

Timothy said nothing. He held my stare until his eyes took on a hollow look similar to his grandmother's. I had the feeling he was staring through me, not at me. The strength left his shoulders as he sagged against the bed. Poor kid looked too tired to even cry. Death can do that to a person. Sometimes it breaks you down a different way. It robs you of the ability to stand straight and function. It's like cutting the foundation out of something.

I placed a hand on his leg. "Timmy, you okay?"

He let his head fall to the side, his gaze going to the window. "No."

I exhaled. At least he was honest.

"It's my fault." His voice sounded like warbling strings. "She's dead because of me, isn't she?" Something cut the strings, replacing them with cracking glass. He was on the edge of shattering completely.

"Oh, kid." I felt like I'd taken a hammer to the gut, heart, and the base of my skull. Survivor's guilt is a terrible thing. Timmy spent who knows how long unconscious. Then he wakes to find a monster double-timing it out of his room, leaving his grandmother—a woman who spent days watching over him—dead. The inside of his mind must've been a blender tearing through thoughts of grief and guilt.

I wasn't going to let the kid be consumed by that. No way in hell. My fingers dug into his calf until the pressure prompted him to turn back.

He stared at me, unfocused.

"It's not your fault."

Timothy didn't look like he believed me.

"It's not." I let stone and metal fill my voice, not leaving any room for argument.

The kid nodded more to himself than me.

"You saw that...thing, right?"

He licked his lips before answering. "Yes."

My voice hardened past what I thought was possible. "That's what killed your grandmother. I don't know what it is, but I promise you when I find it—I'm going kill it." I gave him a fierce smile.

He returned a brittle one.

It was the best I could hope for given the circumstances. I shook his leg and motioned to an empty space on the bed. He gave me a cue that I moved on, lowering myself to sit beside him. "Mind if I show you something?"

"Sure." His voice was strained, like the back of his throat had been clawed. I couldn't blame him.

I shifted on the bed, making it easier for me to flash my forearm. I hooked an index finger against the cuff of my sleeve and pulled. The windbreaker's material rustled as I revealed my forearm. I turned it so Timmy could see the tattoo.

He eyed it and blinked, unsure of what to make of it.

I felt the same way. It was easy to show a random kid my tattoo, but I'd struggled to come clean with Ortiz about it. I figured it out a second later. Lies hurt, but sometimes, the truth kills. People unaware of the paranormal world can't get involved knowingly. When you drag them into it, it's not that easy for them to claw their way free. It ends in death.

I exhaled and decided to give him the light version. "This is important." I prodded the tattoo with a finger. "Let's say it's part of my job, and that job involves me doing dangerous things. What you saw, it isn't normal. That's all I'm going to say. But I'm going to do my job and send it to hell. To do that, I need to know what you saw when you started screaming."

The kid flinched, and I felt like something played my spine like a xylophone. I'm not fond of asking kids to conjure up frightening memories. But I needed whatever info I could scrounge up. That didn't make asking any easier.

His chest rose slowly as he took deep breaths. I saw the focus flicker in his eyes as he tried to figure things out. Timmy's face furrowed. "I heard things, before I woke up, I mean."

I remained silent, rolling my wrist in a gesture for him to continue and explain.

"Voices. My grandmother's first. She sounded scared and excited at the same time, you know?" He groaned and shifted on the bed. "Someone was talking to her, she sounded nice."

She? That was something. Not much, but it all adds up.

"I couldn't make out the words. Or I don't remember them—I dunno."

I placed a hand over my mouth to muffle the sigh. "It's okay, kid; keep going."

"Then, I don't know. I felt fine? Like I had a good night's sleep, and I was waking up. I got up and saw my grandmother twitching." He spasmed like he'd been shocked. Painful memories do that to people.

I squeezed his leg harder, reminding that I was by his side. "It's alright. Go on. What did you see?"

"A devil."

Chapter Eleven

My body felt like it'd been carved from thin ice. I swallowed and stared at the kid until his features appeared to blur. "What?"

"A devil."

I shut my eyes, pressing my palms against them. Devil was a generic term people used when they couldn't wrap their heads around the paranormal. Nightmares and things we can't explain are devils. Sometimes, we turn people into devils when they commit unspeakable acts. It's a blanket term, and not a good one. But given the circumstances, I got why the kid chose it. I only hoped he wasn't being literal.

"What do you mean? What'd it look like?"

He winced.

I stopped and looked at his leg, releasing my grip. "Sorry." I didn't realize how hard I'd been squeezing. Timmy would have bruises. But it was the least of our worries if he was right.

God, don't let him be right.

"It was tall...and dark. I couldn't see it right, really. It had stubby horns, like the tops were cut off. I saw wings, I think?"

"You think?"

He recoiled.

I exhaled, working to calm myself. "Sorry, sorry. Go on."

"I don't know. It just, it was a monster, you know? Not...like the devil from stories, but it wasn't normal."

No kidding. I patted his leg and gave him a reassuring smile. "Alright, Timmy, how about you lie down and conk out, huh?" He gave me a dubious look that I answered with a lopsided grin. "Come on. I swear it." I drew an invisible cross over my heart. "Nothing will mess with you. Last time I checked, whatever it was left after you noticed it, right?"

He nodded but didn't seem placated.

"It's scared of you." I grinned wider.

"You think so?"

"Know so." I pounded a fist on my chest. "Trust me. Monsters and nightmares prey on those scared of them. There's a reason so many monsters operate in the shadows and darkness. They're cowards. Remember that. You're braver than they are. Keep that in mind, and nothing will mess with you."

He smiled and squirmed to relax himself.

Phew. I couldn't do much for the kid, but I could put him at ease and get a little revenge for him. I flashed him a smile before rising from the bed to leave the room.

I passed through the door when a crash followed by screams tore through the hall. My body had sprung to action before I'd finished processing it all. I stopped as soon as I had burst into a sprint. Thirty feet from me, near the end of the hall, was an upturned cart. Food littered the floor. It wasn't alone.

A dark-skinned man lay toppled beside it. He looked fine, except for his neck. It was twisted at a grotesque angle that left no doubt it was broken. I cleared my head and crossed the distance to the scene.

Staffers responded before I could get there. I exhaled and grimaced at the edge of the bustling crowd. A familiar face stood out. I tugged at the edge of her sleeve.

Anna turned to me. Her eyes were unfocused and carried a wet sheen.

"Are you okay?"

She seemed not to hear me.

"Anna?"

The nurse drifted back to reality, blinking away whatever thoughts had seized her. "I'm sorry." She gave me a look like Timmy had, more through me than at me. "I'm a little..." She stopped and turned to the scene. Her hand flew to her mouth.

I pulled her into a tight side hug. "Yeah, I gotchya."

"You know, you see a lot in my line of work, but this is not normal."

She was right. The odds of someone falling and breaking their neck from an upright position is in the astronomical odds territory. The only way that happens is with a little push—the supernatural kind.

"Did you see anything funny or strange before the gentleman"—I gestured to the scene—"that?"

She shook her head. "No, I was just checking up on his wife, and when I came out..." Anna winced hard.

"His wife?"

"Long story, but most of her organs are failing. The shutdown's bad. It's been hard on him. He's always visited though—every day. They shared desserts. It was...sweet. She's been touch and go recently, and it's been hard on him. He couldn't bring himself to go into the room today, so I did it for him. You know, act like an intermediary. I've done it before. Sometimes it's just hard for people."

I nodded sympathetically. "Yeah, I hear ya."

She sniffed once.

I pulled her as gently as I could. "Come on." Nearby staff members had the scene under control and were taking care to handle the poor dude's body. I didn't want to stand in the way of the professionals. I led Anna down the hall, away from the scene. "How's his wife doing?" A change of topics always helps.

Anna's mouth twisted before she choked down a gulp of air. "She's fine. It's a miracle really."

Another miracle. Like Ashton had said, those weren't uncommon in hospitals, but they sure were happening a bit too often for my tastes. "Oh?"

"Yeah, she was completely coherent, like she wasn't sick at all. I didn't have time to run any tests or notify her doctor. And then, when I came out with the news, that happened. It's horrible irony—cruel—is what it is." Her voice snapped like twigs.

A lasso roped around my brain, tugging it from our conversation. Everything that was going on seemed to boil down to something I'd seen before. I've dealt with miracles before and cruel twists of irony. They definitely came at the hands of a devil, or something close enough to one.

But they tended to leave a telltale sign behind. I hadn't seen any soot lying around, so I buried the thought. Too bad a worse one replaced it. Whatever was doing this had some serious mojo behind it. Enough to alter reality, but just how small or large of a scale. Regardless, that was a level of power I did not want to mess with unprepared.

I pulled myself together and gave Anna an extra squeeze. "I'm sorry. Hey, how about I get out of your hair and leave you be, hm?"

She bit her lip but nodded in agreement.

I turned and moved towards the elevator, hunching over to hide most of my profile. If something was lurking around here with enough magic to kill on a whim and grant miracles, I didn't need it spotting me before I was ready for a throwdown.

A light above the elevators flashed as one of them stopped on the floor. The doors parted, and I rushed to hop in. I stopped as the woman exiting nearly bumped into me. "Ortiz?"

She shook her head in disbelief. "Of course. I bump into you just like that."

She took the words right out of my mouth. I gave a thin smile. "Yeah, I've got an uncanny sense of luck."

Ortiz grabbed the front of my jacket and pulled.

I stumbled into the lift. "What gives?"

Her eyes narrowed. "You've already found something, haven't you?"

It was disturbing how she did that. "Yeah, bumped into Ashton, like you said. Found some things out." I jabbed a thumb against the button to take us to the ground floor. The elevator shuddered into movement, and I leaned against the panel. "You get Kelly somewhere safe?"

Ortiz grunted with nigh-masculine skill. "What did you find out about whatever it is we're after?"

We're. Just like that and we were back to normal—sort of. I didn't know how to feel about that. I wanted her help. I wanted her to be safe. I wanted her to forgive me. Three things. I didn't know how many of them I'd actually get. The lift made it down a floor before I was able to say, "How about I tell you what I saw first?" I turned my head to glance at her.

She crossed her arms, leaning back against the nearest side of the elevator. "Sure."

I told her everything.

The lift made it to the ground floor before she

processed it all. "Wow. That is a lot of strangeness to make sense of."

A lopsided grin spread across my face. "That's the name of my autobiography."

Ortiz snorted and moved towards the doors as they opened. "Don't expect a lot of sales."

My face scrunched, and I sniffed in mock indignance. I'm best-seller material. I waved a dismissive hand and fell in step beside her. "Anyway, I've got enough to start putting things together..." I exhaled, shutting my eyes.

"But?"

"But what I've got isn't looking good. It's giving me more questions than answers."

Ortiz sped up, gesturing with a slight turn of her head. "Tell me about it in the car. I'll give you a ride back. We'll make a pot of coffee and go over that journal of yours. It's got to have something in it, right?"

I shrugged. It had a lot in it. That didn't mean it had the right answers. The thing about knowledge is, well, there's so much of it out there. Sometimes what you know can get you killed. Other times, it's what you don't know that gets you tossed into a shallow grave.

Ortiz led the way to the visitor parking lot. We passed a few rows until she came to a stop next to a mid-sized gray sedan that blended in with every other car in the lot. She pulled the keys from her pocket and unlocked the vehicle. "Get in."

I obliged in silence, plunking into the passenger seat. The dash smelled of vinyl polish. The seats had that rigid feel, implying they hadn't been broken in yet. I let out a low whistle as I looked around. "New car, huh? Spiffy."

"Yeah." Something in her voice changed, becoming like sharpened stone. "Crazy accident happened to my last car."

I gulped.

"It blew up, would you believe it?" She leaned forwards and eyed me. "A fireball hit it, and some freak of magical nature—" Ortiz stopped, clapping her hands together before parting them in a dramatic mimic of an explosion. "What are the odds?"

I shrank in my seat and mumbled under my breath.

"What was that?" Ortiz shot me a glare as she started

the car.

"Sorry, but that happened over a year ago. You've got insurance. Not to mention you work for the government."

"Do you know how hard it is to explain an incinerated car to an insurance claims agent?"

"Do I look like I have insurance?" I matched her stare, refusing to back down. "And are we seriously arguing about this right now?"

She smiled. "I know." Ortiz reached out and gave me a gentle prod. "Something to lighten the mood for a sec. This stuff always gets so..." She trailed off and put the car into reverse, easing us out of the parking spot.

"Yeah, it does." I turned to look out the window, resting my head against it. My knuckles tapped against the glass in a staccato beat as Ortiz shuttled us along. "Part of the job. There's a lot of grim and dark to it. Doesn't mean there's not light here and there." I leaned over and flashed her a quick smile before falling back against the door.

"I could use a bit of light right now." She sounded like she'd churned gravel and cement in her throat.

"Lizzie's doing fine—great actually. Remember her? The little, adorable, spacey-headed girl we saved?"

A wide smile broke across Ortiz's face. "Yes, I do. She's an interesting child. I'm glad though. Thanks for telling me."

We exited the lot, and I let my eyes succumb to fatigue. They drifted shut, letting me sort through everything I had found out. A faint pang filled my ribs and I groaned. "What?"

"Don't pass out yet. I need info."

I grumbled incoherently, and my ribs panged again. "I need a nap."

"Sleep when you're dead."

"I can't. I don't even get paid for this job. I need a union—for me."

A series of light breaths left Ortiz's mouth in what I could only assume was a poorly muffled laugh. "Good luck with that."

"Hater." I squirmed into an upright position, allowing the scenery to become a blurred swath of grays and burgundy. A deep sigh left through my nose before I felt comfortable dredging up what else I'd learned. I told her everything I'd heard from Ashton, Anna, and Timothy.

Ortiz suppressed a minor convulsion. "That sounds a lot like our first case together."

"Minus the red mist and vanishing into mirrors, yeah." I made sure Ortiz heard that. She had a point, but I was going to make sure she knew it was the wrong one. That first case put her through a horrible wringer. Ortiz needed to know this wasn't a repeat. She may have moved on, but every nightmare leaves a bit of itself lodged in the back of your mind. They're just waiting for the right tug to resurface. Sometimes it comes from external sources. Sometimes you're the one to dredge them up.

I wasn't going to let that happen. "Hey, remember, no soot. And I don't think anyone's dug up a vessel for an ancient and malevolent spirit lately." I squinted and gave her a comical look. "Have they?"

She laughed. "Not that I've heard of." Ortiz slowed the car to a stop at the intersection.

I exhaled, loosening my shoulders as I sank against the seat again. "Good. Look, I don't know what's doing this, but I know what it isn't."

Ortiz made a sound that could have been a snicker.

I glared at her. "Not knowing is just as useful sometimes. No use chasing down the wrong leads, right?"

She sobered and gave me a nod as the light turned green. "Good point."

I have those on occasion. Too bad I didn't get to savor the occasion. We accelerated, making it to the middle of the intersection when the world jerked to the left. The sound of crashing metal and polyurethane is unmistakable. It's a cacophony of plastic crunches and screeching metals. The world snapped to a halt, juddering my bones and my noggin.

The raucous bellow of horns and panicked screams pulled me from the dazed reverie. "Ortiz?" The airbags hadn't gone off. It was a small blessing. Those things knock more people out than accidents at times. I shook my head clear and fidgeted with my seatbelt. A look out the window showed me a white sedan often used by police officers. The front was reinforced with a metal ram.

This wasn't an accident. The thought galvanized me into action. I let the invisible surge rush through me as I freed myself from my belt and did the same for Ortiz. I gave her a gentle shake. She responded.

"Ugh, the hell?" Ortiz cradled her head.

"Accident. Get out. Not an accident. Move!" My rapid-fire comments snapped her into clarity and she heeded my words.

Ortiz opened her door, and I scrambled over the center console, moving to follow her.

The police car's doors opened and two people exited. They weren't officers. Wonderful. Our assailants were in black rugged-looking pants and matching tops. They wore ballistic vests and armored helmets. It looked like they had plundered riot gear.

Ortiz gawked.

"Less staring, more running!" I tugged on her sleeve, prompting her to follow me down a side street. "Please tell me you're packing a silly number of guns?"

She eyed me like I was an idiot for asking. "After everything you've put me through—yes. But I keep most of them in my car!"

Well, that sucked. I cast a look over my shoulder as my feet hammered against the street. One of the pair drew and tucked a pump action shotgun to their chest. The side of it sported a pouch. I could make out the tips of the ammunition. The thing had a pistol grip attached.

The second of the pair unfolded the stock of a compact submachine gun. A second magazine was fastened to the first with a simple bracket. It looked like something from a movie. Fortunately, they weren't stupid enough to start firing in the middle of daylight at an intersection.

They'd wait till they cornered us somewhere. Then they'd kill us. Yay for being procedural.

Ortiz reached into her jacket, freeing her pistol from her holster. "Who are they?"

"How should I know?" I gave her a brief look of irritation.

"Who did you piss off this time?"

I snarled. "I didn't piss anyone off!"

"You're always pissing someone off."

My snarl faded, and I gave her a flat look. "Yet. I haven't—yet." I stopped short, nearly fumbling when I glanced at Ortiz's gun. It wasn't the Glock she had leveled at me before. It was a polished revolver that would make anyone think twice about messing with her. "Where were you hiding that?"

She gave me a wolfish smile. "Holster against my lower back."

"You scare me."

Her grin widened before slipping away. "We can't start a firefight out here. Someone could get hurt."

I nodded in agreement. "Can we focus on it not being us first?"

She eyed me and took the lead, steering us down a path between two single level buildings. Ortiz slowed and rounded a corner.

I huffed and followed her, hoping she knew what she was doing. My hope turned into an acidic salve against the lining of my throat when I crossed the corner. "It's a parking lot. A dead end."

Ortiz turned without acknowledging me. She backpedaled several steps, her eyes fixed on the entry point—where I stood.

I rushed to her side. "What in the hell are you—"

Thunder cracked, and I flinched.

The pursuer with the shotgun jerked. Ortiz's first shot struck the attacker's vest, staggering them. The second round cracked off. The assailant's leg went out from underneath them and they impacted the brick wall. A spiteful hiss came from the wound above their knee. Blood trickled, steaming as it exited the bullet hole.

I couldn't see their expression through the helmet, but the way they were fixed on the injury made it clear they didn't have a clue what was going on. I did. Blood doesn't tend to sizzle when you're capped. Not unless you're something that goes bumpity-bump in the night. I eyed Ortiz.

"Nice shot. The hell are you using anyway?"

She flashed me a smile that was all teeth. "Hollow points. Copper and steel jacket."

I let out a low whistle. Steel and iron did funny things to creatures from the paranormal world.

The figure struggled, planting the tip of the shotgun

against the concrete. They held hard to it. It wasn't doing them much good with their leg mangled. They realized that and settled for hefting the weapon and aiming it towards Ortiz.

She didn't like people pointing their weapons at her. Ortiz took that personally.

I couldn't blame her.

She fired twice in quick succession. Two rounds struck within a penny's distance from one another; too bad both hit the vest. They drove the attacker flat against the ground.

They flailed and struggled to shift to their side.

I ran towards him.

"Stop!"

I did, turning to stare at Ortiz. "What gives?"

"Look where they're pinned."

I looked back, but couldn't make out the point Ortiz was talking about. My shoulders rolled back in a shrug as I gave her a quizzical look.

"They're on the ground, in view of the alley leading here. Their partner hasn't shown up. They were chasing us together. How much do you want to bet their partner is at the other end of the alley?"

I blinked, swallowed, and turned to stare back at our attacker. She had a point. The thought never crossed my mind. I put a hand to the side of my mouth. "Hey, ass trinket!"

Somehow the bad guys always know when you're talking to them, even when you're slinging insults. It's nice.

The attacker shimmied and turned to brush the armored face mask up. A pair of yellow eyes came into view.

I sighed. "Again? Seriously, what did I do to you freaks?"

The Night Runner managed to raise a single hand, giving me a gesture that needed no translation.

Ortiz crossed the distance between her and me, coming to my side. "You want me to break that finger?"

I snorted. "You're hot when you're all angry and threatening."

She shot me a glare that could've turned steel into slag.

I swallowed what I was about to say in favor of something else. "Take your helmet off and give us some answers."

The Night Runner removed its helmet. They had the androgynous features that most of their race did, leaving me puzzled as to their gender. "Or what?" They racked their throat and spat at the ground. A globule of pinkish white struck the concrete.

"Or I let her do what she does best." I grinned and hooked a thumb to Ortiz.

She moved on cue, taking a step closer to the Night Runner and training her gun at its skull.

"Do you think I'm afraid of dying?" Their lips spread into a thin, strained smile. A crazed light filled their eyes.

"No, I don't. But I think steel hurts a helluva lot, and she's packing enough to make the remaining time you have pretty uncomfortable."

Their eyes widened.

Ortiz took over the interrogation. "Where's your partner?" She managed to keep her eyes focused on the Night Runner while still paying attention to the mouth of the alley. It was an impressive level of awareness.

I needed to learn that.

The Night Runner smiled, sticking their tongue out between their teeth. Their mouth opened wider before snapping shut. They didn't bother to pull their tongue back. The Night Runner's mouth gnashed until most of their tongue fell to the ground.

Ortiz leapt a step back. "Jesus." She pointed the gun at the creature, unsure what to do.

Blood dribbled over the Night Runner's bottom lip. Their mouth spread into a macabre smile.

Invisible metal cords seized my arms, causing them to throb and flare. I snarled and stormed over to the Night Runner. I sank to a knee, twisting to lash out with a fist. My hand connected with the side of their skull, driving the elf's face into the ground.

"Vincent!"

My collar tightened around my throat and I choked. The world pulled away from me as I stumbled back. Ortiz didn't let up on her grip, and I backpedaled the best I could.

A sound like popping bubble wrap through a megaphone filled the parking lot. A burst of bullets hammered into the Night Runner's body. Three buried themselves along the side of their head. The Night Runner went limp.

I would've been caught in that if Ortiz hadn't hauled me back. "Thanks—whoa." My legs crossed as I was shoved to the side. I swung my arms and tried to regain my balance.

Ortiz sidestepped me, moving in a semi-circle to get closer to the corner without breaking her cover. She peeked and snapped back as a torrent of bullets cracked against the brick and concrete.

A shrill cry echoed down the alley. The second black-clad figure hurtled into view. They pivoted and faced Ortiz with insect-like reflexes. The attacker sank to one knee, placing a hand on the ground and lashing out with a boot.

Ortiz took two steps to the side and swatted at the boot with her open hand. She batted the blow aside and leveled the gun. Ortiz fired blind.

The Night Runner's left shoulder and torso snapped back. They fell to their bottom before rolling onto their back.

Ortiz didn't slow, seizing the shift in combat and using it to her favor. She rushed the fallen elf and slammed her heel into the helmet. Ortiz's leg was like a hydraulic piston, driving the helm into the ground with a crack.

Supernatural or not, they had to have felt that. The Night Runner's ears would be ringing.

Ortiz's leg cracked out, sending the tip of her shoe into the Night Runner's unprotected chin. Her strike drove the back of their head against the concrete again.

I made a mental note to lighten up with the annoying comments around Ortiz. At least for the time being.

Ortiz dropped to a knee, gripping the helmet and wrenching it free.

The Night Runner had sharper, more angular features than the last. I wanted to take a chance that it was a woman. Her hair was shaved at the sides, leaving a long mane trailing at the back.

The she-elf flashed me a heated look before staring at Ortiz. "Get your whore off me."

I exhaled through my teeth and shut my eyes. A wet crack rang out, not unlike a fist crashing into a certain elf's face. I opened my eyes and peered at the scene.

Ortiz shook her hand and balled it again.

The Night Runner licked the corner of her lips, mopping up a splotch of blood. "Is that the best you can do?"

I sighed. Some people can't help but antagonize others. I kept my eyes open as Ortiz's second punch forced the Night Runner's head to the side. I clapped. "Nice punch."

Ortiz grunted.

I shut up.

She leaned back and trained her revolver on the Night Runner's face. Ortiz kept the gun out of arm's reach rather than shoving it against the creature to make a show. "Now, you're going to answer his questions." She nodded to me.

The dark elf arched a brow. "Or what?"

Ortiz thumbed the hammer back. "You don't want to die. It's not worth it. Take a look at your pal, at what you did to him."

The Night Runner bobbed her shoulders in a half shrug. "He knew what he signed up for. We both did."

I went over to Ortiz's side and glanced down at the elf. "Yeah, and what's that?"

The elf snorted.

"Hey, you don't have to die here. I could let my hyper-aggressive friend let you go—if you answer some questions." I smiled.

Ortiz flashed me a look that said I was an idiot.

I chose to be an adult and ignored the look. "We want answers. We don't need you. So, here's the deal—listening? Why are you after me? Is there any way short of giving you a handgun lobotomy that we can get you to stop, and where did you get the gear? Black is sort of my thing. It's fashionable and in. I find it slimming, and you know I'm trying to look like I take my figure—"

"Gods and darker things—does he shut up?" The Night Runner's eyes grew to saucer-sized orbs as she glared at me. She eyed Ortiz. "How do you put up with such an insufferable fool?"

I blinked. I'm not insufferable.

Ortiz gave the elf a paper-thin smile. "He's...an acquired taste. Now, answer his questions."

The elf bristled and eyed us with suspicion. "How can I trust you?"

Ortiz froze and glanced at me.

I sank to my knees and locked eyes with the Night Runner. "You can't, but you can trust this: if you don't give us what we want, she'll shoot you. You have a guarantee. It's not the best, but your only other option is telling us what we want. Seems like a no-brainer to me."

The elf licked her lips. I could see her weighing the situation. She exhaled and raised one of her hands in an open palm. "There's a price on his head." The Night Runner tilted to look at me. "It's worth a lot. The contract is not an open offer."

I pursed my lips. "Meaning you were hired specifically. Who?"

She shrugged. "Anonymous, but this might be worth something to you mortals."

I waited but wasn't rewarded.

The elf's smile grew. "Whoever they are, they weren't offering financial compensation."

Ortiz and I traded looks. I rubbed a hand against my face, sighing from the tiresome exchange. "Then what are they paying you with?"

Her lips peeled back to give us a smile that revealed her fangs. "Power. The kind that comes from favors. The kind few can give in the Neravene, but many crave."

My, that was cryptic. I groaned. "How 'bout not being like a crossword puzzle and giving me something straight?"

She didn't reply.

I went for my trump card. "The Grand Marquis isn't going to be happy about some of his folk taking up hits and getting involved in mortal business." I smiled.

She threw her head back and let out a laugh. "I'm Free Folk. I can do as I please, and I've told you what I know."

So much for my trump card.

"That's the best I can do." The Night Runner gave a mild shrug.

I eyed Ortiz. "Is it?"

Ortiz huffed in irritation. "She's telling the truth."

I still didn't know how she did it, but I wasn't going to question her inner polygraph. When Ortiz knew, she knew.

"Fine, let her go."

Ortiz stared at me but didn't move.

"Take her gun, and let her go." I frowned. It wasn't ideal, but it was fair. Sometimes that mattered more.

Ortiz grumbled something under her breath but did as I asked. She hefted the submachine gun and trained both weapons on the Night Runner. "Go. Do anything funny, even look at me the wrong way, and I'll end you."

My spine twisted inside my back. That wasn't chilling at all.

The Night Runner grinned at me and nodded to Ortiz. "I like her." She motioned with her hand, parting the air as a violet Way opened.

Ortiz sucked in a breath and swore.

The Night Runner grabbed her fallen comrade by the back of his collar and dragged him through the opening. It shut as soon as they passed through.

I exhaled and rubbed the back of my head.

Ortiz's eyes never wavered from the spot where the Way had shut. "So, that happened."

I grunted.

"Want to explain that? I'd rather not have to beat it out of you, and I'm kind of on a roll with that." The edges of her mouth twitched.

"Har har." I clapped twice. "What do you want to know?"

"What were those things, and—be straight with me—do you know why they're after you?" She turned her head and gave me an oblique stare.

Ortiz had heard the same story from the Night Runner that I had. It stung to think she believed I was holding out on her. But then, it's not like I didn't deserve it. "You want the short version or the long?"

She moved to the fallen submachine gun, kicking it towards me. "I don't want my hands on that. It's probably unregistered—illegal. I want the short story now, long later. Grab the shotgun too."

I paused, tilting my head at the weapon, then her. "What am I supposed to do with a couple of guns?"

Ortiz stared at me like it should have been obvious. "Use them if—God forbid—we're attacked again. We still don't know what killed..." She swallowed and fell silent.

"Yeah, okay." I nodded and scratched my brow nervously. She was still struggling with everything. Ortiz may have been composed on the outside, but another brush with the paranormal had rattled her. Daniel's death was prodding at her psyche, not having the grace to remain buried until this was finished. I snatched the compact weapon and moved towards the shotgun. "You know, the cops will likely be at the scene of the crash by now. I can't exactly stuff these down my pants."

She shook her head. "Let me worry about that if they're there. Answers, now."

I shrugged my way out of Daniel's windbreaker, unfolding it over the ground. The shotgun fit easily within the confines of the jacket. The machine pistol slipped in comfortably as well. I lifted the bundle and tossed it over my back, tying the front of the sleeves together. "Right, I'll explain as we walk."

Ortiz bowed her head in agreement and set off.

I sprinted until I caught up to her side. "Those things were Night Runners."

She faced me and then rolled her eyes. "And those are?"

"Think elves. Now think dark elves, think literally. Darker complexion as far as most people are concerned. Too many nuances to go into. They're called Svartals. Night Runners are like Svartals' little, not-so-distant relatives. Brothers in appearance that are more like cousins in the family tree, if that makes sense."

"You know the sad thing is...it sort of does." She laughed and broke into a smile that reached her eyes. "What was that about a Grand Marquis?"

I shuddered. Damn, did she pick up on every little detail? I chalked it up to a mixture of Ortiz being curious and her training. I grunted in disdain before answering. "He's a lord in the Neravene."

Ortiz mimicked my shudder. She didn't have good memories of hopping through Ways.

To be honest, neither did I. Anytime I have to go through one of those means something has gone horribly wrong in my case and life.

"So, he's powerful?"

I waggled my hand in a so-so gesture. "He's a political figure for the Night Runners to rally behind. Think of him as their lord, voice, and representative to the other freestanding lords and ladies. I don't know how involved he gets with the higher-up courts and factions."

Ortiz sputtered and gave me a wild-eyed stare. "You're kidding? There are political systems in the paranormal world? They have...what, congressmen and reps?"

I shook my head. "No, when I said lord, I was being literal. Think old school. Monarchies, baronies, and cut-throat stuff. You don't get elected over there. You take power."

She pursed her lips. "That explains a lot. So, when they said they were Free Folk?"

"Yeah, free to do whatever and suffer the consequences. They're not completely free though. The paranormal are bound by non-physical rules and laws governing their nature, mantles, and more. It's complicated."

"Sounds like. Did you learn this through your cases or what?" She let the question linger in the air.

"Some, yes. Other bits, no. Some of it was research. A lot of it was meeting the right, or wrong, creature. It's part of the life."

"Have I mentioned your life sucks?"

I scowled. "Why, yes, you have, multiple times now. Thanks." I stopped myself from uttering a witty retort as I broke past the corner of the block. Red and blue lights cascaded over the wall and my eyes. I hissed. "Uh, guess you're up, Agent Ortiz. I think I'm going to linger here." I pointed to the ground. "Seeing how I'm carrying two—likely illegally obtained—dangerous weapons that were fired—also very illegally—in broad daylight." I gave her a wide smile.

She didn't return it, deciding to frown instead. "Fine, pansy. I'll see if I can sort this out."

"What are you going to tell them?"

"The truth."

My heart felt cold and like it had shrunk a few sizes. "Ortiz, what's a stroke feel like? My face is getting tingly, and my chest feels tight. Are you crazy?"

She rolled her eyes. "We were driving. We were hit intentionally and pursued by gunmen. We have no idea where they are now. I'm going to describe them in great detail, minus their bastard, dark elf features."

I opened my mouth but forgot what I was going to say. It wasn't a bad plan. I felt it best to remain hidden behind the corner, out of sight, and be there for her in spirit. "Knock 'em dead." I took a few cautionary steps back.

Ortiz shook her head and passed me, rounding the corner and flagging down the officers.

I shut my eyes and ran through a series of likely scenarios. Most of them involved running away. Counting seconds turned to minutes as I lingered around the corner and waited. My temples throbbed like they nursed a pair of heartbeats. I winced and massaged them. My hands pressed hard to my skull as the pulsing exploded into a lance of pain. It was like a skewer going through my mind. I shut my eyes and endured the agony.

My body felt stiff, like it was in the act of resting and refused any sudden movements. Opening my eyes wasn't an option. They fought me as I tried to take a peek. The room was dark, but I recognized it. Daniel's bedroom. My breathing intensified—well, Daniel's did. He squirmed and shrugged out of his covers. The room smelled of burning wood and something noxiously sweet. It was thick and choking. Daniel swallowed the saliva in his mouth, trying to alleviate the dryness in his throat. It didn't do any good.

A rush of chilled menthol surged down his gullet as twin orbs of burning charcoal flared to life in the dark. Something rasped like dry leaves being dragged against a metal grate.

"She wanted this, you know?" The voice came from the source of the fiery glow.

Daniel's throat seized, and I felt the panic sweep across him in a torrent of cold waves. He scrambled. His neck ached; the air was cut off as cords of steel dug into it. He managed to scream.

The borough of Queens spun into my vision like a top. I held tight to my head to steady it and stop the teetering. A low groan left my lips. I let myself lean on the brick wall. My chest heaved, and I blinked hard in the hopes of shrugging off the vision.

Well, that was intense. I need to talk to Church about

the special effects.

I knew one thing at least: whatever that nasty was, it had gotten Daniel in his own home. So why bother making it look like a break-in? It didn't add up. All that did was draw attention to Daniel's disappearance and that something was wrong.

The paranormal don't care about the state of affairs after they kill someone. They're not hung up on the law and investigations.

Monsters aren't exactly high up on the plausible explanations for a missing persons case. Shocker.

I grimaced and swung my hand back. The base of my fist struck the wall with a dull, fleshy impact. I sighed.

"Is this a bad time, or do you want to get into it with the brick wall? I think you'd win if you headbutted it."

I turned.

Ortiz smiled as she leaned her shoulder against the wall.

I grunted and made a simple hand gesture. "What happened?"

She exhaled. "I explained it like I said I would. They weren't happy, but there was no one to contradict me. The weapons didn't come up. Everyone who saw the scene scattered."

"Funny how that happens when armed gunmen pop out of a car."

Her eyes narrowed. "Can you blame them?"

I couldn't. It's part of human nature. When trouble goes down, self-preservation kicks in and we scuttle for cover. Humans don't like getting involved. We have a tendency to avoid uncomfortable truths and realities. You run from danger, not into it. I stared at Ortiz and resisted the urge to smile.

Most of us anyhow. There are those people that face the hard things head on. They dive into danger and hope to bring as many people out of it as they can. Ortiz was one of them. I was glad to have her on my side.

"No, I can't blame them. So, what? As far as they're concerned it's a hit and run?"

She nodded. "A hit and run with a stolen cruiser."

I let out a low whistle. That was brazen of the supernatural to steal a cop car. But, if the price was as high as it sounded, grand theft auto was an acceptable risk. "And what about the gunshots?"

Ortiz shrugged. "No one reported them. We were in a parking lot with no cars, so no one was likely there."

I opened my mouth in a silent, "Ah."

She turned and beckoned with a hand. "I called Kelly, went to voicemail. I asked her to come to the apartment when she has a chance. She's probably found something useful by now."

I pressed my lips tight and said nothing.

Ortiz caught the look. "You don't like her, do you?"

"She's weird." I eyed the scene of the accident as we approached. The car had been moved to the side of the curb. Ortiz's vehicle looked the way you'd expect it to. All four wheels were still attached, which was a plus. The passenger front fender was crumpled like a cheap can, close to hugging the tire. The door on that side was battered, and the door jamb wasn't in great shape. I didn't think the car would be able to drive us back. "How come you didn't ask for a tow?"

She groaned. "I need my car right now. Don't start, I swear."

I said nothing.

Ortiz unlocked the sedan and clambered in, eyeing me to do the same.

I grunted and jerked on the handle. It wouldn't budge. I banged on the window.

"Do you really want to be banging on my window after you did this?"

I blinked and thought about my answer. "The hell's this my fault?"

She turned on her seat, bringing one of her knees to her chest. Her foot crashed into the inside of the passenger door and it opened. "Every time I get in a car with you something happens!"

I ignored her death glare and fell onto the seat. The bundle of guns flew over my shoulder as I tossed it onto the back seat. I winced, knowing that my journals had taken a small beating in the action. "Night Runners did this, not me. The first time wasn't my fault either."

She grumbled under her breath before turning to me.

Ortiz's glare could've melted icecaps. The car's engine let out an uncharacteristic throaty burble as it started.

I frowned. "Sounds like your intake or exhaust manifold is leaking."

Ortiz slipped the car into drive and held the glare. "Gee, I wonder why?" The car lurched to the right further than it should've. Ortiz swore, her hands sliding over the wheel as she fought it for control.

I let out a low, long breath through my teeth. "Looks like you might need an alignment too." My eyes remained fixed ahead. It was easier to keep myself from laughing that way.

"Vincent, have you ever been punched in the throat—hard?"

A few seconds passed before I decided to answer the question. "I think you and I both know that with everything I go through that I have."

Ortiz nodded more to herself than me, still fighting the wheel on occasion. "I want you to remember that feeling. When we get back to the apartment, I'll give you a more physical reminder."

"Uh, anger is like holding onto a hot coal with the intent of throwing it at someone. You've got to burn yourself before burning someone else." I grinned.

Ortiz ignored me, wrenching on the wheel to get it to turn far enough to the left. We rounded a street corner with a measure of difficulty, but the car ticked along. "Did you just quote Buddha?"

I frowned. "I think it's from a fortune cookie."

Ortiz looked at me like I was hopeless. She shook her head; her twitching lips made it clear she was about to break into a smile. She did. "Thank you."

"For what?"

"For being an idiot, on purpose."

I opened my mouth and stared in silence.

"I'm not stupid, Vincent. I get what you're doing. The jokes, the over-the-top and asinine comments, all of it."

I bristled in mock offense. "They're not over-the-top." I put a hand to my heart.

She snorted. "You're trying to keep me from focusing too much on what just happened. You're worried it might cause me to slip into a bad place. The cases we worked together and their fallouts. It's a lot, you know that. And they're still on my mind. You know that too. Say it with me: 'Ortiz, you are not an idiot.'"

I said it.

Her smile grew a fraction. "Thank you, for agreeing and for doing what you're doing, but, you can stop. I'm a big girl. Just know I appreciate it."

I nodded in respect. That was fair enough.

"So, can we be serious for a minute, as hard as that is for you?"

I gestured with a hand as a yes.

"What else do I need to know? I can't help but feel I'm missing something."

I ran my tongue over my teeth, wondering what to say. "Trust me, I feel the same way. I'm not sure. A lot is going on, and honestly, I don't think we've seen the whole picture yet."

She swore again and jerked the wheel. "I swear, every time you come into my life, I'm plagued with bad luck."

"I'm getting that embroidered on a pair of oven mitts."

The corner of her mouth twitched, and her eyes narrowed.

I raised my hands in defeat. "Alright, alright." I exhaled and shrugged. "You know as much as I do right now."

"Which isn't much."

I grunted in agreement.

"Do you have any idea on how to narrow down the search for this thing?" There was something in her voice that wasn't quite a plea, but it was close.

I wished I had a good answer. The monster responsible for these deaths had robbed Ortiz of someone close. If we didn't find it soon, it would take many more. That wasn't something either of us could live with. Or would allow. I decided to change the subject.

It took some effort though. I didn't want to sound like I was burying the topic. "How's work?"

Ortiz stiffened. "You mean before today, my one day off since I've gotten back?"

I winced. Oops. It's not as if I'd intentionally dragged her into this. "Um, yeah."

"It's been fine."

I eyed her. "Doesn't sound like it."

The car screeched to a halt.

I tightened and squirmed. "Holy crap, Ortiz! Warn a guy before any and all sudden stops in the middle of the street. I don't know if you remember, but the last time we came to a shuddering halt, we were chased by elves."

Ortiz ignored everything I said. "Do you want to know how my work's been?" She didn't give me a chance to respond. "It's been hell, Vincent, and I'm not using the word lightly. Do you know what it's like to go out, sometimes on raids, and—" She exhaled, breaking eye contact. "It's like you said, those things we've gone through don't leave you alone. They're in the back of my head. I'm terrified they'll pop out right when something bad is going to happen here." She jabbed a finger out the window. "The real world."

My fingers tapped against my thigh. I wanted to reach out, take her hand and give it a reassuring squeeze. I didn't feel it'd be welcome at the moment.

"There are moments when people are counting on me, and I'm not sure if they should be. I can't trust myself at times. What if one of those memories comes back? Those things that no one else believes in and knows about but me? What if I choke when someone needs me, and because of it, I lose them? My job requires me to be there—one hundred percent—no excuses." She pressed her lips together before licking them.

A hollow silence filled the car. I rushed to fill it. "And you're worried that you can't be that person? You think that because of what you've gone through and are carrying...that you can't be there for others?"

She looked at me; her eyes seemed unfocused. Ortiz chewed her bottom lip. It was something she did when she was anxious, deep in thought or confused.

I aimed to clear it all up for her. "Bullshit."

Her eyes widened.

"Look, I may not know you like your friends or the people you've worked with for years, but you know what, I've fought with you!" I held up two fingers. "Twice, Ortiz. Twice. Remember that. You and I have stopped two monsters that were hurting people. Some innocent, some not so much. We've saved lives together. That's no easy thing. And that ain't nothing to scoff at either. We did it even though it was hard. We did it not always at our best—compromised, unsure of ourselves. But we did it. No one's expecting you to be there one hundred percent. How can you be?"

She shook slightly. Ortiz lifted her foot from the brake, letting the car trundle forwards before accelerating.

It seemed like the right time now. I reached out and cupped her hand, squeezing tight. "You're human, and I'm, well, I'd like to think I'm as close as I can be to one." I gave her a reassuring smile. "Look, I get it, trust me. The nightmares don't stop. I told you that once before. But you learn to fight 'em, just like you do the monsters. Here's what I know. You can, and you've been there when it counts."

She sniffed. It was light, almost unnoticeable, and I acted like it was exactly that. She didn't need to know I heard it.

"You were there when I needed you back in Manhattan. You helped me solve Norman's murder. We prevented a whole mess of horrible things from happening, Ortiz. You were there for me, and Lizzie, not to mention her sister, when we all needed you. How many people were in that asylum?"

She shook her head. "I don't know—lots."

"Lots, yeah. That freak was going to kill them all in the end. You and I stopped that, together. You know what? You can't forget? Good. Don't. The bad stuff never leaves, but don't let it hold onto you without remembering the good you did. That's not the way it works. Otherwise, it'll eat you up like you're made of wet cardboard. You'll fall to pieces. And if that happens, you can't help anybody."

"How do you do it?"

"Honestly?"

She locked eyes with me. "Honestly."

"I'm afraid of what happens if I don't. It's like I told you back in the asylum. Someone's got to carry all of this so others don't. And...I don't have a choice." I gave her the goofiest grin I could.

Ortiz shook, pressing a hand to her sides. Seconds later,

the inevitable. She burst into a torrent of laughter. "And I thought my job's work hours sucked."

"Tell me about it. You know I don't even get a pension plan?"

She rolled her eyes. "What a shame." Ortiz opened her mouth to speak, but stopped as we turned onto the street where Daniel lived.

"Yeah..." I trailed off when I saw what Ortiz had seen. "That's never a good sign."

Chapter Twelve

A pair of ambulances were parked against the curb closest to the apartment complex. The sidewalk thronged with people I assumed were tenants. I lurched against the seat as Ortiz gunned her hobbled car down the road. My shoulder throbbed as I crashed into the door from the sudden turn.

Ortiz twisted the wheel, pulling the car into an empty spot on the curb a bit too fast. The vehicle juddered as the passenger side wheel impacted the curb. She wasted no time in turning off the ignition and flinging the door open.

I followed her lead. Well, I tried to. My door protested granting me freedom. I leaned into it. Nothing. A string of obscenities left my mouth as my heel crashed into the door. It opened, but not without a low groan of metal I hoped went unheard by Ortiz. She was going to need to replace some door hinges. I leapt out and sprinted after her.

Ortiz muscled her way past the first few people before pulling out that special little badge that gave her a great deal of power. People pulled away from her like she were radioactive.

The doors of the complex opened. A familiar man was bound to a stretcher. He had dark skin and was dressed similarly to Church—nerd chic. He was out cold, and that wasn't the worst of it.

My vision blurred, replaced by something that looked like flickering screens. Every interaction Daniel had with the man of late strobed by. I exhaled when the vision faded. I hadn't gotten his name before. It'd taken all of this to be able to address him properly. And now it looked like he wouldn't be able to hear me say his name. I pushed my way through the crowd, reaching out with a hand. "Milo!"

The EMT warned me back.

Ortiz pulled up alongside the first responder without

impeding her. "What happened?"

The EMT gestured to the man's hands.

Ortiz arched a brow. "Are those burns?"

"Yes, we've got another coming down. Same thing. Electrocution."

I tried to break free of the front line of the crowd, but the EMT wasn't wasting time. She brought the stretcher to the edge of the ambulance, getting another responder to help her load it. The doors shut.

Another stretcher followed in its wake, heading towards the other vehicle. The woman on it looked like she was in her late fifties. Her hair looked like strands of fine steel wool. She had the same complexion as Milo and enough of his features for me to hazard a guess that she was related— his mother, I assumed. I wished those were the only similarities. She sported the same patterns of burns to her hands and face.

I didn't know what to make of it. They were both alive but needed medical attention—fast. I swore under my breath and stayed out of the way. If all went well, I'd likely be able to pay a visit later and get some answers. I shut my eyes and inhaled.

It's never easy looking at people when they go through something like that. Never. But it's part of the job—the part you learn to balance. Distance yourself too much, and you grow numb. The cases are easy, but it becomes a cold, mechanical process. I know it all too well. I was like that before meeting Ortiz. You have to feel, no matter how hard it is, no matter how much you don't want to. It's like letting yourself be open to everything that happens to others. If you don't do it, you can't help. Not really, anyway. Sometimes the hardest thing you can do is let yourself care.

It's like inviting a hurricane of shrapnel into your heart and mind. But if you don't, you lose out on a lot that can help you. Like anger. We're taught to bury it. It's bad. It's distracting. It's the path to the dark side—whatever. People forget this. It works. There's a hot clarity that comes with it, as well as the renewal of purpose. Whatever works.

I exhaled and made a fist. My fingers dug into the soft meat of my palm, eliciting an acute row of pressure until the area grew numb. It looked like I had a lot of people to settle scores for. I gritted my teeth and made a silent affirmation I was going to give this thing hell.

Ortiz put a hand on my shoulder, giving me a shake. "You alright? You look... I've seen that before."

I eyed her, trying to let the heat leave my stare.

The edge of her mouth quirked like she was trying not to smile. "That's the look you give when you're angry, which usually means you're going to do something impulsive, and stupid." She smirked.

I scowled and nodded towards the building. "Let's go and check it out."

"Check what out?" She arched a brow.

"His place, or do you think people getting zapped like that is normal?"

Ortiz's eyebrows knitted together, and teeth flashed as she chewed on her lower lip for a second. "You're right. It's fishy." She waved her badge at me. "Me first. At least I have a reason to be looking around." Ortiz moved past me and headed towards the apartment.

I took a step after her, and the right sleeve of my shirt tightened around my arm. I glanced over my shoulder. "Oh, great, you." I could have sounded more enthused. It would have been polite.

Kelly stared at me like I hadn't said a word. She slid her thumb underneath the strap of her bag, adjusting it with a tug. "I got here as fast as I could. I'm sorry about..." She gestured to the ambulance. "I can help."

"How?"

She gave me a lopsided smile. "Um, I figured you out, didn't I? I'm also a genius."

I snorted. "Modest much?"

Kelly's face remained neutral.

"Wait, you're serious?"

She nodded.

Oh. A genius on your team never hurts, and I'm not one to push away talent. I just hoped I could keep her from falling too far down the rabbit hole. I cleared my throat. "Yeah, come on." I followed Ortiz, motioning with a hand for Kelly to tag along.

We moved up the stairs in silence. Ortiz leaned against the wall, waiting by the door for Milo's place. Her hand fell to the handle, jostling it. "It's open." She gave me a knowing look.

I pursed my lips.

Kelly looked between us. "What's that mean?"

I looked at her. "Medical responders don't pick locks. Normally when they're called to a scene, they have some measure of access to the person in need. A family member unlocks the door usually."

She stared at me, waiting for me to make it clear.

"So, here's the thing. Both Milo and the woman were hurt...in the exact same way. Keep that in mind."

She nodded.

"If both people in the apartment were out cold, who called for the ambulances? Who unlocked the place?"

Kelly's face scrunched before she went wide-eyed. "This wasn't an accident."

"Bingo, welcome to the world of—"

"Aliens. Thank you for explaining all of that. I have a lot to learn." She patted me on the shoulder and moved towards the door.

My mouth froze half-open. I glanced at Ortiz, whose face was a tight mask of resistance. She was struggling not to burst into a fit of laughter. I scowled.

Ortiz lost it.

My scowl deepened. "It's not funny."

She kept laughing.

Kelly stared at the both of us. "Are we going inside?"

Ortiz's body shook when she stopped. A glimmer hung in her eyes. "Yeah, shall we?" She gave me a look.

I let out a low, animalistic growl and made my way to the door. Brushing aside Ortiz's hand, I took the knob, flinging the door open. I took several steps into Milo's apartment before a familiar smell stopped me. Burning hair and skin have a unique stench. It isn't pleasant. My nose twitched, and I winced as I tried to push the sulfurous odor from my mind. It's never that simple.

Ortiz mirrored me. Her nose wriggled, and she huffed a few light breaths through her mouth. The smell, tinged with the knowledge of what happened to Milo, didn't make it easy to ignore the stink. But we could work through it.

A black leather sofa took up most of the living room.

The standard dresser, no higher than my waist, stood against the right-side wall. An impressive flat screen television hung from the wall. It was paired with a sound system that would make any technology buff drool. The place was filled with the sort of technology you'd find on the cover of a geek magazine.

Kelly whistled and brushed past us. She moved towards a wooden workbench in the far corner of the room. It was littered with battered laptops and computers parts like it was a recycling dump for components. A small, rectangular mirror hung on the wall. She bent at the waist, eyeing the table and its contents with interest.

Ortiz followed her lead, nudging me with an elbow.

I grunted.

She pointed to a deformed box of black composite material. A frayed and mangled cord ran from the back of it into an outlet.

"Kelly, what's that?" I pointed to what Ortiz was looking at.

The young genius spotted the device, and her lips pressed together. "It's a power supply."

Ortiz and I exchanged puzzled looks.

"Uh, it's a pa-what?" I glanced from the box to Kelly, waiting for an explanation.

She rolled her shoulder and let the bag slip from her arm to the ground. "It's what powers something like a desktop computer. It plugs into a wall outlet for constant power unlike a laptop that has a charger but also an internal battery. Something's wrong." She bent over the device, sniffing it before recoiling.

Ortiz and I leaned forwards. I gave Kelly a light prod. "What's up?"

"It's been fried. Hard to tell from the smell though." Kelly wrinkled her nose and waved a hand. "The mirror's giving off a smell like orange-scented glass cleaner. It's overpowering the burn."

"How often do these things fry out?"

She turned and gave me a look that answered my question.

"Oh. So, freak accident, huh?" We all knew it was anything but that.

"They burn out on occasion but this looks like someone started a campfire inside it and I don't know..." She trailed off and pointed to a section of the workbench.

I don't know how I missed it at first. Black lines raced across the wood like vines. "Are those burn marks?"

Ortiz moved to Kelly's side, scanning the table. "That's exactly what they are."

We both turned to Kelly.

"So, what are the odds of one of these things blowing up and electrocuting someone? Because from where I'm standing, I don't see how anything else in here could've fried two people."

Both women looked at me like I was screwy.

Ortiz pouted and shifted her posture like she was uncertain. "I don't know; that's a stretch—a long one. We don't know for sure what caused them to be hurt. Filling in that gap with anything else is just looking for answers. That won't make them the right ones."

Kelly nodded.

I stared at Ortiz. "You're looking for logical arguments. Need I remind you we're hunting a monster? Remember Manhattan? Filling in gaps is what I do. The paranormal don't play by reason and logic."

Ortiz's eyes narrowed.

I blinked and licked my lips. "But I don't think it'd hurt having a look around the place. Think you can work your magic, Geek Squad, and figure anything else out about Milo?"

She rolled her eyes. "Easy." Kelly moved over to the sofa, scooping her bag up on the way. The girl plunked on a cushion and removed her laptop. She went to work fast.

A dull pressure filled my forearm. I turned to Ortiz, arching a brow. "What gives?"

"Vincent, I know your job's not easy, but if we jump to conclusions we could miss out on something important. It leads to chasing ghosts and bad leads. Someone else could get hurt while we do that."

She had a point, but so did I. "I know. But, and this is going to sound asinine, you've done this with me before. How many times have my crazy leads been not-so-crazy?"

Ortiz frowned, balling a fist and putting it on her hip.

"You're right. That did sound asinine. Last name, Right. First name, Always."

I tried to mask the smirk fighting to make its way across my face. I failed. I offered her a half-shrug as an apology. "Look, I don't know what exactly is going on, just that something isn't adding up. They came out with burn marks and the notion they've been electrocuted. I don't see anything else that would point to that except the fried box over there. It's a stretch, yeah, but that's assuming the box was naturally the cause."

Ortiz glanced at the box, then back to me. "You think something gave it a little extra juice? Magic?" She eyed the power supply again, taking a step back from it.

I mimicked her. The thing was still plugged in. If something had given it some oomph, no reason to believe it couldn't do it again. "We've seen stranger things. Our first case, which this is starting to resemble in some odd ways."

"Every case with you is odd."

That was true. I waved it off and leaned against the table, sighing. "I don't know what else to run on, Ortiz. I feel like I'm digging in the dirt with my bare hands and no clue of what I'm supposed to be searching for. I've got fragments of clues that make it seem like a monster we've already ganked." A hollow thud came from the table as my fists hammered it.

Ortiz took hold of one of my arms, pulling it away from the table. "Hey, I know." She licked her lips and breathed out. "I know. It's never easy, I've gone through this myself on cases. When things don't add up, you want to pull your hair out. It doesn't help. It just makes your brain feel like a mess of tangled knots."

That's exactly how I felt. I winced, pretending that the pressure with which I held my eyes shut would alleviate the throbbing in my skull. It didn't.

She squeezed my wrist, pulling me from my clouded thoughts. "We'll figure it out."

I wasn't so sure. I looked at her. "How do you know?"

"Because we don't really have a choice. I can't let a monster run around my state killing people." She arched a brow and gave me a knowing look. "What about you?"

I grinned. "Screw that."

She nodded. "So, let's take this a step at a time. We have a list of things we know—no matter how little sense they make."

"And a list of things we don't know, a pretty big one, to be fair."

Ortiz glared at me.

I shut up.

She went on like I hadn't spoken. "We need to sit down and break up each bit of information on its own—see where it leads us. Then we can treat it like a jigsaw puzzle and put it back together. We might not get all of the pieces, but if we play it right, we can get enough to have an idea of what we're looking at."

It was a smart move, except for one issue. I pointed to my forearm.

Ortiz glanced at it and sighed. "Right, there's always a catch with you."

I shrugged. "As close as I am to it—we can't all be perfect." I gave her a lopsided smile.

She didn't return it. "We have resources. Your journals are loaded with information, right? There's bound to be something in there."

I pressed a hand to my head. "I don't know, Ortiz. There's so much I encounter on a case that it's hard recalling it all, not to mention recording it. My journals have a lot, but sometimes it's not about a lot; it's about what I don't have."

"Well, you won't know until you look." She shifted away from me and looked at me sideways.

I raised my hands in a gesture of defeat.

Ortiz held the look. "So, where are they?"

I looked away before turning back, giving her a weak smile and laugh. My hand went to the back of my head. "In the car, in the windbreaker being used to hide the illegal weapons you told me to take."

Ortiz stared. "You left them in my car?"

There are moments in every man's life where sometimes answering a question is not the best thing to do. No matter how witty a reply I might have had, no matter how simple the answer, it was safer to look at my shoes. They were nice shoes.

Kelly bounced in her seat, thrusting a fist into the air. "Check it out!"

Ortiz turned to her, forgetting about me.

Bless you, you strange, strange child. I followed Ortiz towards the couch, and we hovered over Kelly's laptop. A series of small windows dotted the page.

She looked at us both before trailing her finger over the mouse pad. A single window expanded to dominate the screen. Milo's face sat boxed in the top-right corner of the web page. He looked happy. His glasses sat at an angle, noticeably I might add. It worked for him and gave Milo the definitive geek vibe. It was like looking at a younger, darker, Church, minus all the hair.

"What are we looking at?" I scanned the page but didn't have a clear idea.

"It's his blog." Kelly looked at me like it should have been obvious.

I shrugged. "How's that relevant?"

She pointed a finger to a counter at the top of the page.

I shook my head. "So?"

Kelly let out a resigned sigh. She eyed Ortiz. "How do you work with this caveman?"

I blinked and stared at both of them.

Kelly shook her head, returning to the page while Ortiz fought not to smile.

I released a chest-shaking grunt that would have made any troglodyte proud. "Me smash little computer."

Kelly turned slowly, staring at me the way a large cat might before pouncing on a mouse. "Not if you want to live." Her voice could have made snow feel warm by comparison.

I gave Ortiz a sideways glance.

Her lips pressed tighter together than before. The muscles in her neck quivered as her chest shook. She was enjoying this.

"Bah, tough talk." I waved them both off. "What's the point?"

Kelly calmed and worked her magic, bringing up another site for comparison. "See the hits there?" She flipped back to the previous page once Ortiz and I had acknowledged the count. "Now, Milo's." She highlighted the counter, flipping between the pages so we could compare.

Ortiz and I whistled in unison. Milo's numbers were exponentially higher than the other site's.

"Cool, big numbers. I don't see the importance. Then again, I have trouble with anything after the venerable número trés." I waggled three fingers.

Ortiz shook her head. "Should have watched more Sesame Street."

"Yeah, the monstrous puppet in charge of counting is a vampire." I stared at her, making it clear I wasn't a fan. "I'm not big on that. Go figure."

She rolled her eyes.

Kelly cleared her throat, looking at the pair of us like we were bickering children.

I pointed at Ortiz. "She started it."

Ortiz looked like she was going to bite my finger off.

I curled the finger back and eyed the screen. "I still don't see the big deal?"

The young computer guru dragged the mouse from the counter over to a series of page ads. From there, she pulled the cursor to a donation button. "With the amount of traffic he gets, and the ads, he's probably making a living from this blog alone. Then there are the donations." She pointed to a small box below them and a scrolling script of names and numbers. "He's actively getting money from people. Some are throwing pocket change, others—" She trailed off and clicked on a sum of two hundred dollars.

"For running a website?" I'm sure my eyes swelled to owlish proportions.

"His blog is endless information articles on computer maintenance and repair. It's textbook thorough." It sounded like she was talking to herself as she scrolled through his site. "He's got in depth videos too, not to mention his work hours where people can call in and chat live so he can diagnose problems. Milo's got his blog set up with work order forms so people can even mail units in for repair. He's got a form set up to get permission to remote into people's computers too."

Ortiz and I traded quizzical looks then looked to Kelly, making it clear she was speaking another language.

The young woman's shoulders sunk further. "He has an

impressive blog that lets him make a full-time living as a computer technician without needing to leave the comfort of his home. The only exceptions to that are groceries and other human things."

I don't know why, but I felt like the last part of her comment was addressed to me. I resisted the urge to loom over her and scowl.

Ortiz leaned closer to Kelly, nudging the girl with her elbow. "How does this help us?"

Kelly's face tightened as she thought. "I'm not sure, but I think knowing what people do for a living is useful in your line of work, right?"

Ortiz nodded before giving me a look.

I didn't know what to make of it. Yes, it was a possibility Milo's work had gotten him fried; everything pointed to it. But it was rather coincidental, aside from the unbelievable part. I shut my eyes and swore as it hit me.

"Um, okay?" Kelly looked at me like I was unstable.

To be fair, hunting the paranormal requires a bit of crazy.

"What's wrong?" Ortiz was watching me carefully. She knew I was onto something.

"Yo, Hackers, can you find out anything more about Milo's business?"

Kelly frowned. "Yes, and did you really just reference that movie? You're old."

I sniffed and didn't deign to reply.

She put her laptop beside her and rose from the couch. Kelly walked past us towards the table with the damaged power supply. She picked a hard binder like the sort you'd find in elementary school. Kelly thumbed it open and leafed through the pages. She stopped when she'd reached the final page. "That's weird."

Ortiz and I waited in silence. It's obvious when someone's on a roll, and when they are, you leave them to it.

Kelly held onto the binder as she leaned over the power supply, eyeing it from as many angles as she could. She grabbed the box, turning it over.

I bristled the second she made contact. Fortunately, nothing happened.

Kelly's gaze bounced from the binder to the damaged

power supply and back again several times. "This might be one of those clues you're looking for."

I rocketed off the sofa, covering the distance in a second. Ortiz was a millimeter behind me. I came to Kelly's side, staring at the binder and then the unit, hoping she had something good. The sheet of paper was segmented into horizontal boxes in which descriptions and numbers sat. It looked like an organized list.

"These are his work orders." Kelly tapped her thumb against the final box.

I scanned it and clenched my jaw.

Ortiz mimicked me when she saw it.

"Yeah." Kelly pointed to the power supply. "The part number matches the one on the bottom of the supply he was testing. It was shipped to him for a diagnosis. Intermittent power failure—cutting off."

Power failure was an understatement.

"It's way too much of a coincidence for that thing to blow up, shock Milo, and be the newest job he had." Kelly pointed at another box on the page. It was a date of arrival marker. Milo had gotten the unit earlier today.

I looked up from the binder to Ortiz, arching a brow. "Still think it's a stretch?"

She huffed a breath. Ortiz crossed her arms, and I could see her struggling with the urge to hit me.

I let my face slip into a neutral mask that would hopefully keep her from following through on that desire. "Right, so we've got foul play. A really weird piece of foul play."

Ortiz bit her lip. "But why send this? If it's something paranormal, why bother making it look like a work accident? If whatever it is can do"—Ortiz nodded to the power supply—"that, what's the point of using an item to kill?"

"Weird twist of fate," said Kelly.

A series of thuds came from the door.

We all turned.

The knocking repeated.

Kelly shuddered and clutched the binder to her chest. Ortiz's body stiffened like she was readying for a fight.

My fingers waggled at my side as I ran through the likely scenarios. I decided on a course of action, and that I wasn't too bright. "Ortiz?"

"Yeah?"

"You still packing?"

"Both the revolver and my service weapon."

Of course she was. Ortiz was like my own Rambo, but smaller and scarier. I moved towards the door, letting my hand fall to the knob. My fingers gripped it, and I wrenched it open, preparing for the worst.

He didn't look old enough to be out of high school. A shock of blonde hair and an acne-riddled face that looked rougher than some bumpy roads. He was dressed in a beige uniform I'd expect of a delivery man.

"What?" My lips peeled back in an almost snarl.

The kid shivered, looking like he would piss his khaki pants. His hand trembled as he presented me with an envelope.

I took it and turned it over, eyeing both sides. It was completely blank. I arched a brow and stared. "What gives?"

He shrugged. "I was paid to give it to you."

I thanked him by way of a brusque nod.

He lingered in the doorway, looking at me like there was something else.

"What?"

Ortiz cleared her throat as she came to my side. "He wants a tip."

Both of my eyebrows shot up. "Oh. Right. Uh, stay in school." I slammed the door shut.

Ortiz stared at me, her mouth hanging open. She looked at the door then back to me. "Did you just stiff a kid on a tip?"

I waggled the envelope at her. "Trust me, I don't get something like this unless it's bad news—very bad news."

She arched a brow, leaning against the door. "So, you're going to take it out on the messenger?"

I shrugged.

"You can be such a child."

I stuck my tongue out and flipped the envelope over, sliding my index finger underneath the flap. Paper tore as I dragged the digit across. My thumb and forefinger slid inside, pinching the letter and pulling it free. I unfolded it with a flick of my wrist.

Ortiz pushed off the wall, leaning closer to get a better look.

I eyed her and turned away.

She let out a little growl.

I ignored her glare, going over the letter until the end. It was a short message written in elegant, flowing script. The letter ended with an address and a single initial. One that meant trouble. I sighed. "Hey, Ortiz, do you know where this is?" I read the address aloud.

She shook her head.

"I do," said Kelly. "It's a bar about fifteen minutes from here. Why?"

Ortiz gave me a silent look that asked the same question.

"Because I was right. It's bad news."

Chapter Thirteen

"Pack up and head home, Kelly." I waved a hand at her laptop and bag. My face tightened before slipping into a frown as I realized I had left my spare cash in my windbreaker.

Kelly moved to the couch, collecting her gear and stuffing it into her bag. Once it was done, she rounded on me. The look on her face made it obvious she didn't intend to go home.

I looked to Ortiz for help.

She wore the same look as Kelly.

A groan worked its way up my throat. I stopped it before it left my mouth, turning it into a long, quiet sigh. "This could get dangerous. No, scratch that. It is going to be dangerous."

Both women exchanged a quick look. Their features hardened, as did the resolve in their eyes.

"You two aren't going to leave, are you?"

They shook their heads.

Ortiz crossed her arms. "There is a paranormal creature hurting people. No one else can deal with it, so I'm going to."

I wanted to point out that I could deal with it and planned to. The fire in her eyes made me reconsider voicing that point. "Just promise me that you'll follow my lead. Look, you want to fight this thing with me, come in on my case? Fine. All I'm asking is that you trust me where it counts. I know this world. If I tell you to do something"—I eyed both of them—"either of you—you do it."

Kelly looked to Ortiz as if waiting for a silent cue.

Ortiz nodded.

Kelly did the same.

I exhaled in relief. "Good. I can't make any promises about what will happen; I just know it's not going to be good."

"Is he always this negative?" Kelly shouldered her bag, looking at Ortiz for an answer.

The agent rolled her eyes and moved to open the door. "No. Sometimes he's just a wiseass." Her tone made it sound like more of an insult than a compliment, but I knew she meant it as the latter.

Nothing is wrong with being a wiseass.

Ortiz swung the door open, heading out of the hall without waiting for us. Kelly brushed past me in pursuit.

Something tugged at me to stop and give Milo's place one last look. Part of it was sentimental. The guy had invited me to a movie night, seemed like a good person, and now he was injured. Maybe if I'd been faster in figuring things out, or even getting back, he'd still be fine. He was another person in the long line hurt by the paranormal.

The other half of it was intuition. I walked back to the workbench. Caution dictated that I unplug the little death box from the socket. I grabbed a bit of the cord still protected by its covering and tugged. The plug came free and clunked against the surface of the table. I lifted the box to my face. It wasn't the best idea. I shut my eyes and inhaled.

A resounding thud echoed as the box landed on the table. One of its pointed corners left a pea-sized indent in the wood. The box may have left my hands, but the smell remained. It took me a bit to work through the burnt plastic and smoke. There was an underlying odor that matched the one in Daniel's bedroom.

The creature was smart enough to target people using their livelihoods. That's never a good sign. And it meant I had to brush up on Daniel's neighbors the next chance I had. My fingers closed around the letter until it crumpled. I stuffed it into my pocket. A series of dull knocks sounded from behind me, prompting me to turn.

Kelly's head hung past the doorframe, the rest of her body out of sight as she knocked again. "You coming?"

"Yeah, sorry, had to check something out."

She looked at the power supply, then me, raising a brow. Her lips parted, but she said nothing.

I sprinted the short distance to the door and grabbed

the back of it with my hand. It swung shut behind us as Kelly led the way.

"What did you find?"

I sniffed once. "What makes you think I found anything?"

"Avoiding the question. You've done this before—a lot—according to everything I've dug up. And I'm not stupid." She smirked.

No, she wasn't at all. "Quid pro quo, kid?"

Kelly's brows knitted together, and her face scrunched when she looked at me. "What did you have in mind?"

"I've got questions of my own." We made it down the stairs and into the lobby where Ortiz waited. I slowed my pace and dropped the volume of my voice. "I'd like answers."

"You mean what else do I know about you?" The smirk grew into a smile of self-satisfaction.

She caught on quick. "Yeah." I increased the distance between us as I moved past Ortiz to the door. It opened with a groan of protest from the hinges. I held it until both women exited, slipping through behind them. I looked at the cars lining the streets and rocked in place. "So, whose car are we taking?"

Kelly turned to me. "You don't have your own?"

I looked to Ortiz. "Do I?"

She shook her head. "Subway and public transport were his thing."

I opened my mouth to speak before Ortiz held up a finger. I shut it.

"No." She turned to look back at Kelly.

The young hacker blinked. "Wait, why me?"

I moved towards where Ortiz had parked, beckoning with my hand to follow. Their footsteps were audible as they fell into a light jog behind me. My pace quickened until I reached her vehicle. "That's why." I waved a hand at the crumpled fender and surrounding area on her sedan.

"Wow. You should have that looked at." Kelly bent at the waist, eyeing the damage with an equal amount of shock and admiration. "What hit you, a bus?"

Ortiz scowled. "Monsters in a stolen police cruiser."

Kelly straightened, and her eyes narrowed. "Monsters

and aliens are interchangeable, but it isn't that hard to say aliens."

Ortiz looked to me for help.

I shrugged. "Hey, you're her friend." I rapped my knuckles against the back window and nodded to the coat inside. "Think they'll be safe in there?"

Ortiz stared.

I held up my hands. "Right. Of course. Um, so, Kelly, wanna bring your car around and give us a ride?"

Her shoulders sank, followed by the rest of her posture. "Yeah, sure. It's not like I had better things to do except..." She trailed off as she moved further away. When she was near the end of the block, Ortiz turned to me.

"I heard most of it, you know?" She looked at me like I was supposed to know what that meant.

I arched a brow. "Eh?"

"What you asked Kelly back there." She jerked a thumb towards the apartment complex.

"Oh." I didn't have a better response.

"She's told you everything she told me. Kelly isn't big on hiding things." Ortiz stared into my eyes hard. "Unlike some people."

My left hand tightened into a fist several times. I exhaled in concert with it. "I know. And you know why I did what I did. I'm not going to keep apologizing for it. We're not going to agree on the reasons behind it, but we can agree that this is where we are now. I'm trying to keep you two safe. Sorry, I know that rankles you. Ortiz, I got you killed at one point. No arguing that. I can't watch that happen again, to you, Lizzie"—I pointed towards where Kelly had gone—"her, anyone. This is me just trying my best. I'm not trying to keep you out of this world anymore, not my call. But I am trying to make sure you survive it."

Her fingers dug into both of my biceps and she squeezed. "I know. Thank you. And Kelly and I are going to listen. We need you to realize that we're not stupid. We don't know it all, but we want to help." Her voice made steel seem softer than butter. "We know when to take our lead from you. We expect you to know when you need to shut up and follow ours." The corners of her mouth pulled into a light smile.

I returned it. "Fair enough. Besides, I don't think we have any more time to fight." I gestured to my tattoo with my chin. Forty-five hours remained for us to figure it all out. It was going to have to be enough.

Ortiz gave a micro nod of her head to the street behind us.

A red coupe came to a halt next to Ortiz's car, blocking the lane. Kids.

Ortiz moved around her vehicle and towards Kelly's.

I looked into the window, regretting leaving my journals behind, but taking them would be too risky. If things went wrong—and I had reason to believe they would—they'd end up in dangerous hands. I gritted my teeth and rushed into the street.

Kelly's car was a late nineties Camaro with a pair of glass panels as part of the roof that had been removed to expose its insides to the warmth. The car was the exact shade of red as a fire engine. A color begging for the police's attention. Ortiz's hand fell on the door handle to open it.

I sped up, coming to her side in a second. "Shotgun."

She turned her head, blinking twice before giving me a look like I was a child. Ortiz shook her head and opened the door. She reached down, pulling a lever to fold the seat down.

I smiled, waiting for her to get in the back.

She didn't. Ortiz straightened, waving a hand to the back seat.

I frowned. "Uh, that's not how the rule works."

She arched a brow. "That's adorable. Get in the back."

I didn't have time to argue, even though she was wrong. She stepped aside as I made my way to the door. Getting in was a bit of an effort. My body groaned in discomfort as I twisted through the small space and fell onto the seat. The back of the passenger seat snapped towards me and thunked as it came to a stop. Ortiz plopped down, keeping her head perfectly straight. I hoped she could feel my stare through the headrest. One does not ignore shotgun.

The door shut and Ortiz whispered something in Kelly's ear. The young woman laughed as the car lurched forwards with a basso rumble that could only come from eight cylinders. Ortiz shifted in her seat, turning just far enough to look at me over her shoulder. "Do you think we're going to find any sort of help at this bar?"

My gut felt like it was being stretched and kneaded. It was possible we could get a nudge in the right direction, but I doubted it. My list of contacts wasn't big on doing me favors—unconditionally at least. There's always a catch. And right now, there was a hook in my cheek that was being tugged. "Honestly, I'm not sure. I'd rather not go at all."

Ortiz asked a silent question with her stare.

"This is one of those occasions where not going would make everything worse." I stared back, making it clear that I didn't have a choice.

She bit her lip and nodded to herself before turning to look ahead. "It sounds like one of those things you could use a hand with—or a few hands." Ortiz tilted her head towards Kelly.

"You're right. It's also one of those things that could get all three of us killed. Like I said, I'm not sure what's going to happen. I've got a horrible feeling. Those usually turn out to be right." I regretted saying it.

An awkward silence filled the car. It that made the air feel like a thick gel, deafening me to all other sounds. I decided to end it.

The muscles in my throat ached as I cleared it a bit too hard. At least I got everyone's attention. "So, Kelly, we don't really know each other that well—"

"You could've started this conversation way less awkwardly than that." Unlike Ortiz, Kelly kept her eyes on the road as she spoke. Thank God.

I bristled in my seat and went on as if she hadn't spoken. "It's obvious you've watched way too many reruns of shows involving gate travel or a guy in a fez."

She huffed through her nose. "You say that like it's a bad thing." Kelly pulled the car onto a new street and accelerated.

"I'm just trying to understand the alien thing. It doesn't make sense, especially when I've come clean about what I am and the world I'm involved with." It was hard to see her reasoning. I knew she wasn't doing it to irritate me. There's a certain conviction that colors a person's voice and makes its way to their eyes when they believe in something. When I met Kelly, I had seen and heard that in her. I just wanted to know why.

"It doesn't make sense," she said.

"How so? What reason would I have to lie?"

She shifted in her seat, and I saw her shoulders and upper back stiffen. "I'm not saying you are lying. It could be that you're not aware of what you are. You say you're a soul—science hasn't proven those exist one way or another. How do you know you are what you are? Where's your proof? What's it like when you're not possessing a dead body? How do you know you're not some highly advanced form of consciousness that doesn't need a body to survive?" The questions were delivered in a cold, analytical voice.

Each one pumped another shot of ice water through my body. My brain numbed as I tried to process them.

I know what I am. Don't I? Pressure built within my gums, and my teeth skidded over one another. Church had told me what I was, and I believed him. I trusted him. Do you? The question caused my marrow to feel like it'd been replaced with chunks of burning charcoal. Both hands balled into fists, making the small bones inside them throb. I didn't have proof. I just had what I'd been told, and now I had more questions than ever. I shut my eyes and buried them all. It didn't matter. Belief is a power.

It shapes things and people. It's a defining force like no other. I filled my voice with iron and stone. "It's called a soul, Kelly. I know what I am. The things I've seen and fought are pulled from history—mythology—not space. You can probably make an argument to make that seem like aliens too. I'm not going to try to convince you to see things my way. All I need from you is your word—whatever you believe—that you're going to trust I know what I'm talking about when dealing with this world. That fair?"

She nodded. "Yeah."

That settled it. Like the questions, I buried that part of the conversation. I needed other answers. "How long have you been following me?"

Kelly's arm shot towards the center of the steering wheel. The car released a weak cry like the horn was muffled. "Jackass." Her gaze was fixed on a passing Beetle in horrible condition. The car was an amalgamation of multicolored panels plucked from donor cars likely. "Sorry, and I've been digging into you for a few years now. There are people who've been trying to figure you out for longer. Most of them have a bunch of pictures and videos but not a clue." She laughed to herself.

It was a small relief. But if more people were looking into me, it meant new faces who could get dragged into my messy life. I needed to have a talk to Church about this.

"Most people think you're a secret group of individuals. There are forums about trying to figure out how to join and learn what they know about all the strange events. Ortiz and I were the first to put it all together with what we knew between us." Kelly held out a fist. Ortiz bumped hers against it.

I stared and judged them in silence.

The car burped a series of throaty burbles as Kelly pulled into an empty spot on the curb. We had arrived. Both women exited at the same time, but Kelly paused at the door. She leaned and folded her seat forwards as Ortiz did the same a second later.

I eyed Ortiz until she noticed me. I smiled and scooted towards Kelly's side, exiting there.

Ortiz scoffed and shook her head. "Child."

I ignored the comment.

The bar was nice and small, the sort of thing you'd expect on the corner of a busy city. It was made of gray stone with a series of protruding windows that formed a small nook inside the bar. Smoked glass prevented a look inside. The door sat recessed a few feet into the stone. It was the color of bright rum, dulled and weathered from time and the elements. I peered closer. Thin etchings ran around the entirety of its frame. Each marking was no larger than the pin of a thumbtack. The carvings looked archaic and didn't resemble any language I knew of—mortal or supernatural.

The handle was a metal I couldn't identify, patinated a moss green and bent into an intricate, flowing shape. A banner of crimson hung from the bar, draped around a protruding frame of metal to serve as a cover of sorts. I got a feeling this was one of those places where knocking was appreciated.

Manners never go amiss when dealing with the paranormal and unknown. My knuckles bounced off the door. I felt Ortiz and Kelly drilling holes in the back of my head with their stares.

There was a heavy click from the other side of the door. My body stiffened.

The door opened, and a bald, living mountain of muscle and ink stood in the way. He was dressed in an olive tank top, which showed off arms built with the sort of mass geared for competitive shows rather than function. His skin was sun-kissed and covered in green tattoos that crisscrossed in simple designs.

I looked up to eyeball him. The guy had a full foot over Daniel—at least. I pegged him to be seven feet plus. "'Sup?"

His face twisted into a scowl. That's always a great welcome. His dark eyes narrowed.

"Uh, can we come in?" I looked over my shoulder and hooked a thumb to Ortiz and Kelly. "I promise we won't get too loud with the drunken karaoke. You guys have that here, right?"

Thugzilla growled at me.

My eyes narrowed back, and I stared him down. "Listen, I don't speak that." I reached into my pocket, fishing out a ball of paper. Taking it between my thumb and forefinger, I gave it a quick flick to unfold it. It was a pain to sort out the folded mess, but I managed and turned it over to him. "See, I got an invitation to the cool kids' club." I tapped my index finger to the lone initial at the bottom of the page.

He stared at it then looked over his shoulder to something obscured by his bulk.

"It's fine. I invited him. Let him through," said a voice that confirmed my fears. It was sweet and melodic. A shame the thing it belonged to wasn't.

The rent-a-thug moved out of the way.

I moved forwards, stopping mid-step. I planted my foot to the ground and turned a fraction. "You two stay here." I pointed at a spot just inside the entrance.

Ortiz looked at me, then at the bouncer. "You want me to stay here—with him?"

"Just in case, watch my back, huh?" I grinned, turning to the living roadblock. He glared at me, and I returned it.

"Yeah, I know you can hear me. Behave." I waggled an admonishing finger at him.

"Or what?" His voice sounded like he'd eaten cement blocks and sawdust for breakfast.

Ortiz stepped between us and met his gaze. There was a feral smile on her face. Her hands went to her hips and she shifted. She held the stare.

There was a moment where all the sound died. I felt web-like strands of electricity arc through the air. There's a certain pressure that builds when two people, or even animals, get into it. The air tightens around you; it quivers.

The muscle-bound brute bristled.

Ortiz didn't flinch. Her smile widened, reminding me of a wolf's. "Give me a reason."

Thugosaurus blinked and took a step back.

Ortiz took two towards him, forcing the brute to compensate and backpedal faster than his brain could keep up.

Chairs clattered as his backside brushed against them.

I did my best not to chuckle. My hands fell to my stomach, roaring laughter filled the bar.

The thing about bullies is...they're usually the biggest, meanest things around. They go for extended periods of time unchallenged. That reinforces their ego, which exists to overcompensate for other things—or lack thereof. But big and mean doesn't translate into tough. Trust me on that. They're not used to being stood up to. Even the biggest cat can be made to blink. Sometimes, you just have to stare them down.

The bouncer scowled and took a step towards Ortiz. His shoulder rolled, and a meaty fist sailed towards her. I couldn't recall what followed. Ortiz blurred into motion, stepping to the side as her leg snapped. The tip of her shoe connected below his sternum, causing him to double over. The inside of her palm slid along the outside of his arm and pushed. A loud thud filled our ears as his jaw impacted the table. Ortiz had him pinned by his wrist and the back of his neck.

And sometimes you have to kick their ass. Either or.

I blinked.

Kelly whistled.

He tried to struggle, but Ortiz leaned into him, applying more pressure. "Don't. You just assaulted a federal agent; that's a crime." She leaned back and pivoted.

He let out a grunt that morphed into a whimper.

I placed a hand on her shoulders. "Okay, easy there. What did we say about bullying children?"

Ortiz's body shook, and she released a snort. Her grip loosened enough for the bouncer to free himself. Ortiz stood in place, eyeing him.

I looked past them, paying attention to the bar. It was smaller than most, caught somewhere between the average American living room and a large bedroom. Everything from the walls, tables, and flooring were comprised of a dark wood that reminded me of Guinness. It gave the place a somber look. A mirror glinted like a mirage behind the counter, reflecting the warm glow of amber light. There was no bartender.

I moved towards the back and the figure seated at the furthest table. A black, wide-brimmed sunhat obscured her face, but I didn't need to see it to know who it was. I sat across from her, propping my elbows on the table.

She wore a long dress that looked like it was woven out of midnight skies, sequined with silver starlight. It left her slender, toned arms bare. Her skin reminded me of porcelain.

She removed her hat, and I had to work to not suck in a breath. The woman possessed an ethereal and wild beauty. It was something akin to a hungry cat. Savage, sharp, and entrancing. She flashed me a fox-like smile.

I didn't return it. "Hello, Lyshae."

Chapter Fourteen

Of all the people I could have been summoned by, it had to be her. And I used the term people lightly. Lyshae looked close enough to one. She had hair the color of spun gold, worn loose and falling past her shoulders. The ends of each strand were as white as snow. Her eyes were hypnotic gems of citrine blended with garnet. They reminded me of a fox's. There was a mischievous look in them, one that deepened when she caught me staring. Her lips spread, revealing her teeth. Her canines seemed a bit sharper than they should've been. "You know, it's rude to gawk at a lady."

That jarred me back into my usual self. "Except, you're no lady." I gave her a thin smile.

She lifted a hand, putting it to her mouth as she let out a mock gasp. A pair of triangles twitched atop her head. They protruded from her hair and were trimmed with white fur. Ears that looked like they belonged to an animal. "No, I am not." Her smile widened, and her eyes burned with an inner light.

Lyshae was a Kitsune, a Japanese fox spirit of mischief, information, and illusion. She was also a major pain in my ass.

"What do you want?" It was an effort to keep my breathing steady and my jaw from hardening. Lyshae had helped me before on cases, but the last time we dealt, it came at a cost. Most things do.

Lyshae ignored me, reaching for the slender champagne flute by her side. A liquid of rose-gold sparkled within. She took her time raising it to her lips.

I sighed, waiting for her to finish the sip and lower the champagne. I had the feeling she was watching me over the rim of the glass. A grunt from behind us prompted me to turn.

Ortiz and Lyshae's henchman stood a few feet from each other, locked in another stare down.

I turned back. "Lyshae, think you could get your goon to stand down?"

She arched a delicate brow. Her eyelids fluttered several times. They reminded me of dark soot over snow. "Why?"

I hooked a thumb to Ortiz. "Because I can't promise she won't break him, and what would you do without your muscle?" I smiled.

Lyshae matched it. An amused light shone in her eyes. She didn't need him for anything. It was likely she kept him around to deter mortals, and nothing more. It was easier than making the effort herself. "That's enough, Luther. You're dismissed."

He turned and eyed her before looking back to Ortiz.

"I'll be fine. They won't harm me." Lyshae looked at me, her smile widening until it was discomforting to look at. "Will you, Vincent?"

I looked away.

Luther blew out a breath of exasperation and headed towards the door. I couldn't help but notice that he gave Ortiz as wide a berth as was possible in the tiny bar.

I grinned.

Lyshae looked past me to Ortiz and Kelly. A hungry smile spread across her face. "Why don't you invite your friends to join us? I'm certain they would like to hear the conversation." Her voice carried through the bar. She wasn't trying to be subtle.

I suppressed an inner groan, knowing that Ortiz had heard the invitation. Now I was caught between pissing off Lyshae or Ortiz. Not great circumstances. I leaned forwards, dropping my voice to a whisper. "Uh, I don't think that's a good idea."

Lyshae didn't miss a beat. "Nonsense. I insist."

Of course you do.

She beckoned them with her index and middle fingers.

I looked over my shoulder as Ortiz and Kelly exchanged a quick look. It was an effort to keep my face neutral as they approached. Lyshae wasn't stupid or nice. If she was inviting them to sit with us, it was for a reason. And it wouldn't be a good one. I turned and glared at Lyshae. "What's this about?"

She ignored me, keeping her gaze fixed on the approaching women. Her smile made my spine feel brittle. Lyshae didn't rise to meet Ortiz and Kelly as they stopped by the side of the table. She gestured with a wave of a hand.

The women eyed me then Lyshae. Ortiz's eyes narrowed and hardened. "You." Her jaw tightened. She wasn't a fan of Lyshae.

The Kitsune returned a smile.

I sighed and scooted over. "Sit by me—both of you."

Ortiz and Kelly didn't argue.

Lyshae shot me a look, the edge of her mouth turned up. She thought it was funny.

I thought it was cautious. The last thing we needed was a trickster spirit getting her hands around one of my friends—literally.

Kelly gawked at Lyshae, her hands reaching into her pocket and fishing for something. She pulled out her phone and fumbled with it. "You've got cat ears coming out of the top of your head!" She thumbed the center of her phone several times. An audible snap echoed from it each time.

Lyshae sat and endured the click-fest rather maturely. She took another sip of her drink until Kelly finished.

Kelly's face spread into a smile that morphed into a frown the next second. She squinted at her phone, swiping her index finger along the screen. "That's odd. The pictures are gone." She held up the phone for us to see. The seat and table were in view. Lyshae wasn't.

The fox spirit smiled. I had no doubt she had woven some kind of glamour to protect herself from recording devices. Life's hard for an information spirit if people take your picture every now and again. Kelly seemed nonplussed about it.

I grunted as Ortiz and Kelly scooted along the table, forcing me to grind against the bar wall. A huff of air left through my nose as I shimmied into a more comfortable position. "Alright, we're all here. Wanna tell us what this is about? I'm busy." I raised a hand, flashing my tattoo in her face.

She rolled her eyes. "You're always busy, but that's no concern of mine."

I raised a brow. "Oh? Wow. This conversation's already off to a great start. You don't value my time, my job—hurts a guy's feelings, ya know."

Lyshae gave Ortiz and Kelly a look of exasperation.

They shrugged and returned it.

I sniffed. That was mildly insulting for a silent exchange. Ignoring the denigration, I stared at Lyshae, hardening my jaw.

She exhaled a light puff of air. "Please, you don't have to act tough. I plan to tell you why you are here."

Ortiz wasn't keen on waiting. "Or you could tell us now." She reached into her coat, removing a badge. "I could arrest you."

Lyshae leaned back, steepling her hands on the table. "Oh?"

"You were at the asylum last year. Involved in the deaths of innocent people." Ortiz's voice could've peeled chunks of wood off the table.

The trickster spirit wasn't the least bit intimidated. She waved a hand airily. "Fah, and you can prove this?" She raised a finger. "Better, let me guess: you're going to arrest me on the grounds that I was there at the time of the murders, which as far as public records are concerned, have been solved. You and I both know you are bluffing, Camilla Ortiz."

Ortiz shivered and went wide-eyed. She pulled herself together fast, but I knew Lyshae had caught the reaction. I couldn't blame Ortiz though. Names have power attached to them. Having a paranormal creature, one like Lyshae, say yours could unnerve you. It's like a feather of pure ice trailing its way down your spine.

"As far as your mortal world goes, I don't exist. And when I do, I am generally in control of the situation, which brings us to why you are here." Lyshae turned her gaze to me. "I own you, Vincent Graves."

Oh crap. I knew where this was going.

She held up three fingers. "You owe me a series of debts."

Crap-crap-crap. Lyshae, you bitch.

"I'm giving you a chance to erase one of them. I'm calling your favor, Graves. You're mine."

Dammit. My knuckles ached and my teeth ground. "Lyshae, don't do this. Not now."

She ignored me, taking another sip of her champagne.

Ortiz bristled. She knew what was at stake and wasn't fond of this either.

"Please, I'm on a case—people are dying."

"They're always dying. It's the nature of things. You knew I would come for you. You knew it would be during a case—when else? I am here, as are you. You will do what I say."

I took a series of deep breaths, shutting my eyes as I worked to still myself.

"If it's any consolation, I do apologize for the measures I had to take to ensure you were the right choice." She sipped her booze, eyeing me over the glass in pleasure.

I blinked, and rusted gears turned in my noggin. Everything fell into place. "Oh, you conniving, backstabbing, murderous bitch!"

Ortiz and Kelly scooched away from me until the latter was close to falling off the seat.

"I did apologize, did I not? Besides, Vincent, you've always known who and what I am." She placed her fingers to her collarbone. "When have I ever hidden that from you?" She gave me a smile that made my intestines wind.

"What's going on?" Ortiz looked between us.

I growled and resisted the urge to reach over the table and grab Lyshae. "She"—I jabbed a finger at the Kitsune—"is the reason I've been attacked throughout this case!"

Ortiz crossed her arms as she leaned and arched a brow. "Really?" Her mouth spread into a smile. "And you don't deny that?" She stared at Lyshae.

The fox spirit took another sip. "I do not." She didn't sound worried about confessing. Then again, it'd be a pain in the ass to prove. But if Lyshae was anything, it was most definitely that. "And as you can see, he was the proper choice." She raised the glass in my direction. "Congratulations, Vincent, you passed tryouts."

I grunted. "You had a Night Runner and a troll jump me."

Kelly sputtered and leaned over the table, looking at me, then Lyshae. "Are you serious?"

Neither of us answered her.

"Trolls? And what did you say the first thing was?" Kelly turned her phone sideways in her hands. Her fingers blurred over it like she was taking notes. "So, what are they really? This is so going on my blog."

I sighed and rubbed my palms against my face. "Careful, kid, falling down the rabbit hole here isn't going to lead to fun and whimsical adventures. It'll get you killed."

Kelly stopped typing and licked her lips.

Lyshae let out a rueful chuckle. "Hardly."

Kelly relaxed.

"A girl such as you—young, intelligent. No, you'd be of great use to many creatures. You'd be sold or worse." Lyshae's voice filled with something near need. "You'd be treated well if you cooperated, or... Well, you can imagine what monsters would do to you, can't you, young one?"

Kelly jumped from her seat like she were sitting on burning coals. She took a series of steps back. Her chest rose rapidly, and her frantic breathing was the only sound in the bar.

Ortiz moved to get up from her seat.

I put a hand on her shoulder, shaking my head. She flashed me a quick look that I answered with a firm stare. Kelly didn't need to be here. In fact, she shouldn't have come at all. I couldn't turn her away before, but maybe now I could. I wanted to keep something worse from happening to her. I looked to Ortiz for a split second, and my insides roiled. Kelly didn't need to get involved in this. "You should leave." My voice was cold steel and gravel.

Kelly took another step back, and her breathing slowed a shade. "I could, couldn't I?"

I nodded.

She licked her lips and her thumb brushed against her phone absentmindedly.

Lyshae watched the scene play out with a disturbing level of calm. It almost looked like she was waiting for an answer she knew she was going to get.

I nudged Ortiz with an elbow. She shot me a death glare but turned in her seat.

"Kelly, maybe you should listen. I know I asked you to help me, and you have—a lot. Thank you for that. But no one said you had to come any further with us. This...world isn't nice. It's"—she inhaled and gripped herself tight—"hard. And it's going to force you to make harder decisions. You don't want that."

I stared at Ortiz and grimaced. Part of me wished I could push her out of this world too. The other part of me didn't want my face pummeled. I kept quiet.

Kelly rubbed a hand against her mouth. "If I leave, I miss out on something. That's the way it typically goes."

No.

She took a breath and steeled herself, taking a step closer.

"Kelly, turn around and go home." I kept my voice from becoming a plea. I didn't want Lyshae to hear that or get the satisfaction.

"But if she does that, her curiosity will remain unfulfilled," said Lyshae.

I shot her a stare that could've burned a hole through lead. "You know the old saying about curiosity and the cat."

"I do." Kelly came to Ortiz's side, motioning to sit. Ortiz obliged her and moved over. The computer whiz eased herself down. "I'm in."

I looked to the ceiling before turning my attention back to Lyshae. "Alright, in case it wasn't clear before, I really hate you." My comment didn't faze her. "So, what was with the whole audition gig?"

"Why, I need some help of the brutish variety, and you seemed a fair candidate."

I blinked, and it fell into place. "You were the one watching me out on the streets—the one I couldn't peg."

She looked at me like I was dimwitted. "Obviously."

"You were sizing me up against different nasties. You need muscle, so...I'm your thug?"

Ortiz and Kelly snickered.

I glared at them. "Lyshae, you put me through a series of fights just to snag a role as your cheap muscle? You didn't think I could cut it? No—wait, even if you did, that means you think I'm good for just punching things."

Lyshae's lips went tight, and her eyes twinkled.

"I'm insulted." I turned to Ortiz. "I should be insulted, right?"

"Yes, you're insulted." She shook her head and rolled her eyes.

I turned back to Lyshae. "I'm insulted."

She rolled her hand through the air in a dismissive gesture. "Please, don't see it as being cheap muscle. It's far more dignified than that."

I tilted my head. "Oh?"

Her mouth spread into a wide smile of self-satisfaction. "Yes. How well do you wear a suit?"

"A sa-what?"

Lyshae looked at Ortiz and Kelly. "And you two will wear dresses."

Ortiz's eyes widened.

Kelly's face furrowed like she didn't understand the statement.

I waved my hand in Lyshae's face to get her attention. "Uh, what exactly are we doing? Where are you taking us?"

Her smile grew. "Why, a ball, of course."

Everyone but Lyshae exchanged glances.

"A ball—like with dancing?"

Lyshae pressed her lips together, giving me a look of sympathy. "Yes, Vincent. Dancing. Mingling. A rather sophisticated affair." She tilted her head and gave me a paper-thin smile. "Please do try and be on your best behavior. Your job isn't to start fights; it's to protect me." She placed a hand on her chest in a dainty gesture.

I grunted. Lyshae didn't need my protection. She was more than capable of handling herself. I'd seen her take down a pack of truck-sized spiders with nothing more than an illusion and her attitude. Lying to people and manipulating them was what she did best. It didn't hurt that she enjoyed it. "And where exactly is this ball?"

She gave me a knowing look.

Oh crap. "Um, I've recently developed a severe allergy to the Neravene."

Ortiz shuddered at the word. I couldn't blame her.

Kelly perked up in her seat. "What's that?"

Lyshae turned to her. "A place of magic and wonder. Where reality warps, and dreams become real."

"Not to mention nightmares." My voice was like charred stone. "Don't try to sell her on a lie. This place and all the places within...are dangerous." I gave Kelly a slow, long stare.

Kelly folded her lower lip back and pressed her mouth shut.

At least she was taking it seriously. I turned back to Lyshae. "Alright, we both know I can't exactly say no." My fists had balled before I released them in concert with a heavy exhale. "Let's do this."

She smiled and rose in a fluid manner. "Excellent. Follow me." Lyshae moved towards the bathrooms, except moved was the wrong word. It looked like she was gliding across the floor. The ends of her dress trailed over the floor as she made her way to the men's room door.

I arched a brow and gave her a look. "Uh, pretty sure you shouldn't be walking in there. You might make some guy too nervous to pee."

The women turned their eyes to me, then shook their heads in varying degrees of disregard and disappointment.

Lyshae pushed the door open and stepped inside. We followed behind her. The fox spirit paused, turning her nose up. She sniffed several times and blinked. Her face twisted in revulsion.

Ortiz's nose wriggled, but she controlled herself.

Kelly mirrored Lyshae's reaction, going so far as to cover her nose and mouth. "Jeez, do you guys just eat garbage?"

"I've often wondered how men seem to tolerate the odor." Lyshae looked at me.

I shrugged. "It's an acquired taste of olfactory preference...one we ignore." The explanation didn't stop me from raising the collar of Daniel's shirt over my nose. It smelled like you'd imagine, a men's room but during halftime after a diet of ballpark food. It wasn't pleasant.

Ortiz shook her head and motioned around the vacant bathroom. "Why are we here, and why's this place suspiciously empty? If I were going to ambush someone, this is where I'd do it. Close quarters. One way in, and out." Ortiz's body quivered like she was waiting for a threat.

She had a good point. I stared holes into the back of Lyshae's head.

The Kitsune brushed off the question with a light laugh.

"I own this establishment, one among many. As to the reason we are here—" She waved a hand before the bathroom wall. The air around her hand bent and bowed. Carmine light followed the wave. It lingered over the wall like a translucent blanket. The light bled, sinking over the tiles until it reached the floor.

The doorway of red hung before us, looking like a shower of glimmering rubies. Lyshae bent slightly and waved her hands with a flourish. "After you."

I stared at the Way, then her. "You can't be serious?"

She gave me a look that said she was.

"You think I'm going to turn my back on you?" I held my stare.

Lyshae smiled. "By all means then, let those two go first." She gestured to Kelly and Ortiz. "We can go through together." Her smile widened, and a gleam flickered through her eyes.

I scowled. "Yeah, right. Send them first into whatever danger's on the other side."

Lyshae's expression went flat. "Those are your options. Who do you think will hold the Way open for you? Or did you perchance learn how to open your own?"

My eyes narrowed, but I kept it at that. I couldn't do anything to her—yet. You honor your deals with the paranormal, no matter how crappy they are. If I welched on a debt, word would spread quickly. That'd ruin my rep in the eyes of my contacts. In my world, that's as good as a death sentence. It's not easy to fight monsters and navigate the intricacies of the paranormal world without the right info. I exhaled and motioned with a hand.

Ortiz and Kelly exchanged a look before glancing at me. Ortiz bit her lower lip, her eyes darting from Lyshae to me, asking a silent question.

I winced as an imaginary set of needles pricked my brain. There were no good options here. I turned to Kelly. "Last chance, kid. You might really want to consider sitting this one out."

Kelly mirrored Ortiz's earlier look, glancing at all of us one by one. Her eyes shut as she mulled it over. She opened them a second later. "I'm going."

I was afraid she was going to say that. "Alright. Ortiz,

you first."

She nodded and stepped towards the Way without hesitation. Ortiz stopped just before passing through. She turned a fraction, looking over her shoulder one last time.

I inclined my head. "I've got your back."

Ortiz turned back to the Way. "Kelly, take my hand." The young woman obliged without a word. The muscles in Ortiz's back stiffened, but she stepped into the Way with Kelly.

A halogen white flared through the carmine lens of the opening as they passed through. I eyed the Way, and my stomach roiled. I've got a bad feeling about this.

Lyshae bumped me with her hip, extending a hand. "Shall we?"

I took her hand and led her towards the Way. No matter how much I distrusted her, a little politeness couldn't hurt. Maybe it would put her at ease and reconsider whatever fuckery she had in mind. There wasn't a shred of doubt that she would try to pull one over on me. Anything I could do to give her pause, or better yet, not try it in the first place, was a win. I took a step into the Way.

The sleeve around my left arm went tight like it was caught in a clamp. I froze and turned my head to face Lyshae. "What gives?"

She leaned in close enough that her lips almost brushed my ears. I felt her breath against the skin of my neck. "I know what you're thinking, Vincent."

I tried not to let her unsettle me. "Really? That's a trick, because I don't know what I'm thinking half the time." I let out a weak chuckle.

She didn't buy it. "You're thinking that at some point, I am going to betray you." The smile she flashed was all teeth. "You are right. I will. It's who I am. But that doesn't mean any harm has to befall you or your people."

I bristled in her grip. Most monsters don't tell you they're going to stab you in the back.

You had to appreciate her honesty at least.

She pulled me an inch closer. "But I also know that you are looking for any chance you have of betraying me. I would advise against that. I know you're thinking of a way to free yourself without tarnishing your reputation. That is irrelevant. It won't absolve your debt."

Actually, it would, but something in Lyshae's voice made chips of ice slide under my skin.

"The thing you are forgetting is that you owe two more debts. Two. But you have to ask yourself, Vincent: Do I still hold those debts, or have I passed them on to others?"

The chips of ice made their way to my heart and throat, freezing the areas solid. "What?"

Lyshae stared at me, a crazed light in her eyes.

"You can't do that, can you?"

She smiled. "Wouldn't you like to know?"

I did.

"You will have to earn that knowledge. That means you have to survive what comes next." With that, she stepped forwards and pulled me into the Way.

Chapter Fifteen

A dull impact ricocheted up my legs to settle in my knees. I sank my weight and grimaced through the discomfort. Lyshae seemed unfazed. My sight fixed on her hips and backside, which happened to be in front of my face. I blinked and looked away. Paranormal booty is never worth the trouble it can bring. And it always brings trouble.

I leaned past the view and found Kelly and Ortiz standing a dozen feet from our landing. They were engrossed in the scenery. To be fair, it was the quite the scene. An endless plain of grass. Perfectly flat. A sea of stalks bowed in the breeze. The sky was a dead ringer from one back home. A clear spring morning blue. Sometimes the simple things hold their own unique and entrancing beauty. I cleared my throat. "Lyshae, where are we?"

"Nowhere that should concern you and somewhere we can have a bit of privacy before the event."

I squinted at her. "Well, that was almost an answer."

"It's the only answer you need."

Ortiz came to our side, keeping her head on a swivel and surveying the open field. "At least this place has a good line of sight. Makes it easy to keep an eye out for trouble."

Or for trouble to keep an eye on us. I frowned and rose, staring at the back of Lyshae's head. "Is this neutral ground?"

The fox spirit didn't answer and stones fell into my stomach. I banished them.

Kelly spun in place, holding her phone up as she recorded. "So where are we, pocket dimension or something?"

"Sort of. Think of it as one room in a larger room of rooms in one mega mansion inside an even bigger one." It was the best way to explain it to her.

She stopped in place. "Whoa. That's...big."

I nodded. "As far as I know, the Neravene has no end. It's constantly growing and changing in accordance to the beings that occupy it."

"Yes." Lyshae moved past us all. "Which is why a certain balance must be kept. Otherwise, the Neravene's nature could be upset. If one seeks to change the balance of power, it must be done subtly, tastefully, and preferably, with discretion." She looked over her shoulder to glare at me.

I sniffed at the remark. I could be discreet. Something struck me. Lyshae's tone made it sound like she had plans to mess with the balance of power in the Neravene. I stared at her back until I felt my eyes were boring invisible holes into her. "And what are you after? You still haven't told us." I held my glare.

Lyshae turned as if she had all the time in the world.

I didn't.

One edge of her mouth twitched. "No, I haven't."

My eyes narrowed. "I'm not a fan of being jerked around."

The Kitsune gave me a look that said she didn't care.

Kelly paused, turning to look twenty yards to our left. She pointed her phone in the direction. "Um, are we expecting company?"

I gave Lyshae a sideways look. "Are we?" I had a feeling I already knew the answer.

A ring of amber light crackled into existence. It was like a circular shower of golden-orange fireworks. Ortiz's body tensed as she raised her hands to the side of her face. Her right index finger shuddered like it wished it rested on a trigger.

I was glad she didn't pull her weapon. No telling who was coming out of the Way.

The center of the ring strobed through a gradient of blues that contrasted the outermost edge. A figure emerged.

Kelly's mouth parted. The phone shook in her hands, and she gawked without blinking.

I think she was losing her hold on the aliens theory and accepting the paranormal. It's not an easy thing to acknowledge, but then, strange things never are. That doesn't mean they're not real. Only a fool discounts something because they haven't seen it. There's a word for that.

Faith. I don't operate with or on a whole lot of it, but I've been getting better about it. Ortiz and a few others have taught me to give it more of a chance. I believe in a lot of things, but mostly...people. Some of them disappoint you, sure. But give them a chance, and people can surprise you.

The thing coming out of the Way wasn't a person. He could have passed for one if he wasn't so inhumanly good looking. His face was an artist's rendition of a slender man with perfect, high bone structure.

I already hated him.

He was dressed like he was ready to walk the red carpet at a Hollywood premiere. His suit looked of designer make and probably cost the same as Daniel's monthly rent. It was a two-piece suit the color of weathered tin and had a slight satin sheen to it. The cuffs and collar were trimmed in black. The top of a low-cut black vest barely stood out against his equally black dress shirt. The only thing that let me tell them apart was the muted gray tie. He wore the entire ensemble well. His right arm was bent, and something hung over his shoulder that I couldn't make out.

Kelly stared at him in a manner that made my jaw lock.

Ortiz wore the same look until her gaze drifted to his left hand, more accurately, what was in it.

Pretty Boy held a rifle that looked cartoonishly small even in his slender hands. It was something out of a science-fiction movie. Dark plastic, box-shaped with an obscenely thin-long barrel.

The look Ortiz gave him spoke volumes—most of them equating to the same thing: Try something, and I'll bury my foot in your ass.

I smiled.

The newcomer wasn't fazed. He rolled a hand through the air like he was bored. The sparkling Way shut. He turned to Lyshae, bowing his head before flashing us a jarringly white smile.

He and Church clearly saw the same dentist. I hooked a thumb to the well-dressed and armed stranger. "Who's this mook?"

The gun-toting visitor sighed and shook his head.

"Humans, honestly?" He tilted his head towards Lyshae, eyeing her like he'd rather be somewhere else.

"Yes, and don't complain. Our deal doesn't allow you to question me, does it?" Lyshae's face was cold stone.

I sucked in a breath I hope went unheard. It sounded like she had him by the balls. Whatever their deal was, it must've included a bitch clause somewhere.

The stooge's lips went tight, but he didn't offer any backtalk. Instead, he lowered his other arm, revealing a set of bags you'd find at a dry cleaner. He looked at Ortiz, giving her a thin smile. "You look like you want to attack me."

Ortiz matched his thin smile. "Are you going to give me a reason to?"

His smile widened. "I just want to give you your clothes."

Kelly, Ortiz, and I exchanged puzzled looks.

Lyshae laughed. "You don't expect to arrive at the ball dressed as you are, do you?"

She had a point.

Her "hired" help placed the bags on the ground, straightening up at a cautious pace. His gaze never left Ortiz, and her stare never wavered.

As much as I hated dragging her into these sorts of things, I was glad she had my back.

The sound of a digital camera shutter filled our ear. We all turned to Kelly, who was busy snapping shots of Mr. Paranormal GQ.

He ran a hand through his thick, jet black hair, and somehow managed to make the simple action look like a pose for a cover shoot. A twinkle went through his pale, lime-colored eyes.

"You are the creepiest alien I have ever seen!" Kelly took another shot.

The lackey's face lost all expression.

"I mean you are hauntingly fake looking. It's like someone went crazy with the digital touchups." Kelly waved a hand over her face. "Ease up on the plastic and pretty Skin Sheath. The beautiful aliens are the ones that kill you."

He blinked several times, turning to Lyshae for help.

Lyshae ignored him. She was great boss material. "Fetch

your clothes. Time is dwindling."

I fidgeted and buried the desire to look at my forearm. Lyshae was right. Time passes of its own accord in the Neravene. I had no idea how much had slipped by just standing in the field, and my tattoo wouldn't tell me. It wouldn't update until I was out of the Neravene. I exhaled through my nose and marched over to our new friend. "So, what's a Daoine doing working for her?" I tilted my head towards Lyshae.

His jaw hardened, and his eyes flashed as he glanced at the Kitsune. "Long story."

I scooped up the three giant bags and held them up to inspect. A brightly colored tag hung from each of the plastic carriers. "Whose is whose?" I turned to Lyshae.

"Black tag is yours, Vincent. The red is for Camilla Ortiz, and the last is for the young miss. Do not worry about the sizes; they are accurate." She sounded confident about that.

I waved a hand to Ortiz and Kelly, silently asking them to come over to me. They took their respective bags and unzipped them. I did the same, letting out a low whistle as I pulled the suit free.

It was a match for the Daoine's in every aspect but color. The suit was a shade of smeared charcoal. A black dress shirt and vest were folded alongside it as well as a strikingly bright red tie that was sure to draw anyone's eye. I held up the ensemble and arched a brow at Lyshae. "Do I want to know how you know my borrowed body's size?"

She gave me a smile that made me feel like I was being viewed under an x-ray.

I suppressed a shiver and felt violated. A light wumph sounded to my side and I turned. Ortiz's jacket rested on the ground. She slid her thumbs under the holsters, running them against the leather. "I'm not going to drop my guns until he drops his." Ortiz nodded at the Daoine.

He glanced at Lyshae who inclined her head. His weapon fell to the grass.

Ortiz's holsters joined her jacket on the ground. She put her hands to her waist, grabbed the bottom of her shirt, and wriggled out of it.

I turned away; although, part of me didn't want to. It

could have been a piece of Daniel and whatever he'd felt for her. Or it could've been something else. "Uh, you want a little privacy there?"

Ortiz snorted. "I'm a grown girl. I don't have issues with something like this, you pansy."

I twisted my face into a mock scowl. "You're a pansy."

The air between Kelly, Ortiz, and I bowed and shimmered as light crystallized and showered down. It looked like a waterfall of frosted glass beads. I couldn't see through it. Lyshae had woven an illusory curtain. I stripped out of my clothes, tossing them aside as I knelt to pick up the suit.

Lyshae clapped her hands once. The Daoine turned to her, waiting. "Fetch their shoes, will you? Be quick. I don't want to linger here longer than necessary."

The Daoine's features tightened, but he made no angry outburst. He opened a Way and vanished.

The little act should have held my attention, but that's not what I focused on. Lyshae wanted us to dress up and leave as quickly as possible. When I'd asked her if this was neutral ground, she didn't respond. My neck stiffened, and I turned to look at a portion of the field. Nothing came into view but endless grass. That wasn't comforting. I had a feeling we were trespassing, and whomever this domain belonged to, wouldn't be happy about that.

I wriggled into the pants, leaving them to hang on my waist as I slipped into the shirt. It was a quick process. After buttoning everything up, I fished through the bag for a pair of black socks that I slid into while lobbing the tie over my neck. A series of short twists, and I had a simple knot. The vest fought me as I tried to button it up. It felt a size smaller than it should've been, but I managed to fit into it in the end. I wriggled my toes and gave myself a once over.

I made sure to fish the remaining cash out of my old pants. You never know when or where a few bills can come in handy.

"The vest seems tighter than should be." Lyshae pursed her lips and approached.

I resisted exhaling and possibly ripping part of the vest. Nodding in agreement seemed a better option.

Lyshae pressed her hands to my ribs, running them

against my body.

I stared at her until I felt the constricting fabric around my torso loosen. "What'd you do?"

"I stretched the vest slightly—you're welcome."

The same Way from earlier opened. The Daoine returned with three shoeboxes stacked atop one another. He came to my side, thrusting with his chin to the top box.

I took it and thumbed the top off as he vanished behind the magical curtain. Inside, were a pair of slip-on dress shoes made of black leather. The price tag was still attached. I fumbled with the box, almost dropping it after I read how much they cost. "Seven hundred bucks—for shoes? What's wrong with sneakers?"

Lyshae gave me a look of disapproval. "Uncouth simpleton."

I stuck my tongue out at her and snapped the tag off the shoes as I slipped into them. They weren't even comfortable.

The Daoine grabbed my discarded clothes, unceremoniously stuffing them into the bag that had held my suit.

"Hey, I'm going to want those back. I'm not running around Queens dressed like"—I pulled on the collar of my shirt—"this."

The Daoine rolled his eyes. "Noted, mortal."

There was a sound like tin wind chimes rattling. I turned around. The curtain fell. My jaw followed when I saw Ortiz.

She wore an expensive designer dress that would catch anyone's eye. It was carnation red, held off the shoulder with thin straps. The deep, plunging neckline would cause any man to do a double take and gawk. The end of the dress pooled around her feet. A long slit ran up the side of the dress, revealing most of her left leg. Ortiz was built of the springy, flat muscle that belonged on lifelong athletes. The dress clung to her in all the right places.

Ortiz stared back at me. "So?"

I nodded in silence.

She looked relieved. A hint of color touched her cheeks.

It took me a moment to realize how hard I was staring and whose body I was doing it in. My chest panged like it was a bell wrung by a hammer. The guilt echoed through my torso, settling in my stomach. Ortiz and Daniel had a thing for each other, and now it'd never happen. There was a part of me that wondered if she'd wished Daniel had looked at her the way I'd been doing. I swallowed and turned my head. As hard as it was for me, it couldn't have been any easier for her. And I had no right to get any ideas while wearing his body.

Ortiz crossed the distance between us. A glint drew my attention to her shoes—a pair of red pumps sporting golden leaves that bent towards her ankles. They were adorned with gems of pure, sparkling white.

Lyshae had one hell of a bank account to spring for diamond-and-gold decorated shoes.

Ortiz stopped within arm's reach and tilted her head, regarding me. "You look good."

"Thanks." My voice came out rougher than I expected. A faint glimmer pulled my gaze towards her neckline. A silver chain hung around it, ending in an ornate cross between her breasts. The ends of it were flattened, spreading into what looked like oak leaves. It was fashioned from two different metals. One was clearly silver. The other was like burnt cobalt. I didn't recognize it. A glass bead sat in the center of the cross filled with a sangria-colored resin.

Ortiz caught my stare and arched a brow.

I raised my hands in defense. "I was looking at the cross—I swear."

"Oh, that."

Phew. I had a feeling that it didn't matter much if Ortiz was wearing a functional pair of shoes or designer pumps. She could kick ass in either. I didn't want to test the theory.

I gestured to the cross. "When did you get holy?"

She shrugged. "I've always sort of been. Grew up with it, you know? But..." She trailed off and licked her lips. "I didn't pick this back up"—she lifted the chain—"until after the asylum. I'm not a good Catholic; more of a drive-by one." The smile she flashed me, coupled with her outfit, sent an electric tingle through my extremities.

I tried to rein my simpler impulses under control. "What's a drive-by Catholic?"

She looked away before shooting a quick glance to the sky. "You know, every time you drive by a church, you do this." She moved her index and middle fingers over her head and chest to form a cross in the air.

I threw my head back and laughed.

Ortiz had the grace to flush and turn her head like she was embarrassed.

My arm throbbed a second later. I rubbed the spot and glared at her.

"Hey, I haven't been to church in a long time. This is me working on getting better." She shifted her posture and crossed her arms.

"No judging." I pressed my lips, trying not to burst into a second fit of laughter. "I'm not the one who goes to hell for not being a good Catholic."

She gave me a look that said I would be punched again if I kept it up.

I felt it was a good point to stop.

The remaining curtain of light fell. Lyshae had done an equally impressive job with Kelly's attire. The young woman wore a flowing ball gown of soft periwinkle pressed with a dusting of white sequins that looked like tiny snowflakes. She wore a pair of heels that looked like they were made from golden webbing. Her hair was pinned back with a butterfly clip made of onyx and diamonds.

I turned to Lyshae. "You paid for all of this, right?"

"Yes." She seemed confused about my question. "How else would I acquire the clothing?"

"How much did you spend?" I waved a hand to Ortiz and Kelly.

Lyshae upturned one of her hands, making a dismissive gesture. "An inconsequential amount."

Ortiz ground the tip of one of her pumps against the ground. "These are three thousand dollar pumps." Her voice never wavered, like it was normal for shoes to cost that much.

I choked on air and sputtered. Inconsequential amount. What in the world did she consider consequential?

Lyshae made another gesture. "Consider the clothing a manner of payment, if you will, for aiding me in what's to come."

Ortiz rolled her shoulders in a nonchalant shrug, but her mouth spread into a grin.

Kelly was a little less restrained. "Hell, yes."

I stared at them both.

Kelly matched my look. "What? Because I walk around in jeans and sneakers, I can't like clothes like this? Are we getting our normal clothes back?" Kelly regarded the Daoine who'd snatched up the article and piled them into a small mound.

The Kitsune didn't answer.

I turned back to Lyshae. "Does this mean I can keep the suit?"

Her lips twitched. "You may, if it lasts."

I didn't get to utter a riposte as something made the meat between my shoulders shiver and tense. When you've done as much work hunting the paranormal as I have, you develop a sixth sense when things are about to go wrong. This was one of those moments. I whipped my head around and stared down a length of the field.

Waist-high stalks of grass waved and shuddered like they were under a heavy gust of wind. Except the breeze blew in a different direction than that of the moving grass. A faint crackle of electricity bounded across the tips of the grass blades. It wasn't until I saw it a second time that I believed it was real. I shot Lyshae a heated look. "You never answered me when I asked if we were on neutral grounds."

"Why does it—" She stopped short, catching onto what I had seen.

"Because I think we're about to have company."

Chapter Sixteen

The blue-white currents intensified. Hair-thin tendrils of smoke wafted from the tips of the grass as the electricity closed around us. A violent flash of light rocketed over the field, forming a circle around us.

Everyone took a step closer to each other.

"My guns!" Ortiz turned and glanced at her weapons.

The Daoine moved at speeds that would've shamed an Olympic sprinter. He swept up his miniature rifle and was by Ortiz's holsters before I could exhale. His leg snapped out, catching the leather around his ankle and sending it flying.

Ortiz pivoted and snatched the tangled mess out of the air. She flicked her wrist. The material jerked and opened, allowing her to draw her service weapon. She released her grip and let the bundle fall at her feet. The entire exchange happened in seconds.

I balled one of my fists, waving a hand at my side. "Kelly, get by Ortiz—now!"

She did as I instructed, her dress whisking as she moved to Ortiz's side.

The Daoine positioned himself between Lyshae and me.

Grass rustled and electric discharges sparked around us. They died as a panther-sized, marmalade cat bounded into the air.

"Holy shit!" I took a step back before turning to dive towards Ortiz's holster. My shoulder hit the ground at an odd angle, and the connecting tissue within strained. Nothing tore, fortunately. I rolled and clawed blindly for the holster. My fingers raked against leather. I pulled, sending the bundle towards me and drew her revolver, not bothering to get to my feet.

The giant cat sat before us, eyeing us with the patience of a predator.

Nobody moved. I was glad they didn't.

A trio of growth-hormone-abusing cats burst from the grass and landed to surround us. One resembled a marshmallow-white Scottish Fold. The one to our right was a thin, leonine-looking fella, the color of burnt umber streaked with gingerbread. The last feline was a chunky thing that could have benefited from exercise. Its fur was splotches of carob and hickory, hairs standing on end like it'd been shocked. Its tail was a tiny nub, and its end was notched. Something had bitten it into a stump.

The marmalade cat's chest vibrated as it let out a mrowl that sounded like a large lawnmower starting up.

I looked around the field. "Anyone here speak cat?" I kept the gun trained on the panther kitty. Everyone has different opinions about animals. Some people love canines and are dog people. Some people love cats. Some love both. I was once chased by a tiger made of solid gold down the streets of Manhattan.

I like dogs.

Lyshae raised a hand, drawing the attention of the cats. She moved to my side with relative calm given the situation. "My retainers and I were merely passing through. We carry no ill intent. What can we do for you?" Her voice made sugar seem sour.

I eyed the surrounding cats without turning my head. Cats are apex predators in many environments across the worlds—mortal and supernatural. A simple thing like moving my head wouldn't go unnoticed. Their muscles were tensed like coiled springs. I wasn't sure if I could get off a shot before they jumped me, should it come to it. Kelly was only a few feet from me, and if either Ortiz or I missed, the young woman would be in a world of trouble. I exhaled and restrained myself. It wasn't worth risking. Lyshae would have to handle it her way.

The marmalade cat shivered. Fishing-line cracks of lightning arced over random parts of its body, dying as fast as they'd sparked to life. The cat took several steps forwards and raised its head. Air waved and rippled around it as the cat seemed to liquefy. It moved closer and grew. Within seconds, a woman stood in front of us.

She had a feral beauty much like Lyshae. The former cat

was lithe, and her slender muscles looked carved from wood. She wore a simple, sleeveless shirt of faded black and matching, loose pants. Functional clothing. Her arms crossed in scars that'd long gone white and were a sharp contrast to her tawny skin. She had Lyshae's ears, triangular tufts of hair around a fleshy pink that protruded from the top of her head. That wasn't what held my attention though. Her eyes were the color of polished pennies and slit vertically exactly like a cat's.

"Well, shit." I turned my head a fraction towards Lyshae. "Distant relations?"

Lyshae had the grace to offer me a thin smile and nothing more. She looked like she wanted to twist her face in revulsion. "Bakeneko," she said.

My mouth went dry. Every time I venture into the Neravene, things go sideways. I repressed a sigh. The cat people were seriously bad news, and I got why my relations comment rankled Lyshae. Kitsunes and Bakeneko are distantly related. Emphasis on the distantly.

Something hard brushed against the back of my left ankle, prompting me to look over my shoulder.

Ortiz gave a micro-nod of her head in the direction of the tawny cat-lady.

"Bakeneko—Japanese cat demons."

Ortiz's eyes narrowed. She gave me a silent look, asking me if I was kidding.

I wish I were.

The lead Bakeneko's ears twitched and her eyes focused on me. Her lips peeled into a smile that showed too many teeth. Her canines were long enough to qualify as fangs. It didn't help that she stared at me like I was a juicy burger.

I'm nobody's chew toy.

The cat lady leaned to her side, staring at Ortiz. Her smile grew. So did the crazed, hungry light in her eyes. "Demon is a stretch. We're shapeshifters."

That much was true. Bakeneko, like Kitsunes, could shift into a human form. Rumor had it that they could morph into another form. Something halfway between cat and human, a form that granted the best traits of both bodies without sacrificing the benefits of either. I hoped it was nothing more than wild speculation.

Bakeneko may have shared some resemblance to Kitsunes, but they were superficial. The fox spirits were harmless pranksters at best. At their worst, they were manipulative and self-serving ass croutons like Lyshae. And Bakeneko didn't have a best side. They were notorious hunters, killers for hire, and highwaymen of the Neravene.

When you've got the sight and reflexes of a big cat, why bother working when you can take what you want?

Bakeneko are curious, fast, and tenacious. Lore hinted at the fact they were horribly cruel things that stalked lost travelers in the woods in the dead of night. The Bakeneko would toy with them, terrifying them best they could. When they were done playing with the travelers, they'd tear 'em to shreds and eat them. Some myths suggested Bakeneko went as far as feeding on the souls of those they captured.

I suppressed a shiver. A pissed off monster had once tried to rip my soul out of the body I was occupying. Had it not been for Church, it would have succeeded. I remembered the pain. It was like a million barbs tearing into my flesh. I wasn't keen on repeating the experience. My grip tightened on the revolver, and I exhaled to clear my mind. If the pussycat wanted to start something, I was damn well going to finish it.

"You're trespassing." Wild ecstasy filled the Bakeneko's eyes as she took a couple of steps forwards.

Lyshae tensed and forced a smile. It looked like she was trying to stretch stone. "Oh, I wasn't aware this land was claimed." It wasn't a convincing lie.

It took me a second to realize it wasn't supposed to be. Oh, crap. I hope you know what you're doing, Lyshae.

Lyshae pursed her lips and bent forwards slightly. She looked around the field in mock astonishment. "As far as I know, no one has dominion over this. No lord, nor any lady of the Neravene has claimed these empty fields as theirs." She straightened and gave the Bakeneko a sideways look, shooting her a taunting smile. "Are you perchance a lady of the Neravene? Did you claim this?" Her mouth parted into an O.

The Bakeneko's ears stiffened, and her fingers flexed.

I could've sworn her nails had lengthened for a split second. I blinked and focused on them, but they appeared normal. That was reassuring...

"No answer?" Lyshae put a hand to her mouth to stifle the small laugh. She was goading the Bakeneko. They weren't the kind of creatures to forgive and forget. They were hot tempered and took light teasing as a personal offense. This wouldn't end well.

The marmalade Bakeneko leaned forwards, throwing her arms out in a challenging manner. Her mouth parted and she let out a hiss. The cats around us echoed it. "Of course not. None of us are lords or ladies, including you." She jabbed a finger at Lyshae. "No one has protection—you're fair game."

Guess that settled it on what the Bakeneko were doing here. They were robbers, here to relieve us of our possessions. And I had just gotten the fancy suit.

Lyshae didn't seem the least bit upset by the Bakeneko's declaration. I thought about it and realized she wasn't worried earlier either. Her irritation at wanting us to speed up was nothing more than an act. She had known this place was a targeted spot for bands of Bakeneko. This was planned. She wanted us here.

Bitch.

I turned and glowered at the Kitsune.

She didn't pay me any mind. Lyshae waved a hand in a bored manner. "We are fair game, yes. That does not mean we are easy prey." Lyshae smiled before snapping her teeth at the air. Her smile widened when the Bakeneko flinched.

A sound like a camera shutter snapping went off. Everyone turned to the source. Kelly held her phone in the direction of the female cat-lady. Her hands shook as she took another photo.

Ortiz glanced at Kelly out of the corner of her eyes but said nothing.

The Bakeneko woman had plenty to say however. "What is the mortal doing?"

There was another digital snap. Kelly licked her lips and looked at the other cats before answering. "Taking pictures for my blog."

The Bakeneko blinked several times and tilted her head like Kelly had made a string of strange sounds. Her fingers flexed, and the ends of her nails darkened for a second before returning to normal.

I gulped, realizing that I had been right earlier when I thought I'd seen them lengthen. They had some tricks up their sleeves. But, if I knew Lyshae like I thought I did, she'd have a few of her own. I hoped they were better.

Lyshae advanced towards the Bakeneko's leader. The action elicited a chorus of resonating burbles from the surrounding felines. Lyshae paid them no mind. "If you attack us, we will be within our rights to defend ourselves. This land is unclaimed but well-traveled. It's a popular path to an important location. That's why you prowl these grounds and target passersby, no?"

The cat-lady said nothing but one of her ears twitched in agitation.

Lyshae knew what she was doing. She pressed further. "If you run roughshod over these paths long enough, they will fall into disuse—open to being claimed." The Kitsune's mouth spread into a wolfish smile. "Someone's trying to curry favor with a certain lord, aren't they?" She waggled an admonishing finger at the Bakeneko.

The feline-looking woman recoiled a step and gnashed her teeth. "What if I am?"

"It's pathetic. He wouldn't notice you anyhow. You're trash." Lyshae's tone was acidic enough to eat through stone.

I sucked in a breath. This was not the time for Lyshae to be starting a literal catfight. Her last comment had sounded personal.

The Bakeneko's leader shook. Her fingers splayed as they extended and tapered into dangerous points like claws. Her cheeks sprouted a small coat of marmalade fur at the fringes and her eyes gleamed. "Kill them."

Dammit, Lyshae.

Chapter Seventeen

Guttural rumbling sounded around us. Cats leapt towards us. The air exploded with deafening roars.

Ortiz and the Daoine fired in staggering succession. The difference of caliber in their rounds was like two sets of percussion instruments being played in a jarring overlap. Their bullets hit home.

The air around the three cats shivered like it was made from plastic sheets. Their forms collapsed, leaving behind nothing. Illusions. Blades of grass waved and shuddered.

Oh crap.

The three real cats burst from their hiding spots, rushing towards us and keeping their profiles low.

I sighted on the umber cat and squeezed the trigger before shifting position and repeating the action. The cat moved before the first round left the barrel, managing to avoid the second as well.

Fortunately, Ortiz was a better shot than I'd ever be. She spat at her side and cracked off a round. The bullet caught the freakishly large cat in its left shoulder, causing the beast to lose its balance. The Bakeneko's momentum couldn't be stopped thankfully. Its bulk and speed carried it forwards to grind along the ground. It tumbled and fought to right itself. Ortiz unloaded three more shots into its body.

"How do we kill these things?"

I fired a warning shot towards the marshmallow-colored cat, forcing it to pounce twice and vanish into the grass under a veil. "Keep shooting; that's how. Bakeneko are pretty close to mortal. Resilient suckers, but bullets will do the job."

"Good." Ortiz fired a few rounds into the distance where the white cat had disappeared. Her gun clicked. "Shit."

"Here." The Daoine shouldered his way between us,

holding the rifle with one hand as he handed Ortiz two magazines.

Her eyes widened before a feral smile spread across her face. "Marry me."

The Daoine smiled back.

I growled and glared at him. "How'd you just so happen to have those on hand?"

He nodded towards Lyshae, who stood with her arms crossed in front of the lead Bakeneko, neither of the pair engaging in the fight. "She anticipated the need for weapons as well as the people you would most likely bring and the firearms she"—he gestured to Ortiz —"would likely bring."

Anticipated was the wrong word. Lyshae had set us up. I kept that to myself and spat. "And how did she know that?"

The Daoine shrugged. "It's her job."

I scowled. "Know-it-all."

Ortiz nudged me in the ribs after she'd reloaded. "Don't look a gift horse in the mouth."

"Speaking of looking, where are the two other cats?" I turned in place, keeping my eyes open for any movement in the field.

The Daoine spun and sank to his knees. His gun barked four times. Bullets scythed through air and grass. A pained yowl emanated from twenty yards behind us. The Daoine fired another burst in its direction. "There's one of them. Or...it was."

Ortiz looked at him in admiration, the edges of her mouth turning upwards. She released a low whistle.

Show off. It's not that hard to hit an invisible target when you have superhuman senses, reflexes, and magic amplifying your every action by second nature. Maybe I was just bitter. I glared at the Daoine and his perfect features and decided my feelings were justified.

Lyshae's laugh cut through the field. "Two of your friends are gone. Two little cats left."

I could almost see her smile even though her back was turned to me. She was enjoying this. My spine felt like it was going to twist and knot inside my body. I didn't understand how anyone or anything could enjoy the sudden outburst of violence that had left two things dead. They may have been monsters, sure, but Lyshae looked pretty damn human. Take away the fox-like ears atop her head, and you wouldn't be able to tell her apart from any other vanilla mortal. Not to mention she could glamour herself. Yet her attitude was chillingly inhuman.

It was a good reminder that sometimes monsters look just like us. It's not their appearance that matters. It's what they do and how they do it. She'd orchestrated this. I didn't know how—yet—but she wanted a fight. And she was willing to throw us under the bus to get it. That was all manner of cold and calculating. We were going to have a talk when this was over.

Lyshae turned around, staring into the distance at something none of us could make out. The Kitsune raised a hand, extending her index finger and raising her thumb to make a hand pistol. She shut an eye and tilted her head. Lyshae grinned. "Bang." She moved her hand like she had fired an invisible shot. A lance of lime-green fire erupted from the tip of her finger.

The coil of flame surged over the field, forcing every blade of grass to bow under its pressure. In the distance, the air shimmered and shattered like it was made of cheap crystal. A hickory-colored cat jumped into the air, flailing in panic as the ground beneath it flashed. Green flames crackled over the spot and threatened to lick their way up to the cat. The beast's fur melted away as it took human form. It twisted midair with a gymnast's grace and landed in a crouch a safe distance from the fire.

Everyone was silent. I turned my gaze from the recovering Bakeneko to eye the path the flames had traveled. The tips of the grass looked like they hadn't been subjected to a fire. I smiled. I'd seen this before. Lyshae could weave some pretty impressive illusions.

The Bakeneko in the distance rose. He was a dark-skinned male with thick, shaggy hair the color of honey infused hickory. His eyes were like the female Bakeneko who led the group. Burning like bright copper and vertically slit. He was a husky guy with a build like someone who lifted a lot of weights but could've been tighter with their diet. He was completely nude.

I winced, trying to blot out the giant, naked cat-man.

Things I don't need to remember for one thousand, Trebek. I shook my head and glanced at Lyshae, who was smiling. She shouldn't have been. She may have had an eye on one of the Bakeneko, but there was still one to her back.

The tawny Bakeneko pulled an arm back and lunged. Her clawed hand raked the air, closing in on the back of Lyshae's throat.

Lyshae fell to her hands as the blow sailed harmlessly overhead. The Kitsune tucked her knees to her chest before driving her legs out like pistons. Her heels rocketed into the Bakeneko's stomach. The force of the handstand mule-kick sent the creature tumbling. Lyshae pushed off her hands and landed back on her feet, brushing her palms against each other.

I made a mental note not get into a fist fight with her. That was impressive. It pays to have lived for a thousand years. She must've picked up some fighting tips over the millennia.

A series of heavy barks came from behind me. The Daoine muttered something in a language I didn't think was human. The rifle cracked several more times. Either he was missing—unlikely—or trying to drive the creature away.

The Bakeneko's leader recovered and screamed at Lyshae. It was a hoarse thing that sounded like it tore half the lining in her throat. She didn't attack again fortunately.

Lyshae was unfazed by all of it. She ran her hands against her sides, smoothing her dress. "Then there was one. Do you really want to continue? Or would you rather walk away from this? You have a choice. You can live and scamper back to your king to tell him what happened—how you failed—or you can keep this a secret and live with the shame. Either way, you are no longer permitted here." Lyshae ground her foot against the dirt. "And this is no longer neutral ground."

What? Just when I was starting to think I had her figured out. The Kitsune was working too many angles for me to keep track of. Calling in my favor. Hoping to get us ambushed by Bakeneko and starting a fight. All so she could run them out to claim the land on someone else's behalf. A certain question lingered in my mind.

Somehow, it'd made its way to the tip of the Bakeneko's

tongue. She sneered at Lyshae but kept herself from a doing anything rash. "Then what is it?"

"Mine," said Lyshae.

The temperature felt like it had dropped enough to warrant using the Kelvin scale. All it had taken was one word. Possession is a powerful thing. Declaring something as yours has a small, yet magical effect. People don't realize that. Imagine it: if someone tells you that something is theirs, you remember that. That's my toy. That's my car. That's my cookie. You don't touch other people's things. Nothing is physically stopping you, but there's this invisible barrier that keeps you from crossing that line.

Unless you're trying to start a fight. Or you're a kleptomaniac.

But there's power in claiming something. I just hadn't figured Lyshae for hopping aboard that train. And now she'd snatched a chunk—no matter how small—of the Neravene for herself. Guess whose fault that was? I let her manipulate Ortiz, Kelly, and me into this. The Kitsune had plans of moving up in the paranormal world. From information broker to landowner. I had a feeling I knew where she was heading down the line. I didn't know where she intended to stop, or if I could force her to.

I hoped I wouldn't have to find out anytime soon.

The Bakeneko lost her cool and snarled.

Lyshae shook her hand. An inch of polished metal protruded from her grip.

I never saw her arm move.

Crimson beads soared into the air like they'd been flung from the tip of a brush. The Bakeneko screamed, pawing at her face as she reeled. A gash the length of my middle finger ran down the side of her nose, barely missing the inside of her left eye. The flesh didn't fester or hiss in protest.

I made a mental note that Bakeneko didn't suffer the same adverse reaction to human metals like some creatures of the Neravene. Shame.

The Bakeneko yowled. Its pitch was loud and shrill enough to strip bark and fiber from trees. My eardrums rattled inside my skull as the creature lunged. Her fingers closed around Lyshae's throat. The cat-lady's lower left eyelid twitched like it couldn't handle the strain of keeping the muscle open.

Lyshae stood so calmly that she made stones look like shivering leaves under a stiff breeze. "Go ahead. Kill me."

I could picture her smile. "Um"—I raised an index finger and took a step forwards—"maybe you shouldn't provoke the angry cat woman who's got her hands to your throat. Just a suggestion." I blinked and realized something. "On second thought, never mind—go ahead."

Ortiz hissed, and my shoulder throbbed. "What are you thinking?"

"That maybe if Catwoman there kills the tricksy, manipulative fox spirit, I go free?"

The Daoine grunted and shook his head. "Don't get your hopes up. She's been at this game for too long to screw this up now. She knows what she's doing, and who she's playing."

I eyed him but kept from scowling. "Yeah, and who's that?"

"All of us." His voice was flat.

Somehow, Lyshae managed to let out a small, melodic laugh. "If you kill me, my retainer will kill you. It's not an outcome that favors you."

The Bakeneko bared her fangs. "Or you."

"I'll take my chances. What about you?" Lyshae's mouth quirked at the corners.

The Bakeneko blinked, and her hand tremored on Lyshae's throat. The cat demon released her hold.

"I don't believe it." I gawked at what was happening.

Lyshae had literally set up the Bakeneko's crew to be wiped out by us, insulted her, and maimed her. Their leader had her hands wrapped around the Kitsune's pretty little neck, ready to wring it. And she had let go. There was manipulative and mind-fuckery, and then there was Lyshae, who brought those things to an art form.

Lyshae raised a hand, bringing it to rest on the Bakeneko's shoulder. "I have a question for you before you disappear."

The cat demon took a step back, looking over her shoulder for help that would never come.

Lyshae leaned in. "Can you outrun a bullet?"

The Bakeneko turned and ran. She was twenty feet from

Lyshae when she clawed the air like she was hoping to tear it away.

The Daoine brushed past me, tucking his compact rifle to the center of his chest. A light, like a candle sparking to life, licked around the tip of the weapon's barrel, and a sundering crack accompanied it.

The air parted. Jagged streaks of tangerine light tore through the space. The Bakeneko passed through.

For all the gun's show, it didn't deliver. The round passed several feet wide of the cat demon's last position. There was a sharp sound like the landscape around us had taken a massive breath. The Way vanished.

Everything was quiet—for a moment, at least.

I turned to the Daoine and narrowed my eyes. "I didn't think something like you would miss."

"I do when I'm paid to." He gave me a thin smile. Meaning Lyshae had anticipated this—down to the gritty details of how it could play out. It was time for me to test just how much she had figured out.

"Ortiz, watch her crony, will ya?" I tilted my head in the direction of the Daoine. With a flick of my wrist, I sent her revolver tumbling towards her.

She caught it without looking.

"Crony?" The Daoine blinked and wrinkled his face.

Ortiz shifted her posture and backpedaled a few steps. "What are you going to do?"

I clenched my jaw. "Have a talk with his boss. If he does anything funny, shoot him."

Ortiz's mouth twitched, but she didn't argue. Killing someone, something, in cold blood didn't sit well with her. The Bakeneko had attacked us. It was self-defense, plain and simple. But the Daoine had fought by our side, and truth be told, saved us. Ortiz knew that. The only way she'd pull the trigger was if he gave her a reason to.

I had a feeling that I was going to give everyone cause to lose their cool. It's a specialty of mine. "Kelly, come with me, if you don't mind?" Getting her away from the powder keg that could be the Daoine and Ortiz seemed like a good idea. "Kelly?" I turned and wished I hadn't.

She clutched tight to her phone like it was the only thing she could remember how to do. Her knuckles were white enough to make me think she'd been holding onto it the entire fight. The tips of her fingers were getting close to a shade of purple that came with no circulation. The phone shuddered in her grip. Her eyes were wide and staring a hole through me.

I'd seen that look before. It was a hollow stare that somehow lets a person see a lot and yet nothing at all.

I felt like she was staring at me, through me, and past me all at the same time. Lyshae was pushed from my mind for the moment. I'd deal with her after I took care of something more important. I moved past Ortiz, keeping my eyes locked with Kelly's.

No matter the terrible things that happen, having your eyes on a friend can help snap you back to reality. At the very least, it can help you process.

I placed my hands on her shoulders and rubbed them. "Hey, Kelly?" I gave her a lopsided smile. Never let anyone tell you that a smile doesn't help. They do. Go down the street and flash someone a genuine, honest-to-God smile, and see what happens. Most will return it and brighten up. There's a subtle magic in smiles. They can wash a lot of bad things away, and bring some people out of someplace dark. "Kelly?"

She blinked, sucking on what little moisture was left in her mouth. "Yes?" Her voice shook more than the phone.

I followed my own advice and gave her the most honest smile I could. It wasn't hard. Sometimes you just have to find something you're grateful for, no matter how small, and let it out. In this case, it was the simple fact that she was unharmed. A lot of people don't have that luxury the first time they dive into the paranormal world. Ortiz hadn't. The thought threatened to pull the smile from my face. "You're fine." I rubbed her shoulders again.

"Am I?" She sounded like she was far away and dazed. "That's funny, because I feel—I don't know."

"One word at a time, kid. Just say whatever comes to mind. I know there's bound to be a lot racing up there with what just happened. And here." I slid my hands against her arms until I came to her wrists. "Maybe we should loosen up on this, huh?" My thumbs slipped between her fingers and the phone, prying them apart gently. I folded my fingers over one of her hands and I pushed the phone into her palm.

She closed her hand over it. Her grip was softer. A small relief.

"Better?" I held my smile.

Kelly nodded. "Yeah. What happened?"

"Honestly?" I almost looked over my shoulder to Lyshae but I kept my eyes on Kelly. She needed a friend right now. "That's a good question. Are you sure you want the answers?"

She licked her lips and let out a weak laugh. "That's what I live for."

I shot Ortiz a look before turning back to Kelly. "I've heard that before."

Ortiz stared daggers at me.

The ends of Kelly's mouth turned up in a light smile.

Worked for me. "Then I'll give them to you. But first, trust me, you're going to want a breather. Seeing the things you just did, then trying to process them with the answers I'll give you—it never goes well. Take my word on that one, yeah?"

"Yeah." It sounded like she was trying to convince herself more than me. Kelly broke our gaze, looking past me.

I sighed. I had a good idea of what she was looking at. "Speaking of answers." I whirled around and surged forwards a step. My hands balled around the front of Lyshae's dress, and I pulled her close. "Give me one reason why I shouldn't finish what the Bakeneko started?"

She gave me a fox-like smile. "I'll give you five."

An elongated barrel pressed against my temple. "One," said the Daoine.

Oops.

Chapter Eighteen

A pinpoint of pressure concentrated on my thigh. I looked down without moving my head. The tip of Lyshae's diminutive blade pressed against my suit with enough force to be felt. I had a feeling if the Kitsune pushed harder, the knife would cut into my femoral artery. It wasn't a theory I wanted to test.

Lyshae extended two fingers from her free hand. "Two."

My face felt like drying cement being forced to stretch as I smiled. I didn't want to find out what the other three reasons were.

"Step away from him—now." Ortiz's voice cut through the series of thoughts occupying my head.

Lyshae looked past me. The knife remained in place, to my discomfort. "Why? He threatened me. I'm simply reminding him of his place. Should I remind you of yours?"

I swallowed. Making mistakes wasn't part of Lyshae's repertoire, but she had just made a big one.

"What?" Ortiz's tone could've sanded brick into dust. "I have two reasons of my own." She stepped around us and into view. Both of her guns were leveled on Lyshae. Ortiz didn't make a habit of missing.

I had a feeling Lyshae knew that.

Ortiz glanced at the Daoine, but her weapons remained trained on the Kitsune. "What happens if your boss dies?"

His mouth twitched. "I'm free of my debt." A large smile made its way across his mouth. He didn't remove the barrel of his weapon from my head though.

I took that personally.

"Yes, he would go free, as in fact, would you." Lyshae inclined her head towards Ortiz. "But poor Vincent would not." She lifted a third finger, then a fourth, until all five digits were splayed. "You owe me three debts. One of those belongs to me." She folded a finger back. "Two are in condition to be passed on."

My breathing slowed, and the front portions of my brain felt like a dry sponge crumbling to bits.

Ortiz licked her lips, and her body tremored like she was fighting the urge to move and remain still. "She can't do that, can she?" Ortiz's gaze flickered to me.

I wasn't sure. Debts in the paranormal world weren't much different from the mortal one. Except for the fact if you welched on one, it'd be a monster coming to collect out of your ass, not some guy with a Jersey accent. But, in principle, a debt could be passed on no different than in our world. Tabs were kept on who and what was owed—mostly between the two parties themselves. I don't know how the mechanics worked in the Neravene, but I couldn't count it out. If there was a possibility Lyshae could've sold my debts to someone else—knowing her, someone worse—then I had to take it as absolute fact. It was safer that way.

"Kill me now, and your debts will go to beings that you do not want to be in service to, believe me in that, Vincent Graves. I know you. I know your sensibilities and the kind of man you are. And I know how to break you." She gave me a cruel smile reserved for supervillains. Lyshae's body blurred, and she stood several feet away from me. Her hands went into the air in a non-threatening gesture. The knife had vanished somewhere on her person faster than I could track it.

The Daoine pulled away from me, stepping back to position himself behind me.

Lyshae smoothed her dress like the entire situation was only mildly troublesome. "Now, shall we continue? We don't want to be late."

We couldn't have that.

She gestured with a finger to her retainer. The Daoine fell in step as Lyshae moved down the field.

I blinked and exchanged looks with Kelly and Ortiz before falling into jog behind Lyshae.

"Wait!"

I stopped and looked over my shoulder to see Kelly and Ortiz marching towards me with considerable effort. "Uh, why?"

Ortiz looked at me like I was an idiot. "You want to try running in these?" She looked down at her pumps.

I opened my mouth to argue but caught her glare and decided against it. Bands of leather hung in her left hand along with her revolver. I eyed it, then her. "What's up with that?"

She gave me another look, one that said I should know why she was carrying it. "You honestly expect me to go to a paranormal ball without my weapons?"

"You're carrying them."

"It's a ball, with monsters. I'm no expert in your world, Vincent, but I'm sure they will be twitchy seeing a woman with guns."

I couldn't argue that logic.

Ortiz licked her lips and released a piercing whistle.

Lyshae and the Daoine stopped in their tracks and looked back over to us.

"Pretty boy, give me a hand?" Ortiz lifted the holsters for him to see.

The Daoine looked at Lyshae before he nodded and moved towards us. He came to our side in a matter of seconds and waited for Ortiz to explain.

"You wouldn't happen to have a knife on you by any chance?"

The Daoine bent, pulling at the cuff of one of his pant legs. A thin band of black vinyl held a sheathed blade.

Of course Double-O-Douche had a hidden knife in his suit. I rolled my eyes.

He pulled the blade free. It was made from a faerie metal that was a deep blue like twilight skies. The edge of the blade had patinated to carry a pattern of colors that looked like the Northern Lights. He flipped the weapon in his grip, offering it to Ortiz.

She waved a hand to decline. "Here." She passed her guns to me and fumbled with the holsters. With a quick snap of her hand, she brushed the slit portion of her dress aside, revealing a lot more leg. She pulled the holsters tight between her hands, stretching the material out. "Cut here"—she gestured with nod—"and here."

The Daoine severed the leather bands as instructed.

Ortiz muttered a thanks and bent to fasten the strips to

her leg.

The Daoine knelt, offering a hand. "Let me."

Creep.

Ortiz didn't refuse.

Jerk-creep.

His knife blurred, splitting the ends of the band into thin strips. The Daoine fastened the holsters to either side of her thigh and bound their ends together. He looked up and smiled as he stowed his knife. "There."

"Yeah, thanks. How's about you amscray back to your conniving, two-faced boss now, huh?" I jerked a thumb over to Lyshae, who waited patiently twenty yards from us.

The Daoine's mouth moved like was going to say something. Whatever it was, he considered, flashed Ortiz a grin oozing with faerie charm, and sauntered off.

"Douche."

Ortiz looked at me then the Daoine. "Are you jealous?"

"No, I'm not five." I held up ten digits. "I'm this many." I moved after the paranormal pair ahead.

She snorted. "That explains a lot. He's starting to trust me though."

I faltered a step. "What?"

"I know he's not human. I'm not stupid. You said they were manipulative. I may not know the supernatural world like you do, but I know how to game someone like him. He's not on our side. I know that. But I can make him hesitate to try any funny business. He knows I'm a threat, and I think he likes me."

I grunted.

She shot me a smile that was all teeth before nudging me. "Talk. What exactly is he?"

I looked to my side and found Kelly lingering a few steps outside my reach. She was listening in silence, waiting for answers. They both deserved them. "A Daoine, it's like a high faerie."

Ortiz blinked and threw a hand to her mouth to stop the sputtering laughter. "I'm sorry, he's a what?"

"A faerie, like out of the stories. They're not all tiny specks with wings. The Daoine are the highest of fae. They look just like us, if we were perfect. That's what makes them dangerous. Magic is as normal to them as breathing. They can glamour themselves to look normal, but they're faster than us, stronger, and better at anything we could possibly do."

Ortiz sobered. "You make them sound like Superman."

I gave her a knowing look.

"Oh." Her jaw hardened. "How do you kill one?" Her gaze drifted towards the fae's back, and I shuddered.

"With a lot of luck and a whole lot of iron or steel."

Her lips pursed. "Like the Night Runners."

"Yeah."

She brushed her dress slit aside, running her hands over her guns. "Right. Got it. Anything else I need to know?"

I shook my head. "Not that I can think of. If I come up with something, I'll let you know." I pointed towards the Daoine and Lyshae. "We should catch up. I don't want to give her any more of a reason to be pissed at me." I took a step before five bars of iron dug into my bicep. I looked back at Ortiz, arching a brow.

"Hey, we'll get through this. We'll get you out." She had a look I'd seen in her before, and I liked it. It was molten metal—fire and steel.

"Thanks." My voice was like smoke over gravel. I didn't believe her just yet, but I wanted to. "Let's go."

Kelly came to my side as we walked. She kept pace in silence, looking down to her phone then me.

I didn't prod her. She had a lot on her mind, and if she wanted to let it out, I was going to give her the time she needed to sift through her thoughts. It's never easy tackling the unknown. When the unknown happens to be demonic cat people, it's even harder.

"So."

I turned to look at her but didn't slow my pace. "Yeah?"

"Faeries. Cat people." She swallowed and looked down at her phone again. "It's not easy to believe."

"No, it isn't. You saw it with your own eyes. Pretty sure you felt some things too. You tell me: what do you think?"

"I don't know. That's not easy for me because my whole world is knowing things. It's what I do, you know? I hack. I write. I research. I read. That's my life. This"—she waved a finger at our surroundings—"doesn't fit with what I know. It doesn't add up. I'm trying to make sense of it, to make it work. It just doesn't."

I remained silent.

"Nothing—nothing—gives any shred of proof, or points to the supernatural. The things that do are blurry camera footage of unexplainable events or mythology."

I took a breath and placed a hand on her shoulders. She tremored under the touch until I squeezed just a bit. My hand shook from her deep breathing, but she calmed. "Kelly, if a tree falls in the forest and no one's there to hear it, does it make a sound?"

She stared at me.

"No, seriously, think about it? Just because something goes unseen or unheard, it doesn't mean it's not out there. Just because something doesn't make sense, doesn't mean it's not real. Just because something doesn't fit our narrative or desire of what we want the world to be like, doesn't mean it's not true." I gave her a gentle shake. "Look, the thing is, there are lots of sources pointing to the paranormal. I'm not just talking about your local and dashingly handsome paranormal investigator here." I pointed to myself and smiled.

Kelly shook her head but smiled back. The look on her face said she was humoring me and nothing more.

"Look back through human history, eh? How many times were new ideas put out there—ones that were right— only to be shot down because someone didn't believe? Microorganisms were ignored for the longest time. Oh, the theory about the Earth being flat—how'd that work out once someone figured out it wasn't? Hell, some dipsticks still think it's a conspiracy. You ever go on a thing called the Internet?"

Kelly snorted and rubbed a hand against her face. "Okay, you have a point. But still, how can people go so long without knowing about monsters? Where's the proof?"

I gawked at her. "Kelly, ignoring what just happened, where isn't the proof? You've seen it all around you. Where do you think so many of those horror stories and folktales come from?" She moved her mouth to speak but I waved her off. "No, really, think about it. People are experts at burying the things they don't want to see. It's like skeletons in the closet, but for the mind. You're the web guru. You tell me: you ever come across a monster or paranormal video?"

She nodded. "Of course, they're always horrible quality—fake."

I arched a brow and gave her a knowing look. "Why does horrible quality mean fake? You're saying they should look like Hollywood blockbusters? Think about it. Most people recording a paranormal event are on the fly—not counting those goofs who go looking for trouble. People are likely using their cell phone, like how you were doing back there." I gestured behind us.

Her mouth parted before she shut it. Kelly licked her lips and looked away for a second. "That doesn't explain why things aren't clear. It's almost as if people are trying to hide what's happening so it can't be analyzed."

I didn't know if my eyes could open any wider. "That's what bothers you, the darkness? I know it's a bit of a cliché, but when do you think monsters are most likely to attack people? It's in the dark, Kelly. How good's your night vision, because most monsters I've run into have excellent sight in the dark. Think of all the apex predators you can. Most hunt at night. It's nice when your prey can't see you."

She looked away again and there was a light in her eyes I didn't like. Kelly's body shook once again. Maybe I needed to tone it down. Maybe not. She needed to know.

I pressed her. "Kelly, do you remember what you were like when the Bakeneko ambushed us?"

"I was shaking. I couldn't stop."

"Now imagine you're someone—not unlike yourself just a bit ago—and you're encountering your first monster. You've got a phone on hand and you start recording. How steady do you think your hands are going to be when demon cat-people are jumping around with the not-so-groovy intent of eating you?"

The young woman's head sank. Invisible gears were likely turning in her head.

I wanted to make sure they clicked into place. "Kelly, the thing about this world is that people have seen these things. That's not the issue. Never was. They don't want to believe in them. They just can't. Why? Because no one else does. So, what do you do? You play stupid, denial, until your mind eventually comes up with a fiction that makes it believable."

"You're saying we're conditioned to lie to ourselves."

I nodded. "And we're damn good at it. Our brain makes things what we want them to be—needs them to be. We're looking for answers to explain the unexplainable. But we don't always have them, or we don't like the ones that we find. So, we come up with ones we do like. That's what happens. It ain't right though. Here's the thing about this life, Kelly. It's not up to us to always have the answers, and that's okay."

She blinked like I spoke a foreign language. "How can you not know? Doesn't your job revolve around knowing?"

I shook my head. "No. Knowing helps. It's power. My job revolves around figuring things out—learning. There's a difference, and the latter leads to the former. But to do that, you have to have an open mind. And you need to know that it's okay not to have all the answers all of the time. When you try to have that, you end up forcing the wrong answers to be right. That's a dangerous game and can lead to more trouble. We have to carry on the best we can in the face of danger and the unknown. It's not a great gig, but it's part of being human." I put a hand on her shoulder and squeezed.

She locked eyes with me. "That doesn't make this any easier, you know?"

"I know. But it's not supposed to be easy. Trust me when I say that was never part of the deal."

A light similar to one I'd seen in Ortiz's eyes flickered through Kelly's. "For the record, your deal sucks." She smiled.

I returned it. "Yeah." I dropped my voice so only I could hear it. "And I have a feeling it's going to get worse." I looked to Lyshae.

"What was that?"

I eyed Kelly, keeping my smile up. "Nothing. Do me a favor; hang by Ortiz."

She tilted her head, staring at me, but she complied.

I thanked her and picked up my pace, leaving her behind. Lyshae had let some things slip, but I still didn't know why she wanted this piece of the Neravene. As far as I could see, the place was worthless. I remembered an old adage: Looks can be deceiving. My pace doubled and I came by the Kitsune's side, throwing a quick look over my shoulder to ensure Ortiz and Kelly were okay. I didn't want any more surprises.

Lyshae kept her gaze ahead but acknowledged my presence. "Yes?"

The trickster spirit was adept at spotting when someone was fishing for info. I'd have to be clever. "So, uh, nice field, huh?"

She didn't say anything, but I had the feeling she thought I was stupid.

"I mean, if you were going to claim a field, might as well pick this one, right?" See. Clever.

Lyshae let out a breath but remained silent.

I let out a low, long whistle. "Prime real estate, I hear it's a buyer's market. Needs some landscaping. Place is a bit sparse. Then there's the cat problem. Though, think we took care of that. Pests are a pain." I gave her a stupid grin.

The muscles under her right eye twitched.

"Ayup, and you got the place pretty cheap. I mean you can't beat free land. It's the one thing they're not making anymore. Though I guess in the Neravene, it just keeps on growing. Huh, that going to devalue what you've got?"

"Do you remember when I slapped you?" Lyshae stopped in place, turned, and stared at me. Her chest heaved just enough to be noticeable, and her gaze was frozen daggers.

I blinked and looked up to the sky, putting a finger to my lips. "I think so. I remember you kissing me too."

Her hand twitched, and I felt a sudden urge to step to the side. She smiled. "At this particular moment, I feel that it's going to be a slap—a hard one."

"Heh." I gave her a weak smile. "Don't suppose you're going to tell me why-oh-why you wanted this here piece of the Neravene?"

Her smile widened. "Why, of course."

Both of my brows shot up. "Oh?" I wasn't expecting Lyshae to be forthcoming. It wasn't in her nature. Then again, just when I thought I had her figured out, she'd throw me another curveball.

"This is one of the few paths in the Neravene that can

lead to many places on foot. As you know, there are some places one cannot simply open a Way into." Her teeth gleamed. "This allows me to work around that problem. And it's mine." She sounded hungry. "This is the first of many domains I plan to take, Vincent. I aim to be a lady of the Neravene." Her eyes glowed with a light I couldn't name. It was the sort that took hold of men and women gone mad with power or worse—a crazed gleam.

My insides felt like they were being squeezed by rusted and frozen chains. It took me a second to catch my next breath, and the back of my tongue felt like I'd swallowed a lump of ash. I couldn't come up with a response.

Lyshae waved a hand ahead of me. "We've arrived."

Chapter Nineteen

She wasn't kidding. I don't know how, but the scene ahead wasn't the same as the one behind. The stalks of grass had vanished, replaced by an untouched field of snow. Stones as large as my head raced along either side to create a strip of snow in between that looked like a path. My muscles shivered on impulse. Something felt off.

I squinted and fell to a knee, taking care not to let any snow brush against the jacket. No cold brushed against my fingers as I lowered them against the frost. I blinked and turned to look at Lyshae.

She didn't return my stare, instead keeping her eyes fixed on the endless expanse of white ahead.

I wiggled my index and middle fingers before plunging them into the snow. Nothing. It was like sticking my digits into flour. I shook them clean and rose to my feet. "So, that's not weird at all."

"Sarcasm?" Lyshae glanced at me and shook her head in disapproval.

I made a small gesture with my thumb and forefinger.

"Refrain from that when we are inside with our host." She looked ahead like I was no longer there.

I blinked several times, trying to process what she'd said. "You want me to not be a wiseass?"

"Correct."

I blinked more. "Uh, I think you may have twisted the wrong guy's arm."

Lyshae turned and gave me a smile that made my bowels freeze. "For your sake, Vincent, I hope not. More than your arm will be twisted and broken if you cannot control yourself."

I answered with a thin smile. "By you?"

"Our host."

"Who is?" I watched her for any tell.

"Waiting," she said, moving several steps ahead. "Come."

Lyshae's cryptic answers were getting on my nerves. I paused and considered if this was how Ortiz felt when I wasn't straight with her. Unlikely. Lyshae isn't as charming as I am. I looked over my shoulder to see the pair of women trundle into the snowy field, giving it the same bewildered look I had.

Ortiz stopped, looking down to her feet and back up again. "I'm not a fan of this."

Kelly wore the same look as Ortiz. "Me either."

"Are you two cold?" I arched a brow and waited for the obvious answer.

Kelly frowned and took another step forwards, nudging a small mound of white with the tip of her exposed foot. Her eyes widened, and she glanced at Ortiz. "That's not normal."

Ortiz followed the young woman's lead and knelt much like I had. Her index finger plunged into the snow before she pulled it back and shook it clean. She stared at the snow, then me. "Explain that."

I rolled my shoulders in a light shrug. "Wish I could. I can't. Bet she can though if she chooses to." I tilted my head towards Lyshae. "Come on." I marched after the fox spirit, ignoring the snow that threatened to work its way over my shoe and against my socks. My pace quickened, and I stole another look to see Ortiz and Kelly had done the same. I pulled up beside Lyshae. "Where exactly is this ball taking place?"

"Ahead of us." Lyshae raised a hand and waved it like a television presenter showing off a new product. Except there was nothing there.

If I stared any harder, my vision would cut out from the never-ending stark white. The distant air wavered like a desert mirage. I squinted, eyeing the spot to ensure I wasn't imagining things. I wasn't. The air waved and bent. The masquerade of December skies fell. It looked like the sky rained old, gray stone. I stopped in my tracks as Lyshae continued ahead.

Ortiz and Kelly froze in place just a foot behind me. We gawked in unison as a castle from old Germanic tales came into view. And I thought Lyshae was good at veils.

The entirety of it was cold stone, long worn from harsh winds and moisture that'd found its way into every possible crack to make them worse. Yet it held together. I had the feeling most of its look was there to inspire a sense of foreboding. It did a great job. It was sixty square miles of spooky.

I counted eight capped spires around the main body of the castle. The closest of them had a set of windows that just so happened to be open. I wagered someone, or something, watched us from within.

Slabs of what looked like polished river stones trailed along a small hill leading up to the front of the castle. They continued to reveal themselves from under the veil until they stopped several feet from where we stood.

Ortiz looked down, then to Kelly before settling on me. "That's an impressive welcome mat."

Kelly and I bobbed our heads in agreement. It's normal to be at a loss for words when a castle appears out of thin air.

My left shoulder throbbed lightly. I looked at Ortiz. "What?"

"Any idea whose party this is?"

I looked at Lyshae and then the castle. "Trouble."

One of Ortiz's eyes twitched. "Anyone ever tell you it's annoying when you're vague?"

I held my stare on Lyshae and the dark Hogwarts knockoff. "Yeah, I'm starting to sympathize." Even with all the Kitsune's money and influence, she didn't warrant a castle in the Neravene. Most beings didn't. That was a sign of power you couldn't just buy or trick your way into. I ran through the list of beings that could've called the place their home. The list was short. And the beings comprising it weren't friendly or anything I wanted to meet.

The tendrils of ice worming their way through my extremities had nothing to do with the surrounding snow. I couldn't back out on the deal I'd made with Lyshae. We'd sworn the pact and sealed it with blood. There's magic in mortal blood, and it can be used for all manner of supernatural hoodoo. If I got cold feet now, there's no telling the damage it'd do to me. Not to mention ruining my name.

Information brokers don't like dealing with people they can't trust. I gritted my teeth and clenched my fists several times. If I didn't follow through on this, there was the chance I wouldn't make it back to solve Daniel's murder. I had no idea how much time had passed already or the rate at which it was moving. The only option was getting this over with as fast as possible. I jogged after Lyshae, motioning for the Ortiz and Kelly to follow.

We moved along the path in silence. Lyshae's head remained fixed ahead, but there were micro-movements that let me know she was watching everything around us. That meant she was on guard. But if we were invited, why the need for caution and, more importantly, from what? My stomach sank, and I wondered if we were party crashing. You do not crash your way into anything involving the powerful beings of the Neravene. It's how you end up on the dinner menu.

Ortiz sidled alongside me, shifting her hips and bumping me gently.

"What's up?"

She raised her brows and thrust her chin in the direction of Lyshae. "She's eyeing our surroundings like she's expecting an attack."

"How do you know that?"

Ortiz gave me a knowing look. "Because that's what I've been doing. So, tell me, should I expect danger?"

I huffed a breath and shut my eyes for a second. "Ortiz, we're in a magical realm of monsters where we were not too long ago jumped by cat-people."

Her mouth and nose scrunched. "Good point." She brushed a hand against her thigh, feeling for her handguns, seemingly more for comfort than anything else.

I turned my profile until I was sidestepping up the stairs. Kelly trailed behind, and the distance between us grew. The young woman's head turned in every possible direction like she was trying to commit every detail to memory. Except her eyes were wide and carrying a manic look that comes from stress...or fear. I cleared my throat and inclined my head towards Kelly.

Ortiz caught the look and followed it.

"Think you can hang back and give her a talk?"

"About what?"

"Whatever you can to make her feel comfortable. Any tips that have helped you come to grips with this not-so-nice world I play in? Ortiz, you've handled a lot. Just...share what you feel might help her. Please."

She nodded and slowed her pace until Kelly caught up.

I faced ahead and increased my lead. Ortiz would keep Kelly safe while I kept an eye on our escort. Lyshae wasn't done manipulating us. Running one game was never enough. The setup with the Bakeneko was a warm-up for whatever else she had planned. It was a good bet the ball was what she had really wanted me for. The scene in the green field was just a bonus—a big one.

We rounded a corner and made our way up the final incline. The doors were made from solid wood a color between ebony and walnut. Each one was the length of a city block in height. The dark wood didn't do anything to brighten the bleak stone around it. Whoever owned the place needed a new decorator. Lyshae walked up to the door. Her Daoine stooge followed her.

I crossed my fingers and hoped they'd lost our invite. If she was rejected at the door, I was free. Technically, I had followed her to the ball as asked. If she couldn't get in, it was no fault of mine. It wouldn't free me of the remaining two debts. One down was better than none though. I'd take what I could get.

Lyshae waved a hand towards the door, gesturing for the faerie-Bond to approach it. He did and knocked three times. Nothing happened.

I gave silent thanks and raised a hand into the air. "Well, can't say we didn't try. Shame really. And you didn't even change clothes." I pursed my lips and pouted at Lyshae.

She turned and smiled. "I didn't want to ruin my real dress. I'll change when it's necessary. Besides, leaving now would be rude."

"Eh?" The surface of the snow shuddered, and I took a step back. Ortiz and Kelly came into my view, and I waved a hand, ushering them back.

They didn't listen. Go figure.

The ground tremored like it harbored a secret itching to

burst free. Knowing my luck, it'd be a bad one.

Plumes of snow erupted a dozen feet into the air. Humanoid figures sprang from the ground.

I hate being right sometimes.

They looked like men who had never seen the sun. Their skin was the sort of white that could only be achieved after death and if you were left out in a frozen tundra. They were clad in armor that'd gone out of fashion centuries ago. Darkened steel rings that linked together and furs over leather. The monsters turned slowly to face us, giving us a hollow stare like they were looking through us. The entirety of their eyes were the color of a frozen lake—glassy gray-whites that added another layer of emptiness to their gaze. Frost and bits of ice clung to them in places like a second skin. They shambled in place like they were waiting for something. I counted six of them.

Ortiz brushed aside part of her dress. She hunched a bit and her hands flew to her holsters.

"Wait!" I held a hand and prayed she wouldn't draw.

The Popsicle-people shifted to face Ortiz. The sound of stiff metal and sinew filled our ears with little clinks and cracks.

Ortiz stopped an inch from pulling a gun. She looked at the ice-men then me.

I gave her a weak smile. "I think they'd take it personally."

She lifted her hands and raised them in a cautious manner.

Cold acid seared my marrow, threatening to freeze me from the inside. "Wights." My voice was a whisper not audible over the ice cracking over their bodies. Wights were out of old German myths. The freaks were undead creatures that had managed to cling onto a portion of their soul. Well, whatever was left after centuries of decay and magical bastardization. The soul doesn't hold up all too well after decades in a dead body with strain.

The chill going through my body deepened. Oh, crap. Could that happen to me? I repressed a shiver. I'm nothing like those things. Say it a few more times and you'll believe it. Shut up. After I was done with my mental self-flagellation, I ran through what else I knew about wights.

I didn't have much else. They were strong—comes from being undead and not held back by silly things like self-preservation. The creatures still retained something close to human-level intelligence. And the only way I knew how to kill them was with fire. There wasn't an abundance of that around.

The wight closest to Lyshae raised his head and let its mouth fall open. No noise came out. The creature's chest heaved like it was working air through its lungs and remembering how to speak. A hollow, high-pitched sound left its mouth like wind going through a glass bottle. "Leave."

I don't know what possessed me to open my mouth. "But if you don't buy the cookies, we can't send the girls to Orlando."

The wights turned in unison to face me.

Ooooh boy. Being the center of attention isn't always a good thing. I let out a weak laugh and held out my hands like I had an offering. "We've got snickerdoodles?" I gave them a lopsided grin.

Ortiz's groan was audible.

Kelly sucked in a breath, her eyes wide.

Lyshae looked like she was going to slap me.

The wights offered no other response.

"Don't tell me you're into those mint cookies?" I gave them a look of mock horror and made a retching sound. "Because mint...cool taste...cool...you guys are..." I stopped talking after their empty-eyed stares managed to light with a hint of murder. "Heh."

Lyshae didn't care much for my witticisms and walked towards the closest wight. Everyone remained rooted as she crossed the distance, slow and confident. Either she had something up her sleeve, or she knew something I didn't. Being that it was Lyshae, I'd wager on both. The Kitsune stopped a foot from the creature, and she extended an index finger. She bent it several times, beckoning the wight to come closer. If I didn't know any better, it looked like she was in charge of the situation. The creature obliged her summons, and Lyshae leaned in until her lips were by its ears. She moved them, but I couldn't hear what she'd said.

The wight pulled back like its muscles and joints were

frozen. I had a feeling it was more to do with what the trickster spirit had told him. He blinked once and turned to face his crew. "Escort them."

Oh, goodie.

The wights by Ortiz and Kelly ushered the ladies to my side before flanking us. The lead snowman shambled towards the doors. Deep, resounding thuds echoed from the doors each time its fist crashed against them. The castle groaned like it was a beast roused from a long slumber, and it was angry. Loose particulates and snow shook free of the doors as they vibrated. The groaning intensified, and a sharp keen rang out as the doors opened.

We followed the chief snow zombie as he led the way. A veil of roiling fog obscured whatever lay behind the doors.

How convenient.

The leader of the wights paused before it, allowing the rest of us to catch up. He placed his hand against it, raking the fog like he could tear a piece free. The gaseous barrier dissipated, and a mixture of warm brass and amber lights filled our view.

I squinted against the sudden barrage of brightness.

A cacophony of voices and instruments reverberated through and out over us.

The wight placed a hand to either side of his mouth. "The Lady Lyshae and...escort, Vincent Graves."

The noise died.

Chapter Twenty

My eyes adjusted to the light. The doors opened into a hall that looked like it went on for several miles. The floor looked like the snow had made its way inside and flattened into stone. Flecks of white skittered along the surface like every breeze was lifting bits of the flooring to whisk it away. It looked like it was flurrying upside down. Chandeliers hung in the air suspended by unseen hands. They burned with the golden hues I'd seen earlier. I couldn't make out the number of heavy, ebony wood tables filling the place. Every one of them was packed with beings. All of them stared at me.

Popularity sucks.

I smiled, and the stares intensified. There was a long moment where it felt like my gaze held every single other one in attendance. Thankfully, someone must've said something funny because a chorus of laughter erupted from a far back corner. It rippled along, dying a third of the way down the length of the hall. The joke must've been good because it prompted the guests to return to their drinking and revelry. My shoulders sagged, and a bit of the strength fled my back. I slumped as I exhaled.

Lyshae stepped beside me, taking my hand within hers. "That was well done. Holding their stares without word was better than I expected. I was afraid you would open your mouth."

I glowered.

Lyshae returned a grin. "Good. Hold that—silently."

I narrowed my eyes.

Her smile grew. "Better."

"What was that about? How'd Frosty know my name?"

Lyshae looked at me like the answer was obvious. "Why, I told him."

"You what—why?"

"Because...you have a reputation among many that I seek to exploit. The more eyes on you, the better."

You mean the fewer eyes on you. So, she didn't want me for the muscle. I was a patsy for something I needed to get wise to quickly. There was another thing that needed to be cleared up as well. "What reputation?"

"Word of your cases and the beings you've killed has spread over the years. The flames of that reputation may have been fanned and exaggerated by certain parties." Lyshae's eyes gleamed under the light, but her face remained neutral.

Yeah, I bet.

"Much of the Neravene views you as a juggernaut of sorts. A mortal that can't die for long. Something that always returns and is relentless. Not to mention your particular talent for absorbing punishment."

"Wow. I didn't know I was viewed like that. I mean, I had an idea, but..." I rubbed my face and stared at the countless mass of supernatural nasties. A silent plea ran through my mind, begging me not to test out my reputation. Any one of the figures in attendance had a good shot of being something that could pancake my ass.

"Yes, Vincent. It's taken a great deal of work to build your reputation for my purposes. Don't ruin it before I get my use out of it, because I know the truth about you."

I arched a brow.

"You're a destructive buffoon."

My scowl returned. "Bitch."

She laughed and moved ahead of me with her bodyguard.

My hand shot out, grabbing her by her forearm. If she wanted me to act like a hard ass, she and everyone else would see it firsthand. I jerked hard and pulled her close.

Her eyes widened and flashed with a heat that could've caused burns. "What are you doing?" She kept her voice to a low hiss.

I squeezed her arm harder. An untold number of eyes turned to us, watching in silence. I planned on giving them a good show. "When this is over, I want answers. Screw the garbage you just said. We both know you know something about who I really am—was—before this." I waved a hand over my borrowed body.

Her teeth gritted as her features furrowed. "And I told you whom to consult. You didn't. That is your failing, not mine. Now, let go."

I did.

She had the grace not to yank her arm away from my grip. Instead, she was poised and in control. Lyshae flourished with her hand and waved it from the crown of her head down to her waist. The air following the movement blurred. Her black dress was replaced with a something that belonged on fashion week. It was a strapless, body-hugging number as white as the snow-colored floor. Faint hairline threads of gold ran around the dress and shone under the light. It ended halfway down her thighs. Lyshae didn't bother adding any shoes to the mix, deciding to go barefoot.

"Uh, very chic? What gives? Isn't this a fancy shindig?"

Lyshae gave me a Hollywood smile that was radiant white. "It is. Some of us are more traditional in our appearances. I am not."

"I thought appearances mattered here." I eyed her.

"They do." Her smile faltered before reappearing just as fast. "But remember, appearances can be deceiving, and at other times, they are all that matters." Her tone suggested there was more to what she was saying.

"Shallow much?"

"And what are you without your appearances? Who are you? You don't even know." Her words cut through me like shards of glass.

She was right. I didn't have a clue about my prior life. But everyone else seemed to. A guttural burble escaped my lips. "I'm more than just this." I smacked a hand to Daniel's chest. "I identify with more than this meat suit. I know who I am."

Lyshae pressed her lips together to keep from laughing. "You have no idea who you are...or what. Behave and perhaps you'll come to know a little more, hm?" She shimmied in place and sauntered forwards like she was at a frat party. That was bound to draw attention, which was probably her goal all along. The Daoine followed and moved with the lazy confidence of a predator.

I held out a hand. "Wait!" The Kitsune managed to vanish along with her bodyguard into a nearby crowd. I swore, drawing nearby stares. I stared back. "What?" Some of them averted their gaze. Some didn't. I stopped caring.

Ortiz and Kelly came to my side and gave me looks urging me to err on the side of caution. They had a point. We were in a castle full of paranormal whats-its. The last thing I needed to do was start fights I couldn't finish.

My hand went to my collar. I hooked my index finger inside it and tugged twice. It was a delicate balance. Too much eye contact with the wrong guests, and I'd start trouble. Too little and I'd come off as prey. That wouldn't do Ortiz and Kelly any favors either. I lowered my voice to a barely audible whisper. "Stick close. Don't wander off, and whatever you do, don't accept any gifts or favors. Got it?"

Both women nodded in unison.

It wasn't enough. "I need to hear you both say it." They did, and it was a small relief that let me loosen my posture a bit. "Alright, well, let's mingle." I picked out a nearby table that appeared to have the least threatening attendees.

Compared to the rest of the tables, it was a deserted island. Four beings occupied it. The only problem was figuring out what exactly they were.

The closest looked like a slender Japanese man in his late eighties. He had razor-sharp, gaunt features that made him looked like a shaved hawk. His hairless skull sported a few marks of discoloration that came with his age. He looked up at us and muttered something I couldn't make out. His voice was a resonant baritone, even when hushed, with a hint of thick smoke and dryness that came with years of abusive smoking. He was dressed in a uniform that could have belonged to a Japanese soldier from the Second World War.

The figure to his right was a woman whose skin was dark enough to redefine the word. Nearby light seemed to pull itself to her only to be lost forever in her complexion. She kept her eyes locked on the three of us as she spoke to the Japanese man to her side. Between the clear accent and her features, I pegged her as someone—thing—from the Indian subcontinent.

She wore a sari made of red silk hemmed in a silver

thread so fine and polished it could've been spun from the precious metal itself. More silver adorned her ears in small hoops and studs. It seemed the theme as a slender reef of the same metal ran along her forehead in a simple crown. A heavy, intricate layer of gold links wove over her chest and around her throat. That was a serious necklace.

I waved at the pair.

They stopped talking and rose, inclining their heads to the others who remained seated. They moved towards us.

The muscles in my forearms knotted and the feeling made its way into my fists. A hand fell on my shoulder, prompting me to relax. I looked to my side and gave Ortiz a silent thanks. Despite my muscles being at ease, my heart and temples still nursed a set of boomboxes.

The pair stopped a few feet in front of us. Both moved with an eerie and utterly inhuman precision in even the smallest of their movements. The Japanese man eyed the three of us in a slow, mechanical manner before making a sound of disgust that seemed to shake phlegm loose from deep within his chest.

Classy.

He whispered something to the woman then turned to leave.

Gold rings clanged and jingled along her wrist and forearms as the Indian woman gave him a minor wave. She turned back to face us. Her gaze narrowed in on me, seeming to block out everything else.

The space around me felt tight, like I was inside a bottle being pumped with excess air. I tried to clear my throat, but it sounded like I'd swallowed a dog's squeaky toy. "Um, hi."

The woman smiled. You often hear about things being the color of blood, but it's poetic exaggeration most of the time. That wasn't the case here. Her lips were a disturbing red—wet, like they were covered in something other than lipstick. "I've heard of you." My bones rattled when she spoke. There was a second layer in her voice that wormed its way into my body and threatened to shake me apart.

I cleared my throat successfully. "All good things, I hope."

"Mhmm."

I forced a thin smile. This was going well. Given the

environment of potentially hostile nasties all around me, I figured it wouldn't hurt to make a friend. I extended a hand. "Pleasure to meet you."

She didn't take it. Cold. The woman tilted her head, regarding me for another instant that seemed to stretch forever. "Curious."

"What is?"

"You. How did someone put you together? A little soul in someone else's body—odd."

Kelly and Ortiz traded glances and looked to me for an answer. I wish I had one. Maybe Lyshae had stamped it somewhere on my suit, but it's not normal for creatures to pick out what I am at first glance. I arched a brow and kept quiet.

"It's a wonder you have held together for so long."

"Impressive, huh?" I gave her a lopsided grin.

She shook her head in what looked almost like pity. "You are a broken thing bound to break further. Shame."

I swallowed the lumps of gravel in my throat. She was right. All the years of body hopping hadn't done me any good. I'd lost so many memories and had no idea if I'd ever get them back. But my last case had forced me to consider another possibility. What if there was only so much of this my soul could take before something worse happened? I didn't want to consider it.

"You should," said the woman.

I looked at her and nearly sucked in a breath through my teeth. Her eyes resembled pools of liquid ink lined with hairline branches of fire. It was like staring into dying coals threaded with a hint of flames. "Who—what are you?" I had a feeling I knew, but I had to hear it from her. A part of me didn't want to. But reading minds isn't common. I only knew of one person who seemed to possess that ability.

She leaned close, and the smell of hot spices threatened to choke me. There was something else. An odor associated with dead bodies in the morgue—times a thousand. It was like inhaling a frozen meat locker.

I nearly gagged.

The woman whispered my name, and it felt like my bones were toothpicks supporting cinderblocks. My knees buckled, and I hit the floor. "Do not move." The comment was directed at Ortiz and Kelly. I wasn't sure since my view was fixed on the floor. The pressure increased to the point where I feared becoming a Graves-puddle. It relented a second later.

I exhaled and pushed myself to my feet. My suit wasn't dirty, so there was that. I brushed myself off regardless and tried to look dignified. "Well, that was rude."

The woman smiled and, believe me, I was glad. No one wants an angry god—goddess—on their hands. "It was mildly entertaining to meet you. Perhaps we shall meet again." She inclined her head in a manner that looked like it hadn't moved at all. The woman moved off in the direction of her friend.

Ortiz followed the woman with her eyes before turning to me. "What was that?"

"If I am right—and I have a feeling I am—she's a sign that Lyshae is the least of our troubles."

Ortiz raised a brow. "Meaning?"

"That we should really play nice."

Kelly and Ortiz gave me flat stares.

I held up my hands. "Yeah, I know. Can the smartassery, make nice."

Both women gave me dubious looks.

Playing nice wouldn't hurt though. I turned back to the table. Only one person remained. The other must've left when I turned my back. He had a face that looked carved from white marble. Hard edges and gaunt features that he somehow made work for him. He ran a pale hand through his hair, sweeping it back. Some locks curled around the ends. It was the sort of black so dark it edged near blue. He looked up and caught me staring. His eyes were a gray that belonged to storm clouds moments before they brought the thunder.

I gave him a goofy grin and headed towards him. Kelly and Ortiz followed as I took a seat across from the dark-haired man. "Hey, long time."

He shifted and looked around like he was searching for someone—anyone else to sit with. "Not long enough."

Ouch. "FYI, words hurt."

He rolled his eyes and brushed his long, black duster aside to reveal an equally dark silk shirt. "Acronyms." He spat the word like a curse.

"I know, right? Look, on the DL, I'm working a case and this is really going to cut into my timeline. Feel like helping a friend out? Because I need this wrapped up ASAP. Things ATM are pretty FUBAR, but I'm trying to keep them from getting worse. Uh...hashtag YOLO." I widened my grin.

His eyes narrowed, and I felt that thunder coming on. He reached over, grabbing a chalice fashioned from something like pearl. His fingers closed tightly around it. The material crunched like it was tin. His eyes never broke contact with mine as garnet liquid sloshed onto his hand. "I had forgotten what a pain in the ass you were, Graves. I've killed men for being less than the nuisance you're being now." His eyes hardened into discs of concrete.

I kept up the smile. "Aw, don't be like that. Remember that time I got you pizza?"

A small fountain of liquid leapt from the goblet as it crumpled completely.

I blinked as I took my seat across from him. "Uh, did you not like it?"

"What do you want? Why are you here?" He looked over his shoulder again, likely still searching for an empty seat nearby.

"Long story or short?" My grin slipped, and Ortiz and Kelly took spots beside me.

"Short preferably; the shorter, the better," he said, turning his gaze towards Ortiz. He looked at her the way someone would if they had nothing else better to do. "And you are?"

Ortiz smiled and held out her hand, shooting me a sideways look. "No names, right?"

I nodded.

"Nobody." She kept the smile up.

Tall, dark, and pale smirked as he cupped her hand. He pulled it close and leaned in, brushing his lips against her fingers.

Ortiz shuddered at the touch.

My hand darted out on impulse, fingers closing around the nearest dinner knife. I lunged across the table and pulled his hand from her, pinning it down. The tip of the knife pressed against the soft meat under his chin. "Don't. Don't you fucking dare pull that crap around me, freak!"

The clamor died around us. All eyes turned towards us—again. I wasn't doing a good job of not causing a scene.

My friend sighed and kept his bored gaze on Ortiz like the situation didn't bother him. He glanced at me for a split second. "Manners, Graves." His attention went back to Ortiz. "Call me Card."

She stared hard at him. "I've worked my job long enough to spot a fake name when I hear it."

Card grinned. "It's what he knows me by"—he managed to raise and tilt his eyebrows towards me—"and the best I could do this century." He flashed Ortiz a smile that made me want to push up on the knife a little harder. "And, Graves, you're really pushing your luck. I like you— the way some people like an irritating dog—and you're pushing it now."

"Keep talking, and I'll push harder. Maybe you'll get the point. Get it? Point?" I gave him a wolfish smile.

"Is that really the smart thing to do here? I saw you came with Lyshae."

"So?"

"Tell me: Did she you give her word of safe conduct?"

"Uh..." I looked to Ortiz and Kelly who stared back. Crap. She hadn't. We had no guarantees of our safety with Lyshae other than she needed us. Or so she said. As far as I knew, this might be as far she needed me. But I still owed her two more debts. She wasn't the kind to squander favors or leverage she'd earned. I didn't let Card see my doubt.

"You're a guest in a place of neutrality tonight. You're threatening another guest without provocation—"

"Provocation my ass! I know what you are. I know who you are. You're a threat just because of that." My hand shook just enough that the point scritched against his chin without drawing any blood.

Nearby guests turned in place, leaning towards us in curiosity. It might have been a trick of the light colored with my imagination, but their eyes held hungry gleams. There's a certain feeling when you're being stared at like a meal by big predators. This was that.

I looked around, catching all the looks I could, and

swallowed.

Card didn't relent. "Think hard about where you are. Who could drum up a party with the likes of gods and darker things—some of them nameless? You're here under a promise of no hostility that everyone unconditionally accepted when passing through the doors. You're coming pretty close to breaking that, and you didn't get any oaths guaranteeing your safety." A thin, crooked smile spread across his face like a slit in marble. "Or your friends." He glanced at Ortiz and Kelly.

Moisture built atop the skin of my palm and I felt the knife slipping. I licked my lips and kept the blade in place.

"That means you're fair game, even if you don't put the knife down. If you keep it up, you're going to find yourself in a world of trouble from our host."

I arched a brow and peeled my lips back into a snarl. No fear in the face of monsters. Easier said than done. "Yeah, and who's that?"

Card chuckled. "You're about to find out."

The lights went out, and hundreds of eyes shone like prisms.

Chapter Twenty-One

Golfball-sized motes of blue flame erupted into existence along the walls of the castle. The fires gave off more light than they should have been able to. The entire room was cast into an odd tint reserved for low-grade horror flicks.

It didn't do wonders for the various eyes homing in on our little spat.

"I think I'll lose the knife." I let go of my hold on Card's wrist. The knife clattered atop the table.

"Wise choice." Card pulled his hand back and propped his elbows atop the table, resting his chin on balled fists.

A Way snapped to life at the end of the hall. It was a smooth slit through space that grew by the second. The Way rippled and expanded like a nebulous cloud of white.

Ortiz, Kelly, and I squinted at the jarring brightness.

Flurries raced out of it and filled the hall like they were propelled from the other side by a high-powered leaf blower. It was a beautiful thing to look at, even under the blue lighting. A figure stepped out, and I regretted bringing my friends into this mess.

"No-no-no." My fists balled tight enough to make the tips of my fingers ache.

Kelly scooted closer to me, her hands back on her phone. "It's not a good thing when you say that, is it?" She thumbed a button, causing a vibrant light to spring from the back of her phone.

"No, it isn't." I clenched my jaw and wanted to usher Ortiz and Kelly from the seat. But bailing on a lady of the Neravene's party was one hell of a slight. Bailing on a queen's party was worse. It's an offense that ends up with you being served as chunks out of a tuna can for monsters. I never was a fan of tuna.

The Way shut, and a young woman stood at the end of

the hall with the grace and poise of someone decades older. Although, decades was the wrong word. There wasn't any accurate way of pegging just how old she was. Ancient. Damn ancient was closer.

She was dressed in a long gown the color of frozen blueberries—a dark thing sequined in pin-sized diamonds. A thin cape flowed over shoulders and trailed several feet behind her. It was a translucent mesh that seemed fashioned out of snow. Don't ask me how. Her lips were the color of smeared strawberries and made her fair skin look snow-white by comparison. The soot-dark hair didn't help.

"Welcome, all." Her voice rang through the hall with enough force to drown out a thunderstorm. It helps having a bit of magic. And if I was right, she had no end of it at her disposal.

A chorus of cheers greeted her. There were a few disgruntled murmurs that silenced themselves when they'd realized what they were doing and to whom. Even I shut my trap and joined in with the thunderous applause.

Who says I can't learn?

The applause lost most of its roar but kept on. The queen stood in place, waiting for the lingering sounds to die.

Ortiz tugged on my sleeve. "Vincent, who is that?"

I exhaled. "The White Queen. As fair as snow...and just as cold and harsh."

A rogue beam of light arced over nearby tables as Kelly fumbled with her phone. She muted the light and clutched the device to her chest.

Good move. We didn't want to draw any more attention to ourselves now that the queen was at the center. She could keep it. I'd stirred the pot enough and wanted to get us out alive.

"Sounds like an important person. A powerful person." Ortiz glared at me. "Someone we don't want to start trouble with." The look deepened.

"That's an understatement. She's a freaking queen of winter—a force of nature. She's one of the few beings that can bring the season on...and all of its good or ill."

"Winter has a good side?"

I nodded. "Yeah, think about it. It's when things die; old leaves and animals fall dead and return to the earth.

They nourish the ground and sometimes other creatures. The cycle starts back up for growth in spring. It's necessary and dangerous."

"And I'm guessing so is she?" Ortiz flicked a quick look towards the queen before turning back to me.

"Ortiz"—I turned to Kelly—"Kelly, the White Queen is on par with some gods in terms of power. I'm talking old-world stuff, like the ability to start the next ice age if something pisses her off."

Kelly angled her phone up just enough for the camera to catch the queen's figure. She kept the light off however. The young hacker leaned close, keeping her voice to a whisper. "What's keeping her in check and from doing exactly that?"

"A handful of other beings equally as powerful either working in concert to bring on winter or usher in summer. It's sort of taboo to bring about the frosty end of the world without consulting your peers. Plus, the gods and other creatures behind summer wouldn't take too kindly to it."

Kelly let out a dark laugh. "Oh, well, as long as she has permission and it's not a terrible inconvenience to anyone."

I snorted and threw my hands over my nose and mouth to bury the sound.

"You know"—Card leaned forwards—"if I can hear you, a great many others can as well." He pinched his thumb and forefinger together, dragging them across his lips.

I looked to Kelly. "Yeah, kid, shut up."

She glared at me and shook her head.

Curiosity gnawed at me and kept me from keeping my trap closed. Big surprise. I leaned towards Card. "So, what's this about—the ball?"

He shook his head and let his head fall to the side like he didn't care much. "I don't know. I don't care. I was invited, and I wasn't going to decline."

I raised a brow. "Oh? You here for the food then?"

His teeth gleamed, and his canines seemed a little longer than the average person's. "I'm abstaining. Last time we met you gave me a rather pointed ultimatum."

My fingers drummed against the table, and I inclined my head towards the knife. "I can make it pointier."

"I'm here for the company and the gifts—the receiving

and the giving of them," he said.

The queen waved a hand, and a beam of silver light illuminated the area around her. It was like a concentrated cone of moonlight had decided to focus on her. "I have called the many of you and your guests in attendance to bear witness to, and welcome, a new lady of the Neravene."

If the White Queen didn't have everyone's attention before, she did now.

A new lord or lady in the Neravene was a big deal no matter how small in power or domain they were. Everyone takes note when there's a new player in town. You never know what and when an up-and-coming lord or lady might decide to off you for a bigger slice of power. Being someone of power here meant always having a target on your back. Keeping your friends close and your enemies closer wasn't just a handy proverb; it was a way of life for the lords and ladies. And in the Neravene, it's safer to assume everyone is an enemy.

All guests in attendance watched the queen in an almost hypnotic trance. The air had a static charge quality to it. I had a feeling everyone was going to lengths to either persuade the new member to become friends, or plotting how to dispose of them. Easier said than done. Lyshae was a clever fox.

The White Queen waved a hand to an unlit portion of the hall to her right. "Welcome, Lyshae, new lady of the Neravene."

The Kitsune stepped into the light, her face a neutral mask—respectful. I knew better. Fireworks were going off in the trickster's head. One step closer to climbing the ranks of the unbalanced ladder of power. Part of me wished she'd fall. It was a long way down and a hell of an impact.

There was a moment of silence like after a performer first strums their guitar. A silence of quivering strings waiting to be played again—anticipation.

Card leaned on his elbow, coming closer to me while keeping his gaze on the scene with Lyshae. "When did the Kitsune get her own domain? Last I heard she was working for others." He passed it off as an idle question but there was an undertone in his voice suggesting more. Card really wanted to know how Lyshae had moved up the ranks.

I didn't see why. His place was secure. Hard to want more when you're practically an immortal king. I tried matching his bored tone. "I heard she'd recently came into some land." Very recently. It clicked as soon as I had said it.

Oh, you clever bitch. Lyshae's invitation was contingent on having us clear the Bakeneko out. She'd passed herself off as a lady with no domain and hoped she'd have one by the time we'd gotten to the front door. My fists balled, and the tissue in my wrists felt like steel wire about to snap. We were nothing more than convenient numbers to make it an easier job of eliminating the cat demons.

"Mhmm." Card's fingers tapped a rhythmic beat atop the table. "You wouldn't happen to know the size of her domain?"

I shrugged. "No clue. Could be nothing. Could be ginormous."

He didn't look at me, but I could almost feel his bemused grin. "You're a terrible liar, Graves."

Ortiz nudged me. "He's right. You are."

"Alright, zip it, you two."

"Thank you, lords and ladies." Lyshae's voice boomed through the hall like it was amplified by the same magic the White Queen had used. She pinched the ends of her Skimperella dress and managed to curtsy. That was an impressive feat that demanded applause in and of itself. She spoke again, but I tuned her out.

There was a lot more going on here than just the introduction of Lyshae. This was a ball—a ceremony sure, but it was a networking event. Card had said there was going to be a gift giving party. Time to pucker up and kiss the asses of the powerful and forge new alliances...or enemies. Lyshae would make another power grab now.

Holy crap. From information broker to small freestanding lady to something more all in one day.

She'd have to have one hell of a gift to make that happen.

My stomach rolled and felt like a towel being wrung dry.

"And for my gift to you, oh gracious host," said Lyshae, "I offer you a debt of service I procured."

Ortiz's fingers dug into my arm. "She can't be serious."

I took a deep breath and tried to keep my heart rate

from mimicking a drum solo. "I have a feeling she is."

"I offer you the infamous Vincent Graves."

I hate being right.

Chapter Twenty-Two

The hall erupted into raucous noise, but it was church-quiet as far as I was concerned. The hollering and clamor fell into a distant part of my brain. I buried it. It was like a million electric tendrils arced through my mind, and I could see them all. If only each one didn't numb a part of my noggin as they zipped by.

Card turned to look at me, wearing a stupid, lazy feline-like grin. "Well, that certainly kicked off the party."

"Bite me, Card."

His grin grew wider. "Don't tempt me."

I scowled.

The silver moonbeam died. The blue flames vanished, and the room plunged into absolute darkness.

Card chuckled. It sounded deeper than in reality. "Still want that bite, Graves?"

My eyes hadn't adjusted to the dark, but I held up a certain finger. I was sure Card had no trouble seeing it. Golden light flooded the room and conversations died. Lyshae had vanished from the stage, leaving her highness of all things chilly up there.

"We will continue with the exchange of gifts before beginning the festivities." The queen waved a hand and a wight attendant scrambled towards her, bearing a black box.

The ceremony of paranormal ass kissing wasn't something I was interested in. I turned away and checked on my friends.

Ortiz's hand rested on her thigh, and it wasn't empty. Her revolver sat flush against her leg; the barrel pointed at Card's abdomen. Ortiz's gaze was fixed on the scene by the queen.

Good thinking, Ortiz. I wagered her hand had gone to her gun the second the lights went out. Without making any eye contact in Card's direction, there'd be little way for him to know she was aiming a weapon at him just in case he tried something. The gun wouldn't stop him, but it'd slow him down. It took me longer than it should have to notice the skin of her knuckles. They were near white from her grip.

Being plunged into darkness in a hall filled with apex paranormal predators was not a comforting notion. Couple that with the fact that, not so long ago, Ortiz had done a stint in an institution where living shadows roamed the halls, and you get the idea. A little bit of darkness is just enough for a whole lot of imagination to come into play. And imagination can conjure up some terrible scenarios, especially when you're sitting across from a monster.

I reached out, my fingers brushing over the top of her hand. She tore her gaze away and looked at me when I squeezed her fingers. "You good?"

She licked her lips. "Yeah."

"Good." I turned to Kelly whose face was a furrowed mask, glaring at her phone in uncertainty. "What's up?"

Kelly's lips folded and the tip of her tongue protruded between them. She held her phone towards me. "This."

I scanned the screen and blinked, shrugging.

"Look at the time. It hasn't changed since we left the bar." She pulled the phone back, staring at it. "I don't get it. The camera works fine. But anything that requires internet or GPS is dead." She sounded like it was the worst thing to happen to her.

"Yeah, time moves wonky here. Don't trust your phone."

Kelly's eyes widened as she looked from her phone to me in horror. She didn't seem like the idea of being unable to rely on her technology.

Card's thumbs tapped against the table in a low, rhythmic pace to a beat only he could hear. He stared at me as he drummed. "What did you bring our gracious host?"

Eh? Crap. It's poor form to show up to a shindig in the Neravene without something to offer the host. My mouth moved, but nothing came out. I hooked a thumb to my face. "Apparently, I am the gift." A goofy smile spread across my face.

Card rolled his eyes. "I hope for your sake you brought

something that has some measure of value."

Ouch. I reached over and grabbed a gilded goblet, holding it up for Card to see. "Think she'd notice if I gave her this?"

Card ignored me, placing his hands on the table and pushing off. "Well, enjoy stewing over what to give our host, Graves. I have a gift to give." He turned to Ortiz, flashing her a smile. "And I'll look for you during the dance."

Ortiz blinked and her cheeks flushed. "Dance?"

"It is a ball." Card turned and snapped his fingers. A pair of men came to his side from a nearby table. They were dressed in tailored suits of navy blue.

"Your retainers?" I said.

"As many as I was permitted to bring." Card motioned with his hand and the two men followed behind him as he moved towards the White Queen. The trio disappeared from view.

The attendants—other lords and ladies—followed Card's example. They rose from their seats, summoning their respective posses to gather around. A jumbled line formed, all heading towards the queen. Somehow every being managed to move without jostling another. It was like watching ants moving, strung along by telepathy. Only, any one of those ants could have killed me with little effort.

Ortiz's eyes moved from figure to figure, tracking and absorbing every detail she could. It was a cold, calculating process that made the hairs on the back of my neck stir. Her fingers tapped against her gun as she scanned the room.

Kelly processed it in her own way. She moved her phone in horizontal arcs through the air.

I reached over and tapped her wrist.

"Hm?"

"Kelly, do me a favor. I get this is all exciting blog-worthy material, but don't share it."

"Why not?"

I leaned in close. "These people—things—really like their privacy. Monsters like the dark, remember? Not just in the metaphorical sense. Some of them might take it personally if someone were to out them to the mortal world."

She licked her lips and paused. "Um, how personal?"

I gave her a knowing look. "Like show up at your door personal."

Kelly stopped recording.

A hand wrapped itself around my gut and squeezed. I tried to ignore the pang of guilt, but it wasn't easy. Worrying Kelly wasn't what I wanted to do, but dealing with the paranormal world is like lying on a bed of nails. Sure, if you're careful and slow, most of the pointy things won't prick you. But it takes only one misstep for a nail to pierce you. That's only taking into consideration the one and not the rest. It can get messy. I wanted Kelly as far away from any trouble as possible. Easier said than done.

"So, what do I do with it?"

That was a good question. For once, I had a good answer. "Keep it for yourself. You're a smart kid. Keep a digital journal of everything you've seen. Take notes. Trust me: in this world, the more you know, the better. Just...go slow with how much you try to learn, okay? Diving headfirst into things is a good way to have that head"—I touched my index finger to one side of my throat and dragged it across—"glurck."

"Got it. Thanks for the visual." She shuddered and gripped her phone tight. Her posture loosened a second later. "What now?"

My fingers interlocked and I twiddled my thumbs. "Now, we sit quietly and wait. It doesn't seem like we're actually needed for anything at the moment."

"Except for bait." Kelly stared past me and into the crowd of countless beings.

"Caught that, did you?"

"It took me a while to figure it out, but yeah. I've watched enough television to put it together."

My throat and chest shook as I tried not to laugh. The air buried itself somewhere between the back of my throat and upper portions of my sinuses as a muffled snort.

Kelly's tone turned somber. "You think she's playing you?"

"I know she is." I followed Ortiz's example and turned my gaze on the crowd, scanning for the Kitsune. "I just don't know how yet."

"She's keeping you off your game so you stay out of hers." Ortiz didn't look at me, instead keeping her eyes on the crowd of guests. "It's smart. It lets her use you how she wants and keeps you too preoccupied with your own problems to be one for her." Her face was a neutral mask as she relayed that to me.

I had no idea how Ortiz came to that conclusion, and part of me didn't want to know. I chalked it up to her experience working as a Fed, but still, that was some insight into the cold and calculating mind of a paranormal creature. My lips folded as I thought about it. Ortiz dealt with humans, and at times, we're not much better than actual monsters. Heck, there are plenty of instances when we're worse. I pushed the thought away. She was right though. Lyshae was keeping me unbalanced and doing a damn good job of it.

The hairs on the back of my neck felt like someone brushed a statically charged balloon against them. I turned. Lyshae walked towards us from the right side of the hall, her face a work of almost emotionless stone, save for the upturned edges of her mouth and the glimmer in her eyes. She was pleased with herself for selling me off to the highest bidder.

Bitch.

Question was: What did the White Queen give her besides a title and fancy introduction? *More trouble for you, likely.* I'm ever the optimist.

The Kitsune wriggled her way past a handful of beings and sat at the edge of the table. She scooped up a goblet and brought the cup to her mouth, pausing to watch me over its rim. "Vincent, aren't you going to introduce yourself to our host? I'm under the impression you owe her a favor."

Smiling made my mouth feel like trying to stretch a rubber band past its limit. "Yeah, funny. I heard that too."

The Kitsune smirked and traced her finger around the goblet's lip. "Well?"

It was like being a feather in the wind. I was either being pulled along by something's slipstream ahead of me or being pushed by a gust from behind. This whole case, everything with Lyshae, all of it was putting my mind in a tailspin. It was like having a dozen directions to go down without a clue which to take. All I had was Lyshae's suggestion.

Those always went so well.

My hands brushed against my pants as I mulled it over. I could feel Kelly and Ortiz's eyes on me. "Yeah, okay-sure-why-not." I exhaled before drawing a long breath. "I'll go say hi to the queen." Of all things cold and scary. No pressure. I rose from my seat, patting myself in reassurance more than anything else.

Lyshae reached over to a platter, plucking a piece of peeled, yellow fruit—at least I hoped it was fruit—to plop into her mouth. A bead of juice formed at the end of her lip, trickling down before she lapped it up.

Considering my position, I empathized with the fruit. I sighed and moved past the table and towards the longest line of guests. I wasn't in a rush to meet the White Queen, considering she had me by the short hairs. The closest line happened to be the one with the most guests. I joined the end behind a man in a suit the color of slate dust.

He turned on instinct. Another rule of the Neravene: when someone steps behind you, turn around to look. It's not smart to let unknowns behind your back.

The man was an amalgamation of gray. His tie was expensive silk the color of concrete and matched his Italian leather shoes. The pants were the same shade of slate as his sports jacket. That's not what got my attention.

He had eyes like morning fog—empty, cold. It would have been a lie to say his boater's tan complexion offset his eyes' unsettling look. His hair was the color of ash and iron.

I'd heard of him before. "Father Grey." My voice was low enough for only him to hear.

He inclined his head and opened his mouth to speak. Wisps of smoke unfurled from behind his teeth, rolling through the air before dissipating. It would have been a neat trick had he had a cigar or those fancy electronic things all the kids have nowadays. He was without either.

I swallowed. From what I knew, and I didn't know much about Father Grey, he was in charge of the Order of the Gray. Sort of peacekeepers for the mortal and paranormal world, minus the peace part. They were keen on keeping the balance—whatever the cost. If that meant killing monsters, so be it. The order had the same attitude towards killing Joe Normal, the mortal, if they had to. I wasn't a fan of their methods.

He regarded me in a silence that seemed to stretch out and mute the surrounding noise. "Vincent Graves."

He knew me by name and sight, meaning he had picked me out when Lyshae and I had first entered. I rubbed a hand against my pants and extended. "Uh, hi."

He didn't take it. "I didn't expect you here."

"Neither did I." I shrugged and offered him a grin.

Father Grey had problems smiling or being cordial, it seemed. He exhaled through his nose. "I've heard of your reputation."

I lifted a brow. "Oh?"

He waved a hand in a dismissive manner. "The good and the bad. I'm not fond of either of them, to be frank."

"Who's Frank?"

His lips spread, and it was like watching a snake smiling. It sent a tongue of grease down my spine. "You're not as funny as you think."

"That all depends on how funny you think I think I am."

He exhaled through his nose. "You cause problems wherever you go. You're a stain on the natural order—interfering with the balance of things."

Cracks sounded from my knuckles, and the muscles in my forearms tightened. I didn't make a point of hiding my balled fists. "That's rich coming from the Godfather of Gray Goons."

His eyes narrowed. "What did you say?" Another tendril of smoke slipped out from between his lips.

"You heard me. You and your band of punks decide what gets to happen to who and that's that. You all think you have that right." I leaned close. "You have no right, none. I don't give a damn about the freaks you gank, but don't tell me you don't off normal people now and again."

Something flickered in his eyes and they moved a fraction. He wanted to look away but resisted. He knew I was right.

Father Grey took his tie in one hand, sliding his fingers up to the knot, which he adjusted. "You're right, of course. We do a grave number of things, things you might find unsettling."

"No might about it." I flooded my voice with stone and hot iron.

"We do it so people—things like you—can have a nice life."

"Funny, that's what I tell myself about what I do. Last time I checked, I don't go around sending people to early graves."

He flashed me a cruel smile. "Is that what you tell yourself? That you don't kill people?"

He may as well have pushed me into an ice bath. People had died over the years on my cases. It was never by intent. Yeah, but the road to hell and all that. I told my inner voice to shut up. "Screw you."

Grey rolled his eyes. "Grade school wit, hm?"

I felt like introducing his smug face to my fist, show him grade school up close. Starting fights in a line full of guests with presents wasn't a good idea. I took a breath and unclenched my fists. "I'd tell you not to take this personally, but it's personal. You're a dick. Oh, tell that other guy he's a dick too."

Father Grey's face scrunched.

"Japanese dude. Yay high?" I held a hand around five feet above the air.

"Toshiro." Grey spat the name like a curse.

"Yeah, bumped into him once. Dick."

"He won't bother you anymore." His eyes seemed to cloud a bit.

I stared at him, but he said nothing further.

Father Grey turned and tapped on the shoulder of the guest in front of him. He whispered something. Both of them turned and stepped out of the line. The pattern followed like a ripple through the mass of guests. One by one, they all moved aside, creating a path between them.

I gulped. It wasn't rocket science to figure out who that was meant for. I raised both hands into the air. "No, no, it's cool. Don't let me get in the way of you all meeting Her Highness."

No one stepped back into line.

One does not keep a queen of the Neravene waiting. I sucked in a breath and marched through the wall of beings on either side. It felt like a prison walk. I didn't know who was who and where to make eye contact. So, I did the only thing that made sense. I kept my eyes on the queen and ignored the rest.

Some of the guests shot me stares that felt like desert air brushing against my skin. I shrugged them off, keeping my eyes fixed ahead. Time seemed to slow with every step. I realized, with the next few feet, that time hadn't crawled to a standstill. I had. It took a series of short breaths to regain my courage, and I made my way over to the living force of nature.

Her eyes settled on me, forcing me to steal another quick breath. They were the color of frozen violets, a sheet of gray ice over soft purple and just as cold as they sounded. "Well, well." Her red lips spread into a smile that made the temperature feel like it had plummeted.

I tried to match her smile and think of something clever to say. "Uh, hi." Ladies love witty men.

The White Queen's eyes warmed a bit.

Phew.

She stared at me, waiting.

"Oh right, a gift." I reached into a pocket and clenched my fingers around the contents. My hand shook as I extended the fist, hoping my meager gift would appease her. I opened my hand and showed her the crumpled bills and loose change.

The queen eyed my hand with a look that could've frozen it solid. She plucked the bills from my hand. "Money?"

I shrugged. "For the gal that's got everything, whaddya give her?"

"The debt of a man seems fitting." She gave me a chilling smile that made Lyshae's look warm and inviting.

I gulped. "About that...don't suppose I can ask what you'll have me do?"

"Whatever I desire."

It was a good answer—honest, and just what I expected from a queen of the Neravene. Saying a lot without saying anything is a skill. Someone of her power didn't need someone to scrub floors. If she wanted me to do her a solid, it'd be important—and likely bad. The high-up in the paranormal don't like meddling in the mortal world directly. They have proxies to do the grunt work and to take the blame. Worse, she could have something in mind that involved me going up against another lord or lady. Hell, with her position, it could have something to do with another queen or king.

My mouth went dry. "And if I say no?"

One edge of her mouth quirked. "You can try."

Good argument.

"Whatever I decide depends on if you are even worth keeping." Her voice was like frozen asphalt. Cold and hard.

"What?"

"What use have I of you if you're worthless?"

I had no idea how to answer that.

"Perhaps a trial—entertainment before the dancing begins?"

I didn't like where this was going. "How about you take the dough"—I made a show of jiggling the cash in my hand—"and stop wasting everyone's time." I realized what I'd said a second too late.

Her eyes narrowed into slits. "What did you say?"

The skin around my tattoo suffered from an imaginary pang like it'd been slapped. Time was slipping at a rate I couldn't measure while I was here playing Cinderella. The thought galvanized me into pushing the queen further. Not the brightest idea.

"You heard me." I jabbed a thumb to my chest. "Look, I'm on a tight deadline. People are dying, and if I'm going to be any use to you, I've got to go solve the case I'm working. So you and your trials can—"

She swiped a hand through the air. "Quiet."

My throat seized, and my heart felt like it'd tripled in pace and effort. The muscles in my legs quaked. I fell to my knees. The moisture in my throat felt like it was forcefully evacuated. A plume of winter air left my mouth. The tissue in my throat constricted and froze like I'd swallowed chunks of ice. I tasted salt and iron. Droplets of blood splattered against the floor. Breathing became an effort, and my lungs felt tight.

The queen bent at the waist and extended a finger. She trailed the digit along my jaw. "Speak to me like that again, and I will completely freeze the air, water, and blood in your throat, understood?"

Got it. It came out as, "Gahwhee."

"Good." The queen brushed the rest of her fingers against my gullet, pulling them away with a flourish.

The pain stopped.

Before I could utter a word of thanks, the tip of her shoe pressed against my collarbone. "Now, let us see about your worth. Tell me, can you fight?" She shoved.

I tumbled back like I'd been hit by a linebacker across the upper portions of my body. When the world stopped spinning, I saw a wight approaching. It was the one who'd introduced us to the crowd. The sound of scraping metal caused me to focus on what it was dragging along the ground.

A sword.

I hate swords.

Chapter Twenty-Three

My heels beat against the floor as I kicked away from the advancing undead. Reasoning with monsters is possible; not easy, but it's worth a shot. I held out a hand hoping to slow its approach. "Hey, wait. Haven't you heard violence isn't the—"

The blade arced overhead.

"Holy crap!" I pistoned my legs, pushing off from my heels. I moved back just as the point of the weapon sank into the solid ground inches in front of my feet. My eyes widened. Either the floor was made of foam—unlikely—or that was a seriously sharp sword. I didn't want to find out how keen an edge it held firsthand. I'm attached to my body parts. Call me clingy.

The wight pulled both arms towards its chest, wrenching the blade free from the ground. It cast the weapon into a spinning flourish overhead before the inevitable. The sword fell.

I scrambled to a shaky stand out of the way. The tip sailed by an inch from my shins. It was a small relief. Any closer, and I would've been hobbled. There's little time to size up your adversary in a fight. You have to make do with what little you can gauge of them. Every bit is useful.

The wight pulled its arms in again and thrust. The point darted towards my gut.

I sidestepped and let my momentum carry me away further from the weapon. It wasn't the smartest strategy. Swords have a certain efficacy and that's dependent upon their length. The weapon was the standard, unadorned fare for a longsword. A cruciform hilt and a double-edged blade that totaled a few inches over three feet. The longer I stayed outside that reach, the longer the wight had room to maneuver the weapon. I had to get inside and fast.

The creature worked the sword like a horizontal

jackhammer, driving the tip towards me in short thrusts.

It was a good technique. I gave ground while fighting to maintain a hold of my surroundings and balance. I felt the eyes of every guest weighing on me in anticipation, most notably Her Royal Frostiness.

The queen lingered several feet from her previous position. Guess she wanted a ringside seat.

I muttered a curse under my breath and took a chance at looking over my shoulder. There was a table a few feet behind me. If the wight continued to push me, my back would be against it in a matter of seconds. That wasn't a bad thing if I played it right.

The wight appeared to realize the advantage the table would give it. Flickering lights danced over the length of the blade as the wight cast it from side-to-side.

I inhaled, forcing my stomach to cave in to avoid the tip of the sword. My sudden movements and exertion forced me to exhale and suck down air. I stumbled, my arms going to my sides to keep me from tumbling. Something clattered, and the lip of the table impacted my lower back. It felt like a row of blunted needles had jabbed into a portion of my spine. I winced and opened my eyes in time to see a flash of metal growing closer.

Experience won over thought, and I collapsed. The sword cut harmlessly through the air above me as my elbows absorbed the impact from the bench seat. A chorus of grumbles echoed from the nearby seated guests. Most of them were likely beings I didn't want to piss off. Their discomfort wasn't high on my list of give-a-shits at the moment.

My mind buzzed with thoughts on mythology and lore. Wights didn't feel pain; it's what made them exceptional thugs and soldiers. They were human at one point and retained their intelligence. Wights are essentially smart zombies lacking the desire to munch on brains.

The sword flashed.

I rolled, drawing a grumble from the guest I'd bumped into.

The seat shattered like cheap particle board and dry wood.

I didn't wait for the wight to pull back for another

swing. One of my hands beat frantically atop the table in search of something to grab onto. My fingers closed around something cool and smooth. I pulled and snapped my arm, sending a platter hurtling towards the creature.

The sound of a minute bell rang as metal struck the wight's noggin. It reeled. The monster's footing remained stable.

There were only two ways I could think of to kill the wight and make a good impression on the White Queen: batter the creature into a useless pulp—not as easy as it sounds—or set the freak on fire.

The frozen corpse let out a sound like dry parchment dragging across rough stone. The sword went overhead again, and I knew what was coming.

The guests stood, moving away from the table in a leisured manner.

I clawed at the broken remains of the seat, using it as purchase to haul myself up to the table.

The wight cast the weapon into a long slash.

I pressed flat to the table, sending everything atop it to the floor. The back of my head buzzed as the sword brushed by and stirred hairs. My torso panged as I shifted my hips, extending both legs. My heels crashed into the beast's midsection and sent it toppling. This was the break I needed.

I got to all fours and sprang from the table, my knees absorbing the impact. I turned and grabbed a piece of shattered wood the length of my forearm.

Blue firelight strobed several feet away.

I ran towards it, jabbing the wood into the flames. Nothing happened. The wood refused to ignite. I swore and spat, twisting the former piece of table through the fire. I turned in time to see the wight lumbering towards me.

What the hell? I hefted the piece of wood like an impromptu club. It wouldn't do much against a sword, but if I used it right, it could help me beat the wight senseless.

The creature cut another sideways swath through the air causing me to step back and almost brush against the fire. The wight didn't relent, using the momentum to bring the sword overhead and send it into a flurry of strikes.

I ducked in time to hear metal scraping against stone.

The sword flashed again, threatening to bisect me at the waist. I dove under it, wrapping my arms around one of the creature's legs. The force caused the wight's leg to angle away, and its knee buckled. We crashed into a tangled heap. My hand never left the wooden shrapnel.

The wight bucked in protest and snarled.

"Shut up." I sent the end of the wooden club crashing home against its head.

The creature's eyes looked ready to spin in their sockets. Even so, the wight had the wherewithal to struggle. It lashed out in a frenzy of flailing hands. Its fingers clawed the front of my suit.

"Fuck off. These threads aren't mine!" I beat its hands aside and brought the flat side of the club down on its head. Wood cracked, and flecks of shrapnel fell around the creature's skull. Sadly, it was still conscious.

The wight closed its fingers around the front of my shirt and hauled.

I fell forwards, swinging with my forearm and planting it against the creature's chin. Bracing myself against its face, I pushed back, straining my body to resist its pull.

The thing was strong. Wights possess the uncanny strength that comes with little regard for your connective tissue, joints, and self-preservation. It yanked on my clothing in a cold, mechanical manner.

Buttons popped loose in a cascade from top to bottom. They showered the wight, peppering it in the face.

I heard the fabric straining, ready to give way. I tensed and pulled myself back with all the strength I could. Cloth gave way, and I tumbled backward. The world spun once as I came to rest on my ass.

Bits of my dress-shirt remained in the wight's fingers. The creature gave the fabric no notice and moved to rise.

My fingers tightened around the remaining bit of wood, now little more than a sharp sliver. The ill-fashioned stake retained its length though. Too bad it wasn't as thick as before. If I struck hard at the wrong angle, it'd shatter.

The wight turned its head to regard its fallen sword.

I charged the monster, screaming at the top of my lungs.

The undead warrior turned back in time to raise its

hands in defense.

It did little good as I reversed my grip on the weapon, driving it down towards its skull. The blow didn't land as I had hoped. The monster stepped into the strike, digging its fingers into my throat. "Hurgkh!" I gasped but followed through, sinking the large piece of shrapnel into the spot between its neck and shoulder.

Its body sagged as a dry sigh left its mouth. The wight's grip on my throat loosened.

I returned the earlier favor and grabbed tight to the front of its body. With a twist and heavy push, I turned and sent the wight staggering past me. The force of the shove drove the monster into a nearby wall.

It recovered the second it impacted, turning around and giving me a death glare.

I swallowed and eyed the creature's sword. I raced towards it, managing to lower myself without stopping. My fingers brushed against its hilt and closed around it. There was a second where the blade protested the action of being dragged against the ground. The sword scraped and screamed as I pulled it along.

The wight released a hollow cry and rushed to meet me.

I raised the sword and swung from the shoulder. The wide blow swept through the air towards the monster's arm.

It turned its profile towards me and met the blade with its chest. Metal rings shrieked and clinked as the blade severed them. The sword buried itself into the sternum of the creature and stopped a couple of inches in.

The wight didn't seem the least bit concerned with the fact that its chest was being used as an oversized knife rack.

Details.

The wight snatched me by the shoulder and pulled hard.

I staggered towards the same wall I'd driven the creature into moments ago.

Monsters don't let up. The wight shoved hard, adding extra force into the action.

The side of my face smacked the wall. My vision wavered. The area around my left brow erupted into a razor-sharp row of heat. Something warm and wet pooled at the corner of my eye. Part of my mouth went numb and felt like it'd been scoured with sand. I tasted copper.

I looked over my shoulder. Everything blurred like daubs of paint in water. Two things stood out: the approaching wight and the pulsating blue flame to my side. I placed a hand against the wall and pushed.

I wasn't fast enough.

The wight surged forwards, driving its mass against the side of my body.

My ribs bounced off the wall. I winced and opened my mouth in a mute cry. The back of my skull erupted into pins and needles as the hairs went taut within the wight's grasp. My head got another close-up with the wall.

I reached out blindly, slapping my hand on anything I could find. My fingers found purchase against the crook of the wight's elbow. I squeezed and wrenched.

The creature was forced several steps to the side.

My whole body felt like it'd been a punching bag for the ball. I shut my eyes for a second and buried the spreading numbing sensation and the bone-deep weariness. Something deep and hot stirred inside me like my gut was nursing molten globules. I drew on them. I opened my eyes and plowed forwards.

The wight turned, the still buried sword waggled in the cavity it had carved.

I extended my arms, crashing my palms into the monster's chest just above the weapon. My legs screamed from the effort as I pushed against the creature. I succeeded in shoving it against the small orb of blue.

The fire flashed like it had been fed gasoline.

I released my hold and backpedaled without stopping.

The wight screamed a sound like dying machinery. It was a sharp, dry wail of seizing metalwork. Fire licked its torso, spreading over its body without pause. The undead monster beat itself, working to subdue the fire.

I reached the table and stopped to watch from the safe distance.

The blue fire engulfed the wight as its movement slowed. Its arms no longer windmilled in panic. The creature sank to its knees before toppling over. The fire crackled and hissed spitefully over its body.

I breathed a sigh of relief and turned to the queen. Crumpled bills sat in one of her hands. I smiled and imagined it was a macabre thing to look at. Blood welled at the corner of my mouth and made its taste apparent. "Keep the change."

The queen blinked, and, for an instant, I thought she was going to make good on her threat to freeze my insides. She smiled. With a quick flick of her hand, the cash vanished, and she clapped.

The hall exploded into applause that could be felt in my bones. My head spun as like each clap sent my brain into a tumble.

"Well done." Her voice cut through the clapping and silenced the hall in its wake. "At the very least, you have proved useful for the baser things that require a degree of physicality."

I grunted in between my panting. "Me...hit...things good."

One of the queen's eyes twitched. "I hope you can do more than that, Vincent Graves."

"Try me." It was the best I could I do to not come off intimidated.

"Oh, I intend to." Her smile grew, and an arctic chill rolled through my veins. "But for now, enjoy the ball for as long as you can. Now, let us dance." She extended a hand.

I took it. "Sure, why the hell not?"

Chapter Twenty-Four

The White Queen pulled me to the front of the hall where she had made her entrance. She waved her free hand.

The guests rose and stepped away from the tables in unison. Every fixture sank into the snowy-looking ground like the floor had developed a hunger for them. With that, the cavernous hall was cleared for the dance.

Oh, goodie.

Her Royal Highness of all things shivery twined her fingers within mine. "Your other hand goes on my waist." It wasn't a suggestion.

"What?"

She gave me a smile that made it clear her patience was being tested. "Put your hand on my waist, Vincent Graves."

I did just that.

"You can listen. Good. Now, can you follow?" She didn't give me a chance to answer as she stepped back. Before I could adjust, she moved again, gliding to the side.

The sound of thrumming strings and wind instruments flooded the hall, echoing as they loudened.

She pulled again. It was a gentle tug, but that's not what I found odd.

My body felt like it was being towed through water. Every little bit of force she exerted acted out several times stronger than it should've been. Dancing with the White Queen was like being pulled along by a hurricane pretending to be a breeze. She'd give my hand a gentle tug, and I'd glide after her.

Her intensity increased, and it felt like holding onto a giant pinwheel. The music followed her lead, picking up in tempo. The instruments quickened their pace again and, this time, the queen followed. It was like they were both building to a crescendo that would never come.

My body ached, and every sinew felt like sizzling meat.

The White Queen kept her eyes locked on mine the entire time. She kept the pacing up and showed no signs of slowing.

Periwinkle flashed at the edge of my vision. I focused on it and spotted Kelly. A gaggle of guests crowded her. Some were a bit too eager in seeking her attention for a dance. I wagered others wanted something more than just a waltz—like a meal. Some folks—paranormal or not—don't know how to take no for an answer.

The queen pulled again, and I felt like an elastic band about to snap towards her. I planted my feet, clenching my jaw as I resisted her tug. My heels dragged against the floor. "No."

"What?" Her mouth parted and her eyes lost their focus. She was genuinely confused. The queen kept pulling regardless.

My feet skidded across the floor. The juddering rolled through my ankles. I ground my shoes against the floor, fighting for traction as I pulled back. I stared her down.

She met my look and held it. "Interesting. Why?"

I gestured past her towards Kelly. "My friend."

The queen turned to regard the situation and opened her mouth into a silent "Ah." She faced me. "And? You brought the mortal here. Surely you did not think she would go unnoticed?"

"You're right, and I intend to bring her out of here. And I don't have an issue with her being noticed. My problem is what those freaks will do to her. I'm not a fan of the possibilities."

It felt like layers of plastic wrapped around me. My hearing dulled like I was submerged.

The queen's eyes narrowed. "Those freaks are my guests." She gave me another light pull.

I resisted. "And that girl is my friend. That trumps your paranormal circus."

Her hand slipped from mine, and the area above my wrist throbbed. She squeezed, making it feel like my arm was being crushed in five separate vice-grips. Each point of pressure felt like a cold bar lancing through my forearm.

I winced and fought to keep my knees from buckling. "Go ahead. Crush it. I'll heal."

"You're resilient—reckless."

My teeth ground. "Flatterer." I clenched harder. "Here's the thing: I know I can't overpower you. I know you've got me with that favor Lyshae gave you. I can't wriggle out of it. But you know what? I can fight. I can be a pain in your ass, Your Highness. Maybe it's not smart. Maybe you'll snap your fingers and freeze my borrowed ass. But it'll cost you. You'll be out a useful tool. And make no mistake, I am damn useful."

She tilted her head. "Oh?" The queen dug in with her nails, her grip tightening.

"Yeah." I gritted my teeth harder. The pain felt like frozen skewers going through skin, meat, and bone. "See, I figure it like this. If you didn't have even the slightest interest in keeping my favor, you would have tossed me aside in an instant. Why bother making me fight Skeletor?"

She stared.

"The wight."

The queen opened her mouth in silent recognition, waving a hand for me to continue.

Easier said than done when she was using her other hand to crush the bones in my forearm.

"You could have rejected Lyshae's gift. It's not like it would have hurt your reputation, only hers."

"Yes."

"So, why not do it? What do you need me for? Unless, you wanted someone who's part of the mortal world. Someone not bound by your rules, no allegiances to courts, lords and ladies. You wanted someone free of all that. Someone who can take a beating. And I'm not all that slow on the draw either. You're setting something up."

Her face was a frozen mask, but her eyes flickered with an amused light. "You are indeed quick. Yes. That was all for show. I do want you for something. But that time is long away. For now"—her grip tightened and my knees almost gave way—"it would be in your best interest to behave. Many of my guests are watching. I veiled this conversation."

Ah. That explained the plastic sensation. Veils could do more than obscure sight. They could blot out people listening.

It made sense. Hiding our scuffle from sight would have

been a clear indication something had gone wrong. That wouldn't have been good for her reputation. But muting the sound? At the most it probably looked like we had stopped dancing. Not counting the death grip on my arm.

"Let them watch." I stared daggers at her.

She returned the look. "Not wise."

Kelly's eyes were wide, and her skin paled. Random guests drew closer, working to corral her somewhere out of sight for who knows what.

"I'm not interested in being wise right now. Threaten me all you want, but you know who and what I am. I don't have much aside from this." I glanced at my body. "And this is temporary. The only thing I have—and for the record, they're rather new—is friends. I'm not letting anything happen to them. So, let go."

Her lips spread into a wide smile. "Lyshae did well in gifting me your favor. You will prove useful." The queen's fist clenched.

My knees failed me. The floor thudded against the bones as my arm felt like it'd been stripped by miles of twine.

I don't know how good the veil was. I hoped it kept my screams subdued. My throat felt like I'd gargled bits of glass and nails.

She released her hold and bent. "That was for disobeying me and making a scene before my guests."

I wanted to tell her to go screw herself. I managed a pained whimper instead.

Her smile grew, and she put a finger to my cheek. "It's a shame no one has laid claim to your soul. It would fetch quite the price. Maybe something still will. Maybe something will find a way to pry you free from your little suits. And, no, I do not mean this one." Her finger slid down my throat, reaching my collar until she dragged it to the middle of my chest. "Thank you for the dance."

The air expanded, giving the illusion that I had more room to breathe than before. My hearing fluctuated like I had plugged my ears and now they weren't.

The White Queen flashed me one last smile. Then she was gone.

There was no sign of movement, no visible magic. She

disappeared like I'd dreamed the entire thing up. I blinked away the welling moisture and pulled my sleeve up.

The area above my wrist was the color of blueberry on its way to becoming plum. I tried rolling my wrist. The action sent fireworks and a swarm of wasps through the area. It wasn't completely broken, just fractured. It'd heal.

I struggled to my feet and ignored the staring crowd.

Kelly looked past the guests, seeking a way out of the tightening net of bodies. She spotted me, and I saw relief flood her face.

I braced my good arm on my knee and hauled myself up to a shaky stand. Leaving my friends to these monsters was not an option. My teeth clamped until the only thing I could feel was the pressure through my jaw. I stumbled the first few steps before straightening my back and walking with poise. The pain refused to leave my mind.

Sometimes you have to work through the pain. It's more than a cliché. It's true. Things grow from attention. It's another form of power. Paying something attention is feeding it an awareness it can thrive on. Pain is no exception. I'm not saying you can simply forget about it. The aches, burning, and throbs will be there. But you can put them in a place where they can spur you on. And, if you do it right, they can give you something else to draw on for strength.

Angry resolve.

People say there's no power in anger. That it can be dangerous. They're right. But it depends what you do with it. Lashing out blindly can get a lot of people hurt, including yourself. I wasn't fueled by blind anger. I was angry—for Kelly. That she was stuck surrounded by gods and darker things.

I exhaled and slipped by the first guest comprising the semi-circle around her. The rest were a blur as my attention fixed on her. Stretching my mouth into a smile was a task, but I did it despite the pain. "Hey."

Her mouth trembled like she was fighting to remember how to speak. "H-hey."

I extended my good hand. "May I have this dance?"

She looked at me and then leaned to look past. "Yes. Thank you."

I glanced over my shoulder, flooding my voice with my anger and pain. "Beat it."

They didn't.

"Now!"

A few of the guests exchanged disgruntled looks and grumbles, but they left nonetheless. The handful who remained eyed me for a moment, each shooting me varying degrees of death looks.

"Go ahead. Start something, right here. Think our host is watching? Think she wants you messing with her new toy?" I smiled.

The lingering guests departed.

"Douche-coasters." I glared at them until I was certain they had no intention of returning.

Kelly sniffed, and her face shook like she was about to burst into laughter. "Do I want to know what that means?"

I shook my head. "Nah. Sometimes knowing is overrated. Ignorance is bliss."

She shook a bit more, pressing her lips tight to keep from letting loose. Kelly settled herself with a long breath. "Didn't you say knowledge is power?"

"Yup. But over something silly like this, let it go."

Kelly eyed me. "Did you just say that...in a palace belonging to a snow queen?"

I blinked several times and started, waiting for her to clarify.

"You mean, you haven't seen the movie?"

I kept staring.

"Oh, God." She put a hand to her mouth. "Never mind."

"Um, okay." I waggled my good hand.

She smiled and took it. Her gaze fell to my other hand. "What happened?"

I licked my lips and looked around on instinct. The White Queen was nowhere in sight. "Her Highness has one helluva a handshake. Don't worry, it'll heal with time."

"Thanks again, Vincent. I was..." She trailed off and looked to the ground.

I recognized the look as her stare went hollow and her mouth twitched in silence. Shame.

I traced my thumb over her hand. "Hey, what's up?"

"What's up? I'm freaking out—still." Her breathing picked up. "I'm surrounded by monsters and magic, and I don't have a clue what to do. I don't know what will happen if I say or do the wrong things. I don't even know what the wrong things are. I'm...I'm afraid." She made the word sound like a curse.

"I'm scared too, Kelly. And you know what? That's okay."

She looked at me like she wasn't sure if she could believe that.

"It's true. We're surrounded by supernatural creatures out of folklore and legend. Some of these things are gods and things far worse—trust me. Yeah, I'm freaking out, but I may not look like I am. That's the difference."

"How?" Her eyes held a silent plea that strengthened her question.

"By knowing it's okay to be afraid. I know I'm making it sound easier than it is, but don't go thinking it's a lot harder than it might be either. This world isn't normal. Heck, our world isn't so normal a lot of the time. Surprises happen; things scare us back there too. When those happen, what do you do? You give yourself permission to be scared. It's no different here."

Kelly looked past me, eyeing the crowd. "I kind of think it is."

She had a point, but I had one too. "Being scared is okay. It's a reminder you're human."

"That's what scares me here. Being human—normal— in a place where everything is a monster. You didn't see how they were looking at me." She shivered, pulling her hand from mine and hugging herself.

"I know, Kelly. I saw enough. For what it's worth, I'm sorry you had to experience that. But this is where we are. Nothing can change that, but you can change how you process it. Let yourself be scared, but don't let it stop you from doing what you have to. Being scared is natural, keeps you alive. Don't let it trap you though, Kelly."

"Yeah?" Her voice shook. "I'm open to suggestions on where to start."

I took her hand in mine again and tugged gently. "How about right here?" I took a step back, leading her into a slow, rhythmic, back-and-forth shuffle. It wasn't anything fancy. That wasn't the point. It'd keep her mind on something else.

Kelly tried to keep her eyes on me, but the allure of our surroundings and company proved to be too much. She glanced around us every few seconds. "It's a lot to process. They all look so normal, but—"

"They're not. I know. How do you want to process it?"

Her lids fluttered, and she faltered for a step. "I have a choice?"

"Sure you do." I led her into a small circle of easy footwork. "You always have a choice."

"I don't know. Things make sense, like math. It's logic, rules, numbers, and formulas. You plug things in and get results. It's not like that here."

I shook my head. "No. No, it's not. That's okay though. There are other rules, and, if you take the time, you'll learn 'em. You like having things add up. They won't always in here, but that doesn't mean you can't make sense of a lot of it. You're a blogger—a recorder, right?"

"Yeah?" She quirked a brow.

"Process it like that. Take it all in, take it all down, and make notes. Keep a journal for yourself. Works for me."

"Like an encyclopedia of the paranormal?" Kelly slowed and I could see her working through the notion.

"Exactly like one."

Her expression softened, and she looked, dare I say, at ease. "I think I can work with that." She smiled.

I returned it. "Glad to hear it. Change of subject. Ortiz. You see her around?"

Kelly gestured with her head.

I followed the direction to spot a flash of carnation.

The Daoine and Ortiz were locked in a fast-paced dance set to a different tune than the one being played in the hall. A large smile was plastered over her face.

I must've stared longer and harder than I thought because Kelly pulled on my hand. I turned to her.

"You just had this look on your face," she said.

"What kind of look?"

"Like your puppy died. You looked like you wished you were dancing with her."

My insides ached, and images of Daniel and Ortiz flashed through my mind. I suppressed them. "Yeah, it's part of the fine print with the job. I'm bumming Daniel's body. He had some strong feelings for her."

Kelly opened her mouth but said nothing.

A part of me—a part of Daniel, I wagered—didn't want to move on from speaking about Ortiz. I ignored that part. "You have any idea where our foxy invite went?"

Kelly stared past me and then gave me a knowing look.

My shoulders sank and I sighed. I glanced over my shoulder. Lyshae was several feet away and drawing closer. "Speak of the devil."

Lyshae rolled her eyes. "Now, now. Better the devil you know—"

"Than the one I don't? Like the one you sold me to." I glared at her.

She exhaled through her nose and mouth in a heavy huff. "Please, don't be so melodramatic. Besides, there are more than enough devils for you to deal with back in New York." A lopsided, self-satisfied smirk spread across her face.

I didn't have a clue what Lyshae meant by that. But it was clear she felt I should have gotten it. Perhaps she was toying with me. It's not as if it'd be a new thing for her..

Her smirk vanished as she eyed my injured arm. "What happened?"

"Our host." I held my glare.

"Vincent, for your own good, and—more importantly—mine, would you please stop angering the beings I need?"

I waggled a finger in admonishment. "It's not always about you and your needs. That's selfish."

"One of these days, Vincent, you will learn that a little selfishness is not a bad thing. It goes a long way."

"Like being a lady of the Neravene?" I eyed her.

Her smile made its way to her eyes. "See? You are learning. Exactly like that."

"Yeah, and in case you'd forgotten, those kind of power-plays always come with a cost. They always come back to bite you in your ass."

"Are you still sour over your debt being handed to the

White Queen?" She had the grace to give me a look of mock shame.

"Sour?" I was sure my eyes doubled in size as I gawked at her. "You traded me like I'm not worth a damn thing. Heck, don't you know regifting is rude?"

Lyshae's mouth hung open. She stared at me like she was caught between laughing and disbelief. "Vincent, the very reason I sold your debt to her is because you are worth something." She jabbed a finger into my chest. "Besides being useful as a blunt instrument, you are a soul."

My brain went blank, and I was certain my facial expression mirrored that.

"I thought you would have learned this by now. Everything is for sale. You would be surprised what can be bartered. Even you—what you are—is a commodity in this world. A valuable one, I'll have you know. What do you humans have to offer? Your bodies? Surely, they are worth something. But you, Vincent, you have something more precious." That uncomfortable, hungry light returned to her eyes.

"I resent that remark."

"No, Vincent, you resemble it. That is the point. You humans think your souls are something priceless. It is time you learned that nothing is sacred, and sometimes, the things you believe to be the most sacred of all—priceless— have a price indeed. Many are willing to pay it, sacrifice it for something else. Those who know how to cultivate that demand, even create it, can garner great power and fast." The light intensified to the point where I felt her eyes would start smoldering.

I gave her a sideways look that I hoped would temper her creepy, hungry stare. "Why do I have the feeling we're not just talking about what's happening here?" I made a circular motion with my hand to encapsulate our surroundings.

"I am talking about the Neravene and the mortal world. Do you understand?"

I didn't, but I didn't want to give that away. I nodded.

"They are linked. You know this. Mortals are among the most eager and foolish to embrace what the Neravene can offer. Their lives are fast and fleeting—driven by invisible leashes of impulse pulling them to their next desire. Emotion, not logic, rules their lives. It makes them...what is the word? Suckers."

My good hand balled into a fist.

Lyshae noticed it. "Vincent, after hearing all of what I said, now what do you think of souls? That is when you are really worth something. Your bodies decay. Your souls do not...entirely, at any rate."

What? My heart skipped before doubling in pace.

"That is why I am here. Because you had value to me. Two-fold. Your body for the White Queen's use and, your soul, in the event it comes to that." She gave me a smile that revealed her canines. "Remember that."

My teeth ground as I caught Kelly's look.

She'd been hanging onto Lyshae's every word and processing it. Her face said she was close to believing it. I wasn't going to let her.

My voice and the look I shot Lyshae could have extinguished the blue flames around the hall. "You're wrong, you know. We're worth more than that. Stick around, and I'll show you."

Lyshae took a step back and averted her gaze. "I think this party has gone on for too long. We should leave."

I arched a brow. "Oh, why?"

The familiar sensation of a veil surrounded me.

"Because I have robbed the White Queen."

Not how I wanted to die.

Chapter Twenty-Five

"You did what?"

Lyshae hissed and shot me a reproachful look. "Quiet, fool! I cannot veil our conversation long enough for you to calm down."

I bristled. "This is monumentally bad. Hell, throw in a heap of suicidally stupid as well."

Lyshae's eyes narrowed, and she looked around in panic. "Are you quite done?"

"No..." I trailed off as I realized why she was looking around.

The Kitsune had veiled us from sight as well. Something that, ironically, would not go unnoticed. A party of paranormal beings and gods take note when some of the guests pull a Houdini and vanish.

It's frowned upon. There's no end of skullduggery one could get up to if they disappeared. It meant many of the guests would be working to take down her veil...possibly listen in.

If any of them heard what Lyshae had done.

Oh, crap.

The next instant, the air seemed to pull away from me. Lyshae's veil had been torn from around us.

"Whoa, where did you two go?" Kelly looked between us.

I swallowed and ignored her question. If we had reappeared, someone was behind it.

"They were having a conversation—in private, it seems." The White Queen seemed to appear out of thin air. She stared at Lyshae and me, her lips spreading into a smile. "What about, I wonder?"

I bit my tongue to keep from mouthing something witty that'd get me killed. "We were just leaving. The food here has given Kelly an upset stomach." I leaned towards the queen, putting a hand to the side of my mouth. "Between you and me, it's bad." I should have tried harder about keeping my mouth shut.

Lyshae's eyes widened like she wanted to hunt for a foxhole.

Kelly glanced at me, then the queen, catching on quick. "Yeah." She pressed a hand to her stomach. "I'm not feeling that great."

Bless you, kid.

I stepped back, taking her by the arm. "See? Poor gal. So, thanks for the grub and the dance. Five stars. Hospitality gets a three and a half on account of the wight and this." I waggled my damaged arm. "Can't win 'em all."

Lyshae used my blabbering to move from the scene. She wasn't as stealthy as she thought.

The queen blurred past us, stopping several feet ahead of the Kitsune.

Lyshae froze and exhaled a sharp huff.

The White Queen walked towards Lyshae in slow, measured steps. She placed a hand on Lyshae's shoulder, and the fox spirit quivered.

I'd never seen Lyshae intimidated like that. It spoke volumes about the queen. It said more about Lyshae's decision to rob her. The Kitsune wasn't stupid. Whatever she'd stolen must have been worth a lot, and not in the monetary sense. There wasn't much that appealed to the trickster. Money—she had tons of that.

Lyshae had dragged us here for a power grab. The thing about power is, there's always more up for a grab if you're willing to pay the price. Lyshae seemed willing.

So what did she steal?

The White Queen appeared to loom over the Kitsune. She flashed Kelly and me a look. "You two may leave. The little fox and I have something to speak about." A cruel slit of a smile spread across her face like a gash in a block of ice.

I almost felt sorry for Lyshae, then I remembered what she'd done, and I got over it. "Well, you girls have a nice talk. I'll be taking my friends and going." I smiled at Lyshae.

Her look was a silent plea. It stopped me in my tracks.

I shut my eyes and exhaled in resignation. When I opened them, Ortiz and the Daoine were walking towards us.

The pair had enough sense and caution to stop several feet away from Lyshae and the queen's conversation.

The faerie bodyguard appraised the situation and stepped towards the pair. He addressed the queen without making eye contact. "What's happening here?"

One of the queen's brows twitched, as did a corner of her mouth.

"Oh Queen and host." The Daoine gave her an apologetic look.

"The newly risen Lady Lyshae and I are going to have a talk. I've given your party leave but for her, of course." The queen looked to Lyshae.

The Daoine bobbed his head in acquiescence. "Of course. We should be leaving then." He turned to Ortiz without pausing to give Lyshae a second look.

Damn. Talk about loyalty. Then again, the Daoine gave the impression that he was under a deal much like mine. Doesn't make a guy sympathetic to the woes of a tricky fox spirit.

It was highly unlikely the White Queen would kill Lyshae. If she meant to talk, that's exactly what would happen. That meant Lyshae would walk away, and walk away pissed. She'd remember who left her ass to hang and who didn't.

The Kitsune had me on a few debts. I doubted she'd let me go, but if I played this right, she'd remember that I came to her aid. I could cash that in somehow.

Two can play when it comes to brokering deals and earning favors.

I moved towards the queen and Lyshae. "Ladies, I'm sure what you two have to talk about is important, but do you mind if I borrow Lyshae for just a few moments?" I gave the queen my best smile.

I'd seen more emotion in frozen patches of sidewalks than the look the White Queen gave me.

"I would mind, awfully, as a matter of fact."

My smile slipped at the thought of irking the queen further.

The queen dug her nails into Lyshae's shoulder, causing the Kitsune's legs to quake.

I don't know what possessed me to rush to the Kitsune's side. "Stop!"

The White Queen did. Her fingers flexed and straightened, leaving Lyshae's shoulder. She gave me a flat look. "Excuse me?"

"You made your point. Lyshae can't leave. You want to have a girl-to-girl talk, got it. You don't have to hurt her to get the point across. We all got it." I showed her my injured arm. "You're powerful. All your guests know it. No need to rub it in our faces."

Her eyes narrowed, and I got the feeling another piece of me might end up fractured. "Be careful, Little Spirit."

I reached out with my good arm, sliding it around Lyshae's waist to help brace her. "If whatever you have to say can't wait, then say it here and now, in front of all of us."

The White Queen gave me a look that could've made a sauna feel like an ice bath.

"Very well." The queen leaned forwards, keeping her eyes on Lyshae. "I know what it is you took."

Oooh boy. My heart felt like it had somersaulted and failed to right itself.

Lyshae's body went taut in my grip.

"I am inclined to let you keep it, Lyshae." Her voice was disturbingly flat and hollow.

Lyshae's ears twitched, and her lips trembled. "At what cost?"

"One that I choose." The queen smirked. "Perhaps none. Perhaps you are trading one mistress for another." She gave Lyshae a knowing look.

A flood of questions raced through my mind.

Lyshae nodded and muttered a thanks that I almost didn't hear.

The queen stepped back. "Now, you may leave. I advise you do so before your theft is discovered by the party that gifted it. It would not do to anger another power in the Neravene tonight, Little Fox."

I looked at the pair before settling my gaze on the queen. "You know you said that aloud, right?"

Both women flashed me a look that said I was an idiot.

"Explain it to him, will you?" The queen waved a hand at Lyshae before turning to leave.

"She veiled us, Vincent. From sight. From sound. One that I didn't even notice until she had dropped it."

I let out a low whistle. "How about we follow her advice and get out of here before you tick off anyone else, huh?"

"Yes, thank you, Vincent. Things could have gotten unpleasant."

I pointed to my discolored arm. "Too late. More moving. Less talking." I led the way, beckoning the others to follow as I headed towards the way out.

The Daoine and Ortiz moved to the outside of our party, sandwiching us between them. They did have the best sense of awareness. It was a smart move on their part.

I picked up my pace, keeping my gaze fixed on the exit alone. A small prickle atop my left forearm almost forced me to look down. I ignored the impulse, but a part of brain refused to let go.

Just how much time have I lost?

I shook my head clear and passed out of the castle. A quick glance over my shoulder showed me my friends had made it through without issue. I breathed a sigh of relief.

Ortiz led Kelly away from the paranormal members of our group and came a few feet from my side.

Lyshae and the Daoine stopped in front of me. The former stared at me and then over her shoulder into the castle.

"Well, that was mildly unsettling." Lyshae fanned herself with a hand, downplaying the torrent of anxious thoughts I imagined rushed through her skull.

"Yeah, that's one way to put it. You robbed a freaking Queen of the Neravene. She's going to take it out of your ass, you know?" I cast an unwary look at the castle as well.

"Vincent, please keep my ass out of your thoughts. Besides, it is not anything I cannot handle." Her voice shook just a note near the end.

My eyes narrowed. "Of course you can. But...in the off chance you can't, remember my debts are tied to you. If you go down, I get handed over to another of your contingency debt holders. Kind of tacky if you ask me. I'm not big into being shared."

Lyshae gave me a weak smile.

"So, what is it? Spill."

Ortiz stepped up, staring between Lyshae and me. "Robbed?" Her gaze settled on Lyshae and hardened.

Lyshae flashed Ortiz the same weak smile. "It sounds worse than it is."

"What. Did. You. Take?" I took a step towards her.

The Kitsune's shoulders sagged as she exhaled. "Show them."

Her Daoine attendant stepped between us and reached into a pocket in his pants. He withdrew a box the size of a deck of playing cards.

It was made from what looked like white oak, unnaturally smooth and clean. Endless, flowing script covered every inch of its surface in an archaic language I couldn't make out. Some of the lettering bowed and scrolled across the surface.

I blinked before leaning forwards and squinting. "The lettering moved." I looked up to Lyshae. "What the hell is that? Who did you steal it from, really?"

Lyshae's smile morphed into something more authentic. She seemed pleased with herself. "That, Vincent, is something I need. We will leave it at that. As for whom I procured it from..." She left the answer unsaid.

I scowled.

"But I'm not wholly unappreciative of what you did back there for me. Remember what I told you about prices and power. About a soul's worth and how people are all too willing to give them over."

"Okay? Why?" I tilted my head, glancing at the box and then her. I couldn't work out if there was a connection between the box and what she meant.

"Because I pay my debts, however small. And you could use a clue." She winked and waved her hand.

A stream of flurries followed her gesture, coalescing into a thick wall. Crystal clear water trickled from the top of the formation as most of it solidified. The water ran to the center where it stopped and twisted like a stopper being pulled from a filled tub.

I let out a low whistle. "I thought you said you couldn't open Ways here. Holding out on me?"

Lyshae laughed. "Hardly. And you are right. You cannot

open Ways to get here, and most cannot open Ways out. It just so happens I have recently become elevated in stature." She exhaled through her nose, and her lips spread into another smile. "I can open a Way out."

"Yeah, I noticed." I arched a brow and eyed her. "How? This going to take us through a path or plop us back somewhere of your choosing?"

She held her smile. "Somewhere of my choosing."

Great.

Lyshae motioned at the Way. "After you, Vincent."

I didn't have much choice, not if I wanted to get back to my case. I hoped I still had enough time left to get to the bottom of it.

I passed through the Way.

* * *

The men's bathroom in the bar came into view with the accompanying aroma of industrial cleaner. At least someone had gone through the place in our absence and rid it of its previous odor.

A small patch of skin on my left forearm flushed with heat.

I glanced at the reddened area and swore.

Ortiz exited the Way in time to hear my curse and looked at me. "What's wrong?"

I held up my arm.

She sucked in a breath. "That long?"

"Seems like." Forty-five hours had remained when I'd confronted Lyshae in the bar. Our meet-and-greet session had cost me thirteen hours. Only thirty-two remained.

My teeth ground. A little less than a day and a half left. It'd have to be enough.

Kelly popped out next and wobbled over the floor. Her arms went to her sides to help grant some balance. "Diving in and out of those things in heels should be an Olympic sport. Not easy."

I snorted, and Ortiz shook her head trying to stifle a laugh.

Lyshae and her Daoine exited last. Her faerie boy-toy

carried a familiar set of bags over a shoulder.

He eyed me and inclined his head. "Your clothes." The bags fell unceremoniously to the floor.

"Uh, thanks. When did you grab those?" I looked from the bags to him.

Kelly didn't wait for his response. She gave him a look asking the silent question as to which was hers. When he gave her a quiet nod to the bag, she snatched it and marched into the nearest stall. A near retching sound emanated from within a second later.

"Oh my God! What is wrong with some men?"

I buried my face in my hands as she flushed.

The toilet sounded, followed by a string of muttering.

I laughed a bit harder and snatched up my bag, heading to the stall beside Kelly's.

It was easy slipping out of the ruined portions of my clothes. I let them fall to the floor without a care as the stall to my left banged shut. Ortiz, I wagered. Within a handful of minutes, I'd slipped into what I'd been wearing before. There was something comforting about the clothes.

I exited the stall and frowned when I saw the paranormal pair standing there. My gaze fell to Lyshae. "Still here?"

"For a moment. I wanted to wish you luck on your case. Do your best not to die. I will have further need of you."

My frown morphed into a scowl. "So long as you get your use out of me, it's all good, right? Never mind the fact people are getting hurt here." I waved an arm to my side.

She shrugged. "That is none of my concern. I've done what I can for you. If you are too dense to realize it...so be it. You have no idea what you are dealing with, Vincent. The sooner you put it together, the better for you and those involved." Lyshae clapped her hands twice. "Chop-chop, I believe?"

I bristled and restrained myself from taking a step closer. My thoughts turned to everything I could recall on my case, and most of it added up. There were a few holes. One stuck out more than the rest.

"Before you go, I need to know something."

She lowered her head a fraction.

"Two Night Runners attacked Ortiz and me. They

literally came in guns blazing after trying to wreck us in a car accident."

"They succeeded in the car part!" Ortiz's voice echoed within the stall.

I hooked a thumb in her direction. "Yeah, that."

Lyshae arched a brow. "I'm not hearing a question."

"Having goons jump me in the dark and out of sight fits you. Two fae gunning for us on a contract? Not your style. So, who's behind that?"

Her eyes smoldered, and she stared at me.

I bit down on my lower lip. "If it's not you, then it's what I'm hunting, isn't it?"

The light in her eyes grew, followed by a satisfied smile.

"Okay, fine. That means there is some manner of payment up for grabs. They didn't say cash. I doubt Night Runners have much use for money. So..." I trailed off when I noticed Lyshae's stare growing deeper and hungrier.

"Oh, holy crap." I shook my head, and my jaw ached as I pieced more of it together. "All that talk about debts and payment. That's what this is about? That's what's going on here too? That's what's up for grabs if something takes me out, right? Someone gets a big honkin' favor?"

Lyshae tapped an index finger to her nose. "Something like that."

Something like that but not quite, huh? It wasn't enough to give me the answer I needed. But, if I was smart about what I did next, it'd help narrow things down.

"So, how are they collecting these favors or power?"

The Kitsune chose to remain silent.

I stepped towards her and reached out.

A hand of cold iron clamped around my good arm and squeezed.

I gritted my teeth and glared at the Daoine. "Back in the Neravene, you were willing to ditch her. Now you're protecting her?"

He gave me a lopsided grin.

Self-serving bastard.

"It's quite alright. Let him go." Lyshae placed a hand on the Daoine's arm, gently pushing against it.

He released his grip.

I shook my hand and kept my eyes on the Kitsune.

"Give me something, please?"

She shook her head. "I've given you enough. I like you, Vincent. But there's only so much I'm willing to do, even for you. This is something you need to figure out. If you can't put it together, then you're not going to be of much use to me come the future." Lyshae turned and walked towards the door with her Daoine in tow.

A ring of pain flared around my injured hand as I tried to ball it into a fist. My fingers hesitated before complying. At least I was getting some movement back, even if it came with a cost. A door slammed to my side, prompting me to turn.

Ortiz stood dressed in her earlier attire.

"You hear all of that?"

She put her hands on her hips and nodded. "What's our next move?"

Kelly exited her stall a second later, back in her normal clothes as well. She had a bag over her shoulder and fixed me with the same look Ortiz wore: the look of wanting answers.

I blew out a breath through my nose and let the weight sink from my shoulders. "Honestly, I'm not sure. I feel stretched in too many directions." My good hand fell over my face as I rubbed, sighing into my palm.

"Well"—Ortiz pursed her lips—"we have a victim we could pay a visit to, if he's in a stable condition and a talking mood."

A flicker of hope surged through me.

Milo had been injured when the paramedics took him and his mother. The burns had looked severe, not fatal though. There was a chance he, or his mother, had seen something—knew something.

"Good point. That's why they pay you the big bucks."

Ortiz scoffed and rolled her eyes. "You haven't seen a government salary paycheck recently, have you?"

Ouch.

"If it makes you feel any better, I don't get paid a dime." I gave her a weak smile.

She shook her head, pressing her lips together to keep from smiling. "It takes the sting off a bit. Alright, let's head back, grab my car, and we can visit the hospital."

A clap filled the small bathroom.

I turned to its source, eyeing Kelly. "Something to share with the class, or are you just feeling the Holy Spirit?"

She ignored my quip. "I forgot to tell you what I found out about Daniel's neighbors."

Ortiz and I exchanged a look before turning back to her.

"They're all recent move-ins into the complex—"

I waved a hand, cutting her off. "I already got an inkling of that earlier."

Her brows knitted together, and her eyes narrowed. "But, uh, go on."

"They've all filed for taxes as independent businesses." Kelly made it sound like it was important. For the borrowed life of me, I couldn't see how.

"Okay? That means?"

She rolled her shoulders and had the grace to look at the floor before turning back to me. "I don't know. You're supposed to be the detective."

I opened my mouth to reply, but Ortiz held up a hand. I shut my cakehole and waited.

Ortiz tilted her head and gave Kelly a stare I was sure she used when interrogating criminals. "How exactly did you come across their tax records?"

Kelly's cheeks flushed, and her body quivered. "Well, you know, people leave those things lying around on the web." She looked to me for help.

Ortiz didn't turn around, but I had the feeling she was shooting me a glare anyway.

I looked away from Kelly and towards the rather interesting grout between the tiles.

Seconds passed before Ortiz relented with a heavy sigh. "Please don't make me arrest you, Kelly. I like you."

"Got it." Kelly rubbed her index finger against her nose and looked to the ground again. "Next time, I'll just lie."

I snickered and threw my hand over my mouth to muffle it.

Ortiz turned slowly to stare at me. "Start walking. Car. Hospital."

"Yeah." I buried the laughter, but it still filled most of my face. "Sure thing." The last traces of amusement left my face as I made my way to the door. My elbow bumped into it, sending it open. I planted myself against it, holding it open for my friends.

Ortiz and Kelly exited the bathroom, taking the lead out of the bar and to the car. I had to jog a few steps to fall in behind them. We exited Lyshae's establishment.

Night had fallen over Queens while we were away. The perfect time of day for monsters to come out and play. The idea caused a tremor in the pit of my stomach as I made my way over to Kelly's Camaro.

I cut in front of the women, gesturing with my injured arm. "Dibs up front. I'm handicapped." I smirked.

Ortiz shook her head in resignation. "Fine, baby."

I stuck my tongue at her and made my way over to the passenger's side.

Kelly unlocked the vehicle and fell into her seat.

Because I'm a gentleman, I bent and folded my seat forwards, gesturing for Ortiz to slip in behind me.

She clambered in and fastened her belt. "What would I do without you?" Her voice was dry.

I snapped the seat upright and wriggled into it. "Most likely get your butt kicked by monsters." My seat juddered while I fumbled for my seatbelt.

Kelly spun in her seat, glaring at me then Ortiz. "Behave, kids." She turned her gaze back to Ortiz. "No kicking my seats." Her gaze returned to me. "No antagonizing the other passengers."

Ortiz and I mumbled half-apologies.

"Good." A smile of self-satisfaction spread over Kelly's face as the car thundered to life with the snarling percussion only a V8 could produce. The vehicle snorted as it lurched forwards and snapped into the lane with the sort of torque you'd expect from a muscle car.

The fingers of my right hand felt like grains of sand tumbled through them. Every imagined piece sent a tingle through the area. I shuddered and winced, closing my hand tight. It hit me a second later.

I flexed my fingers and stared at my arm. It looked like someone with a particularly strong grip had grabbed me. That had been the case, but the only signs were slight bruising. My lips went tight, and I shut my eyes in anticipation as I rolled my wrist.

The injured limb twanged like it had been sprained, but nothing more. It was functional again.

Kelly urged the car down the street at a speed that wasn't legal by any standard. She slowed just enough to round the corner without losing control of the backend.

I yelped and leaned into the door, reaching up with my healed hand to cling to support. "Holy shit, slow down!"

"We're pressed for time, aren't we?" Kelly looked to my tattoo before turning her eyes back to the road.

"Time's irrelevant if you get into a smoldering car accident. What's this thing made out of anyways"—I kicked the glove box to make a point—"fiberglass?"

"Feet off my car!" Kelly glared at me. One of her hands jerked, causing the wheel to snap to one direction. The car followed.

Rubber screeched in agonized protest as it fought for grip against the street.

I sucked in a breath, and Ortiz muttered a curse.

Kelly righted herself, both hands going to the wheel as she reined the vehicle back under control.

I let out a wheeze that sounded like a broken vacuum. "Jeez. I'll keep my feet off the dash if you keep your eyes on the road and don't pull another Ortiz." My head snapped forwards and the small of my back ached as my seat shook. I twisted, glancing over my shoulder.

Ortiz sat with her legs crossed, eyeing me like she wished she could have kicked something more than just the seat.

I made a childish face at her.

Kelly's face tightened as her lips pulled into a frown. It didn't last. Her body shook and she broke into laughter. "I swear, you're both kids. One second you're fighting monsters and helping me unfreeze, then you're fighting each other."

I grinned and had a feeling Ortiz did the same behind me. "That's the thing about fighting monsters though. Sometimes you need to fall back and have a laugh. If you don't, things can get pretty dark. You have to enjoy the bits in between the long, dark patches. Otherwise, what's the point? Laugh a little when you can; it won't kill you." I widened my grin and shot Kelly a wink.

"Good advice," she said.

"I've been known to spit some words of wisdom."

Ortiz sounded like she'd choked on her own laughter.

Smartass.

The atmosphere changed after that. The air felt a bit more spacious and there was a faint hint of hanging electricity—the good kind. All it would take was something mildly funny to set us off again.

Sometimes life isn't lived in the hectic moments of doing things. Sometimes it's lived in the moments between all the noise and commotion. It's in the quiet times where you can just sit back and be with friends. The moments where noise is silent, and something else takes its place. Something like laughter.

It's one of those things I never get to enjoy as much as I should.

Hunting a monster with Kelly and Ortiz towing along reminded me of that.

My forearm prickled. I glanced at it. Thirty-one hours left.

Laugh when and as much as you can because time has a way of slipping away from you.

Kelly brought the Camaro around the corner and onto the street where Daniel lived. Her foot came off the accelerator halfway down the block, letting the car roll to a halt on its own. She left it running as I unbuckled myself and swung out of the door.

Ortiz bent over, fumbling for the lever to drop the passenger seat. She scrambled out a few seconds later and glowered at me.

I shrugged, hitting the sidewalk hard and making my way towards her mangled car. My right hand seemed functional enough to warrant a test. I made a fist and rapped my knuckles against the rear passenger side window.

Ortiz huffed as she pulled open the driver's door, unlocking the others as well. "What happened to riding up front?"

I gestured to the coat on her back seat. My journals lay hidden beneath it along with the weapons we'd confiscated from the Night Runners.

"Think you can figure out what we're after now that you've been around the block a bit?" There was a hint of expectancy in her voice. She wanted for me to have the answers. Even if I didn't share them with her, as long as I had something—a plan—that would have been fine with her.

I hated the idea of disappointing her again.

My mouth spread wide almost on default. "'Course. I've got a good idea of where to start."

In truth, I had half a decent notion. Part of an idea is better than none at all.

My fingers closed around the windbreaker. I tugged it free, slipping into it before patting the sides where my journals rested. Snagging the shotgun was tempting, but it would be more of a hindrance than anything else.

Hospital employees frown upon people toting weapons in their workplace.

I stepped away from the door, shoving it shut with the heel of my palm.

Ortiz started the car, lowering the windows and turning on the headlights. "Get in."

My hand was on the handle when the muscles in my lower back knotted like a spasm. I shuddered through it and blinked.

Time leaves an impression. Do something over and over at the same time of day, and it ends up ingrained in you. A part of you syncs up with that. Your body remembers.

Something about that moment triggered a tug in the back of Daniel's mind.

"You going to stand there all night? Get in." Ortiz leaned over and opened my door for me.

The tug became a noose, pulling my attention to the building behind me. I looked up at the apartment complex. Pale yellow lights dotted the brick building.

My fingers drummed against the car's door panel. "You know what? Go on without me and keep an eye on Kelly."

A moment of quiet passed between us.

"What are you going to do?"

I turned back to face her. "I think it's time I stopped by and checked out movie night."

"Be careful. So far everyone harmed or targeted has been a resident of this place. Daniel..." Ortiz stopped and vinyl squeaked as her fingers tightened against the wheel. "Milo. Whatever we're dealing with has it out for people in Daniel's life."

The lining of my throat felt like frozen flecks of glass. Swallowing hurt. I did it anyway and fixed Ortiz with a knowing look. "That means you too."

Her mouth pulled into a thin smile. "I know."

I sighed. There wasn't much of a choice. Splitting up put all of us in danger, but if we didn't cover enough ground and get answers fast enough, more people would die. There wasn't any question about that.

That didn't make it any easier to swallow. If something happened to Ortiz again, it'd be on me. She was more than capable of handling herself. But the paranormal world had no guarantees. Even with my experience and knowledge, monsters still managed to get the drop on me at times. And it only takes that one creature to do it right.

"You've got this look on your face."

I pulled out of my trance and stared at her.

"I never saw it on Daniel's face, but I've seen you pull it on the other guys before. You're debating about letting me go it alone." There was a hint of stone in her voice. She wasn't angry, but something about my look had bothered her.

"It crossed my mind. You made it clear it's not my call and you're right. Doesn't mean it sits easy with me."

"Likewise. Think how I feel. You're about to go into a room where there might be a monster. A monster that—for the record—killed my friend. It's dangerous, Vincent. In my job, I don't let people walk into danger. I'm supposed to keep them safe." Something in her voice sent waves through my body. It was like hearing clear, ringing brass dull and lose its tone.

Nobody walks in and out of this life without scars. Ortiz was earning hers. I hated that.

I shut my eyes for a second and exhaled. "I hear you. So let's do something about it? Get to the hospital. Check up on Milo and find out what you can. I'll see what I can find here and we'll meet back at Daniel's place soon as possible."

She inclined her head in a silent yes.

I stepped away from the car, waving as she put the car in drive and pulled out. Time may have been pressing, but I stood fixed to spot and watched the car until the taillights passed out of sight.

Seeing the car vanish did something to the air. It wasn't cold, but a wave rolled over my body that made me give the windbreaker a tight pull.

Right. Nothing to it.

I made my way into the complex and up the stairs. A mantra rang through my head reminding me that this was simple. All I had to do was pay a visit to some of Daniel's neighbors. We'd do nothing more than enjoy a movie and some food in an enclosed space.

It just so happened that any one of the guests could be a monster.

I came to Ashton's apartment door. One hand fell to the handle while the other tapped against the door just loud enough to be heard over a movie.

The handle jostled and the door cracked open. White light flashed through, strobing in the dark room.

Somebody screamed.

I hate it when the monsters start the party without me.

Chapter Twenty-Six

Years of monster-hunting took hold, and my leg came off the ground. I twisted and pistoned my heel into the door.

It crashed back, meeting with resistance as it thunked against the person behind it.

I barreled through the gap and came to an abrupt halt.

A shrill scream cut through the room again.

I turned to the flashing projector screen then to the group of people seated on the lengthy sofa who eyed me like I was there to rob them. My hands went into the air in a silent apology as I turned to the guy on the floor.

Ashton lay on his side, clutching his left arm and staring at me like I was nuts. "What the hell?"

I cast another look around the room. "Uh, sorry. Long day. Uh, lots of art stuff. Fumes. I heard screaming and panicked."

Ashton ran his hands over his chest, smoothing out the rumpled dark shirt. He scrambled to his feet and dusted off his gray sweatpants. "Were you making with the paint or sniffing it?" His face broke into a wide grin, and he ran a hand through his hair while extending the other.

I took it and squeezed. "No hard feelings, right?"

He shook his head and stepped towards a small kitchen island in the corner of the room.

His apartment was the same size as Daniel's and should've been crowded, but he made the lack of space work for him. The seating was broken into two long sofas large enough accommodate a decent gathering of friends. A pile of cushions lay scattered on the floor, some resting under the bottoms of other guests.

Most of the remaining furniture was sleek, metal, and polished. Nearly everything was tucked away if not in use. A table sat folded in half to my left. It was an efficient setup.

Ashton plucked a whiskey glass from the island and filled it with a fizzing orange soda. "You look beat, man. You okay?" He nodded to a spot over my shoulder.

I followed his look and found myself staring at Daniel's face. The skin under his eyes looked thin and darkened. His hair was disheveled. His mug looked peaky.

My gaze stayed fixed on the mirror. A citrus scented candle burned on the board below it. Its waning fire cast a tint on the mirror's reflection. A tint that worsened as Ashton came into view through it.

His skin seemed to pull tight—gaunt—like it was nothing more than a flimsy mask. The whites of his eyes carried the fire's glow.

I sucked in a breath and pulled away from the mirror.

Ashton nudged me with his elbow. "What's up? Look like you saw a ghost." He passed me the drink.

I accepted it and took a swig. "I thought I did too."

His brows pulled together, and he looked at me like I wasn't making sense. "Right, well, come on." He led the way to the couch and bent to retrieve a thin remote sitting on the arm rest. With a push of his thumb, he paused the movie.

I stopped a few feet from the sofa and took in all the faces I could.

A woman sat at the end of the couch closest to Ashton. Her hair was the platinum blonde that pop stars went for and worn past her chin. She reminded me of plump, mother-like figures on cooking channels. The screen glow cast enough light on her face to bring out some red in her pale cheeks. She looked closer to her forties if I had to guess.

Ashton cleared his throat, drawing the attention of the room. "So, now that we're almost all here."

Almost. Someone was missing.

"I figure this might be the closest we get to a full party. With that, has everyone heard what happened to Milo?"

The rest of the guests murmured in agreement.

"Seems like a good time to wish him well and for a speedy recovery, right?" He looked around at everyone in the room.

A chorus of well wishes filled the air, and I joined in.

Ashton waved me over, and I heeded the summon. "I

know it's been a while since you've come to one of these, especially since the gallery's been picking up in traffic and sales. You're a busy man."

I guess I was.

"Yeah." I gave a mild shrug. There wasn't much else to do.

"There are some new faces, recent move-ins that you haven't bumped into...or cared to." There was a hint of accusation in his voice.

"Like you said, I'm busy."

"Always make time for your friends. Come on." He grabbed me by the elbow and led me closer to the group. Ashton prodded a young woman on the floor with the tip of his foot. "Get up. Say hi. It's rude to chill on my floor and not introduce yourself."

The "rude" woman pulled her knees to her chest and bound to her feet in an impressive display of athleticism. She had dark hair pulled into a single tail. Her clothing was loose and functional but showed off her fit physique. She'd earned her tan naturally, no doubt, from spending time outdoors. She could have been featured on a fitness magazine.

I held out my hand. "Daniel."

She gave me a smile that reached her brown eyes. "Ariel."

We traded grips.

"What do you do?"

"I'm an artist, you?"

"Fitness vlogger."

I blinked. Again with the internet things. "I get the first half of that."

Ariel laughed. "I run a web channel teaching healthy cooking and home workouts you can do on a budget to get in shape."

My mouth fell open, but I didn't have a response.

But someone else did.

The perky, plump blonde on the couch snickered. She tilted her head, her lips pressing tight as she fixed Ariel with a look of contempt. "If you call that cooking, and I don't."

You can feel it when there are two different temperature extremes. The blonde woman's voice was hateful-cold, like being caught in a subzero winter in your undies. Her look was arctic daggers.

Ariel cocked her head like she'd been slapped. "Whatever you say, fat ass." Her tone was a hot fire poker pressed to flesh. Sizzling heat.

The blonde placed her hands on the couch, shoving herself to a shaky stand. Pearls shook around her neck like glistening orbs caught in the screen's glare. She jabbed a thick finger towards Ariel. "I'm sorry. Isn't my show doing better than yours? Which one of us makes more money again?"

Show? A countdown went off in my head. Milo ran a freelance repair center out of his home. Ariel was a one-woman health channel. And the snooty blonde sounded like she was in a similar business—likely cooking—given her jab at Ariel.

Three for three in the same line of work. Kelly had said that everyone had filed as some form of freelancer. It didn't mean much, but that didn't mean it meant nothing either.

Occam's razor. I was overly complicating things. Everyone had one thing in common. A single thread. I just needed to pull on it and see what unraveled.

Light flooded the room, and the women's conversation paused.

Ashton stood near the door, putting a hand to his mouth as he cleared his throat. "Alright, movie night's on hold for obvious reasons. Things are getting a bit heated. Maybe we should take a break, chill, eat some food?"

I had to give it to him; he was good at defusing situations. Likely a talent he'd acquired working at the hospital. Not an easy job.

I thought on it and crossed him off my list of suspects. Daniel and Ashton were the only two who had jobs requiring them to leave their home. If anything, it made them easier targets—exposed. Not that the confines of an apartment made one safer. Milo was proof of that. One thing still nagged me. Daniel's finances had turned around too fast for my liking. He'd gone from struggling entrepreneur to successful quick enough to be suspect. It seemed to be the trend.

Something fit about that theory; I just wasn't sure what

yet.

Instincts aren't something to be discounted though. The brain's an amazing machine, processing and filing away more than we could ever pay conscious attention to. There's a part of us working away in the background, sorting through it and tossing us the bits we can use.

I jumped in to make the best of the new situation. "You heard our host. Let's break it up, ladies." I flashed them the best smile I could and stepped between them.

Both women exchanged a glare before stepping off to opposite corners of the room. A small relief.

I turned my attention to a rake of a man sitting next to where the plump blonde had been. He had the look of a young Hispanic man somewhere in his twenties. His hair was a curly, dark mess that looked like it needed a salon-grade shampoo. A thin, wiry patch of hair made its way across his face and wasn't filling in properly. It made him look younger than he actually was. More prepubescent than adult.

He shifted uncomfortably on the cushions. The young man gave both women a squirrelly look of anxiety that they didn't notice. He likely feared getting caught up in the drama.

I moved over to the spot left open by the uppity blonde and plunked down. "Hey."

My new pal turned to me and thrust his chin up in a simple hello.

Everything in sight slid away to be replaced by another scene.

Sunlight came down in a pale glow too weak for it to be the afternoon. A small, white, round table stood outside an old brick building. Two men sat across from each other in cheap, plastic folding chairs. The man opposite me was the same sitting on Ashton's couch. It looked like a nice lunch out between friends. A name came with the vision.

So did a feeling like thumbtacks pressing into the space behind my eyes. I winced, and something wet rippled against the skin below my lids.

"You okay, Dan?"

I shook my head and rubbed my palms against my eyes. "Yeah, Eddie, I'm great. Bad headache. Too many hours working, you know?"

He leaned back and nodded. "Tell me 'bout it. The radio show and site are killing me. I'm spending more time in a chair than is good for me." He shut his eyes and reached to massage his lower back. Eddie's complaining intensified, making him sound like a caffeinated squirrel.

I tuned most of it out. Another person made my list of freelancers.

"Diagnosing and fixin' cars over audio calls and comment posts ain't easy. Half the time I'm puttin' up preventive measures so I don't have to bother so much with fixes."

I grunted in agreement. "You don't get out much, do you?"

He shook his head. "Not anymore. When I started, yeah. I was working a day job as a simple lube tech. Oil changes all day. My business was shit. Luck's a funny thing though. Boom"—a slap rang out as his fist struck an open palm—"my site exploded."

I stared. "Just like that? Overnight?"

"Yeah, man. I know my stuff. Good stuff always finds a way to the top. Remember that."

I didn't know much about making a living as a single-man business, but it didn't seem that easy. Random strokes of luck resulting in overnight successes were rare. Too rare for it to be coincidence.

Dammit, Graves.

Favors. Lyshae hadn't dragged me all the way to that ball for the power trip and trading me off. It was about everything happening there and here. While she was working her way up in the Neravene, something was working their way up in the mortal world. That thought couldn't have sat well with her. Not after she'd worked and risked her butt climbing up the ladder. Nothing sucks like getting promoted and finding out you've got competition.

Lyshae wanted me to figure out my case, despite her nonchalant attitude. All the talk and hints about trading favors, costs, and power. The people here were doing a little quid pro quo for some kicks in their personal lives. And with those kinds of deals, the cost's always high. People were paying with their lives.

But what did the paranormal party get out of that? What favors could a bunch of mortals do for a monster?

A lot of the paranormal crowd were bound by rules preventing them from directly interacting with the mortal world. Night Runners clearly weren't on that list. But the higher ups fit the bill. They could use a mortal on a leash to interfere on their behalf. I didn't see the endgame though.

My fingers flexed and knuckles cracked.

"Daniel." The voice pulled me from my theoretical musing.

I got to my feet without thinking.

The woman couldn't have been out of college long. Early twenties with a long, freckled face. Her hair was a mess of frizzy black springs that bounced with every shift of her head. She looked at me with a hint of hesitation.

Another rush of images flooded my mind. It was like a carousel of washed-out pictures moving too fast to see. I focused on what I could.

Daniel and the woman—Caroline—worked to hang a series of art on his gallery walls. Day turned to night on the streets of Queens, but the pair worked on. They sat cross-legged on wooden floors eating and laughing over what looked like Chinese takeout.

The scene broke apart like a clump of sand in water. A familiar hallway replaced it. Just outside Daniel's apartment.

Caroline was dressed like you'd expect of an artist. Simple olive pants stained in pastels and oils like they were a canvas. She wore a gray half-sleeve tee that was dusted in charcoal from artist's pencils, no doubt. The woman pressed herself against Daniel and leaned in.

Daniel didn't shy away. His hands slipped around her waist as he pulled her tight. Their lips brushed and stayed close. I felt my borrowed throat get warm. A cold rush of liquid menthol flooded Daniel's body and numbed my mind. The Daniel in the vision snapped rigid and pushed Caroline away, staring at her like she was a ghost. He pressed a hand to his head and held his other out to stop her advance.

Daniel gave her a look that was a solid "no" in any language. He grabbed the handle to his door and made his way inside. There was no effort to keep the door from slamming shut.

Cold.

My stomach felt like a dry towel wrung of all moisture. I thought Daniel had had a thing for Ortiz, but there he was kissing Caroline. He may have been dead, but I had to sit and pick up the tab for his guilt.

Feeling everything the original owners of the bodies do is a mixed blessing. It helps keep me grounded in being human, in remembering why I do my job. Other times, it sucks. It makes me wish I could be empty—free—and just hunt monsters.

People's problems complicate the job.

"Daniel?" Caroline's mouth spread into half-smile. It was a weak thing but carrying a bit of hope. A light glow made its way into her eyes. It was like looking into pools of watered-down brandy.

"Sorry. A lot going through my head right now."

She pursed her lips and looked away for a second. "I know. I feel the same. We haven't... It's been a while. I thought you stopped showing up to these because of what—" She broke off and shrugged.

I assumed she meant the kiss in the hall. It wasn't a subtle letdown.

"No, you're good—fine. I'm sorry."

She looked mollified by that. Her posture loosened. The baggy clothing she wore seemed to hang off her. If any more dried paint speckled her sleeveless shirt, it'd be passable as a Pollock work. She brushed her hands against her macaroon-colored canvas pants. It was a nervous gesture she repeated.

"Our last conversation ended abruptly." I rubbed the back of my neck and looked away. It was true.

"More like awkwardly."

"That too. How are things?"

Her face tightened. "You mean after I pulled my work from your gallery? Not good." She followed the comment with a bitter laugh. "Going solo online and on commission hasn't been great. I'm barely eking by."

Another freelancer. Something didn't add up. She hadn't had a lucky break. Caroline made it clear there was no wind of fortune on her side.

Maybe she hadn't made a deal with whatever I was

hunting.

She took a step closer, reaching out with an unsteady hand.

My nose twinged under the smell of something that tried too hard to be perfume. It was an overpowering chemical cocktail.

Sunuvabitch. I shut my eyes and thought back to Daniel's apartment. During my earlier search, I'd come across a series of drawings by the man. One of them was a picture of a beautiful woman that was none other than Camilla Ortiz. Another figure hung in the background at the edge of a street corner. A woman with frizzy hair. A woman Daniel had some affection for.

And a monster loomed over them both in the drawing.

Caroline was involved somehow.

Daniel suffered through what I had thought was a nightmare involving the monster. I bet he had thought it was nothing more than a dream as well. It hadn't been. The poor guy had woken up to find it stalking him.

Stalking him the way Caroline appeared to have done.

It wasn't difficult to pin her perfume to what I had found while searching his drawers. Besides the financial statements, there were a handful of letters that I hadn't opened, but they reeked of the same odor. Letters from her no doubt.

I needed to skip out on movie night and go through those envelopes. Missing something wasn't an option.

Someone knocked on the door.

Ashton clapped his hands together. "Took her long enough." He jogged over and opened the door.

Anna stood there.

Chapter Twenty-Seven

Seconds ticked by before I realized my mouth hung open in silence. It should've occurred to me that she might have shown up. Ashton was her colleague, so it wasn't a stretch to figure they were friends.

I didn't know if she fit into this, and if so, how. Anna wasn't one of Daniel's neighbors, but if she came around to movie night often enough, it might have put her in the monster's crosshairs.

She looked good. That was saying something considering she hadn't bothered dressing up. Anna wore a simple clover-green shirt under a slim-fitting leather jacket. She had on the kind of jeans you could pluck cheap from a discount store, and comfortable sneakers. Some people can make casual look great.

Anna caught my stare, giving Ashton a warm smile before heading my way. She looped her thumbs through the belt hoops at the front of her pants and rocked in place. "Looks like you're going to have that chance to get me a tuna melt after all." Her voice was strained, like she'd spent a lot of time yelling. The skin under her eyes looked like she hadn't slept well the night before.

"You look like you need a solid eight hours of shut-eye more than a sandwich."

She shrugged and returned a weary smile.

"Long day?"

"Yeah. It's getting better though. I didn't expect to see you here."

The feeling was mutual.

"Back atchya."

I needed to find a tactful way to ditch the little get-together, especially since Daniel had missed a couple of these already. People would notice if I slipped out without a word. Anna gave me that way.

"Hey, did you just get off?"

She waggled her hand. "Been a little more than an hour. I changed at work, then hopped the metro down here."

If she'd just come off a shift at the hospital, there was a chance she had an update on Milo. Being one of Ashton's coworkers, she might have some idea about who his friends were. I hoped that was the sort of thing that didn't go unnoticed in hospitals.

"Mind if I ask a work-related question?"

She exhaled through her nose. "Damn, a girl can't catch a break."

"Sorry, but it's important."

"Important as in about you and Ashton's mutual friend?"

Phew. A silent thanks ran through my head for her diligence and attention to detail.

"Yeah, him. How's he doing?"

I would have killed for her to give me that weak smile from moments ago.

Anna's gaze fell to the floor like it was an interesting thing to look at. Her face went through a series of empty motions. They were the kind that came with a lot of practice in working up to relay bad news.

An oily hand squeezed my guts and twisted. I worked to bury the discomfort and worry. "Anna?"

"Your friend, Milo—things didn't look good for him when I checked up. The burns aren't fatal." She swallowed and looked back up at me.

"But?"

"But it sounds like they were caused by electrocution. Whatever it was, it left his heart in bad shape. I don't know if he'll recover. If he does, he might be living with a pacemaker. I'm not a doctor, but what I heard didn't sound good."

I shut my eyes as countless obscenities rang through my skull. Each one toned like a hammer striking a gong.

It was my job to stop things like this from happening.

My marrow felt like it was set to boil and that I'd soon burn from the inside out.

It took a trio of breaths to get my mind sorted enough to work through things.

I held out my hand towards Anna. "Mind if I borrow your phone? Mine's, uh, broken."

She didn't miss a beat, reaching for the hefty burgundy purse hanging from a shoulder. Anna tugged the zipper aside and dove in with a hand. She produced the phone in seconds, turning it over in her grip and passing it to me the right way up.

I took it and tipped it in her direction as a way of silent thanks. I glanced at the phone and realized she'd left it unlocked and opened to her address book. A particular number was highlighted: work.

"I figured you wanted to call in and check up on him. I don't know if he'll be able to answer the phone. His mother seemed in better shape though. It's sometimes hard to tell with people's age, you know? But she was coherent, talking, and eating. All good signs." A modicum of cheer returned to Anna's voice and face.

"Thanks. Any idea how I might be able to get in touch with someone else?"

She arched a brow.

"I've got a friend who went in to check on Milo."

Anna's hand went to her hair, tugging on it compulsively. She licked her lips and looked like she was struggling to process. "Right. If they're still there in his room, you...you can have your call directed to the in-room phone. Hopefully they will pick up. It'd be easier to call them directly though."

I shrugged and gave her an apologetic look. "Her number was on my old phone. Can't recall." I tapped a finger to the side of my head.

"Right." Anna fished a pocket-sized flip-mirror from her purse. She thumbed it open, glancing at herself. "I'm going to go to the bathroom and freshen up. You weren't kidding. I could use some sprucing up."

I held up a finger. "I definitely did not say that."

She waved me off. "It's okay." Anna didn't give me a chance to reply, passing by me and heading down the narrow hall away from the kitchen.

I moved over to a corner of Ashton's apartment. Satisfied there were no lingering ears in my direction, I swiped away from the address book and brought up the dialing screen.

There was another way to get in touch with Ortiz despite not knowing her number. I had committed another one to memory after a particular case in New York. Rummaging through my journal to retrieve a number wasn't convenient or always an option.

I dialed the number, crossing a pair of mental fingers that they would be in a helping mood. The line trilled with no sign of ending. I blew out a breath.

"Hello." The speaker sounded like she was on a helium diet.

"Get Gnosis on the line."

There was a pause.

That always bodes well.

"He's not speaking to you."

I blinked. "He's not what? You tell that curmudgeonly garden ornament to—"

The line clicked.

"Hello? Smurfette? Shit." I redialed and stretched my mouth into a wide and artificial smile. "Be nice. Be nice. It's not that hard. She's just the help. Don't shoot the messenger." I mumbled the mantras to myself as the phone rang.

At least it wasn't sent directly to voicemail.

The line went live, but there was no sound.

I exhaled loud enough to ensure they heard me. "So, that started out wrong. Hi. Can you put me through to Gnosis, please?"

Silence.

"Tell him it's in his best interest. If I end up whacked by a monster—permanently speaking—he can forget collecting on what I owe." I flooded my voice with enough stone to bluff a career gambler. "And the way things are going, there's a good chance I might not make it out. Your call."

The silence endured.

"Wait one moment." The living squeaky toy put me on hold.

I sighed.

The phone got halfway through a ring before someone answered.

"Graves." He sounded like he made a habit of drinking

a cocktail of smoke and gravel.

"The one and only. I need a small favor, Gnosis."

I imagined the patriarch of all gnomes was lounging in an expensive leather recliner while he listened to my plea. The bearded little creature probably had a smug smile plastered over his face. I had no doubts that he was contemplating how he'd squeeze another IOU out of me.

"I'm listening, Graves. What is it?"

"I need you to connect me to Camilla Ortiz. My timeline's running short. I've got bits and pieces of clues, and something big is at work."

Gnosis inhaled, sounding like he was taking a long drag of something. A cigar, I wagered. "Define big."

I bit back the short joke on the tip of my tongue. "As in something's trading favors for favors, and I'm not so sure the stakes end there."

"They usually don't. Clarify what you mean by favors."

"Like people are getting big breaks in their luck overnight, and I can't pin down what exactly they're giving up to earn them. But a credible...ish source hinted that it's favors. Good enough."

"My assistant said you threatened to balk on our deal if I didn't do this. Blackmailing me isn't a good idea, Graves."

"I said there was a chance I might not make it out of this alive. If that happens, your deal's nixed. Difference."

"You're lucky I desire that favor."

I opened my mouth to counter with a witty retort.

The line clicked and morphed into the unmistakable sound of a dial tone.

"Hello?"

"Ortiz, it's me."

"I never gave you my cell number. Daniel's is busted. How are you calling me?"

"Magic." I waggled my fingers.

I could almost hear her blink on the other end of the line.

"I swear, if you're waggling your fingers in that stupid gesture, I'm going to break them."

"I'm not." I stopped moving my fingers. "So, what have you got?"

She exhaled. "You're not going to like it. I know you

didn't know him, but Daniel did."

No.

"Milo's gone."

Silence returned. I only wished it permeated my skull and chest. Two different kinds of beats filled me. The sound of my heart was like listening to someone pounding on a plastic bucket. A cheap, hollow sound. My temples chimed like a xylophone playing without pause.

A minute passed before I could summon the words. "Oh." It wasn't much in the way of words, but my usual hyper-verbal self couldn't be bothered. "How'd he go?"

"You won't believe me, but...he just sort of passed on."

It took me longer than I cared to admit to process that. "What do you mean? He just flatlined?"

"Yes. His heart was doing fine. He was recovering."

Which contradicted what Anna had said.

"The doctor said he'd recover. I flashed my credentials and explained I was a personal friend as well. Kelly and I sat outside his room. Fifteen minutes later, people rushed into his room because he was crashing. I got worried when everything went quiet."

I held my breath, waiting for her to go on.

"One of the nurses—Anna—came out and gave us the news. She—"

"What? You sure that was her name? Describe her?"

Ortiz took a sharp breath. She was miffed about being interrupted. But she summed Anna up.

Each word was like a cold stone dropping into the pit of my stomach. She pegged Anna the way only a federal agent could. We were talking about the same woman.

"Ortiz, that's not possible. She's here—right now—at this party. I'm using her phone."

"Shit, you don't think..." Her voice hardened.

"I'm about to find out."

"Wait, Vincent. There's something else." She went quiet after that.

I swallowed, hesitant to ask. "Uh-huh?"

"Kelly went to go check on Milo's mother. The doctor said it was like Milo's body had fully shut down. His heart didn't seem to fail so much as everything did. Breathing and heartbeat went out together. They were even monitoring his brain activity. There was a worry he might have taken some damage from the electrical shock. His brain shut down at the same time. It was like someone flipped a switch and turned Milo off."

I rubbed a hand across my face. "Right, and Kelly feared the same thing could happen to his mother. She's off on her own...while we have a monster loose."

"Find Anna. I'll grab Kelly and get out of here. We'll head back to Daniel's place."

"Stay on the line." I turned on my heel and raced towards the bathroom, ignoring the odd stares from the other guests. A silent hope filled me that I'd find Anna before Ortiz did.

I stopped in front of the door I believed to be the bathroom and formed a fist. My knuckles bounced off the door several times. "Anna?"

No reply.

My fingers closed around the knob and I turned it, pushing the door open.

The bathroom was cramped. A sink over a wooden counter that jutted out too far and was made from cheap wood. The pale yellow curtains were pulled back to reveal the shower. It was a plain setup like you'd expect for a bachelor's place.

There was one problem. No Anna.

I hadn't seen her mingling with the group.

The room smelled like someone had emptied an entire can of citrus cleaner.

My eyes widened, and I turned to the mirror.

Shit. Of course.

This freak could go into mirrors. What's to say it couldn't move through a network of them? Things started snapping into place, and I had an idea of what we were dealing with.

I put the phone back to my ear. "Ortiz, tell me you found Kelly. Tell me you're getting out of there."

"I found her. News isn't good. You don't sound great yourself. What's wrong?"

"Stay away from any mirrors."

"What?"

"Do it. Get out of any rooms that have them. Start

moving now. I think I know what we're up against, and it can move through mirrors—any mirrors."

"What is it?"

"I'm not sure, but I've got a—" I stopped as the mirror shimmered. A flare of molten orange light rippled through its surface. The light coalesced into twin orbs, hanging a few inches apart from one another. They looked like eyes.

Eyes of glowing, fiery orange are never reassuring.

The smell of citrus increased.

"Clever boy," said the freaking mirror. It was Anna's voice.

I snapped my recently healed hand towards the voice. Scalding hot glass shattered. Heated daggers bit into the skin of my fingers and knuckles.

The pungent smell of oranges died with the light.

My chest heaved while I panted, waiting for the voice to return.

It didn't.

I sighed in relief, putting the phone back to my ear.

"Vincent. Vincent! What the hell was that?"

"Trouble. And I think it's heading your way."

Chapter Twenty-Eight

"Got it. We're heading out now. Kelly, move!"

"Keep your eyes open. Avoid any mirrors in the hospital. I don't know how far and fast these things can move. Oh, and if you smell anything like orange cleaner, run faster."

"What?"

"Just trust me." I thumbed the phone off and stared at the broken mirror. There was no resurgence of the light or smell. I sure as hell didn't hurt the creature, not like that.

My fingers twitched and stung as I plucked bits of glass from them. The injury would heal soon enough.

The door knob turned.

I whipped around, stowing the phone in my pocket before cradling my wounded hand.

The door opened. Eddie stood there, puzzled for a moment. He eyed my hand, then the mirror. "We...uh, heard shouting and then glass breaking." His gaze drifted back to the mirror. "Are you okay? What happened?"

Part of me wanted to confront him with the truth. At this point, there wasn't much hiding the fact that the group here had somehow landed a deal for success. They were all freelancers who blew up instantly. That could backfire, and I had a feeling it would.

I was injured and didn't know what their deals entailed. Could be they were nothing more than desperate people ready to deal at any cost. Could be they were all in on it. If that was the case, it was possible they could have killed Daniel together.

I threw the notion away as quickly as I'd thought it up. None of them seemed freaked out by Daniel's return. Everyday humans aren't great at keeping cool when people return from the dead, or the river.

Which means none of them know what happened to

Daniel.

Oh, hell. These poor bastards struck deals with that freak, and none of them knew that each other had. This monster was screwing them all. Set them up for success, then snatch it away from them.

That wasn't enough to put the nails in the coffin. Whatever favors the creature had asked for had to be temporary. There's little point in asking for something and offing the person before you can collect.

So, quick favors for quick success. An opportunity too good to be true. Which meant anyone else who'd signed on had a short timer. And that clock was going to be punched—fast.

I stuffed the phone into a pocket and surged towards Eddie. My fingers closed around the front of his shirt, and I hauled. He spun with me as I pulled him into the bathroom, driving him against the wall.

"Whoa, Dan, what the hell!"

A quick kick with the side of my foot shut the door. I leaned closer, eyeing him with a hard look that could've sanded stone to dust. "What did you do?"

He sputtered and looked to the door, likely dreaming of escape.

I shook him. "What did you do? And don't lie. I know what's going on and how your little work-from-home business took off."

His eyes ballooned several times over.

Homerun, Graves.

"I don't..." He cast another look at the door but made no effort to fight me off.

"Tell me what I'm dealing with. What did you do, Eddie?"

"I can't. Man, that thing, that's some El Diablo shit." He made a series of quick gestures in the shape of a cross over his body. "I swear, if my mom knew the crap I was messin' with—"

"Your mom's not here. And she sure as hell ain't going to be here to save your ass when this goes sideways. And in case you haven't noticed, it's already getting messy. Or do you think Milo stuck a knife in a socket for kicks and giggles? What about his mother?"

I didn't think his eyes could widen any larger. I was wrong.

Eddie's feet beat and scrabbled against the wall as tried to backpedal. "You don't know what you're talkin' about."

I snarled and shoved harder. "Don't give me that. Milo's dead!"

The words had a sobering effect.

His posture shrank, and the fight left his body. The wide-eyed look was replaced by one of frosted glass. Eddie's face lost all expression. He looked hollow. "What?"

"Milo's dead. Understand? Our friend is dead."

The color left his face as it morphed into a mask of horror. "You don't know what you're dealing with."

"Then tell me, dammit. You made a dirty deal, fine. If you don't want to get bitten in the ass for it, give me something to work with. Help me stop it." I gave him another shake.

"How the hell are you going to stop that thing?"

"By you telling me the truth. What did you sign up for? What'd it cost you? Tell me everything—hell, anything."

He licked his lips and wore a look that said he wanted to be anywhere but here. "Alright. I don't know what that thing was exactly, okay? It was like some giant bat-looking monster."

I took a breath, working not to interrupt him. I had no clue what that meant, and my mind ran away with ideas.

"It had orange eyes, man, like fire. It got into my room one night. I don't know how, man. Don't ask. I freaked out, you know? It told me it could offer me anything I wanted. Anything. Who can do that for you? Man, I knew it was something dark, but..."

I finished it for him. "You didn't care. What have you got to lose, right?"

"My soul." His lips trembled with a shake that made its way through the rest of his body.

That tremor found a way from his body into mine. My hands quivered as his shaking made its way through my muscles and into my bones. Taking a breath made a painfully cold ache lance the back of my throat like it was layered in cracked, frozen glass.

"Come again? You offered this thing your what?" My

hands moved from his collar to his shoulders. Every one of my fingers dug into the soft tissue with renewed vigor.

He flinched from the pressure and had the grace not to look me in the eye. "My soul, man. That fiend asked for my soul. Said I'd have whatever I wanted for it. It's crazy, right? I mean who believes that? I didn't think it was a big deal. Next thing I know, I'm talking without thinking. I tell it that I want my career to take off, right? That's not so crazy."

We had a different idea of what crazy was.

"I didn't think this thing could do it, you know? But..." Eddie licked his lips and swallowed. "Then, things got weird."

I blinked and shook him once. "Weirder than the devil in your room asking for your soul?"

He bobbed his head frantically. "Fire just whoomph"— he mimed an explosion with his hands—"right into my room like fireworks went off or something. There's a piece of paper in its claws, and it's got smoke coming off it."

I stared at him, waiting for an explanation.

"It was a contract. A real thing. Paper, terms, and everything."

I kept staring.

"Look, I didn't know what to do. I figured what the hell, might as well."

"Right, because nothing bad would come from you striking a deal with a freaking monster that popped into your home and conjured a freaking contract out of fire."

He looked to the floor and shrugged. "A part of me thought it was still some crazy dream."

My eyes narrowed and I leaned closer. "But you signed anyway."

Eddie lowered his head further. "Yeah, man. Next day, my site traffic is through the roof. I'm making money, and it stays that way. I was making enough to quit my day job, man."

"And all it cost you was your soul. Good thing that's not important, right?"

He sulked further. "I don't know what to say. I made my bones, alright? You don't question things like that."

I released my hold on Eddie and shook my head. "Maybe you should."

The not-so-lucky man brushed himself off and turned towards the door. He stopped as his hand went to open it, looking over his shoulder at me. "What's it matter to you? You didn't lose yours, did you?"

Buddy, I wish I could tell you.

"It matters because there's some questions left unanswered. Questions like, when does this thing get your soul?"

Eddie froze. "What?"

"You heard me. When's it due?"

His face lost all expression, shifting into a frozen mask of horror. "I..."

"You don't know, do you?" I rubbed my face with a palm. "Did you even glance at the contract?"

The look he flashed me answered my question.

"Of course you didn't." I ground my palm against my face harder. "So, for all you know, there is no timeframe for when you've got to pay up and kiss your soul sayonara."

"I mean, no..."

I exhaled. Wonderful. There was no telling when Eddie's clock would be punched. Or anyone else's for that matter.

"Oh, shit. You think it could come after me?" Eddie's skin paled, and sweat beaded his brow.

"Yeah. I think whatever you dealt with is back and collecting its dues." My stare hardened, shooting Eddie a silent message. "And I'm banking that this freak's working on a sooner-rather-than-later idea."

Eddie swallowed and looked around the bathroom like he was seeking a bunker to hide in. "What do I do?"

A chorus of screams and shouts filled the air.

I hate it when I'm right.

I forgot about Eddie and flung the door open, rushing towards the living room. A cold slurry filled my veins, pushing me to barrel into the room at full speed.

The plump and haughty blonde lay on the floor. Her rosy coloring fled her face by the second.

I scanned the room.

A stream of scarlet peppered with bloody rivulets went from the entryway mirror to where she stood now. Pieces of apple lay on the floor. The mirror face was cracked, but not broken. Ariel stood by the projection screen, a hand over her mouth, rooted in place by shock. Caroline was nowhere in sight.

I glanced back and rushed to the blonde's side.

Ashton's phone lay on the floor by his side. The small mirror on the back was cracked, likely when he'd dropped it in response, and sported a small smear of blood. He pressed a compress to Renee's throat. His composure was a working lesson in how to be an ice sculpture, cool and unflinching.

Crimson splotched and bled through the towels. Blood pooled over the floor.

Ashton was acting on instinct and nothing more. It wasn't the sort of injury you could save someone from.

"What happened?" I leaned over to get a better look, but Ashton gave me a cold glare that told me to back off.

"Carotid's been severed." His voice was gravel and grit. The following look was enough to let me know what he was thinking.

She wasn't going to make it.

"How'd it happen?"

Ashton ignored me. "Renee, can you hear me?"

Renee's skin reminded me of bone. Her features were gaunt. An alarmingly small amount of blood seeped from the wound.

"Renee?" Moisture welled under Ashton's lids. A second later, beads collapsed and rolled down his cheeks. He held her in silence.

"Oh, God," said Eddie.

I wanted to tell him God had nothing to do with this, but didn't think it'd be a welcome comment at that moment.

Ashton's body quaked as he held onto Renee.

I slipped my arms under his and helped him to his feet. A miniature balloon inflated inside my throat in tandem with my heartbeat. I exhaled and looked over my shoulder to Eddie.

He caught my stare, his gaze going to Renee before he swallowed.

I racked my throat for whatever moisture I could and looked to Ashton. "What happened?"

He cleared his throat, blinking and struggling to speak. "Suicide, what else?"

I didn't buy it.

"Why the hell would she..." I gestured to her throat.

He shook his head, tears still lining his face. "I don't know. What else could it be?"

I had an idea. My gaze wandered over to the broken mirror before coming back to the grizzly scene.

"You tell me, Ashton."

"I was on the couch with Ariel. Eddie went to see what the hell you were doing in my bathroom." He gave me a cold, sideways look.

I shied away from it.

"There was a sound like glass breaking. Ariel turned around and started screaming. I go into work mode and clear the couch before making sense of it all. Renee's dropped the knife and apple she was cutting. Her throat's bleeding, and she's not even trying to stop it. I've never seen anything like it. Self-preservation. Even with something like that, she should've tried to do something." His eyes went back to the deceased woman.

I cleared my throat but remained silent, unsure of what to say. It took me longer than I would have liked to work up the courage to speak again. "Where's Caroline?"

He shook his head like he didn't know or care. "You all should go." Ashton's voice was harsh.

"I'm sorry, but do you think that's a good idea?"

He flashed me a glare that said he wasn't in a mood to argue.

I bit my lower lip and nodded.

"I phoned 911 the second it happened. Cops and medical services will be here any minute. I'll talk to them. For now, everyone...please get out of my home." His face twisted into a series of pained expressions.

"Yeah. Sure." I cleared my throat and eyed Eddie one last time before heading towards the door. My forearm itched. I rolled up my sleeve and glanced it, swallowing a curse.

Thirty hours left.

Great.

At least I had an idea of what I was working with. I just needed a moment's privacy to flip through my journals so I could figure this out.

A part of me wanted to remain, despite Ashton's wishes. Chances were any of them could be targeted next, but I couldn't tail each person as they left. Not without knowing for certain what I was up against.

My walk back to Daniel's apartment consisted of racking my brain to piece everything together and spitting an endless string of profanity. I went inside, leaving the door unlocked for Ortiz's arrival.

My knees quaked, and the fatigued muscles in my legs threatened to give way. It wasn't as easy as willing away the bone-deep tiredness at this point. I felt like I was made of wet cardboard about to collapse.

I fished my journals out of the distended pockets, tucking them under an arm as I made my way to Daniel's bedroom.

His bedroom was refreshingly free of the orange scented odor I'd come to associate with the monster.

I covered the distance to his bedside drawer in lengthy strides, grabbing the handle and pulling. The drawer slid out with enough force to leave it askew on its mountings. My fingers closed around a bundle of envelopes, tossing aside the earlier bills. All that remained were the letters of a personal nature. The letters, I assumed, were from Caroline.

I fanned them out on Daniel's bed, plucking one up. My index fingers parted the already opened seam and I pulled the first letter free. I scanned the letter.

It was from Caroline as I had suspected.

I thought handwriting had gone out of style in the modern age, especially for personal letters.

Caroline must've found it romantic, the nature of the letter suggested as much. The following ones were of the same sort. Each was a pronouncement of how she felt about him. She wanted to be with him. They were both artists on the way to success.

Given what I'd heard from her about her career, that wasn't exactly true.

I snatched up the final letter.

Dark splotches marred the letter. Some of the ink had smeared in places. Tears, likely.

The script was hastily scrawled, possibly in anger given the message. Caroline was furious with Daniel. So much so that she'd pulled her art from his gallery, even though the letter indicated it had been selling well.

Why ruin your big break because of a falling out?

It went on to mention how she felt her feelings were reciprocated at first. That he cared. The letter quickly morphed into accusations of him leading her on and made it to the point where she hoped his gallery would fail.

If that wasn't hate mail, I didn't know what was.

I balled the paper in my hand as I thought about everything I knew. My gut, and the evidence—what little there was of it—told me she was involved in this somehow.

The sound of a door slamming drew my attention.

I hadn't heard anyone open it. The final letter fell from my grip as I hustled to the living room, hoping I wasn't about to have company of the monstrous sort.

Ortiz stood in the center of the room, hands on her hips. She eyed me as I ran in. "Please tell me you've figured this out."

This mess bothered her as much as it did me.

"I hope so." I pulled Daniel's drawings from my lore journal, presenting them to Ortiz. "Go through those. Tell me if anything makes sense. You knew the guy. Maybe his art has a hidden message?" I regretted saying it a second later.

Ortiz's hand trembled as she took the paper. Her gaze fell to the drawings, looking more like she was staring through them to the floor.

"I'm sorry." I reached towards her shoulder.

She shook her head and waved me off.

A change of subject seemed in order. I gestured to the nearby seating. "Where's Kelly?"

Ortiz took a seat, unfolding the various artwork over a knee-high coffee table. "Sent her home. There's only so much we can drag her into. It's safer for her." She sounded distant, like she was only paying me half a mind.

I couldn't argue with her logic. "Isn't that what I've told you before? This work's dangerous. It'd be safer for you too if—" I stopped talking when she flashed me a look that said it was better for my health to remain quiet.

They say silence is golden. I was learning why.

I plopped down beside her, thumbing my journal open.

Pages tumbled by as fast as I could glance at them.

Ortiz took the occasional peek at the flipping pages.

I returned the favor, glancing at the drawings.

She traced a finger over a certain image. The one depicting her and Daniel on a street. The now-recognizable and unmistakable figure of Caroline lurked in the background. A menacing bat-like figure hung above the three of them.

My eyes hovered on the image as I continued flipping.

"Stop!" Ortiz's gaze narrowed on my journal.

I froze, following her gaze. A crude drawing filled the page. It was an image of something halfway between a man and an oversized bat. Rudimentary doodles from German fairy tales sat below.

"Vincent, what the hell is that?"

I sucked in a breath. "A Faust."

Ortiz stared at me, waiting for a clearer answer.

"A devil."

Chapter Twenty-Nine

"Devil?" Ortiz's eyes widened, and I could imagine her pulse beating in her throat.

I knew where she was going with the idea. I waved a hand, hoping to pull her attention away from her train of thought. "Not, The Devil, a devil. As far as I know, that guy doesn't exist."

Ortiz arched a brow before her gaze fell to the cross hanging from her neck.

I shrugged. "Hey, in all my years of work, I haven't found a shred of proof that ol' horns and brimstone is lurking around."

"And what about these things—Fausts—what do I need to know?"

My head tilted to the side. I didn't know what to tell her, but the truth seemed like a good idea.

"Honestly, I don't know where to start." I scooped up my journal, flashing the pages in front her. "Look at my notes."

Her lips curled before forming a frown. "There's not much."

I shook my head. "No, not much at all. There's a reason for that."

Her frown deepened. "I'm not going to like this reason, am I?"

"No. The thing is, I didn't believe in them until now. I mean I've only heard stories—scraps of lore that I've cobbled together, you know? Bits and pieces here and there. And those never really add up to anything concrete."

"Rumors, you mean."

I nodded.

"Well, it looks like they're true. So, we need to figure out as much as we can fast. Start talking."

I sighed, racking my brain for where to begin. "They're

devils—demons in the sense of what they are. At least that's what the scattered history of them suggests."

Ortiz rubbed a thumb and forefinger against her cross.

I pretended I hadn't seen it, looking back to my journal instead. "How much do you know about the legend of Faust?"

"I've heard of the Faustian bargain, but that's about it." She leaned back, resting against one of the armrests of the couch.

"Right. General rundown of the story goes like this." I cleared my throat and recounted the retellings of the myth best I could. "Man named Faust—highly successful, and intelligent—discontent with his life. He wants more."

Ortiz gave me a look. "That's how it always starts, isn't it?" There was an undertone to it like there was more to the statement.

I caught the look and tried to shy away. "You mean like our first case?"

Her lips pressed together as her face and body tightened. "Yes."

"Yeah. Something about us people, I guess. Some things are never enough. Faust certainly thought so. The guy decides to make a pact with the Devil."

Ortiz's eyes narrowed, giving me a look that said, "I told you so."

I waved it off. "Yeah, yeah. Anyway, what's he got to offer that'll please the Devil? His soul." The words fell with iron weight.

Silence followed.

Ortiz's hand tightened around the cross, letting go almost as quick. "I didn't know you could trade something like that."

I shrugged and gestured to myself. "Me neither, until now. How do you think I feel?"

"Good point." She rolled a hand in a lazy wave, motioning for me to continue.

"Right. The tale goes on to say that he traded his soul for unlimited knowledge and pleasure. Not a bad bargain, especially if you're the kind of person who doesn't believe in the soul. There's a problem with the story though."

Ortiz eyed me, waiting in silence for the answer.

"Like every story in the mortal world, it's been told over and over, twisted each time."

"You're saying it's wrong? Or part of it is?"

"Yes. Way I've heard it a few times through sources and cases I've worked is like this: Faust wasn't the name of the man. That was something that happened after the telling of the original tale. It was spun enough to where things got lost and it was eventually published. Kind of like how you tell a story enough times by word of mouth and it's no longer the same when it's finally written down. Faust was the name of the kind of creature. From what I've heard, no one actually remembers the man's name."

Ortiz picked up on what I said. "Kind of. Meaning there's not just one of these out there?"

I shook my head. "They're a species, from what I can gather. Fausts are behind the origins of stories like selling your soul and paying the devil its dues. And now the devil's here to collect."

"That's what Kelly meant when she said that all of Daniel's neighbors are freelancers that made it big." Her eyes widened in realization. "You don't think they all struck deals?"

I lowered my head, looking at her out of the corners of my eyes.

She rubbed the heel of a palm against her forehead. "Of course they did. Milo, the rest of them..." Ortiz trailed off when her gaze fell back on me.

I avoided the look.

"No. Daniel did not make one of these deals." Her voice was cold iron, unflinching and hard.

I wished mine could have sounded the same. It came out more like worn stone about to crumble under its own weight. "I never said that he did, Ortiz."

"But you're thinking it." The metal in her voice quivered.

It hurt hearing that, the possible doubt in me and in her friend Daniel. She had already lost him. Ortiz didn't want anything tarnishing his memory. That was a different kind of pain, something that sticks—lasts.

I shrugged. "I don't know what to think. There was no reason for Daniel to be killed. Only way Fausts get involved is if you deal with them. From the bits of lore I've got, they can't reach out and affect you unless a bargain is struck."

"Maybe Daniel found out, found something about the Faust? If someone's butting into its business, isn't that enough cause for it to want to kill him?"

It was possible. I didn't want to admit that because I didn't know where it would lead. Maybe it was the wrong thing to do, but I swallowed and gave Ortiz what she wanted.

"You're right. There's no telling why it did what it did. We'll figure that out when we do. In the meantime, we have to find a way to kill this thing."

Her lips went thin and she gave me a look. "And do you know where to start?"

My mouth mirrored hers, going tight. "Not much of one."

All of my time working paranormal cases led to more information about creatures than I had time to dedicate to learning. I jotted down notes and lore in the few and fleeting moments I had between hunting and being hunted. My journal contained tons of information that I'd never have a chance to properly go through. It made memorizing every monster a pain.

I inhaled, tilting my head side-to-side, eliciting a series of small cracks. "I know one thing: Anna is the Faust we're looking for."

"Now we just have to find her and a way to put her down." Ortiz flashed me a look of heated daggers.

I shied away from it and turned to my journal. "Yeah, easier said than done. Fausts can move through mirrors." My finger trailed over my writing until I found a short scribble that touched on what I'd learned. I tapped the spot, drawing Ortiz's attention to it. "Apparently, they can utilize them like a network of roads leading to certain destinations."

Ortiz's jaw hardened. "Like someone's home. Like Daniel's home." She looked around, her eyes widening as she did.

My gaze went past her to the bathroom door. A hand of cold stone wrapped around my throat as I understood how the Faust had entered Daniel's home before.

I bolted from my seat, snagging my journal as I raced towards the bathroom.

"Where are you going?"

I ignored the question, slipping into the room and pulling my right fist back. A series of imaginary needles lanced through my fingers and knuckles. Silent reminders of the mirror I had broken earlier.

I'm not a fast learner.

A shrill crunch filled the room as cracks shot out from where my fist struck. Silver-black lines webbed out from the point of impact as chunks of glass showered into and around the sink. No errant pieces bit into the already tender flesh of my fingers. A small relief.

The digits did, however, cry out as the surface of my skin flared in a hot reminder of the earlier pain.

Ortiz cleared her throat, eyeing my hand then the mirror. She leaned in the doorway, arms crossed, putting it together. "With that broken"—she licked her lips—"is there any other way for the Faust to get in here?"

I shook my head and hand in unison. "Not that I'm aware of. To be honest, I'm not so sure it could have returned through the mirror."

Ortiz arched a brow, waiting for me to explain.

With the tip of my journal, I batted the faucet handle for cold water. My right hand slipped underneath the spout and cool relief flooded over my raw skin. It wouldn't do much but provide a temporary comfort but, sometimes, that's all it takes to get through a rough patch.

Ortiz's arms tightened around herself. One of her fingers tapped against one of her biceps.

I caught the gesture of irritation and cleared my throat to respond. "Right. Well, from what I can gather, Fausts can move through mirrors that have some connection to their power and the deals they've struck." I regretted my words a second too late.

Ortiz's finger stopped tapping and her look turned to hot steel. "So, you're saying it could have gotten to Daniel because he did make a deal."

The water felt colder than it was in reality. I pulled my hand from underneath the faucet, not bothering to turn the tap off. "No. What I'm saying is that's one way they work.

Everything I can piece together suggests that Fausts can read desires. They pick up on it like a dog with a scent. These freaks can follow that trail to where it leads. A home usually."

Ortiz's finger tapped twice, but she remained silent.

"Thing is, I'm not Daniel. Not really. So, I don't think a Faust could still connect to his home." I took a deep breath, hoping my next words would settle Ortiz's nerves about her departed friend. "I don't think the Faust came into his home because of a deal he made."

Her posture softened. I saw the stiffness leave her shoulders and back. Ortiz's mouth parted, and her head leaned a fraction to one side. She was curious and relieved.

Good.

"I think it came to strike a deal. That's the working theory. But I've got a hunch they can work the whole mirror thing to enter a home and offer a bargain. If they're shot down, they have to leave."

Ortiz's lower lip folded and her teeth almost bit down, but she refrained from chewing. "Why do you say that?"

"Think about it. There's no point coming into someone's home to kill them if you're a Faust. They want—need—deals. They want souls. A Faust can't take yours if you don't sign it over. Enticing you is part of the deal. It's a bit hard if you're breaking into the place to threaten a human. Besides, there's something else at work too."

"And what's that?"

I pointed towards the living room. "Head back there and I'll show you."

Ortiz's mouth twitched, but she did as I asked.

I followed her out and stood in the middle of the place, waving a hand around us. "What do you see?"

Her hips shifted as she leaned a bit more to one side. "A room."

I sighed. "Is that all?"

"Daniel's room."

"Right. Daniel's room. His. It was his. That matters. This whole place"—I waved again—"is his home."

A blank expression took over her face. "You've lost me."

It wasn't an easy concept to explain, but I figured it was

worth a shot. I rubbed the back of my good hand against my mouth before exhaling. "Alright, short and simple version's like this. There's power in homes, particularly a home that you own. There's a force of permanence there. It's a house, solid. All homes are built on foundations, right?"

She nodded; her eyes narrowed, but they lacked a certain focus. Ortiz wasn't following me. Not yet.

"Homes are a place of foundation in one's life. You sleep in them. Grow in them. Raise families, make and share love, create memories. You leave them in the morning and look forwards to returning as quickly as you can. They're a strong part of our lives. A constant part. That creates a form of power around them. They're yours. A home is part of your identity in a way."

Ortiz's eyes widened. "Let me guess: Monsters can't cross into your home unannounced. It's like the myths about a vampire needing an invitation."

"Right and, well, wrong. Monsters can cross through without an invite. They leave a huge chunk of their power behind in doing so however. It's not always worth the risk. I've got the feeling the Faust was thinking along the same lines."

"Why's that?" She quirked a brow.

"Because they exist to strike bargains. They're dealers, paranormal loan sharks. A debtor's power comes from what they hold over you. The only reason she could have come into Daniel's home is to strike a deal. Do something to get that hold over him, you know? Without that, they're vulnerable. The Faust, Anna, would be coming into his home with little power to call on. That's dangerous."

Ortiz's mouth wriggled. "That means they have to be cautious with who they make deals with."

I nodded in agreement. "Yeah. And what better disguise to wear than a nurse at a hospital? Hell, what better place to work than somewhere where people are ill, injured? A place where they and their loved ones are desperate for a miracle."

Ortiz's mouth went thin, and her lips twitched to one side. "Miracle isn't what I'd call it." She made the word sound like a curse.

I shrugged. "Desperation drives people to make all manner of deals. The kind that don't end well for everyone."

My words caused Ortiz's mouth to pull down into a frown. "It's part of human nature. Sometimes we're all too willing to do something bad for a faint glimmer of hope that something good will come out of it. Not saying it's right, but I sure as hell can't say it's horribly wrong. Given the situation some of these people are in, what would we do?"

Ortiz looked away to the far wall, staring more through it than at it. "I don't know." Her voice sounded like something obstructed her throat. "Like you said, it doesn't make it right. People are paying for these deals, and not only with their lives. Other people are getting hurt because of them." She cast a glance my way. Ortiz's eyes seemed to lose a bit of their light as she stared at Daniel's body. She gave me a thin, hollow smile.

I wished I could've returned an authentic one. I looked away for a moment. "Yeah, they are. And they're going to keep paying if we don't stop this freak."

Ortiz's jaw hardened. "Then I hope you have a way to put the Faust down." One of her hands went to her hip, where she had reattached her holster in a shoddy fashion. "Otherwise, I'll do it my way."

I blinked and stared at the gun for a moment. "Your way?"

She bared her teeth, giving me a wolfish smile. "What did you once tell me about bullets and blood?"

A series of cold pins pressed into my spine, causing me to squirm. Gnosis had confided in me a secret he claimed could hurt a great deal of paranormal creatures. A secret that could potentially harm him as well. Taking that into account, he made me promise not to use it recklessly. There was also the caveat of the word hurt. It didn't mean kill.

I wasn't sure if a Faust fit under the "great deal" grouping of supernatural creatures. It was a risk. One that, if used, would surely find its way back to Gnosis' ears, letting him know that I'd broken my word.

In my world, my word is my bond. It's one of the few currencies I can count on. There's a list of creatures that deal with me, trade information and favors, solely because of my word. If I give it, I keep it. End.

Breaking it, even slightly, by letting Ortiz being the one to pull the trigger, would get around. It'd make my contacts wary of working with me.

I relied on the information they provided. Without that, I'd be in serious trouble.

And all of that was selfish to a degree.

How much of it was about me making my job easier? How much of it was about helping me?

I told myself six of one and half a dozen of another.

Gnosis had said that bullets coated in the blood from someone pure of soul could put a serious hurting on a number of monsters. It had less to do with the bullets and more with the blood I figured.

With Ortiz's blood, we had a shot at putting the Faust down. It would save people. Anyone the Faust had dealt with would be free of their contract, I hoped.

I thumbed through my journal, scanning as fast as I could.

I wanted there to be an alternative.

Ortiz's way could work. But the cost would be losing future information that could help me save more people down the line.

Trading lives for now versus lives later. It wasn't a choice I liked weighing.

I sent another page tumbling by, stopping when I came across the final page about Fausts. An image took up most of the page.

The design was of a palm-sized star contained within a circle. Lines intersected the star, breaking off portions to form isolated triangles lined with archaic script and symbols.

A seal. A particular one. Similar to something I'd used on my first case with Ortiz.

I'd recorded the seal through rumor and whisperings of lore. The stories indicated it was one of many created by King Solomon out of legend to contain a variety of monsters. I knew they worked because Ortiz and I had used a similar one on our first case together, binding a creature to its vessel.

The only problem was I didn't know what to bind the Faust in. My journal was noticeably blank on any useful details beyond the seal.

I frowned, turning my attention towards Ortiz.

She stood over the kitchen counter. Ortiz had rolled

one of her sleeves up, resting the bare arm on the zebrawood counter. A fillet knife rested in her right hand. Her fingers gently tapped against the handle, noticeably shaking.

"Uh"—I rose from my seat and held up a finger—"now might be the time for me to make a knife-safety disclaimer."

She gave me a wan look with an equally forced smile. "I'm waiting for a better idea."

I exhaled through my nose, wishing I had one. "I've got part of one. And I know, that's not the same as a good one."

"It's not, but thanks." She steadied her grip, and the knife became as unshakable as her resolve. Ortiz brought the blade to the top of her exposed forearm, shutting her eyes as she murmured something. She touched the fillet knife to her skin, dragging it across the surface slowly. Her lips folded under her teeth and she bit down. No sound of pain or protest left her lips.

Beads of scarlet swelled from the skin before running together to create a thin stream along the shallow cut. Ortiz dropped the knife into the metal-plated sink, reaching out with her now free hand to open a cupboard above. She plucked a translucent plastic bowl, letting it fall onto the counter with a hollow thump. Ortiz held her arm over it, squeezing just below the bleeding area to force the blood to drip faster. It pooled in the bowl.

I went over to her side, moving in silence. She didn't need my help, and both of us knew it. That's not why I did it though. I reached out, grabbing her work-issued firearm and pulling the magazine free.

The magazine had been fully reloaded. I blinked and stared at her. "When did you..." I waggled the item.

"After I parked at the hospital, just in case trouble came our way." She tilted her head and eyed me. "For the record, it usually does when I'm dealing with you."

I gave her a lopsided grin and thumbed bullets free from the magazine and into the bowl.

There wasn't much blood, but past experience taught us that we only needed a touch.

I placed the handgun on the counter, leaning and reaching past Ortiz to snatch a corner of a hanging paper towel. The reel spun as I tugged on the edge, refusing to tear free from the rest of the papers. A perforated line widened and tore free several sheets above the one I pulled on.

Ortiz grabbed the lip of the bowl, shaking it to roll the rounds through some of her blood.

I opened the tap and ran the paper towels through the cold water before wringing them. The wet paper struggled to keep its shape as I folded it and placed it on Ortiz's cut.

She shivered once, not making eye contact.

I held the makeshift compress in place before balling it up to mop away the blood.

Ortiz remained still through the process. "Thank you."

"'Course." The word came out rougher than I'd wanted. She wouldn't need any dressing for a cut so shallow. It'd heal in its own in time. I opened my mouth to say something as she rolled her sleeve back down.

Anna's phone rang.

Ortiz stared at me and then my pocket.

I plucked the phone from its place, staring at the screen. A blocked number. I answered the call. "Hello?"

"Hello, Daniel." The voice belonged to Anna.

My fingers tightened around the phone to the point I worried about cracking the screen. The back of my throat felt layered in snow. I took a breath, steeling myself. "Anna." I thumbed the speaker so Ortiz could follow the conversation.

"Mhm. Imagine my surprise to find you alive and well, walking into my work."

The phone shuddered, threatening to flex under the increasing pressure from my grip. Anna had all but confessed to killing Daniel. At the very least, she made it clear she knew the man had died.

Heat and gravel filled my voice. "Maybe next time you should do the job better."

Anna let out a small, self-satisfied laugh. "How about this time?"

"What?"

She didn't reply. An assortment of indistinguishable and barely audible noises came through the phone. It was like she'd moved it away from her mouth.

I struggled to listen.

Someone sniffled.

"Hello?"

The sniffling stopped. "Daniel? I'm so sorry, man, please—"

Oh shit. Eddie.

"Hello? Eddie?"

No reply.

"Eddie's tied up at the moment—literally. I've never been that sort of woman, but I wanted to make a point."

"And what point is that?"

"That Eddie's life is in my hands."

She had one hell of a point.

"That goes for everyone else who's dealt with you. You're not stopping with Eddie." I exhaled, letting the anger flood my voice. "You sure as hell didn't stop when you were ahead."

"Oh?"

"Renee." I dropped the name with lead-like weight. I hadn't known the woman for more than a few fleeting moments. She'd been pretty stuck-up. It didn't mean she had deserved to die.

"Everything has a price, dear."

"Everything has a consequence, too. When I find you, I'm going to kill you."

Monsters usually hang up when I threaten them on the phone.

The line stayed live.

"That's a shame, Daniel, because I want to talk."

I waited to hear her out.

"I want to deal."

Chapter Thirty

I regretted having not smashed the phone. It would have spared me the ridiculous offer. "You want to what?"

"Deal." She sounded serious.

My stomach shook and laughter rolled out. "You're joking? You want me to make a deal—with you? I know how that'll turn out. Spoiler, not in my favor."

"You're mocking me." Her tone could've stripped the bark from trees.

I laughed harder. "Hell, yes I am. Why would I make a deal with a Faust?"

The line went quiet.

Crap. I swallowed slowly and hoped it wasn't audible. Anna might take her frustration out on Eddie. He may have dug himself into that hole, but he didn't need me making things worse for him.

"Because I'm the one who can free Eddie from his contract. Provided, of course, you do as I say."

I took a deep breath. The proposition had its share of risks. I could get Eddie off the hook if I played my cards right. That meant getting close to the Faust. Easier for it to try to kill me.

I wasn't a fan of that.

Technically, Eddie's problem wasn't mine. He had made his bed and dealt with a loan shark from hell, but Church and Ortiz had reminded me that my job involved trying to save people, regardless how bad they messed up.

I exhaled and shut my eyes. "When and where?"

Anna gave me the address and time.

I didn't know where it led, but I planned to find out before heading there.

Stepping into anything unprepared is a recipe for disaster. Doubly so when it involves monsters.

"I'll be there. Remember, if you hurt Eddie—"

"I know, you'll kill me." Anna's smile found its way into her voice. I could almost hear her grinning. "Do you even know how to hurt one of us?"

I gritted my teeth. "I'm resourceful. I'll figure it out."

Anna let out a little chuckle. "Best of luck then. Don't keep me waiting." She hung up.

Bitch.

I stowed the phone in one of my pockets and turned back to Ortiz.

She stood, arms crossed, and arching a brow.

I shrugged. "You heard her. If I show up, she's offering to let Eddie go."

Ortiz's forehead creased and her brows knitted together. "You don't believe that, do you? It's a trap."

I opened my mouth but Ortiz cut me off as she jabbed a finger towards me.

"Don't say it."

I bit back my Star Wars reference and sighed. "Fine. Yes, it's probably a trap. But we know where she'll be, if she isn't there already. That's something. It means we can get close." I gestured with a hand to Ortiz's gun.

"Close works." She gave me a knowing look. "It also means she could come after you if things go sideways."

I frowned. "I know. Better me than you or Eddie. I've got this." I tapped a finger to the binding symbol in my journal. "Let's hope it's enough."

Ortiz patted her gun. "Same."

"I don't like it. Feels like we're going in blind."

She raised her brow higher than before. "We sort of are."

"We have an address..."

Her mouth pulled into a lopsided smile. "We do, and I have an idea where it is. But it's not much, to be honest."

"I know. I'm pulling at strings here. We've got an hour." I glanced at my tattoo. The time remained the same as before. A small relief.

I eyed the binding symbol again, out of compulsion more than anything else. A knot of worry formed in the front of my brain, almost pulsating like a miniature heartbeat. Between Ortiz and I, we had two big gambles to play, and those had a nasty habit of never paying off.

But sometimes you have to play the hand you've got and hope your opponent has got a worse one.

Not likely with my luck.

I swallowed the pessimism of the bile that had built in the back of my throat. "Let's go." I took both of my journals, tucking them beneath an arm as I moved for the door. "You still got the shotgun in your car?"

Ortiz gave me a reproachful look. "Yes. I'm not a fan of lugging it around though."

I stared at her as I reached for the door.

She rolled her shoulders in a mild shrug. "It's illegally modified as far as the state of New York is concerned. It was used in a crime, Vincent. That makes it evidence."

I froze as my hand fell on the knob. An undertone filled what Ortiz had said. I'd almost ignored it in my haste to rush to Eddie's aid.

The rules and laws of the justice system weren't just guidelines or suggestions for Camilla Ortiz. They were ironclad and a source of her strength. She believed in them. Ortiz believed in doing the right thing by them and the people she took an oath to serve.

There's a power in that, serving a system.

And every time she'd gotten involved with me, that belief and oath were tested. Even the small things pushed and prodded her convictions. Something like toting around a weapon she shouldn't have.

But so long as Vincent Graves needed it, why not?

The bile returned, feeling like the acid tinge from an alkaline battery.

I racked my throat to clear it before giving Ortiz an apologetic glance. "Thanks for hanging onto it nonetheless. I wish you didn't have to do these things, but the supernatural don't really play well with mortal rules. And if we want to stop them, we've got to consider doing the same." I hated saying it, but it was the truth.

"Careful, Vincent. That sounds like the start to a slippery slope. The kind I'm not comfortable with." She kept her voice soft and low, but there was enough of an edge to let me know I was pushing too far.

I pulled the door open and stepped through. The awkward silence followed as Ortiz passed me by. I locked up behind us and moved down the hall, carrying the quiet with me.

Ortiz fell by my side, looking from me to her hands before eyeing me again. Her fingers closed around mine in a tight, brief squeeze. "I didn't mean it to come out like that."

"I know. Doesn't change the fact you're right."

"I am?" She sounded surprised by my admission.

I bowed my head. "I hate to say it"—I flashed her a quick smile—"but you've got a point. That's the problem with my world. You get pushed and pulled along, and sometimes to even the odds, you have to fight dirty. Black and white starts to get a little gray. Then, like you said, slippery slope and all." I squeezed her hand back. "I lose track of that sometimes. Thanks for the reminder."

Ortiz's eyes shone, and she returned my earlier smile with one of her own. "Of course. This kind of work isn't easy. I've gone through my fair share in the field and it gets to you if you let it. The things you see and do stick with you. Some of them rattle you deep down. Eventually you start to wonder if there's a way to skirt around the rules and make things work in your favor. It never ends well though." Her voice was like brittle stone at the end.

A cold slurry rolled through my gut as I caught the shift in tone and guessed what prompted it. I asked the question anyway. "Someone you know?"

Ortiz looked down the hall and didn't turn back to face me. "Once. We're not going there. You still have things you don't want to talk about. This is one of mine. Respect that, please."

I could do that. God knows I'd asked her enough times to respect the parts of my life I couldn't share. I opted for changing the subject as we made our way down the stairs. "How fast do you think you can get us there?" I arched a brow.

Ortiz's mouth twitched once as she mulled it over. "Fast enough, why?"

"Fast enough to park a bit out of the way? I'd like some time to scope out the place. Maybe I can figure something out."

She gave me a silent look that seemed to question the maybe part. Ortiz paused as we reached the doors leading out of the complex. "Do you really have something in mind?"

I shook my head. "No, but I know someone who might."

She held her look, waiting for me to divulge any info about who I meant.

I smiled and opened the door, stepping onto the dark streets of Queens.

Ortiz crossed the few steps between us and caught up. "And they're willing to help...you?"

I sniffed at the implication, rolling my shoulders in a mild shrug. "Can't hurt to ask."

Yes, it can, Graves. I cleared away the negative thought as fast as it had sprung up.

We made our way towards Ortiz's car before I to reached into my pocket and retrieved Anna's phone. My thumb slid against the screen until I'd brought up a number I'd dialed earlier in the night. I pressed it, bringing the phone to my ear.

Ortiz glanced at me before stopping by the driver's side of her car. She unlocked it and got in, eyeing me as she fastened her belt.

I made my way around to the passenger side, getting in as someone answered the line. "Hello?" I could've sworn there was a sigh on the other end of the line. After a moment of silence, I chalked it up to my imagination.

"What do you want, Graves?"

"Oh, you know, small talk. How was your day at work?" I muffled a general groan of discomfort as I opened the door and fell into the passenger seat.

"I don't have time to waste with you." Gnosis sounded like he'd doubled up on the smoke and gravel diet.

I pressed a hand to my chest in mock offense. "Waste? I'm hurt."

"You will be if you keep this up." He wasn't playing.

I swallowed and realized something was up on Gnosis' end. He didn't mind my lip most of the time. "What's up?"

"Problems."

Ortiz watched me carefully, waiting for an answer.

I wish I had one. Instead, I mimicked turning the keys with my hand.

She got the gist of it and started the car. Ortiz pulled out and hit the road, not looking in my direction again.

I had a feeling her ears would be on the conversation however. "What kind of problems? Anything I can do?" I regretted the words the second they left my mouth.

Gnosis let out a dark laugh. "No. And really, you'd offer to help me? Is this some way of trying to get out of your debt?"

The thought hadn't crossed my mind, but it wasn't a bad idea. What better way to get out of Gnosis' grip than saving his tiny hide and calling it even? I'd done it before.

Except there wasn't a life hanging in the balance.

Eddie couldn't wait for me to putter around. I quashed the idea of freeing myself and got to the important matter. "I need your help..."

"Why else would you have called?" His tone could've grated stone.

Don't be a smartass, Graves. Too much at stake. I bit back a snarky reply for something a bit tamer and to the point. "What do you know about Fausts?"

The sound of clinking glass rang through the line. Nothing else followed.

I waited, eyeing the passing buildings.

Gnosis smacked his lips and released the sort of wet cough that came after a strong drink. "Why do you want to know?"

I opened my mouth to speak.

"Never mind. You're hunting one, aren't you?"

"Yeah." I shot Ortiz a quick glance.

Her face was fixed straight ahead, but she gave me an equally quick look out of the corner of her eyes.

I turned away from it, hoping Gnosis had something useful for us. He usually did. The question was: What would it cost me?

The gnome exhaled like he'd taken another swig.

He was really going at that bottle.

"Maybe you should take it easy on the descent into alcoholism. I kind of need you to be, you know, useful?"

Gnosis scoffed. "What you need...is a miracle."

Ouch. Shots fired. I waited for him to explain why he thought that.

"What exactly do you know about Fausts, Vincent?"

I took a deep breath and tried to settle my fried nerves. Ortiz and I didn't have time to waste with a boozed-up contact. I told him what little I knew, making sure to tell him about the seal as well.

Gnosis let out a series of coughs that he quickly muffled. He cleared his throat and acted like I hadn't heard. "That's a decent enough understanding of them. They operate in similar circles to my own. Only they don't barter so much as lie, manipulate, and take advantage of people." An edge of jagged glass filled his voice.

I wanted to point out that Gnosis didn't seem all that different to me. He'd once used a moment of desperation to wrangle a debt out of me. I let it go.

"They don't play the long game the way I do. They want souls. End. They'll do whatever it takes to get one. So long as a mortal signs on the dotted line, so to speak, it's all fair. In my business, besides information, we want those in our debts to live. It's more conducive that way. Some come back to pledge new debts for new favors. No one gets hurt—generally—and everyone profits."

I kept quiet, waiting for him to get to the point.

"Graves, are you aware—truly—of the value of a human soul?"

I had an idea, and I wanted to be wrong. "Last time I read up on my religious books, the sum came in as priceless."

He grunted in what I took to be an affirmation. "Yes. Do you know why?"

My mouth shut as soon as I'd opened it. That was a new one. I had an idea, but I stayed silent, figuring Gnosis would fill me in if I didn't answer.

"Do you know about the law of conservation of energy?"

"Yeah..."

"Energy cannot be created nor destroyed, Graves. What, then, is the human soul?"

Holy shit.

"I'll take your silence as understanding. You know its power. Power that cannot be replicated. Identity springs from it, forms around it. People. Love. Anger. It's unique.

It's energy. It's made, somehow. I won't get into the metaphysics of it all with you. I doubt you could handle it."

I squinted at the insult. That was more like the Gnosis I knew. "Thanks, that's very big of you to spare me the high science." I smiled more for myself than anything else.

The gnome blew out a sharp breath that came through the receiver as a static crackle. "You're quite lucky that this is a rather peculiar situation, Graves."

Why is that, I wonder?

"Souls are currency not only to Fausts but to many paranormal beings—old things—older than me. Do you understand?"

I nodded, not that he'd see it.

"There are far too many uses for the human soul, but they offer Fausts untold leverage. Souls are a rare form of power that can go unequaled, if properly harnessed, in the paranormal world. Fausts, as you've no doubt figured, can tap into that power. That is why I'm going to tell you how to stop one."

The hammer was about to fall. I winced in anticipation of his price.

"For free, Graves."

Chapter Thirty-One

"Uh, say what? Free? That's a French word, right?" I let out a weak laugh.

"You heard me right." Gnosis' voice sounded like freshly solidified molten rock—hot, hard.

"And why are you being so generous?" I shouldn't have asked, but I was glad I did a moment later.

"They're a blight. They interfere in what I do. They don't play by the rules, Graves. Not ones any in my business adhere to anyway. But most of all, I hate them for what they are. Parasites." The heat in his voice intensified.

Hate has its own power. There's a speech by a wise, diminutive puppet that'd warn you otherwise. He'd have a point. It's got its catches, but it doesn't detract from the point that it can make you dangerous.

Gnosis had a personal axe to grind against Fausts. I'd heard the hate in his voice when he'd spoke. It was the kind that stays long buried only to slip out on occasion.

Somewhere along the line, it sounded like one—or a few—had crossed him. Their mistake. I committed that to memory.

"And that's the only reason?" I kept my voice neutral.

His laugh came out as puffs of air leaving his mouth and nose simultaneously. "Of course not. If you deal a blow—however small—the paranormal community will hear of it."

That much was true. Word always got out amongst the supernatural. My name already carried a reputation. That rep grew by the case. Bit of a shame it wasn't always in a favorable manner.

Sometimes notoriety works wonders if you're a paranormal investigator.

"Besides the personal aspect and satisfaction, it's good business. They're competition." A stone-cold undercurrent flooded Gnosis' voice. "And you know how much I dislike that. If I help you take down a Faust in any capacity, I keep my investment alive, and I'll make sure everyone knows it was me who pointed you in the right direction."

Translation: Mess with me, Vincent Graves takes you down.

He wanted to play the angle where I looked like his hitman. Gnosis wanted it known that if anything irked him, they'd be dealt with by the not-so-friendly neighborhood soul.

It wasn't without its problems.

"Yeah, and that puts me in everyone's crosshairs, doesn't it? Your old enemies become mine. Their issues with you hang around my neck, that right? Keeps me too busy looking over my shoulder to ever square things with you."

Gnosis didn't miss a beat, answering me in a voice of smoke and whiskey. "Odd how things work out like that, isn't it?"

I gritted my teeth. "Yeah, odd."

"You can, of course, hang up."

You know damn well I can't. Otherwise, I wouldn't have called you.

"It's tempting."

"But you want to do your job. You have someone to save." He made a condescending clucking sound. "One of these days, Graves, your proclivity for helping the little people is going to get you killed."

"Not today," I said. The resolution was more for me than him.

"No, not today. I have too much vested in your success for you to fail."

I bet.

"How to kill a Faust: In short, you can't."

My insides felt like they were pumped full of liquid nitrogen. I glanced at Ortiz, my eyes falling to her side. Her pistol was tucked there. It was a gamble, one we were betting on. "What do you mean I can't kill one?"

Ortiz turned to look at me, arching a brow.

I hadn't said the most reassuring of things to be fair.

"As in mortals can't kill a Faust."

I frowned and figured at this point it was worth asking the question on my mind. "You once told me about a one-size-fits-all way to handle monsters."

Gnosis made a sound like he'd sucked in a pocket of air through clenched teeth. "I did. I also stated that it could harm a great deal of creatures, not all."

I grimaced. "Let me guess: Fausts aren't on the list of things highly allergic to magic bullets?"

Nothing. No sound of Gnosis taking another sip, no exhale of breath—nothing.

"Hey, Shortstack, you still there?"

Gnosis exhaled. "Graves, have I ever told you how much I detest your short jokes?"

"Bullshit. That's the alcohol talking. That's what you get for pounding back thimbles of liquor. You love my jokes."

He let out a dark, brittle laugh. "You know what's really funny?" His voice sounded like it was on the edge of cracking.

A chill passed through me and I didn't want to answer. "No?"

"I don't know," he said.

"What?" For a second, I felt as if I'd misheard. Gnosis failing to know something was an oxymoron. His entire job was to know. He was a literal being of knowledge. His freakin' name meant "knowledge."

"I don't know."

Hearing him say that a second time didn't help.

"Do you know what a Faust truly is, Graves?"

I shook my head, realizing a second later that he couldn't see me. "We've gone over the general bits about them. Why do I get the feeling you're about to tell me something worse?"

"They're demons of desire. Fausts are a force of nature springing from the greed and want of humans and paranormal beings alike. They can alter reality so long as an accord is struck."

I swallowed as I caught onto what lingered between the lines. "Created from desire. Meaning so long as it exists, so do they?"

"That's what I believe. And in all my years of life, I have yet to find a way to kill one. From what I understand, should you even manage to vanquish one, they'll return. It may take years—decades or longer, but a Faust can return."

I paused, drawing several long breaths. "Okay, but you just said there was a way to stop these freaks."

"I did. You have your seal. It will work. Trapping a Faust isn't a permanent solution. They're like sharks, and they work together. If you imprison one, another Faust may find a way to set its fellow free. The only thing I know of that can kill a Faust is another of its kind."

Great. That was going to be all kinds of fun.

"How am I supposed to pull that off?"

"I believe that is your job." He paused, inhaling loud enough to come over the phone with a tinge of static crackle. "Graves, be careful."

I blinked. Gnosis wasn't known for being sentimental, and especially not for giving a shit about me. He was cold, practical business.

"As you can imagine, Fausts have their own domain in the Neravene. From what I've heard, it's expansive—near endless, in fact. It's what allows them to pass through and into nearly any place with a reflective surface. I don't know what their home looks like, and, to be frank, I don't want to. But, if you were to find a place to trap one, Graves, inside the Neravene will be your best bet."

That gave me a whole lot of info without telling me what I needed to know. It was better than nothing though.

"Uh, thanks. Last question before you run off to a meeting for the little people."

He grated his teeth just loud enough to be heard.

"So, these mirror Ways… Any chance they're two-way? Let's say a dashing, daring, and ever-so-brave paranormal investigator—"

Ortiz snorted.

I turned to eye her, but she kept her face neutral and fixed ahead like she hadn't made a sound at all. I squinted before returning to my conversation with Gnosis. "If I wanted to pass through one of them, how'd I do it?"

"Pass through a mirror? It's not unheard of. Humans have done it before, by accident more than anything else. I wouldn't recommend it, Graves. I would say your only chance would be to do it the same way they do."

"Which is?"

"I don't know." His lips smacked together like he'd

taken another gulp of strong liquor.

"Alright, fair enough. Thanks for giving me something to work with."

"I'm not doing it for you, Vincent. Remember that. Investment." He dropped the word with lead weight, stressing it to ensure I knew he still had that favor. "And one more thing—"

"Yeah, yeah, I know. Be careful—"

"No. Don't screw up and have this come back to me. I want to hear of a trapped or dead Faust, not one that is alive and coming after me." He hung up the line.

Dick…

I stowed the phone and glanced to my side at Ortiz. Her gaze was fixed ahead in a good effort of pretending to be solely focused on the road.

"So, you heard all of that."

"It didn't sound great." She gave me a thin, lopsided smile.

"It wasn't. Deal's this. My contact doesn't know if the whole shoot 'em up routine will work. His info says we've got two options: lock the Faust up or find another Faust to kill it."

Ortiz pursed her lips before folding the lower one to chew on it. "Silver?"

I shrugged. "Don't know. Nothing in the lore suggests it'll do anything. If it worked, I'm sure my information broker would have mentioned it."

The car slowed as we rounded a corner onto a street lined with small, commercial property. Buildings with worn brick faces and siding yellowed from age and filth. Ortiz wrestled the steering wheel as she pulled us over to the curb.

She parked and gestured down the road to a spot I couldn't clearly make out in the dark. "That's the address, best I can guess. They don't make it easy to find things here at night."

I grunted, letting my head thwap against the window to rest it. A small area of skin on my forearm felt like it'd been held too close to a candle. I grimaced and rubbed a hand over the spot. "Hit the lights for me?"

Ortiz didn't question the odd request, smacking a small interior light switch with her hand.

The newfound brightness didn't do me any favors. My tattoo had changed: twenty-nine hours left. Our conversation in the apartment and the trip here hadn't taken that long. The case was running me ragged, leaving me to catch glimpses of my shrinking timeline just as it changed.

Ortiz caught me starting. "It's longer than you've had when we've faced down with a monster before." She offered me a hopeful smile.

"Yeah, how well's that worked out for us before though?"

"Then let's make the best of it. What's the plan?" Her hand went to her side, almost touching her jacket before she realized what she was doing. Ortiz stopped before patting her sidearm.

I figured it was an unconscious gesture of reassurance. "I don't know. I do know this much, if we don't show up, Eddie's dead. I can't have that on me." I stared at her. "And I know you can't have it on you, either."

"Hell no." Her lips spread in a smile that'd make a wolf think twice about messing with her. A faint glow shone over her face from the rear-view mirror. A mix of moon and streetlight added a haunting radiance to her feral grin.

I almost felt sorry for the Faust. Almost.

Ortiz unbuckled and patted herself down before exhaling. "I don't like going in without a plan. If we mess this up..."

"Yeah. But, if we do nothing, Eddie's a goner. We're doing the right thing. Even if all we do is buy him some time to get away."

That settled it. Her face hardened, an old glow of fire and metal filling her eyes made more intense by the shine of light.

It hit me like a sledgehammer. I stared at the mirror. The look of realization must've shown.

Ortiz's smile faltered. "What's wrong?"

"Nothing." I broke out into laughter. "I think I've got a plan."

She quirked a brow, waiting for me to explain.

I reached up and wrapped my fingers around the rear-view mirror.

"What are you doing to—"

I wrenched hard, fighting the well-mounted mirror. A second forceful tug broke it free.

"My mirror! What the hell, Vincent? Banging up my car's body wasn't enough?"

I got out of my belt, opened the door, shooting a look over my shoulder as I turned to get out. "Come on. I think I'm onto something." I sprang from the car, hitting the street in a full run.

Ortiz swore—notably directed at me—and sprinted after me.

The night air felt thinner as I sucked it down as fast as my lungs allowed. I kept my eyes to the building, scanning them for a match of address. Most everything blurred in a mix of faded light, concrete, and stained metal.

Ortiz caught up in seconds, pointing twice to a small building ahead.

My legs juddered as I adjusted my pace suddenly and they bore the brunt of the action.

It didn't take much detective work to know we were at the right place. The automotive shop was dinky compared to neighboring buildings. It consisted of a two-bay garage, currently shuttered. A lone office sat on the side of the building, looking like a hastily built addition of old siding and drywall. Old oil and tobacco stained it much like the garage doors. Two billboards sat atop the building. Their white backgrounds were a mash-up of nearly a dozen different shades of white, all of which were flaking.

One name stood out in bright red: Eddie's Automotive Services. A series of the jobs performed at a garage were listed below.

I looked at Ortiz, then jerked a thumb in the direction of the makeshift office.

She got the message and moved to take a look.

The place looked empty from the outside. At the very least, it should have been.

Which is exactly why she chose it. Pay attention.

I took my own advice and eased up to one of the metal shutters barring the way.

Ortiz hissed, drawing my attention. She pointed towards the office, shaking her head.

I had suspected as much. It was small quarters—too

cramped to set up an ambush in. The likely bet was inside the garage itself. Plenty of room to start a fight, or worse. Or Anna could lock the place and leave us trapped with a running car.

Who knows? The paranormal are good at that sort of stuff and are creative about it.

A little positivity wouldn't kill you, Graves. No, but being in tight quarters with a freaking devil will.

"Shut up, brain, I'm thinking."

Ortiz stared at me, her lips curling at edges. "Yeah, I figured you didn't use that much for your thinking. Nice to know I was right."

I squinted at her.

She didn't say anything further, but her smile grew.

Ignoring her, I leaned close, just shy of my left ear coming in contact with the old and unhygienic garage door.

I didn't make it this far into the case to be offed by a hideous ear infection.

Ortiz placed a hand on my shoulder, easing me back. "Let's try it your way, hm?" She banged her knuckles against the door several times. "It was either that, or you could have kept at being Listens to Doors All Day."

I scowled. "Quiet, smartass. There's only room enough for one of us."

She shifted her hips, one of her hands going to her gun.

"Or two's cool. It's cool."

Ortiz blew a breath out her nose and laughed.

It was cut short as metal rattled and a mechanized groan cried out through the night. Both doors shuddered in unison before lifting upwards. They slid up and retracted along the roof. The insides of the garage were impenetrably dark.

The kind of dark that doesn't happen on its own.

I traded a glance with Ortiz. "Well, that's reassuring."

"Didn't you once tell me your job was to step into the darkness so others wouldn't have to?"

I had said that.

Time to live up to it.

We stepped into the darkness together.

Chapter Thirty-Two

The sound of grinding gears and aged motors returned. Metal clunked and shook as the doors closed behind us.

"Well, that's always a good sign." I frowned and nudged Ortiz with an elbow.

"Stop being so negative—"

Overhead lighting flickered to life with an electric crackle of protest. The light did a poor job of illuminating the place, leaving some of the garage shrouded in semi-darkness.

It was a simple and small place. A row of cherry red toolboxes, standing high above me, ran along the far wall of the place. Their silver-lipped handles gleamed like their owner took special care to clean and polish them after a shift.

The usual deep sink and mirror hung in a far corner.

A less impressive black toolbox sat against the left wall. An orange, waist-high machine of some sort stood beside. Whoever operated in that area had left an old, grime-covered computer between them. Various cables and hoses hung from it. A pair of ramps leading up to a set of rollers dominated the space near the computer. Another mirror hung behind the contraption, placed at the height of a vehicle's headlights.

The center of the garage should've been bare apart from the intruding legs of automotive lifts. It wasn't.

My fingers tightened around the stem of the rear-view mirror as my gaze fell on Anna.

She hadn't changed her appearance at all.

Eddie was bound to a chair by a mix of chains, extension cords, and duct tape. His clothing was marred by dirt and a mix of fluids. Mostly clear stains with a tinge of pink. Some kind of automotive fluid, residue that had likely made its way onto the chains and cords now binding him.

His face looked like he'd come back from batting practice, and his mug had been the ball. One cheek sported a bruise more purple than blue. A finger-length gash made its way above his left eyebrow and was swelling. His right eye was puckered shut.

My stare made its way to his fingers, and I stopped. The whole of my upper body stiffened like I'd been lined with lead.

Eddie's fingers were like misshapen sausages. Each digit was crooked, shaking, and discolored.

A one-inch breaker bar hung from Anna's right hand. She smiled when she saw me notice it before turning her stare to Ortiz. "Do you think that's going to make a difference?"

I turned to follow her gaze.

Ortiz stood, legs spread and arms out in a shooter's position. Her pistol sat comfortably in her hands—index finger stretched along the barrel. She wasn't willing to shoot, not yet. Ortiz cocked her head to the side, like she was weighing the decision. "I'm not sure what will happen. I'm curious though." Her earlier feral grin returned.

Anna blinked.

I made a note not to play poker with Ortiz. That was a hell of a bluff.

To her credit, Anna recovered quickly. She sank to her haunches behind Eddie. Her head came to rest on one of his shoulders as she held the bar across his chest. "Be careful now. You wouldn't want to hurt poor Eddie, right?" She placed her lips next to one of his ears and crooned into it.

I took a step forwards, hoping Anna's attention was more fixed on Ortiz. "Seems like you've done a good enough job on that." I nodded at his injuries.

Anna let out a sound like a low purr. "What can I say? You kept me waiting. It's rude to do that to a girl, you know?"

"Except for the part where you're not really a gal."

She shrugged. "No, I guess not. Would you like to see what I really look like?"

I traded a glance with Ortiz. Last thing either of us wanted was for Anna to feel threatened enough to take on her true form. Things would only go downhill from there, and Eddie was likely to get caught in the crossfire.

"Not really. I've got a great imagination. See, I picture a giant, ugly bat thing."

Anna's eyes narrowed.

"That about right? Leathery skin—total opposite of the whole young and hot nurse thing you've got going on. Flabby body, big ears, veiny lookin'. Tell me, do you have a thing for blood...or bugs?"

The metal bar flexed in her grip, and the cherry coloring in her eyes deepened.

Gulp. That was new.

Ortiz shot me a look to knock it off.

It was good advice.

Anna took a breath, calming herself. "Keep talking. I'll kill you."

I waggled a finger and clucked my tongue in a chiding manner. "Now you're just being batty."

The breaker bar quivered between her hands before the inevitable. It bent into a slight hump. Anna didn't relent with the pressure, contorting the bar into something reminiscent of a Krazy Straw.

I guess I could add enhanced strength to the list of abilities Fausts possessed.

"Wow, someone's been eating their spinach along with their human souls." I gave a weak chuckle.

The light in Anna's eyes brightened. "Oh, you have no idea." She flicked a wrist, tossing the ruined tool aside. It clanged against one of the paint-chipped legs of the car lift.

I glanced at Ortiz out of the corner of my eyes, moving them to look at the far end of the garage in a subtle gesture I hoped she caught.

The only response was an equally careful micro-twitch of her mouth as she took a measured step to the side.

"I'd prefer it if you both stayed in place." Anna moved her hands to Eddie's shoulders before sliding them up to his collar. She spread her fingers, wrapping them around the base of his throat and giving a little squeeze. It looked like she was giving him a gentle massage. The underlying threat was clear.

"And I'd prefer it if you took your hands off him. I thought you said you wanted to deal?"

Anna released her hold on Eddie, bringing her hands into the air and splaying her fingers. "I did."

Ortiz and I waited for her to go on.

"It took me a while to figure it out, you know?" Anna turned her head, giving me a sideways look.

I didn't have a clue what she was talking about, but Eddie looked like he'd spent the night as Anna's physical outlet and didn't need any of my lip making things worse. I nodded silently.

Anna turned her gaze to Ortiz, smiling. "But it didn't take nearly as long once I started digging around. Imagine my surprise when Daniel came back from the dead."

Ortiz bristled. Her jaw tightened, and the gun shook for a second in her grip before settling. Whatever deep, cherry light burned in Anna's eyes was dwarfed by the heat in the glare Ortiz shot back.

Tension. Thick. Knife. Cut.

I sucked in a breath. This was going well.

Anna rolled her wrist as she went on. "I asked around and heard the rumors about dead bodies coming back with a second chance—a vengeance. It didn't take long for rumors to turn into stories and eyewitness accounts. You've left quite the impression on people, little soul."

Ortiz looked at me without turning her head. Her index finger slipped inside the trigger guard.

Whoa-kay, things were escalating and the situation called for my classic charm and tact to defuse things.

I clapped louder than necessary to draw Anna's attention. "Leaving impressions is what I do. Now, if you're real nice, I won't be leaving one of you in the wall."

See, tactful.

The Faust tilted her head, giving me a dubious look.

As long as her attention was on me. I caught Ortiz shifting her hips and posture as she moved another half step towards the other end of the garage. "Well, congrats on figuring it out."

Anna eyed Ortiz again briefly. "It wasn't hard."

Ortiz gave her a brittle smile. Her finger looked like it was exerting pressure against the trigger.

I swallowed. Ortiz may have been professional and well-trained, but she had a limit and a temper. I didn't need the

Faust pushing her buttons. I snapped my fingers to get her attention.

It worked. Anna focused on me, a curious look on her face. She was waiting for me to ask a specific question.

I had an idea of what it was and felt it was time to cut the pussyfooting. "What's the deal? What's it going to take for you to let Eddie go?"

Anna's lips spread into a smile belonging to fox walking into an open chicken coop. "Why, you, of course. Or rather, your soul."

Chapter Thirty-Three

"You're joking..." I said.

Anna's stared at me stone-faced.

"Oh God, you're not joking!" My stomach shook. I had to double over, placing my hands on my knees as I laughed.

The Faust lost all color and expression in her face, going so far as to give Ortiz a quizzical look.

Ortiz shrugged. "He's crazy. Takes some—a lot of—getting used to."

"You should see your face." I let out a light sigh and straightened my posture. "You want me to trade me"—I jabbed both my index fingers to my chest—"for him? Why would I do that?"

Anna's eyes widened, and her mouth moved soundlessly for a moment. She blinked twice before composing herself. "Because that's what you do, Little Spirit. You help people."

I held up a finger. "Okay, first of all, enough with the 'Little Spirit' thing. I'm a big spirit. A big, badass spirit that puts freaks like you in the ground."

Ortiz snorted before turning it into a poorly masked cough.

I glowered at her, then redirected it towards Anna. "Second, I don't know where you heard that. Most things that talk about me mention how I've ganked monsters. I've got a rep for it. A good one."

Anna nodded in agreement. "I've heard those stories too. I've also heard the ones where you risk life and limb to protect people like this." She ran her fingers through Eddie's hair and shook his head.

She was right. Ortiz and Church had reminded me not so long ago what my job was about. It was to protect people like Eddie, even from their own screw ups. Though I didn't know how much the Faust knew about that and how much was rumor she'd come upon.

Time to test a theory.

I waved my hand in an exaggerated and dismissive motion. "Rumors, greatly exaggerated, so on. You get the idea. Tell me, in everything you've heard, where's it said that I save people like him?" A hand reached deep into my gut, pulling forth the anger, guilt, and everything in between, into my voice. "People like Eddie who've made a selfish decision with no thought about the consequences? People who've pulled others into harm's way. People like me? Like her?" I tilted my head in Ortiz's direction.

Anna's eyes widened and she licked her lips several times.

I could see her mulling over what I'd said. She wasn't certain and I had one heck of a point.

Sometimes the unknown frightens monsters as much as it does normal folk like you and me. It's the unlimited range of possibilities. Some of them meaning you were wrong and the consequences that would follow. Consequences like the uppity soul would risk sacrificing your human leverage and come kick your ass.

Well, if I knew how to kick her ass that was. Another blessing of the unknown. Anna had no idea I was clueless on how to put her away for good.

I rolled the rear-view mirror in my grip, hoping my idea would work. All I needed was an uninterrupted moment without the Faust close enough to hurt Eddie. Or with her eyes on me.

I figured I'd have better luck wishing for Church to make my next case something involving the murderer being within arm's reach the second I bounced into their meat suit.

A soul can dream.

The Faust positioned herself on Eddie's side, shrinking low again so most of her body was shielded behind his. "No, I don't think that's it at all. After all, you're here."

"I'm here, yes." I'm the king of witty dialogue.

"And you've got this deal all wrong, Daniel." She placed considerable emphasis on the name. But she hadn't called me Vincent. Meaning there was a good chance she hadn't come across much else about me besides the rumors.

It wasn't much, but it meant I could stretch some of the

truths she'd learned, however small they may have been.

"Yeah, and what exactly do I have wrong?"

"The details. The little things. The ones that matter." She gave me a smile that chilled deep into my marrow. "You know, the ones that poor Eddie didn't check up on. If he did, he might not be in this situation."

I exhaled. That much was true.

"Alright, talk. What details? What exactly is the deal?"

She smiled. It was a crooked thing that I imagined loan sharks gave to people they were about to collect on—and collect big. "One precious, immortal soul that's made quite the reputation over the years, for one slightly used— damaged—automotive blogger and bad negotiator." Anna patted Eddie's cheek lightly. "Don't worry. It won't be immediate."

My eyebrows shot up at that. "Oh no? What, act now and you'll throw in getting screwed with a rusty poker? How about this counter offer? For three easy payments, go fuck yourself!"

Anna's smile slipped, and she grabbed Eddie by his hair. "You're not as funny as you think." Her lips peeled back into a snarl.

While she was busy threatening Eddie, she hadn't noticed that Ortiz had inched her way into a darker corner of the garage and was mostly out of sight. I didn't know how good the Faust's night vision was, but her attention wasn't on Ortiz. That was enough for me.

"I'm freaking hilarious. Ask every monster that's gotten in my way. They'll tell you that my jokes are killer. Geddit? Because they're dead...and I'm funny."

Anna's eyes narrowed into slits. "I take it back. You won't get any time. After I finish with Eddie—in front of you—I'll make your death quick. It's a shame though, wasting something like you."

Crap. I needed to find a way to stall Anna and get her away from Eddie. At least far enough so Ortiz could pop her without risking Eddie's life. Not that he was in great shape.

"What do you mean something like me? Last I checked, I'm a soul." I pointed to Eddie. "He's got one too. Where's the difference?"

Anna's mouth fell open. She gave me a look of incredulity.

A lot of people were giving me that look of late. It was starting to rankle me.

"You still don't get it, do you? You're not like them." She jerked her head towards Eddie. "You're not human."

I sure as hell was.

As far as I saw it, I was just missing the skin suit. Other than that, I was most definitely human.

I didn't let the doubt show on my face.

"You're what comes after a life as a human, but you shouldn't be here—able to do this, what you do at all. But you are. Something put you here. And you keep bouncing around, meddling, getting stronger."

Stronger? I hopped from body to body, getting my ass kicked and kicking my fair share of asses back. But stronger, that was a new one.

Sure, I packed more of a punch than your normal human. And I could take one hell of a beating, not to mention my recovery speed. But I didn't get stronger from each case.

"What do you mean?" I took a step towards her. Caution advised I stay planted, but curiosity took over. She had answers...or something. Sometimes that's just as good.

Her eyes widened. "You shouldn't be able to linger here. But you do. You shouldn't be able to hold onto and in bodies, but you do. As a soul, the only way you can keep doing that is if you're getting stronger. That's not possible. Souls are static; they come into this world, and then they leave. That's the end of it."

Church had never mentioned that. My fingers tensed around the stem of the mirror. If I squeezed any harder, I risked cracking the cheap plastic. I needed to have a talk with him after this case. A long one.

"You should be falling apart after each of these jaunts in someone else's body. You're not. If you're not getting stronger, then something else is holding you together." A thin, cruel smile spread over her face. "Now, I wonder what happens if that force decides to let go. Do you just vanish? Cease to exist?"

I gulped and wished it had gone unheard.

On my last case with Ortiz, I'd experienced something like what Anna had described. It was prompted and pushed by a paranormal hallucinogenic, but the experience still clung to my thoughts. My body had fallen before my eyes, like whatever force kept me together couldn't manage it any longer. The experience had shaken me to my core.

Anna's face lit up in glee. The reddish-orange in her eyes seemed to brighten despite the poor lighting. She knew she'd struck a nerve, and she went after it with renewed vigor.

You have to hate the tenacious monsters.

"Do you remember what it was like, losing your body? What it was like having your soul flit away? Any lingering memories of that? What about what it was like in nothingness? Anything?" Her smile seemed to grow larger with each sentence.

My scowl deepened with every word. Bat bitch.

"No, but I remember the parts where I've come back and iced freaks like you." My retort didn't lessen her enthusiasm.

"Do you want a first-hand look?" Her eyes morphed as she leaned closer to Eddie. What were small hints of red and orange now came to dominate them, growing in intensity by the second. It was a burning light, the color of a wood ember about to burst ablaze.

"Um, not really." I took a step back, glancing at Ortiz's position. "I think you've got something in your eyes. Looks hot, and um, like it might burn." I scratched the skin below my right eye to make my point. "You should have that looked at, you know?"

"Mhm." Her smile took on a Cheshiresque quality, stretching further than what was normal.

That's always a good sign.

The skin of her lips thinned, looking like they were flattening against her gum line and receding. It wasn't long before the area darkened into a shade caught somewhere between charcoal and a deeper black.

I brushed my finger against my lips. "And, uh, you should really get lip balm for that. No offense, but they aren't as kissable as they were a few minutes ago."

"Careful"—her new smile revealed a row of sharpened

teeth framed by a set of four larger fangs—"you'll hurt a girl's feelings saying things like that."

I had the notion she aimed to hurt a lot more than my feelings. Seemed like the least she could do was tolerate a light jibe.

Some monsters are oversensitive about their looks.

"If you feel so strongly about the way I look now, what will you think when you see the rest of me?" Anna's skin wrinkled far more than normal. Her face had lost its healthy color, resembling her darkened mouth more and more by the second. The fire-like glow in her eyes continued to grow and stand out against her blackening skin.

"I'd rather not find out." Keep her talking, Graves. Keep her focused on you. I just needed to get her to come closer to me. It wasn't the brightest of ideas.

She dug her nails into her clothing, tearing them apart with ease.

Most men would have been pleased to get a look at what was underneath.

I'm not one of them.

Anna stripped herself bare in time for me to see her skin sagging like it was a semi-fluid layer. It was like watching flesh-colored wax dribble off of her.

I gave small thanks that my stomach was close to empty.

Projectile vomiting in the face of monsters isn't something the intrepid paranormal investigator does.

Anna's skin split in odd places along her joints and sides, falling to the floor like it was poorly glued-on latex. Bits of sinew and grayish oils fell alongside the skin. The mass impacted the floor with a wet squish.

My stomach roiled.

That was all kinds of nasty.

"Uh, I think you lost your Skin Sheath."

A Skin Sheath was a second skin some members of the supernatural community could generate to conceal their forms. It was literally a layer of skin and other tissue bound over their true form, aided by a bit of magic. In some senses, it was a better camouflage than glamour, which could be dispelled. In other cases, it was downright disgusting.

Anna didn't seem to share that opinion. "I thought it

was time I shed some loose weight."

Heh, it was a good joke. Too bad it came from a butt-ugly monster. I had to say, Daniel was pretty accurate on pegging how hideous Fausts were.

Anna stood—hunched—at well over six feet. She was a nightmarish cross between a woman and a bat, standing on two, scrawny legs that shouldn't have been able to support her. Her toes were elongated far more than any bat's should have been, resembling a reptile from the Paleolithic era. Claws tipped each digit and looked like they'd have no problem shredding the steel tool boxes lining the walls.

Great. It's always wonderful when a monster can not only steal souls and pass through mirrors, but comes equipped with their own industrial can openers for tearing up bodies.

Anna's body reminded me of early renditions of werewolves. Disproportionate mass that tried to incorporate the dimensions of a person's torso but with the figure of a bat. It didn't work well. Her stomach was concave, showcasing ribs pushing against loose skin. Dark fur lined her sides and face, which was an odd cross between a gibbon and bat. Her snout was thumbed up and framed by ridges in the flesh.

"Hate to say this, but I think I preferred the old Anna."

The Faust pressed its bat-like claws to its flabby breasts. "Aw, I'm hurt." Her voice warbled like she had a second set of vocal chords resonating at a higher pitch and her throat was full of water.

"Ah, well, you know the old saying. Sticks and stones—blah, blah, holy hell, are you ugly!"

Her lengthened and tapered ears twitched in a sign of silent umbrage. She tilted her head towards me, giving me a better view of the pair of horns protruding from her skull. They were twice the thickness and length of my thumbs. The protrusions were ribbed and curved towards the back of her skull.

She was really working the Devil motif. The thin skin stretched between her arms finished off the bat-devil hybrid look.

I could see where the stories and images came from.

Somewhere in a cave far away, a fictional playboy

billionaire was taking offense at the bat motif gone wrong.

The garage smelled of burning citrus and brimstone. It was the smell I'd caught at the hospital, lingering around some mirrors, and in Daniel's home. It was the kind of distinct scent one might try to cover up with perfume.

Anna took advantage of me being rooted in place and gawking. She cradled the unconscious Eddie's jaw, giving it a little shake. The Faust pulled his face close to hers.

I'd seen this before and wasn't a fan of the monster make-out session. "Oh God, please don't. And no tongue either. This is disgusting."

Anna's face twisted into something that could've passed for a grin. "Sorry, you're not getting that kind of show, perv." Her voice warbled more than before.

I narrowed my eyes. "Yeah, well, you sound funny, and you smell." I could've sworn there was an agonized groan from where Ortiz lurked.

Anna didn't care much for my snark. "Part of being a Faust. Orange eyes and we smell a little. Comes with the job. You shouldn't tease someone over things they can't control. It's rude." She pulled Eddie's face closer, a hungry smile on her face. "Kiss Eddie goodbye."

I hate it when monsters make better puns than me.

Chapter Thirty-Four

A lot can happen in just one bad moment. People sign deals of desperation and make bad choices. Greed or fear cause you to step into something you're not quite ready for. There isn't enough time to be rational. No amount of thinking and decision-making will help. Sometimes it's fight or flight.

It was time to fight.

A frozen cocktail of adrenaline and fear surged out from my heart, knocking my brain and body into action. My chest shook, and a long-buried scream filled the garage. I rushed the Faust, figuring the rear-view mirror was better served as a blunt instrument now.

Anna broke contact with Eddie, her face a quickly morphing mask of shock, confusion, and finally calculation.

Some monsters think fast.

I twisted and swung my right arm in an upward arc. The back of the mirror sailed towards the underside of the Faust's chin.

Monsters move fast too.

Somehow, the gangly and awkwardly shaped freak pivoted her hips and leaned at an angle like she was quadruple jointed. The crude, plastic club zipped by her face. Anna caught a glance at the mirror and stumbled back.

Interesting. I burned that detail into my mind. I didn't know what it meant, but her reaction was enough to let me know it was important.

I shifted my weight, swinging in reverse. The mirror shuddered at the end of its plastic arm, threatening to shake free.

Anna pulled away from the blow and snapped a scrawny arm towards me.

The front of my ribs flared in dull agony. I winced, stepping back a few feet from her. My free hand went to my side, clutching the area. The short exchange hadn't gone in my favor, and I hadn't expected the Faust to pack quite a punch in her spindly arms.

But I didn't need to win the fight. I just needed to move it away from Eddie. Easy enough. I took another look at the Faust's burning eyes and reconsidered the easy part.

"Go again?" I twirled the mirror with a flourish.

Anna's mouth spread wide, and a tongue twice as long as my middle finger lolled out. As far as goofy smiles went, that one took the cake.

"I said no tongue!" My face twisted in revulsion.

Anna wiggled the organ before pulling it back into her mouth. "What do you think is going to happen if we drag this out?"

I opened my mouth to speak, but Anna cut me off.

"Here's what. I beat you bloody and broken, far past what your little tricks can do to put you back together again. Then, you beg me to stop." Rows of sharp teeth somehow picked up the faint garage light and gleamed.

"Let me guess, you won't, and you'll kill me. Heard it before. So unoriginal. You monsters use the same book or something?" I flashed her a toothy grin.

Her smile grew monstrously wide. "No. I'll stop. Then I'll offer to put you back together again. All of you. The real you."

Say what?

A block of cement wedged itself in the middle of my gullet. My lips felt like I'd rubbed them with coarse sand. I licked them and waited for Anna to explain.

"So, that's what it takes to shut you up." Her eyes glowed, literally. "I can feel it, you know, the little tug inside you. It's not something you can brush off. You want this. At least, a part of you does. You know what it will cost you, but then, so did he." She waved a clawed hand at Eddie. "But you know I can deliver."

My mouth went on autopilot. "Yeah, to be fair, I think it's a shitty delivery service." I nodded towards Eddie. "The part where you come through clearly got lost."

Anna chortled. It sounded like she was choking on water. "Eddie didn't read the contract. He just signed on the dotted line like a good boy. His fault. I get the sense you're a bit smarter than that."

I shot a quick look to Ortiz without turning my head. "A bit."

"Think about it. You can walk away from all of this. The being torn from whatever sleepless, sightless place you go to in between running around in someone else's body. No more pain and terror. No more going up against nightmares like me. And, believe me, if things don't work out between us, I can be your nightmare. You don't enjoy this. Who would? It's not an easy life. In fact, what kind of life is it at all?"

She had a damn good argument. Heh. Every dirty salesman did. They knew how to hook you. The only problem was, that hook led to a table where they skinned and filleted you before dumping what was left into a hellishly hot place.

It would have been wrong of me to say the thought didn't cross my mind. I could step away. Have an identity— a damn name, a real name—my name. My old life. Answers. My problems wouldn't be monsters and horror. They'd be a flat tire, spilling coffee, or a sports team losing a match.

Normal.

A single word that could change my world.

And all I'd have to do is sign away my soul and leave people like Eddie to hang.

The right things are never the easy ones to do. But easy was never part of my life.

My knuckles popped as I balled my fist. Something dark and fiery, like hot coals, filled my voice. "It's my life, that's what, you two-timing, greasy loan shark."

The bat freak's posture slumped. A soft sigh left her lips like she was actually sad over my refusal. "Shame."

Come on.

"Funny, that's what I was going to say about you." I forced a crooked smile over my face. The sharp ache in my ribs made even that small action a chore.

The Faust bristled. "What's that?"

"It's a shame that something with your kind of power— warping reality—has to scrape, beg, and entice people for scraps. I mean, that's what you're picking up, right? High mileage, desperate and broken souls. Heckuva prize, right?

It's a shame you're nothing more than a used car salesman. A pretty bad one, too, if you have to pluck up spares like struggling artists. What's a desperate soul cash in for?"

"Let me show you." Her eyes narrowed.

What?

Anna swung the back of her hand. The ridged knuckles struck a blow across Eddie's face that sent thick, red-tinged spittle into the air. "Wake up, Eddie."

He didn't. Guess he was a heavy sleeper. It comes with being tortured.

My knuckles felt too large for their skin, threatening to grind and burst free as I made a fist. The muscles in my neck contorted as grit and rough stone entered my voice. "Leave him alone."

"Can't do that. I'm going to show you just what a soul is worth and a little more. Wake up." She traced the back of a finger against Eddie's cheek as she exhaled. Orange mist puffed out from her mouth, clinging to the surface of Eddie's skin like sweat. The wet sheen disappeared in seconds, absorbed by his pores.

Eddie jerked like something had prodded his back. A groan followed before he roused, his good eye struggling to flutter open.

Anna leaned closer to him and turned her head towards where Ortiz lay in wait. She winked in that direction.

Anna knew what I was trying to do. She wasn't moving an inch from Eddie if she could help it. I'd have to make her move.

Fine by me.

Eddie groaned again, his mouth moving wordlessly like he was struggling to breathe and speak at the same time. A hacking cough shook his chest before he was able to mutter anything. "Dan—"

Anna pinched her fingers around his cheeks, cutting off anything further. "You're not here to talk, Eddie." She chided him with a tsk. "You already did enough of that, well, the important parts. Now, it's time to pay the bill." Anna's tongue made an encore appearance, tracing a viscous path around her lips in a sign of hunger.

The Faust brought her face to eye level with Eddie's, giving me a quick sidelong glance before turning back to him. "It's the eyes, you know? The windows to the soul. That's how we do it. Interesting, right? Some say if you look deep enough, the more magically inclined humans can see straight into someone's soul. I've never found out if that's true, but you can certainly pull one out through them. Watch."

I didn't want to, but my body felt chained in place. Fatigue, curiosity, and a bit of anger made a hell of a mix. There was no denying a part of me wanted to sit there and watch—glean any extra bit of information about Fausts. Something that might help me gank her.

It'd only cost Eddie his soul.

And he wasn't the only one that had traded his away. I could save more people if it meant he finished the mess he'd started.

I mentally clawed at the thought until nothing remained.

Anna and Eddie locked eyes. His body shuddered and straightened. He fidgeted like he was trying to break eye contact but couldn't force his body to comply. His color paled and his posture slumped a tad.

There wasn't much to see. No stream of ethereal, silver-white light leaving through any orifice. No angels singing or anything of the like. Just a look in both of their eyes.

Eddie's good eye grew glassy and hollow. The fire in the Faust's eyes deepened and burned brighter.

So did the fire inside me.

I opened my mouth and let it out. The roar shook my core but went unheard by Anna. The mirror fell from my hands. I bolted forwards, arms wide, reaching for the paranormal parasite. I wrapped them around her in a hydraulic grip, digging my fingers into her arms as I wrenched. A quick twist of my torso and hips was enough to upset both our momentum.

I hauled her away from Eddie, toppling us to our sides. My body slapped into hers as the concrete impact rattled our bones. A pained yelp from Anna drowned her fleshy crash. I rolled to my side, using the motion to launch the back of my elbow into her blunted snout. My joint throbbed as it met her tissue and bone.

She yowled, thrashing like a thing possessed.

I flailed, lashing out with my legs. My ankles hooked

around her oddly angled ones. I pressed myself flat against her, pinning her in place. "Ortiz!" I pushed myself clear as fast I could.

Twin cracks of thunder roared from a corner of the garage accompanied by brief flares of light. Anna jerked as one of her arms and her other shoulder burst into plumes of blinding light.

I smiled.

Who'da thunk the old trick would have worked again?

My smile slipped as the lights waned out of existence. Blood, the color of sangria, seeped from the wounds. Most of the tissue and surrounding mass remained irritatingly whole.

Anna wheezed.

I took a step forwards, snapping my foot out. The tip of my shoe met the side of her skull, forcing her neck into a bend that'd leave her with one hell of a headache.

Ortiz's weapon barked in triplicate. Each round elicited another spasmodic jerk from the prone Faust. Blossoms of light followed.

If only they'd lasted.

They fizzled out nearly as fast as they formed.

Ortiz stepped out of the dark corner of the garage, leveling her weapon at the monster's center. She quirked a brow and gave me a quick look.

I couldn't answer the silent question, but Anna lay like sack. An ugly, monstrous sack that sucked souls and salty wang...but an immobile one. I could live with that.

"Doesn't hurt to be thorough." Ortiz sounded like she meant that more for herself than me.

As if I needed any other reason for her to pop off a few more shots.

She did exactly that, pumping another pair of rounds into Anna's sternum. No flashes of light accompanied the new wounds.

Uh oh.

Ortiz and I exchanged another glance. "Do you want to explain that?"

I shook my head. "Can't. And if I could, I'm not sure the answer would be great." My words had a sobering effect.

Ortiz took a step back, eyeing me, then the Faust's

body. Her gun remained trained on the monster. "She could be dead." Ortiz didn't sound certain.

Truth be told, neither was I.

Another train of thought crossed my mind. One I didn't want to entertain. The rounds had done something at the start but failed to perform like they had on our first case together. Maybe there wasn't anything wrong with them. Maybe something had changed in Ortiz. And not in a good way.

My stomach threatened to flip at the notion.

I didn't like nursing any reservations about Ortiz, so I did something to cheer myself up. I booted Anna's injured shoulder.

Pettiness is beneath the seasoned paranormal investigator. I was checking if she was dead or not.

I booted her again.

Thoroughness is important.

Anna's wings tremored.

Oh crap.

"Ortiz, move!"

She was already in motion by the time I'd finished uttering her name. Ortiz moved with liquid grace in a crescent-like arc; smooth, controlled steps angling away from the Faust at a pace that didn't compromise her aim. Her handgun cried out once. The round buried itself in Anna's skull.

Her brain must have been located in her ass, because Anna exploded into the air. She launched a fist towards the base of my jaw.

I stepped back, clapping my hands together in hopes of catching her head between them. My balance faltered, and Anna seized the moment a bit too literally for my taste. Her arm snapped to an angle of double-jointed fuckery, and her fingers closed around my throat.

"Bwurk!" I sputtered in a freak moment of trying to exhale and steal breath at once. Five acute points of pressure filled my neck where her talons dug in. She hadn't drawn blood yet.

Ortiz moved at the edge of my peripheral vision. Her gun stayed fixed on the Faust as she circled us slowly.

Anna ignored her, glaring directly at me. The intensity in

her eyes doubled. "What exactly was that?"

I did my best to answer. It came out as a garbled mess.

The orange light in her eyes dimmed before flaring back up.

I took that as a blink.

She loosened her grip enough to allow me to breathe properly. "Let's try that again."

I swallowed a fistful of air. "It was a bad idea...bitch."

"I'll say. That was a numbing experience."

"Kind of wished it was permanently numbing."

Anna grinned. "It didn't hurt so much as made me sleepy."

So, Gnosis' little distinction proved true. Fausts weren't on the list allergic to bullets and blood.

Another shame.

"Maybe I just didn't shoot you enough." Ortiz stopped moving and gave Anna a glare of cold steel.

I arched a brow, giving Anna the best smile I could.

Sometimes when you're staring down monsters, it's best to smile them down. Don't let them see you shake. Don't let them catch onto the fact you might be scared. Sometimes, nothing bothers a monster more than having you smile in their face. It's a tad unsettling.

I stretched my smile wider. "Maybe you should back off, Anna." I inclined my head a fraction towards Ortiz. "She really wants to do as the cool kids do and pop a cap in your ass. My guess is several of them."

"I really do." Ortiz matched my smile. "Do me a favor and don't put him down. Give me a reason to shoot you some more."

Sometimes gunslingin' gals like Ortiz make the world go 'round.

"What's the worst that happens? Maybe she'll get lucky and go from being a New Yorker to Swiss. Get it, because of the bullets, holes—cheese?"

Anna's lips peeled back, revealing a bit too much fang for my taste. "Good point."

Oh no.

She snarled, twisting her body hard and wrenching me along.

Ortiz wasted no time. She fired without stop.

Anna wailed.

I lost track of what happened. A side effect of sailing through the air. A hot, blunted knife seared the outside of my left bicep. My vision flashed as the back of my neck and most of my back struck something soft.

Ortiz huffed out an oomph as she tumbled back and we crashed to the floor.

"Ow." I blinked until the spinning stopped.

"Get off me." Ortiz shuffled beneath me, letting out a groan.

I scrambled to my side.

Purplish fluid raced down Anna's legs and back, spattering the floor as she ran towards one side of the room.

My fingertips brushed the concrete floor as I pulled myself to a shaky stand. I broke into an instinct-driven sprint in pursuit of the Faust.

Anna shambled in an awkward gait, favoring one of her legs as she closed in on the deep wash sink.

The mirror. Sunuvabitch!

She aimed to bolt into the Neravene.

Three guesses where.

I shouted without looking over my shoulder. "Ortiz, get Eddie out of here." I don't know if she heard me. My only response was an ungodly roar that dwarfed the one made by her handgun. I chalked it up to her revolver.

Anna clawed at the air in front of the mirror like she aimed to tear it away. An earsplitting crack emanated from her shoulder blade, now sporting a pinky-width hole. The momentum of the shot sent her into a stumbling spin towards the reflective glass.

I caught up, just within arm's reach. I lashed out at her.

The surface of the mirror bowed and shimmered like a mirage.

Anna leapt, passing through it.

I jumped towards the glass with no idea if I'd follow or crash.

Not my brightest idea.

Chapter Thirty-Five

I shut my eyes, bringing my arms before my face to protect my borrowed mug. The world before me pushed back with a hint of resistance like I'd dived into a pool of gelatin. My momentum carried me forwards through a slog of air, fighting to push me back. The resistance ceased and I fell.

"Oh, fu—uff!" Pain radiated through the bones of my forearms and my sternum as I bounced off the ground. The burning sensation across the surface of my left bicep hadn't stopped. My eyelids fluttered open after a second of labored breathing. The throbbing of my arm stole my attention.

I'd caught a stray from Ortiz's gun. A finger-length wound that clipped the surface of my skin. I opened my mouth to swear, but the sight in front of me stole the words.

The borough of Queens stared back at me, though not as it was supposed to be. New York was painted in a palette consisting of dark, earthen browns and washed-out grays. An unseen hand had warped some of the architecture into that reminiscent of a hundred years ago. Antiquated and dilapidated structures intermingled with modern buildings. A few skyscrapers looked like they'd been stretched taller without any regard for proper proportions.

"The hell?"

"Not exactly." Anna watched me, her eyes narrowed slits. "But stick around, I'll make sure it's just as bad for you. And it'll be your final resting place."

"Drama queen much?" I exhaled through my nose, forcing a crooked grin. My expression slipped when I noticed a faint sheen to the air in places. I tilted my head to get a better look.

Mirrors. Countless fucking mirrors that, if lore served me correct, led anywhere—everywhere!

They hung frameless and unsupported, bobbing slightly

in the air. Formless things that were made of what looked like liquid glass.

The harder I stared at them, the clearer they became. It wasn't long before half of the airspace reflected images of the twisted Queens in a mass of mind trickery.

A seamless twist of space and distance.

Everything became harder to gauge.

Maybe I should've smashed the mirror from the outside.

"It's a lot to take in, isn't it?" Anna looked around, sniffing the air.

I stayed quiet. Her wounds had stopped oozing and were less grisly than before. They weren't healing as far as I could tell, but they didn't seem to bother her either. Something to take note of. Fausts felt pain but weren't hindered by most injuries.

That didn't leave me with much of an option. Not to mention I'd left my alternative plan behind. Punching my way through a Faust didn't seem like a good bet. But stalling did.

"Your home looks like shit." It wasn't wittiest thing I could have said, but when in doubt, cheap insults work.

Anna wrinkled her nose. "Funny, I was about to say you look like that."

I gawked at the creepy bat devil. "Did you just 'I know you are, but what am I' me?"

Her mouth spread into a dog-like grin, tongue hanging out of a corner.

Bleckh.

I needed information—fast. The longer I putzed around the Neravene, the more time would slip by in the real world and on my case. "Where are we?"

"The Hall of Mirrors." She stared at me like it was supposed to be obvious.

"Isn't that something from a carnival?"

"Your ignorance astounds me."

"Me too, on occasion. What's new?" I quirked a lopsided smile.

She froze, unsure of how to react to that.

I glanced around to the mirrors floating everywhere. "This is a whack version of Queens. Why?"

Anna held her stare.

I thought about it, putting together what I knew of Fausts, how they operated, and my limited understanding of the Neravene. "It's a reflection of where you operate. The when and where getting a bit blurred along the way. It's like Queens that is, was, and can be?" It was more of a question than a statement, but the logic seemed to fit.

"Obviously." Her voice was sharp enough to crack any of the mirrors around us. "It's how we pick up on desires. Watch." She waved a hand to a mirror just a few feet out of her reach.

It shimmered brighter as if pulling in more of the weak light offered in the twisted world.

I leaned to my side, thankful for the reprieve, and stared at the paranormal glass. A torrent of images raced through the mirror. My eyes and forebrain ached trying to process the mental onslaught of blurring colors and faces. The pressure built between my temples, making its way to the center of my brain. I was acutely aware of the moisture forming in the corners of my eyes and trickling down.

Desire welled inside me. My core tightened and fluttered as my brain raced into overdrive. I felt no end of wants, carnal lust, ravenous hunger, the kind of desire spurred by loss—a return of something or someone taken. My body threatened to collapse under the weight of it all. I tore myself away.

"Holy fuck!" I brought my palms to my eyes, grinding them to relieve some of the pain. The swell of thoughts and yearnings subsided, but the nausea didn't. I stood there, pressing harder against my face. Seconds passed before the pain and mental knots vanished. "What the heck was that?"

Anna's wing membrane spread under her arm as she gestured to our surroundings. Every mirror flashed once in unison as if responding to her motion. "Them. Everyone— every desire they have. Every want at once. All the things and what they're willing to trade for them."

I gritted my teeth. "Yeah, except you only accept one form of payment."

She shrugged as if it were no concern. "True. It's a lot to take in though, isn't it? For something like you, it must be like trying to keep track of a million gnats all at once."

My teeth ground as I tried to ignore her comparison between people, what they want, and being nothing more than insects to her.

"For Fausts, it's like being handed a menu. We can filter through it and then"—she reached out to the closest mirror—"just pluck." She pinched the air, grabbing some unseen object.

The images flooding the mirror stopped on command. One person filled the glass. A child, pre-teen, huddled without a care in a bed filled with pastel-colored pillows and a blanket. Her hair was a mess, bunched against the pillow with a quarter of it flopping over her skull to fall before her nose. She didn't seem to mind. The kid fidgeted like she was in that place before complete sleep took her. Maybe she was trying to dream without letting go.

It was an odd angle, like the lens we were viewing this through was mounted just an inch above the height of her bed.

I figured it was a mirror set on a children's dresser.

A barbwire band wrapped around my wrists as my hands tightened to the point I feared something would pop. The heat built and my fists shook uncontrollably. "What is this?" I could've cracked stone if I'd raised my voice any higher.

"A demonstration." Anna tilted her head towards the child without breaking eye contact.

No.

Anna turned and moved.

"No!"

Too late.

The Faust's body crashed into the mirror. Its surface rippled like it was nothing more than reflective water.

I buried my scream, letting it push me to run harder. The small bones in my ankles protested as I adjusted to face the mirror and lunged. I crashed into the surface, a dull vibration running up my forearms. I blinked several times.

Anna slipped into the dark room, looking over her shoulder at me.

My palms struck the mirror, sending a weak ripple through it like it was made of acrylic instead of glass.

The Faust moved along the side of her bed, raising a

finger to her lips. She didn't have to say the words.

And I sure as hell didn't listen. I screamed, sending another fist into the mirror. My knuckles throbbed and the surface flexed again, but there was no give. I pounded again. And again.

Anna stopped by the child's side, reaching out with a hand as if to brush her hair.

"Don't you fucking touch her! Don't you dare!" My fists pounded a chaotic drum solo against the mirror. I lost track of how many times I struck it, but I sure as hell felt every blow. The space between my knuckles felt taut and dry as needles pricked the skin. Twin splotches of blood smeared the mirror in a thin veneer.

I pulled my hands away, looking at them. Blood welled atop and between my knuckles where the skin had split. My hands shook in something besides anger.

Anna smiled. "Keep your voice down. You don't want to wake her."

"I'll fucking kill you." I hammered my fist into the mirror again before taking a step back to try another approach.

"You can't. But don't worry, now that I've got you here, I have all time in the world to take your soul. Let me just start with hers." Her smile was replaced by a look of mock concern. "She can't hear us—me, at least. I won't wake her for this." She touched a finger to the girl's temple.

Every angry shade of red imaginable swarmed my vision. The insides of my ears pulsated with my heartbeat, drowning out my own roar. I rushed forwards, kicking out and sending my heel into the mirror.

Ripple.

Flex.

Crack.

Crack?

The anger subsided in a surprise that flushed my nerves cool. I stared at the mirror. A spider-web of cracks filled an area smaller than my palm. Shimmering particulate matter flitted out from the cracks, catching the odd light from within the Neravene.

Anna stopped like she'd been jolted by a current. She looked through the mirror at me. Her face was an immobile mask. Getting even a shred of emotion out of her was a pain.

Whatever I'd done gave Anna cause for pause. I held onto that, hoping it meant something deeper.

Anna's lips folded in consideration before she looked away.

I caught the hesitation.

She touched the kid again, waving her other hand in my direction.

The cracked mirror flared and color rushed to fill the glass. A young girl, the same in bed, stood before me. She wore what looked like a mix of leather and metal armor fashioned in a comic book representation of an Amazon warrior. A band of dull gold ran around her head. The red and blue leather suited the tiny warrior.

She hefted a short sword, clearly made to her size, and smiled at it.

One little force to be reckoned with.

I couldn't help it, seeing the tyke like that forced my lips into a goofy grin. "What am I looking at besides a kickass kid?"

"What she wants." Anna's grin almost matched mine.

I sobered and stared hard at the image.

"And something she's willing to give up her soul for."

Glass cracked, and a tremor shot up my leg to settle in my knee. I pulled my heel back from the mirror and sank it in again. "She's. A. Kid!"

Anna nodded. "She is. One who knows what she wants and is in control over what to give. The matter isn't up to you. It's up to her."

I screamed again, bringing the base of my fist down against the corner of the mirror. It wobbled, the action making its way to the horribly cracked portion. More lines appeared as the glass stressed further.

Anna's mouth twitched.

A theory popped into my head. Breaking the mirror could likely stop the two-way connection between the Neravene and the child's room. But if I did that with Anna in the kid's room, she could end up trapped there. A devil hanging over a child.

I clenched my fists. The torn tissue over my hands

burned in response. It was the best bit of restraint I could manage.

Cool it. There's a kid in trouble. Be smart. Be patient. Think this through.

Anna worked to break my calm. "She wants to be a little hero. I can give that to her."

"Yeah, and for how long? A week? A month? A year? I call bullshit. I've seen how you treat those you deal with."

"Oh, don't take Eddie as the norm. He made a mistake, a stupid one. The others paid attention and negotiated. They played. They lost." Her smile stretched further at one corner of her lips.

"I caught that with Milo. Did he sign up for that shocking twist, or was that an accident?" I already knew the answer.

"Milo." She rolled his name around her mouth like she was remembering how to say it right. "I believe he got five years. But, yes, accidents happen."

My eyes turned to slits. "I'll bet. Doesn't that go against your contract?"

Anna didn't miss a beat. "Only if I'm the one to do it."

Oh shit.

"The Night Runners." I'd almost forgotten. "You hired them to take us out."

She gave me a look that said it was obvious.

"And with Fausts, it's a binding contract. You can't break it yourself if you want."

Anna held the stare that said I was an idiot.

I ignored it.

"The Night Runners were your cat's paws. You followed the letter of your contract. You, the butt ugly you, never did a thing to hurt Milo. You just put him in a position to be. And somehow you found a way to make it look like an accident—even to mortal authorities and doctors."

Anna said nothing, but the corners of her mouth quirked enough for me to notice.

I planned to wipe the look from her face.

Something else crossed my mind. "But wait..." I shut my eyes for a moment and rubbed my forehead with my thumb and forefinger. "Milo died in the hospital. You were there, and you killed Renee."

Anna kept up the silent look.

I was missing something. My head felt like an old television turned to a dead channel. Crackling static took over, so I changed the subject.

"Get out of her room, now." My voice could've flayed skin and sinew.

"Why would I do that?"

Good question.

"Because if you don't, I'll shove my shoe so far up your ass the laces will tickle your tonsils." It wasn't the best answer.

"Or I could stay here with little Shawna, and we could have a talk about what it costs to be a warrior princess."

Glass wailed and cracked in protest. A few shards bit into my hand that had suffered earlier in the day.

I hoped Church signed up for the super regeneration insurance package. My hands were going to be pulped if this kept up.

"I'm not going to let you do that to a fucking child!" My fist crashed into the glass twice more. The mirror flexed from the assault, and the cracks spread across much of the surface. "What happens if I break this and you're on the other side with a kid you have no claim over? She hasn't signed a contract yet. She's worth nothing to you." All I had to do for the moment was show Anna the kid wasn't worth the hassle.

Anna's grin could only be described as monstrous. "Why don't you let Milo tell you what's worth what?"

What?

"Daniel?" said a voice I'd heard only a few times since beginning my case.

I turned towards the source.

He was a scrawny kid that sported the computer geek image down to the way he dressed. The rectangular glasses sitting at crookedly on the bridge of his nose didn't help. I first pegged him at being in his mid-twenties, and his only redeeming feature to most was being over six feet.

I'd also seen him get carried out on a stretcher after being electrocuted.

The air left my lungs, freezing in my throat. "Oh, damn.

Milo...”

Chapter Thirty-Six

He hadn't changed much since I saw him. The burn marks were gone. That was something at least.

"Hey, Daniel." He gave me a thin, pained smile.

I don't know who hurt more at that moment, him or me. I swallowed the moisture in my throat and croaked out a reply. "Hey, you're looking..."

His smile found a way to look thinner.

I turned away from the image of Milo and glared at Anna. "What is this? No bullshit. I want answers."

"It's Milo, or the part I laid claim to."

It took me a while to find the courage to wrench my gaze away from the Faust. That wasn't Milo.

It was his soul.

I looked at him until I felt like I was looking through him. He didn't look like any definition of a soul I'd ever come across. No ethereal glowing spirit, nothing vaguely ghost-like. He looked complete and whole. I could have gone up and put a hand on him. I wagered he would have felt solid.

"No, you're lying. He's some spun-up concoction of this place." I waved a hand at my surroundings.

"If that's what you want to believe." She didn't sound like she was yanking my chain.

But then, monsters never do. They know how to play people. It's how they do what they do. Fausts would be among the best at that. Wheedling people out of their immortal souls isn't an easy job after all.

"Why's he look normal—real?"

Her mouth fell open in an awkward, over-stretched manner that I assumed was a gawk. "The Hall of Mirrors is showing him to you the only way you can possibly process it. Believe me, what's left of him looks very different to me. It's like looking at strands of cloth around pieces of the original. It's tattered, shredded, and what's left is bare thread. Those are the strands of value anyway."

My knuckles popped, and my fingernails buried into my palms.

She was talking about souls. People's freaking souls. The things that made them—you, me—unique. The very idea of people and what they could become. Possibilities, infinite choices that could go on and resonate in the world. All of that came from the soul.

Identity. The idea you get to be who you want to be. You earn that through the good choices and the bad.

And to her, it was nothing more than a damnable fucking payment—a cash card.

Milo was dead. Whatever I was looking at, soul or not, got shoved out of my mind.

My fists shook. "You're wrong."

"What?" Anna sounded like she was in disbelief.

"About the bits of his soul you have and them being of worth. You've stripped that worth. People are always worth something—always. You took him out of this world. You have no idea what he could have gone on to do. Who he could have touched and inspired. What differences, small or large, he could have made. That mattered!" I turned and swung my fist at the mirror.

Her ever-so-ugly Faustiness exploded from the mirror, clawed hand wrapping tight around my throat. My blow skirted past her cheek harmlessly as her momentum drove me back. She plowed forwards, driving me off balance. Anna thrust hard, forcing me to the ground and riding the move all the way down.

My body screamed six different ways as her body crashed atop mine. Her hand cut off my scream, reducing it to a sputtering cry. Sepia tones splotched and blurred through my vision as I tried to focus. I sent the back of my fist into a blow against her forearm. It connected but failed to free my throat of her grip.

She squeezed harder. "What's the matter? No righteous retort?"

"Hugurk!" It was the best I could do. I thrashed my lower half, lashing out with my knees. One struck her lower back, getting a quick huff of frustration out of her. If I didn't figure out a way to stop the batty choke, dry-hump session, I'd suffocate.

Some people pay for that...

I'm not one of them.

Anna pulled me by my throat, lifting my head a hand's breadth from the ground. "Look at them."

My head hung back a bit, limp as the muscles in my neck struggled to hold it upright.

Them?

I groaned and stared behind me. Aw, hell. Milo wasn't the only one watching me.

His mother stood to his side, unaware of everything. Her gaze was hollow, almost like she was blind. Silence left her mouth despite her moving it in an effort to speak. She turned directly towards Milo, looking through him to another mirror.

Her son stared back, fully cognizant that his own mother couldn't recognize him. His expression said it all. The electrocution wasn't the worst pain he'd endured.

Seeing the remnants of your dead mother looking through you like you're not there—that has to sting.

And I wished she were the only one who'd sprung up.

I pegged the newcomer as being in her late seventies. She was exactly the same as when I'd seen her in the hospital. Only her nose had been bleeding then. The old lady's crocheted shawl was coming undone, and much of the yarn was frayed. That was new.

Her glasses sported micro cracks that weren't deep enough to compromise the lenses but enough in number to be an annoyance. The old woman's eyes matched Milo's mother's. Glassy, unfocused things.

Some things added up. A small boy went out for a joy ride, crashing a car in a way that should have ended his life. He got his miracle. His grandmother ended up dead. And now I knew who was behind that "miracle."

It wasn't a stretch to figure grandma had gotten one hell of an offer to save her grandson. She was aging, probably didn't have long in life, and most of all—loved her family. Of course she was willing to sign over something intangible so he'd live.

Love does that to people. It's one of the most powerful

things out there, and people are willing to give up almost anything for it. It's a power that's toppled gods and darker things. Broken empires.

Never forget that.

Seeing her there and what she'd done reinvigorated me. I screamed to fuel myself and arched my back as much as I could. My fists arced down in a pair of hammer blows directed at Anna's forearm. Both struck in staggered succession, shaking her hold enough for me to wriggle free. I put on an animated and nasally Jersey accent. "Heads up, Bat Brain!" I twisted and put as much force as I could into my next punch. My fist met the side of her skull behind her right ear.

Her head rocked to the side. Anna's mouth parted in shock, and a globule of spittle flew free as she yelped.

Yelped?

Anna had felt the blow. Heck, it had rocked her.

I followed up with another punch to the same spot, putting more of my weight into it. The second strike drove the Faust off of me, sending Anna to her side.

She groaned, shaking her head.

I scrambled to my feet, processing it all. "Holy shit, you were shrugging off bullets back there. You're vulnerable here, aren't you? Why? Wait, scratch that—ooph!" My midsection felt like I'd been tackled by a Smart Car with arms. There was enough speed and mass behind her to make me worry about my ribs as she continued to push.

I sank my weight, struggling to ensure she wouldn't upset my balance. The more I lowered my center of gravity, the more she struggled. She hadn't lost her strength, but she definitely worked harder to put up a fight. I'd take whatever I could get. I straightened out and lifted an elbow before dropping it onto her spine.

Anna threw her head back and snarled. Her momentum faltered, and she released her hold, swiping up with her talons.

"Whoa!" I leaned back as the claws hissed spitefully by my chin. My hands clasped tight to her wrist, and I pivoted. I twisted harder, using more strength than proper technique to pull the Faust off balance. My hips braced against hers, and I yelled in effort.

Anna left the ground, sliding over the side of my body and to the ground with a weighty crash. A pained uff left her mouth, and the thin membrane of her wings shuddered.

I capitalized on the small blessing and dropped to a knee. My fist rocketed towards her bony rib cage. A hollow thud greeted me as my fist landed. I followed up with a succession of twin punches to the same spot. All that mass and weight being held up by a fragile set of bones meant that with enough force, I could make the act of just standing up a pain for Anna.

I was fine with that. My arm wound back as I cocked it for another punch. Her short snout seemed as good a place as any to bury my fist. "This is going to hurt."

Anna's mouth spread into a shaky smile. "Funny, I was going to say the same thing." Her eyes flashed.

What?

I lashed out.

Anna rolled, sending her wing's bulk crashing into me. She used the rest of her bulk to topple me onto my side.

I clawed at the ground and scrambled to my feet as she rushed past. "Chicken!"

She ignored my jibe and dove into the nearest mirror.

I chased after her, doing my best not to let my sight be stolen by the departed and lingering souls. I didn't need the distraction. My feet skidded against the uneven ground as I came to a halt before the mirror.

Anna wasn't visible inside it.

Everything within was shrouded in black.

Someone needed to Windex that thing.

A sound like sticks trailing against concrete prompted me to turn around.

Anna closed in, somehow having got around me. Her clawed feet scraped against the ground as she hurtled towards me.

It didn't take me long to do the math. She'd entered the mirror, found another one in the mortal world, and hopped back in. Wonderful. A maze of mirrors.

Just my luck.

I'd been thinking about mirrors the wrong way this whole time. I had picked up the car mirror earlier thinking it was a one-way thing. You look in, and the image is reflected.

I'd viewed them all as a one-way object.

The Faust had shown me they were doors. And the thing about doors is that they may open in a single direction, but you can pass through them either way.

So, if you shut the door with someone still in the room...

I knew what I needed to do.

And it was going to hurt.

I raised my hands like I was ready for a fight. One I planned to lose.

Anna's fingers spread wide, the talons picking up glints of weak light from the Neravene. It didn't help them look any less menacing. She snarled and swiped at me.

I gulped, stepping into the blow to avoid the worst of it. Her bony forearm clipped my skull. Better that than her skewers. My head snapped to the side as a dull throb filled my temples.

"You don't think you can keep this up, do you? Going head to head with—" Anna was cut short by a sickening crunch as the front of her snout deformed, and my forehead ached. She yowled in a mix of pain and fury.

I pulled my noggin back, rubbing the sore spot. I guess I take things too literally at times.

Trails of ichor—mucus and blood—dribbled from her nostrils.

I needed to be the one bleeding for my plan to work. Anna aimed to help make that happen apparently.

She lunged, grabbing hold of my shoulders and spreading her mouth wide.

I winced, and instinct drove me to struggle. "Gyah!" Curved, saw-like needles ripped into the flesh between the base of my neck and shoulder. The area of muscle screamed and tremored as she shook her teeth. I swallowed the whimper trying to leave my lips.

If this kept up, she'd chew her way down to my pelvis.

It's not as fun as it sounds, kids.

I pistoned a fist into her gut to little effect. She seemed keen on using me as her chew toy. I buried both sets of fingers into her throat, digging into every point I could.

Anna's eyes widened, and she released her hold, gasping. Her wings beat in a frenzy as she raked her claws against my chest.

I broke my grip, reeling back and pawing at my front. I panted and pulled my hand away from my chest. A coating of blood acted like syrup, trying to glue my hand to the shredded bits of my shirt.

Well, step one done. Bleed.

Ow.

Anna released an animalistic burble and swung with the back of her closed fist.

The clay-like tones of the Neravene flashed out of sight, replaced by electric streaks of yellow and red as my head whipped to the side. My mouth ached, and the ground moved below me. I tasted salt and iron. Her backhanded strike had split the inside of my cheek. My body hit the ground, and I rolled several feet before coming to a stop.

Muted shades of brown and dull color flooded my vision. A dribble of blood leaked out of one corner of my mouth, refusing to fall to the ground. I racked up a bit of saliva and spat it out to force the blood to follow. A brief groan left my lips, and I pushed myself up to a shaky stand. It was short lived.

My lower back exploded in pain and the muscles around it seized in response. I lurched forwards off balance, turning to look back in time to act. My hand shot out in instinct. The inside of Anna's wrist struck my forearm, but it wasn't enough to deflect her attack. Razor blades and hot coals raced over my left bicep, leaving small furrows that ran red.

There was such a thing as bleeding too much for the cause.

I felt it was time to put up a better fight. Especially since Anna wasn't batting one hundred percent in the Neravene.

I gnashed my teeth and gritted through the pain in my arm. I reached out with a hand and sunk my fingers into her wing. With a quick yank, I tore the membrane.

She screamed. It was a high-pitched trill—any louder and it would've been beyond human hearing.

Flesh stretched and strained, fighting back until the semi-elastic tissue couldn't hold any longer.

For the record, I was right. Anna's howling intensified into something that nearly caused my ears to bleed before I couldn't hear it any longer.

Scraps of thin skin hung from my fingers. Bits of the membrane acted almost like they had a mind of their own, clinging tight and almost wrapping around my digits. I shook my hands free of filth. A rogue piece held to one of my index fingers.

"Bastard!" Anna's mangled mouth twitched before her lips peeled into a snarl. Blood tinged teeth greeted me.

I suppressed a shiver and replied in kind. My smile wasn't as intimidating, but it made a point. I dangled the loose bit of former wing hanging from my finger. "Got your nosey...erhm, well, wing bit. Ew." I flicked it free.

She shrieked and sent her claws into a frenzied flurry. It was like being attacked by a pair of douchey paranormal blenders.

I backpedaled, relying on years of instinct and borrowed skills to avoid the worst of it. My clothing suffered each time I shifted my weight and body to narrowly miss being turned into Graves tartare. I lost track of how many times my eyes shut and my jaw locked to drown out the pain during our exchange.

Anna pushed harder.

I don't know where she drew the strength to keep up. Maybe I'd pissed her off to an extreme degree.

I have that effect on monsters.

Anna swiped at my throat, aiming to open an extra airway in it.

On the account that I was breathing fine as it was, I elected to leap towards her. I grunted as the inside of her arm batted my already wounded bicep. Angry heat flared through the spot but I took it and wrapped my arms around her. I set my jaw and squeezed my arms as hard as I could. The bear hug wouldn't do much to hurt her, but it'd keep her from trying to turn my face and throat into mincemeat.

She thrashed in my grip, and my muscles burned in response.

I just needed to haul her ass to the nearest mirror, and I could get to work.

The fire in my arms was winning out.

Anna dragged a set of talons over my thigh.

My grip broke, and the Faust turned, sending a bony elbow into my face. Red and bright white streaked through my eyes again. I staggered back, glancing at my right leg. The slashes weren't fatal, but they'd be bothersome for a while. I'd live and heal fine.

Anna hobbled towards another mirror not more than a dozen yards from us.

"Like hell you do." I slapped a hand to my thigh, squeezing the wound tight in hopes of stemming some of the blood. Weariness and pain sought to drag me to the ground like lead weights. I shook my head, trying to dispel the fatigue. My adrenaline rush had come and gone. But, if I didn't stop Anna, more people would lose their souls.

And maybe a little girl would never grow up to be a warrior princess.

I chased after her, wincing as every step sent a shock through my injured leg.

Anna passed through a mirror.

I snarled, picking up my pace and pulling a fist back. A dark mass hurtled by at the edge of my vision. I slowed, turning my head and shifting my body to address it.

The Faust had shambled out of another mirror, heading towards Milo and his mother. Anna was hopping through the reflective objects faster than I could keep up. She closed in on Milo faster than I would have liked.

I buried the pain in my leg, telling myself I'd deal with it later and set off after Anna.

Milo saw her coming but he did nothing to avoid her. His lips pressed tight, and his features pulled into a resigned mask of expectancy. He knew what was coming, and didn't intend to fight it.

I only wish I knew what was coming.

Anna raked a hand at him, passing through him like he was nothing but condensed fog. The center of his body parted, and the Faust snapped her jaws as the gaping hole. She tore into his spectral form like a shark gorging on chum. Anna was tearing into the remains of his soul.

The tendons in my body turned into rebar, refusing to move. My joints froze. It didn't last. My heart sped up, pumping like an electric arc furnace sending rivulets of hot metal through my veins.

I raced towards her with renewed vigor as she remained ensconced in the act of devouring a soul. My scream ripped what little moisture I had left in my throat, threatening to tear the lining.

Anna turned her head towards me. Her eyes were a mix of almost drug-induced ecstasy and wide-eyed confusion.

I aimed to settle the confusion part for her. I leapt, throwing my fist out with all the weight, anger, and momentum I could. It felt like a brick had come down on my last two knuckles. I winced and followed through with the blow.

Anna stumbled sideways a couple of steps, relinquishing her hold over Milo.

Correction: what remained of him. And it wasn't much. His form had lost all shape and color. It was like looking at tufts of the cheapest cotton shredded and tossed into the wind. Ghostly, pale-blue strands flitted into the air before dissolving entirely.

My imagination likely fueled the Neravene into showing me the scene unfold that way.

Anna had killed Milo. She'd taken his soul. Even that little bit was gone now. The Faust had completely removed a person from the life and the afterlife.

Something snapped in the darker parts of my brain.

I twisted, sending my left fist into a quick, short uppercut. My fist cracked into the front of her ribs. I repeated the blow before pivoting and sinking my weight as I brought my elbow onto the back of her shoulder.

She staggered, doubling over further and nearly falling to her knees.

My throat wasn't up to another scream. I spat, muttering a curse and driving my heel into the side of her head. "You freak of nature." I punctuated every word with a kick to her ribs. "You killed him—twice!" The following blow struck her chest with more of my shin than my foot.

Anna endured the assault in silence. Her body shivered throughout the ordeal. Puffs of air left her nostrils and mouth in staggered succession. They increased in intensity.

I stepped back, eyes widening as I realized what she was doing. "Stop laughing." I fell to a knee, bringing my fist down against the back of her skull. My punch drove her face into the ground. I expected the sickening sounds of breaking cartilage and fractured bits of jaw.

I was wrong.

Anna laughed harder through the pavement sandwich.

I took a step back when my anger subsided, and I noticed the rest of her body. Her wings were whole. No clawed-out portions, which I certainly remembered doing. The sides of her snout were fine, whole, and not deformed from the battering.

She'd been restored.

"You know"—she laughed harder—"the claims about soul food being good for you aren't exaggerated."

Anna had just made a pun about snuffing out a soul...and a bad pun at that.

I threw another punch.

The Faust sprung to her feet in a burst of preternatural speed. She brought an arm up, catching the inside of my forearm against her elbow. Her hand shot out, closing tight around my throat once again. She shifted and pistoned her arm, throwing me without effort.

I flailed, struggling to adjust for the fall. The back of my heels touched the ground, and I tumbled backwards, twisting to take the brunt of the landing across the broad of my back and shoulders. My body cried out as the jarring impact rattled through me. I rolled over completely. My knees banged against one another as I came to my side. I lay within arm's reach of the mirror I'd entered the Neravene through.

Unlike the bat freak, my injuries hadn't recovered. I bled well enough to do what I needed. I groaned, clawing at the ground, and hauled myself within a hand's breadth of the mirror.

Swearing beneath my breath, I brought my right hand to the bleeding tissue beneath my shoulder and neck. The blood had turned sap-like, not quite dried. It'd have to do.

I traced a finger against the lowest corner of the mirror that was obscured by my body. The symbol from my journal waned from the mental image I tried to keep in my mind. I shut my eyes tight, fighting to keep the picture clear. It was more of a psychosomatic action than anything else. But it helped.

My finger shook in a mix of fatigue and pain as I dragged it along to create the intricate details of the symbol.

"I wanted to offer you something. A chance to have a life." Anna's voice was tinged with smoke and heat. She sounded pissed I'd spurned her offer.

Oh well.

"You didn't have to be so stubborn. You could have avoided this."

I rolled over, pressing my back to the mirror. My lips spread into a toothy, blood tinged smile. "Maybe I'm a tough negotiator?" I widened my smile and shifted to hide the symbol behind my lower back. My index finger continued to scrawl away. It wasn't easy trying to replicate the design while facing in the other direction.

"You're so funny." Her tone implied she thought I was anything but. She lifted her foot and kicked out.

Three points of acute heat blossomed over a tight cluster on my chest. The tips of her talons tore my flesh.

She leaned into me.

The talons dug deeper.

"Ffft." I bit down on my tongue to choke off the pained cry.

"I could have given you answers. You could have had a normal life—a new one, if you wanted. All you had to do was give up something—a state of being you're not even enjoying. Do you like living this?" She put more weight against me, talons burrowing deeper into the muscle of my chest.

I winced, panting before I could dredge up a reply. "A little roughhousing can be fun." I gave her a toothy smile and winked.

Anna ground her foot against me.

I screamed.

"You're not funny. You're irritating, irrational—maddening!"

I coughed hard in pain and an effort to clear my throat. "First, you hit on me. Then, you hit me. Now, you're flattering me. You'll confuse a guy."

She wrenched her foot away, her talons hurting nearly as much on the way out as they did in.

I stayed silent, letting the agony fuel the glare I shot her.

Come on. Stop throwing a hissy fit and look into the mirror.

A deep burble formed in Anna's throat, one she swallowed. She bent and grabbed my jaw and hauled.

The place where my spine met my skull cried like it was going to snap. I lashed out with a kick to the inside of one of her thighs.

She took the blow without any signs of discomfort.

I guess chowing down on Milo topped off her tank.

Her fingers squeezed my lower jaw with enough strength for me to worry about her turning bone to dust. She loosened her hold, transferring her grip to hold me by the top of my throat. "Got anything funny to say now?"

"Heh. I know you are, but what am I?"

She slammed me against the mirror, my head ricocheting off it with a crack that surely came more from me than the glass. Anna pulled me close enough to breathe on me. "What happens when I kill you? Will your little soul flit away to another body? Will you die for real? Maybe, maybe if I kill you here—in my domain—maybe you'll stay here. Wouldn't that be fun? Just you and me, repeating this all over again. Except, this time, you'll be a little less resilient." She pressed her thumb to one of my puncture wounds and ground.

I gritted my teeth and stared her down. "I'd still kick your ass."

"Still? Is that what you think has happened here?"

I flashed her a crooked smile. "Looks that way to me."

"Hm. I'll tell you what it looks like."

Indulge me, freak.

"It looks like you've lost. That you're stalling, trying to catch a second wind that won't do you any good. But let me tell you what I see."

This should be good.

She turned me around and thrust me against the mirror.

I twisted to avoid crashing into it face first. One of my cheeks smashed against the glass, and my temple throbbed from the impact.

"Look in the mirror."

I struggled, placing a hand on the glass surface to push away from it.

Anna figured out what I was going for and used her other hand to grab me by the wrist. She pulled my arm, straightening it out and shoving me harder against the mirror.

"Look!"

"I've got this funny feeling if I do, I'll see a hideous batty monster."

My face pulled away from the mirror before crashing back into it. I almost saw stars.

Guess Anna didn't appreciate the lip, so she settled for trying to split mine.

"I'll tell you what I see." The surface of the mirror flashed like it harbored an inner light. "I'm going to step through this and leave you here. I'm going to find Eddie and tear him apart, slowly. You're going to watch his soul end up in this place right before I devour it. Then, I'm going to go back and fetch your friend Ortiz. Can you guess what I'm going to do to her?"

I grunted and struggled in her grip. "Maybe you should look closer in the mirror, and I'll tell you what I see!" I pulled hard, slipping my extended arm free from her grip. I snaked it behind her waist and pushed. The sudden maneuver caught her off-guard, and her skull bounced off the mirror. Her hold on my neck broke and I stepped behind her, pressing her forehead against the mirror so she'd look straight into it.

Anna thrashed and placed a hand against the glass to push against it. Her hand stuck like it was bonded to the surface. She huffed in agitation and pushed. The mirror acted like a pool of silvery glue. It refused to let go. She pulled against it. Tendrils of liquid glass peeled away from the mirror before snapping back, taking Anna's arm with them. She slammed into the mirror.

"What did you do?"

I pointed to the symbol I'd scrawled on the bottom left corner. "I got to thinking about what you said. The eyes are the windows to the soul, right? Lore says that mirrors are reflections of more than just our physical imagery. They're reflections of what's inside of us—the good, the bad. Things like our desires and our thoughts. Things like our souls."

Anna put her other hand on the mirror out of instinct. She pressed hard and leaned back.

It didn't do her any good.

The mirror fought back, pulling her arm in like it was mercury-colored quicksand.

"No. No-no-no." Anna's shook her upper body, thrashing around like the act of doing so would deny her fate.

"It didn't take me long to put it together. If Fausts can pass through mirrors and if mirrors hold that level of significance in lore, it stands to reasons you can trap one of your kind in them. After all, what can be opened, what can be passed through, can be shut and locked. The rest is what you gave me. The bit about taking souls through eyes. I figured if I could get a Faust to look in a mirror with a seal, well, your own magic would trap you in your own doorway. Neat, huh?"

She shook her arms, still fighting in futility. "Stop this, please!"

Please? That was rich.

I placed my foot against the small of her back and pushed. "Uh, I'm going to go with a big 'No' on that one." I pushed harder.

"I can save Eddie!"

I stopped and pulled my foot back. It wasn't much to help her predicament, but she noticed it. "I'm listening. Talk fast, before you end up as a talking novelty mirror."

"I can cancel his contract. I can free him!"

I had a feeling she could do that.

But at what cost?

Her freedom, likely. Meaning she'd no doubt ensnare someone else down the line. Knowing her, there'd be no end of people. Back to square one. One soul damned to this place in exchange for keeping Anna from snagging countless more. It wasn't good math, no matter how I looked at it.

After all, what's the worth of one immortal soul?

Anna slipped further into the mirror. She kicked it and leaned back. Her foot stuck to the surface and followed suit with her arms. "Help me. Help Eddie. Think about it."

I did and took a step back.

The mirror pulled half of Anna's body into itself.

"Help." Her pleas grew weaker. It was almost like she was begging.

I wondered how many people had given her that same

line. I wondered how many she'd ignored while delighting in taking the last bit of their individuality—their existence— from them.

Anna's face touched the mirror. Her body spasmed in the kind of frenzy a drowning man would exhibit.

I'd know.

A second later, she passed wholly into the mirror. Anna's form didn't look much different. She stared at me, seething. "I'll kill you for this."

I tapped a finger to the mirror. "Yeah, I don't think so. But, maybe, if you play nice, we can see about letting you out."

She threw her head back and scoffed. "Forget it. You had your chance to save Eddie. We'll still get his soul. He and everyone else is ours. We made the deals. We set them up. We're going to collect."

We. She had said, "We."

The last piece fell into place.

There were two of them.

Ortiz and everyone else was vulnerable.

And I'd trapped Anna in my only way out.

Chapter Thirty-Seven

"Shit." I put my hands to the side of my head, rubbing my temples.

"Just figured it out, did you? You're stuck. That gives us all the time in the world to sit and talk. Maybe make a deal? How long do you think has passed, by the way, in the mortal world? A day? A week? Long enough for the rest of your friends to end up here? Maybe—"

"Shut up." I banged the base of my fist against the mirror. My anger wasn't in the blow. It was to make a point.

Anna didn't get it. "Strike a nerve? It's not easy to pass down our deals, you know? Not when we're handing everything someone's wanted on a platter. People can't turn that down. They rarely do in fact."

"Shut. Up." I slammed my fist harder, punctuating each word with a bang.

The surface of the mirror flexed like weak plastic, and Anna's eyes flicked from side-to-side. She made the effort to suppress a shiver.

The Faust had been freaked before when I battered a mirror she was on the other side of, but she'd been safe in someone's home then. She was nothing more than a fixture in one now.

I smiled. "You're right; we should talk."

Anna matched my smile, pressing herself against the glass.

I took a step back. That wasn't an image I needed to see.

She picked up on that. "Sorry, is this better?" Her features rippled, and muscles flexed like snakes under her skin. It was like watching a contortionist wriggle every bone and sinew at once. Milk-white sap oozed from her pores, covering the entirety of her body. The fluid constricted her mass, and fleshy tones bled through it.

Anna stood in the mirror as I'd first seen her. Well, sans the clothing.

It wasn't a bad view. But given that I knew what lay underneath, I couldn't exactly appreciate it.

"Uh, beauty is definitely skin-deep in your case, Anna. But kudos on the nifty Skin Sheath."

"Superficialist." Anna turned and gave me a chiding look over her shoulder.

"Only on the outside." I pinched my borrowed cheeks and pulled them.

"Mhm. Let's skip the witty banter and get onto what's really on your mind—deals. You want something. I want out. Talk."

"Aw, but the witty banter is the best part. Can't make deals without a little foreplay."

Anna's smile thinned.

"Alright, fine." I cleared my throat. "You want out, and I want Eddie's contract nixed. Oh, throw in a Way out of here too."

Her smile vanished, and she shook her head. "No deal."

"What?" I gawked at her.

"One or the other. You're not getting both. You can save Eddie and make yourself comfortable here. Or you get a way out of here, let me out, and maybe, if you're lucky, save your friends. Your mistake is thinking you have a lot more leverage than you do. You don't. I won't be trapped here forever. You know that. You're not the only one who can let me out." Her smile returned with a hungry light coloring her eyes.

Damn. She was right.

I exhaled and leaned against the glass, forcing a smile on my face. "Yeah, but will you get out in time?"

Her face went flat, and she shot me an oblique stare. "In time for what?"

I clenched my jaw, bracing for the pain to come. My fist rocketed into the glass. The mirror vibrated and flexed without giving.

Anna's eyes shot wide. "What are you doing?"

"Testing a theory." I slammed my fist into the glass again. "What happens if I break a mirror with a Faust inside? I've got a feeling it's more than a few years of bad luck for you." I winked.

Anna's lips pressed tight, and she swallowed. She looked over her shoulder for some place to escape.

Thud. Thud. Thud. My fist smashed into the glass. The small bones in my hand throbbed and threatened to give out after all the abuse they'd suffered of late. I kept it up regardless. Thud. Crack!

Heh. Lines as fine as fishing line spread through the glass in the area around my fist. Barely audible cracks continued to sound off as the breaks spread and deepened.

"Well, I guess we're about to find out about my theory, huh? Still going to be a tough negotiator?"

Anna's eyes looked like they were quivering in her sockets. She licked her lips and panted.

"Going once." I drove my other fist into the glass near the already cracking area. It buckled and flexed before giving. Mini fissures spread through the glass, some of which raced to join the previous cracks. "Going twice." I stepped forwards and brought my elbow into the mirror. A hideous, deep crack snapped into life and split across the upper right corner of the glass. If it grew any larger, it'd break a portion of the top clean off.

Anna pressed her hands to the mirror, bringing her face close. "Stop it! Please, just stop."

I stepped back, tensing a leg and making my intention clear. "Yeah? Give me a reason to."

"Alright, alright." She leaned away from me, holding out a hand in a gesture to calm me. Anna turned her other hand palm up, twisting it like she was unscrewing a jar lid. Tendrils of flames sparked into life around the base of her wrist. They snaked up her fingers, spreading wide and flat into the air above. It was a short-lived fire show.

The flames crackled and dimmed, their color fading. A sheet of soft taupe parchment took their place. Aggressive, bold cursive lined the page. At the bottom, a series of scribbles that were clearly a signature.

It didn't take a detective to guess whose.

Anna took the contract by its corner, pinching them tight between her thumbs and forefingers. "All I have to do is tear. That good enough?"

I opened my mouth, then shut it just as fast. I'd almost

fallen for it.

There's a lot in the rumor mill about contracts and dirty dealings. One bit stood out in my mind. It may have had nothing to do with Fausts, or it could have had everything to do with them. I'd learned that some clichés came from paranormal origins.

I followed the hunch. "No, do me a favor and tear it into a bunch of tiny pieces."

Anna's eyes narrowed, and she looked at me like I was odd. She did as I asked however, shredding the contract into countless scraps. "Satisfied? Now, let me out, and I'll throw this to the wind." She rustled the bits of paper in her hands.

"How about you eat them." I smiled.

"What?"

"You heard me. Eat the contract."

Anna's mouth shut, and I could hear her swallow saliva. She licked her lips a second later. "That's crazy."

"Maybe, I've been called that before. Doesn't change my demand. Eat it."

She scowled, shooting me a look that could have turned steel into molten scrap. But she took a fistful of paper and shoved it into her mouth. The Faust chewed and swallowed, repeating the process with the remaining scraps. "You're smarter than I gave you credit for."

"I have my moments and..." Something moved at the edge of my vision. I shifted my body without fully turning.

She was a bit plump, and her platinum blond hair hung just past her chin. The hint of red in her pale cheeks had fled. She looked tired—ghostly, even.

"Renee?" Instinct, stemming from Daniel and his memories of her, urged me to reach out towards the woman. My insides felt like cracked pieces of the mirror wormed through them. A mix of slicing heat and sharp jabs filled me. I shut my eyes and worked to separate Daniel's latent feelings from my own. Renee had been his friend, not mine. But that didn't mean a part of those pangs weren't my own.

I exhaled and turned from her hollow stare. She wasn't really aware of anything by the look of it. "I think I'm going to renegotiate our terms." My fingers dug into my palm as my fist tightened.

Anna's gaze flicked from Renee to me. "What?"

Glass cracked. My knuckles ached and screamed as bits of mirror carved through my flesh.

"Stop!"

I didn't. Both of my fists rained blow after blow against the mirror. Each strike made glass cry. Chips of former mirror fell to the ground. Blood trickled down the sides of my fingers, and my hands twitched of their own accord. I took a step back, eyeing the mirror.

It was cracked throughout, yet remained together.

I planned to fix that.

My heel smashed the middle of the mirror, shattering it into pieces.

Anna's scream was silenced as her image fell apart and shimmering glass rained to the ground.

My hands shook harder. I squeezed my eyes, trying to ignore the pain.

"You bastard!"

I opened my eyes and stumbled back. "What the hell?" I looked down to the source of the noise.

Anna seethed inside a piece of glass the size of my shoe. "When I get out of here—"

I raised my foot.

The Faust held up her hands.

"I've got a feeling you won't be getting out any time now." I brought my foot down, stopping just before crunching the glass. There was still another Faust out there.

Gnosis had told me one of the best ways to stop these freaks was to get them to kill each other.

And now I knew how to make that happen.

I pulled my foot back and eyed Anna. "How do I get out of here?"

She gave me the finger.

Fair enough.

I racked my brain, thinking over everything I had read in my journal. It didn't give me much on this portion of the Neravene. Gnosis had given me his best guess on how the Fausts hopped through mirrors. Anna had built on that, but it still wasn't a concrete answer.

You can't open Ways with a wave of your hand. Not without power and a whole lot of knowledge.

I didn't have the luxury of not figuring it out. Ortiz and Daniel's other friends were in trouble.

"'Kay, think."

"Don't hurt yourself." Anna sounded like she was enjoying my predicament.

I glared at her. "Maybe I should crush you into specks of glass."

She shut up.

"I saw you open a Way when you entered here. You didn't just dive into the mirror, you did something to it. You bridged it to this part of the Neravene."

She didn't answer, but I hadn't expected her to.

"But once you were here, you were hopping through mirrors without issue. Heck, you didn't do a single visible thing to them. You just went on about desires and picking up on mortal wants and..."

Son of a bitch. Gnosis had told me the way to operating in here was exactly how the Fausts did it.

"That's it, isn't?"

Anna remained silent.

"You weren't kidding about the menus thing. This place is an all-you-can-eat buffet. You have to open a door to get in, but once you're here, it's just a matter of knowing what you want and reaching out for it."

The Faust's body tensed, meaning I was onto something.

I rubbed my hands together. The action sent a small jolt through the damaged tissue and likely battered bones. I gritted through it and trained my eyes on another mirror. "Be seeing you." I gave a two-finger salute to Anna and marched off towards the glass I'd eyed a moment ago.

The mirror shuddered, and a ripple went through its surface like it wasn't solid.

Magic is weird.

I placed a hand on it, running it along the glass. Blood trailed behind and marred my reflection. I'd expected to see something more, like the way out.

Anna perked up as if on cue. "It's not that easy."

I ignored her. No one ever said it would be. I placed my fingertips against the mirror, leaning into it.

Desires.

We all have 'em. Sorting them out is another issue.

Unchecked and rampant wants flooded me. Every desire I nursed deep down, and Daniel's as well. The mirror responded in kind.

Its surface quivered like a disturbed body of water. Images rushed by in a blur like a flipbook going too fast. My navel felt like it'd been hooked and tugged as the swirl of desires went through the mirror. The pull grew stronger the longer I stared.

"It's even harder focusing, isn't it? You want it all. You need it all. It's a very mortal thing, desires—unchecked ones. Why settle for just one thing when you know I can make them all come true?" Anna's voice went up a few notches in delight. She enjoyed watching me flounder.

I clenched my jaw and fought the urge to stomp her into bits of nothingness. The mirror flashed faster.

That bitch!

She wanted me riled up, unable to think clearly. Anger fuels desire just as well as other things. Often, more so.

It's easy to get angry and let it carry you away. A whole new set of wants, driven by rage, that overwhelm the others. Keeps you from focusing on what needs to be done.

I shut Anna out and pushed aside the distractions. This was about getting back to Ortiz. I just needed to make that desire stronger than all my others.

Easier said than done.

Fear welled inside me, sending a cold static charge over my skin. If I didn't get back, Daniel's friends, my own, would be in danger.

This affects whatever's left of you just as much as it does me.

I hoped the lingering bits of Daniel's thoughts and memories got the message. I pushed with a single hand against the mirror. Come on. One image dominated my mind: Ortiz's face.

I need to get back there—I want to. It was my job. My responsibility. My desire.

Gentle heat filled my palm, radiating through my fingers and up my arm. The mirror flashed into a mural of porcelain white tiles that shifted without stop. It was like looking at a kaleidoscope.

"Guess this is it."

"Are you sure about that?" Anna's question hit me harder than I'd expected. "What if you're wrong? What if it leads somewhere worse?"

She had a point. The Neravene wasn't exactly tourist friendly. But I didn't have a choice.

"Could be worse. I could be stuck here, like you." I flashed her a wink before pushing against the mirror. My hands passed through, which was good enough for me. I stepped through the glass.

* * *

The brown of the Neravene washed away into jarring whites, forcing me to shut my eyes. My heel clipped something smooth and hard. I tumbled forwards.

"Fuck—" I hit the floor, cool tiles pressing against the bare bits of my skin. I blinked until the red and yellow spots cleared.

Smooth, antiseptically clean flooring that matched the tiles. A white sink that I had no doubt caught my foot on. My surroundings were a dead ringer for the bathrooms in the hospital where Anna had worked.

Meaning Ortiz was here.

Oh crap.

My heart lurched into overtime. I scrambled to my feet and addressed the tingling sensation spreading over my forearm. Twelve hours had passed in the Neravene. Half a day—gone. Seventeen hours to find Ortiz and nail the remaining Faust.

Just what had happened in all that time?

I turned and leaned over the sink, opening the cold faucet with a smack of my hand. Walking around the hospital battered and bleeding wasn't a good idea. A generic, white hand towel hung from a silver ring. I yanked it free and ran it through the water. Satisfied it was cold enough, I wrung it until it was damp, pressing it to my various wounds.

I bit back the curse that made its way to my lips and endured the pain in the tender areas. The process was dull and methodical, but I kept cooling and cleaning my wounds until they looked a tad less grisly.

I'd heal, and that's what mattered.

My shirt was useless scraps, so I ripped it clean and tossed it in the nearby metal bin. I'd find something on the way out. First things first: find Ortiz.

I moved out of the room and cast a quick look around.

My hunch worked out better than I had hoped. I'd landed right where I'd wanted to be. And the proof lay in the bed within arm's reach from me.

Eddie lay in traction. The bruising had worsened, or at least the coloring had. It didn't do wonders for how his face looked. But he was still breathing. And he was free.

I placed a hand on his leg, saying nothing. Finding the right words wasn't easy. I hoped the simple gesture counted. A train of thoughts ran through my mind.

Eddie had gotten to the hospital. Likely manner, Ortiz. Neither of us had called for help prior to my jumping into the Neravene. Made sense that she dragged him here or at least alerted medical services.

If I knew Ortiz, that meant she'd be nearby. She wouldn't risk going to what would now be considered a crime scene, assuming Eddie's condition was chalked up to assault, of course.

No, too many variables. Simplify.

Eddie was here. Ortiz would do the smart thing and keep an eye on him in case I'd failed and Anna showed up. Content with my logic, I headed for the door.

The handle jostled and I tensed.

The door opened.

"Vincent?" Ortiz's eyes widened. She looked well rested, more so than me at any rate.

Even a few hours of sleep would've done me good. But part of my job meant burning through bodies and their limits until the case was over. It wreaked havoc on me, but I didn't have other options.

I opened my mouth to speak, but she cut me off.

"What the hell happened to you?" She shoved me inside, closing the door behind us. "Never mind, not here."

"I, uh—"

A plastic bag rustled in her hand. She thrust it against

my chest. "Here."

"Thanks, I—"

"You've been gone for half a day. Tell me you got her. Your body is... Are those bite marks?"

"Ortiz! Holy shit. Sorry. Yes. And yes."

She glared, and I found myself wishing I was back in the Neravene with Anna.

"Explain." Ortiz held her glare, waiting for answers.

I hooked a finger against the lip of the bag, tugging it open. A clean change of clothes sat folded inside. I snaked the simple black t-shirt free, not bothering with the rest of the clothing. "Oh, you know. I tussled with a crazy gal. She was into dress up, nurse role-play. She was kinky—a biter. Kind of batty, you know?"

Ortiz gave me a thin smile. "You know, I can make it so you really will need a stay in here." Her smile widened.

I wriggled into the shirt, holding up a hand to calm her. "Uh, one rough session is enough for me." I told her everything that had happened.

"So, it's over? You trapped Anna for good? Eddie's free?"

I shook my head. "Not exactly."

Ortiz stared.

"Think about it. Anna couldn't break her own contracts."

Her eyes widened. "Unless someone else did it for her."

I nodded. "Someone who also happens to have access to the patients here. Someone who happened to have access to Daniel's friends. Someone who happened to be standing in front of my face the whole damn time!" I clenched a fist several times before stopping. "Let's go find Ashton."

Chapter Thirty-Eight

Ortiz spun and swung the door open. "He's not here today. I told him to call off. I was worried in case Anna gave you the slip and came back for Eddie. I didn't want any of Daniel's friends getting caught up in anything nasty."

"Too late." I followed her out of the room, moving to her side as we hustled to the elevator. "Please tell me you have an idea of where he might be?"

Ortiz pursed her lips and shook her head.

"What about the others?"

She answered my question with a silent look.

It wasn't an answer I wanted. "Shit, Kelly?" The young woman had a habit of making risky choices.

She stopped cold outside the elevator.

"Ortiz, what's wrong?"

"Kelly." Ortiz took a breath and pressed the button to summon the lift. "She said she wanted to check some things out. You've gotten her curious about this world. Too curious, in my opinion."

A chill settled in my stomach. "Yeah, I had that worry with you, for the record."

She gave me a thin smile. "Kelly told me she was going to dig around Daniel's life to see if she could find anything that might be useful."

Oh no.

"And let me guess, she ruled the apartment out because we've pretty much tossed that place."

Ortiz nodded.

"Meaning she headed to the art studio. The only place left that makes sense. Dammit." I poked the button several times as if it'd bring the elevator to us any faster.

"It's also where I'd head if I were Ashton." Ortiz gave me a knowing look. "You said these monsters pick up on desires. Kelly's new to all of this. A girl who wants answers badly. Someone Anna and Ashton haven't tempted yet."

I should have seen it coming.

The elevator sounded off. A clamor echoed from inside it. The doors opened, and Ortiz and I barged in to the dismay of the exiting people. The lift emptied, leaving just us.

I eyed Ortiz. "I don't suppose you have Ashton's number."

She shook her head. "I knew him vaguely. We weren't close. I bet Anna had him on speed dial though."

I blinked, reaching into my pocket for her phone. The device had held up better than I had. Some of the plastic sported little chips and nicks. The screen was lined with hairline cracks, but it displayed well enough. I thumbed through her contacts. Thankfully, monsters didn't bother with obscuring info.

I dialed and put the phone to speaker.

The line rang for a three-count before going live.

"You know you could've contacted me through any mirror. Why bother with a phone?" said Ashton.

He thought it was Anna.

"Sorry, Anna can't come to the phone right now. She's stuck in a permanent selfie. Don't worry though; you'll be joining her soon enough."

Silence. Kind of figured. It's not every day you tell a monster you trapped his partner in a piece of glass. Maybe they made a Hallmark card for it.

Ashton finally got his wits together. "You."

"Me," I chirped. "Surprised?"

"A little. I expected Anna to have taken care of you."

"Well, she tried. Doesn't count for much though, does it?"

"Not since she failed, no."

Brr. Cold.

No loyalty among thieves.

"Well, here's your chance to do the job right. All you have to do is tell me where you are, Ashton."

"Is that all?"

"Yep. I'll even bring myself over there wrapped up for ya—bow tie and all."

"Well, when you put it like that, how can I say no?"

Ashton's voice was all ash and grit.

A pained whimper made itself barely audible through the line.

My breath solidified in my throat. I had a bad feeling about that.

"Quiet, you'll get your turn." Ashton's tone made it clear that wasn't directed at me. He was chiding someone else.

The elevator hit the lobby, and the doors opened.

Part of me felt glued in place, but I followed Ortiz out and took the phone off speaker. "Who else is there with you?"

"That's a loaded question. Let's see…" He trailed off, and I could imagine him pausing on the other end for effect. "There's Ariel, fit little number. You remember her."

I did.

"Oh"—a finger snap echoed through the line— "Caroline. That's right, your lovebird."

I gritted my teeth, glad that I'd taken the phone off the speaker. Ortiz didn't need to hear that.

"Well, I should say Daniel's quick flame. Looks like that burned out fast. Back to the Fed? Tell me, does she bring out the cuffs—"

"Shut the hell up."

"Touched a nerve? Shouldn't bother you much. You're only borrowing his skin, right?"

The phone squirmed in my hardening grip. "Keep talking. When I find you, I'm going to leave you like I did Anna. Trust me; it's not pretty."

"Speaking of pretty, there's someone else here too. Yeah, we're admiring the art together." He broke off and muttered something I couldn't make out. "Kelly, that's her name. Know her?" His voice made it clear he knew damn well that I did.

Plastic and glass cracked, and the insides of my fingers ached. I loosened my grip on the phone. A rainbow-like blur washed through a portion of the screen. "Yeah, I know her."

"I found her trawling your gallery alone. It's not safe to go out by yourselves these days, especially in a world of monsters. Didn't you tell her that?"

I quickened my pace, giving Ortiz a silent look that told her to hurry up. We bustled by the front desk, heading towards the lot. "I did warn her."

It was the truth. I'd told Kelly to stay as clear as she could of this world. It didn't make things sting any less. She was in trouble because of me.

We went through the sliding doors and entered the lot, hitting the pavement hard and fast. Ortiz's car wouldn't be parked far.

Ashton inhaled deep enough to come through the line. His breathing sounded like he was excited. "I almost thought it was you, you know? I felt Kelly ringing out through the Neravene like a trumpet—so clear. All those questions she wanted answers for. Needed answers for. She was willing to do anything for them."

Was?

I faltered for a step. Ortiz's battered sedan came into view.

She sped up and crossed over to the driver's side as I hustled over to the passenger's. We entered in unison. Ortiz didn't wait for me to buckle up before she started the car and slipped it into drive. Tires screeched as we pulled out fast.

"What did you do to her?" I kept from squeezing the phone any harder.

"Nothing, yet." Ashton's voice was a bit too put on.

I didn't buy it.

"She's a little roughed up at the moment, nothing too bad. I just wanted to make her more receptive to my offer. I can give you everything you want. Anything you want to know—all of it." His last two comments were obviously addressed to Kelly.

"Yeah, and a Nigerian prince has a million dollars for me!" Kelly cracked back.

I snorted. At least she was okay enough for snarky retorts. It also made it clear she wasn't going to take his offer. Small relief.

A sharp smack sounded off.

Asshole.

"She's stubborn. No worries. I've enticed people far more resolute in their convictions. I've been doing this for quite a while."

"Everyone's got to retire sometime." I placed a hand on the speaker to keep him from hearing the next bit. "Ortiz, Dan's art gallery—fast. He's got Kelly and the others there."

She gave me a wide-eyed look before snapping her attention back to the road. Her foot stomped the accelerator.

The sudden burst of speed sent me back against my seat. I pulled my hand away from the speaker. "Don't hurt them."

"That almost sounded like a plea. Try again. Don't hurt them, why? Give me a good reason." Ashton was probably smiling at the other end of the line.

"What do you want, you freak?" I shot Ortiz a glance—a silent request for her to step on it.

She did.

"I want you. I want them. Why settle? I've always been able to have and give it all. I'm going to make you pay for what you did to Anna. Maybe after I'm through with you, and if I'm satisfied, I'll think about letting the others go." Ashton's voice was all acid.

I took note of the venom in his words. He was riled up, meaning he could be made emotional. He cared about Anna, enough to get angry. Angry people—and monsters—could be manipulated. I could work with that.

I cleared my throat, weighing my next words carefully. "I'll be there." I didn't expect him to honor his bargain, but then, I didn't plan to lie down and die for him either. He didn't need to know that detail.

"You've got thirty minutes. Don't be late, or I'll start pushing the girls harder. One of them will break and give in. I don't like torture, but some people will sell their soul just to make the pain stop. Thirty minutes." He hung up.

Plastic and glass gave way as the screen crunched completely. "Dammit!"

Ortiz stared at me in silence.

"We've got thirty minutes to get there, or else Kelly…" I trailed off.

Ortiz reached over and squeezed my shoulder. "We'll make it, and then we'll stop this thing. We've done it before. We'll do it again."

"Thank you."
She said nothing, but smiled and gunned it.

Chapter Thirty-Nine

We pulled up to the studio. Pale morning light gave the place a cool, muted look. The glass panels added to that.

Ortiz unbuckled and leaned over, reaching past my lap.

"Uh, whoa there. You haven't even bought me dinner—ow." The area above my hip throbbed as Ortiz's fist pulled away from the spot.

"Smartass." She opened the glove box, pulling out my journals and tossing them into my lap. "Hold those a sec."

"Yeah, sure." I ran a hand over the journal containing all the lore I'd come across. There was something warm and comforting about holding it again.

Ortiz rummaged through the compartment, pulling out a rectangular box made of hard, black composite plastic. She thumbed it open. Two loaded magazines lay inside. She fished them out, stowing them inside her jacket.

I watched her quietly for a second before my mouth got the better of me. "And for your next trick...pulling a bazooka out from under your seat?"

"After putting up with your world, believe me, if I could, I would." She cracked a smile that set me off into a torrent of laughter. Ortiz joined in.

I lost track of how long passed before it died into a series of light huffs and snorts. "If you ever do get a bazooka, dibs."

Ortiz let out one last laugh before cutting it off and giving me a somber look. "No. You razed a hotel to the ground—"

"Did not! Almost, the caveat matters."

"Almost, fine. And you did that without an explosive weapon."

I sniffed and turned my head to look out the window. "You're never going to let that go."

"Never." Her smile widened.

"I can live with that." I stowed my journals in the compartment and held out a hand. "Mind giving me a piece?"

Ortiz tilted her head to the back seats.

I followed the gesture and grinned. Something sat wrapped in a small plastic tarp across the backseat. Ortiz had likely hidden the weapons from earlier within the bundle. I could work with those.

Ortiz seemed to have read my mind. "You know how to use them?"

I stared at her.

Her face was a neutral mask, but a light gleamed in her eyes.

"Yes. What do I look like?"

The light grew, and the corners of her mouth twitched. "You don't want me to answer that."

I glowered. "Ha, ha. Very funny." I reached back and flipped open the canvas, grabbing the pump-action. A quick twist followed as I maneuvered an arm through the weapon's strap. My fingers scraped against the end of the compact machine gun, and I pulled it into my grip. A gentle itch filled my left forearm.

My tattoo changed. There was no way we'd lost an hour on our way over here. I'd been tracking the digital clock housed in the car's center console. We had ten minutes to spare, meaning I'd arrived back in the mortal world a bit into the last hour.

Sixteen left.

I crossed my fingers that I wouldn't need 'em.

Ortiz caught my look. "Let's hope we won't need that long."

I nodded.

She reached over and tugged on the submachine gun, and I arched a brow. "Maybe someone with more firearms practice should use this?"

I opened my mouth to protest, but thought it over. She had a point.

Machine pistols and the like looked great and fun to use on television. In reality, they were different animals. Sure, they could rain down lead, but that doesn't do you any good. They excelled in coordinated, short bursts to pepper targets.

Otherwise, you ended up with a spray of bullets that would turn innocent bystanders into Swiss cheese.

I forked over the gun. "You okay using this? I know you've got problems hauling these things around." I gave her a sympathetic smile.

Ortiz gave me a feral grin as she took it from my grip. "For Kelly, yes. Now let's stop this thing."

Worked for me.

I checked the pump-action, satisfied it had enough shells left in it for me to wreak some havoc, I swung open the door. "Let's." I stepped out, keeping the weapon low and tucked to my side.

It's not recommended to go out in broad daylight toting weapons in front of an art gallery. That sort of thing gets you funny looks.

Ortiz did a better job of making her way towards the front entrance while concealing her weapon.

Showoff.

We exchanged a quick look at the door. A beige canvas hung inside the doors with a hastily painted message across it.

"Closed?" Ortiz quirked a brow and looked at me.

I shrugged. "Good way to deter random people from coming by. I bet you the door's unlocked."

Ortiz pursed her lips before frowning. "No deal. People see a sign saying an expensive gallery is closed, they'll listen. Five bucks says he's expecting us to come in the front. I'm betting ambush."

"Not taking that action. You're probably right."

Ortiz smiled.

I tried to match it, but the fatigue was getting to me

My healing abilities can only wash away so much. Right now, they were taxed stitching me back together from my fallout with Anna.

I flexed both of my hands, grimacing through the light twinges. They'd recovered enough from the battering. The part of my shoulder Anna had bitten no longer sported angry puncture marks. A row of purplish bruising was the only sign I'd been injured there.

Ortiz nudged me with an elbow, giving me an inquisitive look. "You alright? You look…" Her mouth twitched, but she didn't continue.

"Tired, beaten, sleepless?"

"Like shit. But those work too."

I gave her a strained smile. "I feel like it. I'll recover as more time passes."

She pursed her lips. "That's not a healthy way to do this kind of work. You'll run yourself into the ground, and next time you might not get back up." Her voice took on a leaden weight.

"Tell me about it. But that's what it is. Ortiz, I'm literally occupying someone else's broken body. It's already done with and by all rights should be in the ground. When I'm stuffed into one of these things"—I tugged the neck of my shirt—"they often end up in worse shape than they were before I came along."

"I figured. Doesn't change that fact that you're wearing my friend's body. It's him—a part of him, anyway—that you're running ragged."

Jab.

She wasn't wrong though.

Ortiz folded a corner of her lower lip, chewing on it for a microsecond. "I'm sorry. That was harsh. I'm just worried. You're no good to anyone if you burn out. Whatever you may be able to do and come back from, there are limits. You have to have them too."

Twist.

Right again. I did have limits, and if I was lucky, I'd never have them fully tested. Hell, I'd come close over the years. But there's always that extra step you never want to be forced to take to find out what those limits are.

"You're right." It came out rougher than I'd desired. "We'll talk after this is through. We agreed on that much earlier, yeah?"

She nodded.

"Let's just figure a game plan to get us through this and then deal with whatever comes next. There another way in?" An image flitted through my mind the second I'd finished asking the question.

A path ran along the left side of the building. It led to an emergency exit on the first floor. A keypad access hung near the door, allowing it to be opened from the outside without tripping the alarm and alerting the authorities. It'd also let us get by any measures Ashton might have set up to watch or booby trap the front entrance.

Ortiz opened her mouth to speak.

I waved her off. "Never mind, got it." I tapped a finger to the side of my head. "Dan's memories."

Her nose twitched, and a corner of her mouth quirked. "Showoff."

I gave her a more authentic grin than I'd managed before. "Come on." I hustled to the side of the building, following the wall about two-thirds of the way to the back of the structure.

A simple steel door, generic gray in color, barred our way. Just like in my vision, a keypad of the same metal and color hung beside the door.

I flipped the latch holding its cover in place and opened it. A standard ten-digit number pad sat in place. An endless amount of combinations were possible, and we didn't have the time to guess through them. I shot Ortiz a look.

She shook her head.

"Damn." I took a page out of Ortiz's book and chewed on my lip for a moment. The temptation to point the shotgun at the pad and blast it away was awfully tempting.

That sort of solution works great on television. In reality, it'd draw the cops and leave the door non-operational.

I brushed my fingers against the cool metal buttons in the hope of coaxing something out of Daniel's buried memories.

It worked.

The sheer tactile sensation dredged up an act conditioned to be near automatic for him.

My index finger acted of its own accord, jabbing the buttons in perfect imitation of the sequence I saw in my mind.

A minute dot, nestled within the pad, flashed green.

I placed a hand on the door and tugged it open.

Ortiz lingered, staring at the pad before turning her gaze to me.

"What's up?" I pushed the door open further as a silent invitation for her to hurry up.

"The code you entered—it's the date Daniel took me out for the first time." Her voice was the definition of forced neutrality.

Awkward.

I couldn't imagine the thoughts and emotions running through her. So, I did the next best thing. I held my hand out, letting the door rest against my hip. "Come on, we've got people to save. Let's go be big, shiny heroes." I stretched the goofiest grin possible across my face.

She rolled her eyes, but took my hand and followed me inside.

I squinted down the darkened hallway, trying to gauge what was ahead. Overhead lighting flickered in the throes of dying out.

Great.

Long, dark hallway; shoddy lights; and a monster was about.

"Side-by-side, stay a step ahead of me, and keep the shotgun high." Ortiz moved a foot to my right and back a step. She sunk her weight a bit.

I didn't argue. It was a smart tactic. One that allowed us to move down the hall without putting one of us in another's line of fire.

We moved in tandem through the hall. The sporadic bursts of fluorescent lighting played hell with my vision.

All I needed now was for a giant freaking bat to jump me in the dark.

I felt a small pang of sympathy for the goons jumped by Batman in the comics.

"Except you ain't no Batman."

Ortiz stopped, giving me a look. "What?"

"Nothing." I picked up my pace, taking long strides towards the end of the hall.

"Tell me you have a plan that's more than us shooting everything we have at Ashton." Ortiz's voice was cool and level, but I picked up on a note of something underneath. She was anxious. She'd never been a fan of going in unprepared.

I couldn't blame her.

"I have a plan."

She bristled. "Is it one of those plans I'm not going to

like?"

I fought not to smile. "Yeah, you're not going to like it."

Ortiz stifled a groan. "I thought as much. Let's hear it."

"I'm going to drive Ashton into the Neravene, trap him, and get him to null all of his contracts."

She didn't miss a beat. "That easy?"

"Hell no. Easy's got nothing to do with it. I don't have an option. Besides, I've got a feeling Ashton's already set up a way for him to bolt if things get hairy. In fact, I'm counting on it. And it's the only place a Faust's really vulnerable."

"As in killable?" She kept her gaze fixed ahead, but it felt like part of her managed to eye me as well.

"I think so. I didn't get a chance to test that out. What I do know is they can't take as much of a licking in there."

"I hate that place."

So did I.

We came several steps from the end of the hall. The room ahead was unlit and too far back into the gallery to receive any sunlight from the front windows.

Wonderful.

I held up three fingers for a countdown.

Ortiz nodded.

I folded my middle finger. My ring finger next.

My heart felt like it beat harder in the moment before I lowered the final finger.

I curled my pinky finger and made a fist.

We stepped into the room, my hand smacking against the side of the wall in search of a light switch. I found it and gave it a quick flick.

Light flooded the room.

Someone shrieked.

A sectional wall sat in the center of the room, leaving enough space to look past it and into the room where the scream had come from.

The area was much like the others. Canvas paintings, works in pencils and pens, and some physical pieces as well. An oversized mirror hung on the far wall. It was framed in old, worn wood and stretched wider than several canvas pieces put together. The thing looked like it'd been picked up secondhand from a yard sale.

I broke into a singsong voice. "One of these things doesn't belong."

Ortiz glowered at me then tilted her head to the monster in the room.

Ashton stood near the far wall in his human form. Caroline sat with her back against the same wall, a dozen feet from the Faust. Her hands and feet were duct-taped. Mascara bled from her lashes as tears streamed over her cheeks.

It was easy to see why.

Ariel, the brunette fitness video blogger, was a living piece of abstract art. Her body was bound to a rack made of metal pipes much like the piece I'd trashed in my tussle with the troll. Her wrists and ankles were the only anchor points, leaving much of her body limp as it hung from the metalwork.

That wasn't all.

Blood pooled from a fresh gash in her throat.

Ariel didn't struggle. She didn't look like she was capable of putting up much of a fight anyhow. Dark bags hung under eyes like she'd gotten the worst night's sleep. Her skin quickly lost its color.

We were too late.

Chapter Forty

Ashton held a folding knife with a serrated edge. Ariel's blood trickled down the weapon, beads dripped to the floor.

My teeth ground, and the shotgun flew to chest level as I trained it on him. I slipped a finger over the trigger going so far as to exert pressure. It wasn't enough to squeeze off a shot, but the urge was overwhelming.

Ortiz hissed, giving me a look that advised restraint.

The small muscles in my hand shook. It felt like someone had flooded my marrow with lighter fluid and ignited it. Part of the rage came from me, the other half from what remained of Daniel.

It's never easy seeing your friends murdered. Doesn't matter if they've asked for it or even dug the hole; it's not something you can lie down and accept.

I exhaled and pulled my finger away from the trigger.

Ashton waved the knife in a gesture of admonishment. "Now, now, not too fast." He held the weapon up, examining it under the light. "You don't want to do anything hasty." Ashton pointed the tip of the blade at Caroline. "She won't come out of this in one piece if you do. Not to mention…" He trailed off and pointed the knife to the far wall.

Ortiz and I advanced slowly, keeping our weapons trained on him.

We passed the wall dividing the two rooms with different exhibits. Kelly sat against the wall Ashton pointed at. She rested on her knees, legs folded beneath her. The left corner of her lips was swollen and discolored.

That wasn't what made my heart feel like a rung bell. Her eyes were wide open, staring both at me and through me. Kelly's mouth hung half-open like she wanted to speak but couldn't find the words. She wore an expression of disbelief, either at her current predicament or that we'd actually come to help her.

My finger twitched, itching to pump as many rounds as I could into Ashton's chest cavity. None of which would free Caroline from her contract or ensure Kelly's safety.

All it would do was piss off the bat.

I put that out of my mind and focused on what mattered: Kelly. "Ortiz, watch him." I nodded my head towards Ashton.

She took three steps away from me, keeping the Faust in her sights while giving me some room.

I took a step towards Kelly, lowering the weapon so its weight came to rest on my shoulders via the strap. "Hey, Kelly." My mouth refused to stretch into a smile. I made it happen anyway.

She licked her lips, casting a darting glance to Ashton. Her shoulders shook once.

What the hell did he do to her?

"Hey." Her voice cracked and sounded like rougher than broken asphalt. "I'm sorry—I—"

"No, hey, none of that crap." I cut a swath through the air with my hand. "I'm sorry for letting you get caught up in this. Don't blame yourself." Every word rang that bell in my chest a little harder. "It's my fault."

Ring.

"I could have sent you home at any time, kept you away from all of this."

Ring.

"I knew something like this could happen." My voice dropped lower. "It always seems to."

Ring.

Kelly gave me a broken smile. There was no light or life in it. "Nobody makes me do anything. I chose this." She forced her smile wider. Her cheeks quivered as she did.

Ring. Crack.

She was trying to make me feel better. The kid was sitting there as a consequence of my world, and she was trying to make me feel less guilty.

My hands balled into fists, shaking at my sides.

"She's right, you know?"

I turned to Ashton.

He waggled the knife again. "She didn't come here

because of anything to do with you. Okay, that's not entirely true. She did. Curiosity is one of the greatest mortal pushes. It drives them into all sorts of dangerous things. They just have to know." A Cheshire-like grin spread over his face.

Ortiz took a series of smooth, almost gliding, steps in a semi-circle towards Caroline.

Ashton pivoted, stretching out his arm to point at Ortiz with the knife. "I wouldn't." He looked over his shoulder without turning. "Don't feel too guilty. Kelly wanted answers for herself. She wants to be a part of this world. That's what I gave her."

My heart fell into the pit of my stomach. There must have been a look on my face, because Ashton sensed what I was thinking.

"Oh, no. She hasn't made a deal, yet." His smile grew. "I just decided to show her what monsters were like up close. I gave her a peek at some of what this world has to offer. The ups, the downs. How rough it can be."

I pointed the weapon at him. "Yeah? Do tell."

"I gave her a taste of what she wanted. Showed her all the knowledge she could dream of. Every bit of the paranormal world. And then, I took it away." He tapped the side of the knife to his temple. "The mind remembers, you know? There's a part of her that's going mad at the fact she knew it all. Somewhere buried inside her, at one point at least, were all the answers to all the questions she ever had. Well, many of them anyway."

My finger exerted a modicum of pressure on the trigger again. Blowing him away would only jeopardize Caroline. She was too close to him. It wasn't a stretch to believe a Faust would be able to take a slug or two to the chest and still make it over to her in time to kill her.

I didn't need any more dead bodies. Not if I could help it. "And you just took those away from her? You ripped memories, knowledge, thoughts, right out of her freaking mind?"

He nodded. "It sounds a great deal more violent when you say it like that."

Ortiz took another step, trying to position herself between Caroline and Ashton. "I could show you violent." She flashed him a wolfish grin.

Ashton shook his body in mock terror. "Oh, I bet." He
hooked a finger to his collar, pulling it like he was afraid.

Ass muffin.

"I just offered what was on her mind and in her heart.
And I did it without charging her. I think that was pretty
decent of me," said Ashton.

"Yeah, you're a real charitable soul. Oh, that's right, you
freaks don't have those. Only way you get them is by
stealing them."

He bucked at my comment. His lips peeled away from
his teeth, the skin under his eyes wrinkling. "Is that what
you think?" He thrust his hand towards Kelly. "You think
we kill people just because?"

I nodded to Ariel.

He waved me off like that was inconsequential.

It wasn't. And I was keeping score. I was going to make
sure he paid for that.

"Making these deals isn't a crime. They give us their
souls by choice. Do you understand that? They are. Them.
We're completely up front about it, what it costs, and when
it's time to pay up. It's not pretty. But for whatever amount
of time they get, they get what they want. They get what
they asked for." His body quivered in rage.

It's always the crazies, the monsters, who get bent out
of shape in self-righteous anger.

"Doesn't make it right." My voice was cold stone.

"Right? Is that what your problem with this is? Right?
What right do you have? This is their choice. Free will.
People make choices that kill them all the time. Drugs.
Alcohol. Stupid, reckless acts. Hell, some of you kill each
other just because you can." He smacked his hands to his
chest. "At least we give them something for it. There's
consent. They asked for this. Each and every time—they
asked!"

"Yeah, preying on desperate, broken people who need a
miracle. You're nothing more than a parasite—a fucking
leech. You and your supernatural skank of a partner find
people so low that they're willing to trade anything for a
little high in life. Something to take the pain away. You—"

Ashton screamed and whipped his hand around. The
knife hurtled free, tumbling towards Ortiz. He used the

distraction to move in a burst of freakish speed and rushed me.

Ortiz reacted faster than me. She twisted and unleashed a short burp from the automatic weapon before the knife struck her. It hit her shoulder hilt first. The speed and impact caused her to wince and stop short with her attack. The rounds cracked into the spot Ashton had been standing in.

Caroline screamed and flinched as drywall and bits of canvas dusted the air.

Kelly kicked at the floor as if she could backpedal through the wall behind her.

I steadied the weapon in my hand.

Ashton zigzagged as he closed the distance, too close for Ortiz to let loose with another salvo without fear of hitting me.

I squeezed the trigger. The shotgun thundered, a round striking Ashton in his core.

He lost his momentum and tumbled back like he'd take a sledgehammer to the chest. The Faust rolled head over heels. He landed flat on his back, looking up at the ceiling and blinking.

I pumped the forend of the gun, ejecting the spent shell. I took a short step towards Ashton, aiming the barrel at his fallen form.

He lay there panting. His hand shook as he tried to bring it to the wound. It was a nasty thing, like someone had driven a spike through a ripe melon, splitting it open. The center of his chest needed more than a few stitches.

It was a good look for him.

"You know…" He coughed blood, choking off any further comment.

"Ortiz, get Kelly and—"

Ashton surged to his feet and drove his palm into the area below my sternum.

The air left my lungs, and I fell to my side.

He followed me to the ground, staying too close for Ortiz to fire.

Smart bastard.

Ashton slid to the floor with sinuous grace and smacked his hand out. The shotgun was ripped from my grip and slid across the room. His wound still wept blood and other internal fluids. Some droplets landed on my new shirt.

Of course.

The torn mass of his chest knit itself together before my eyes. Skin and sinew spread like vines, intertwining until whole. A healthy color flooded the area of gray mass, taking on its original flesh tone.

He leaned in too close for comfort, bringing his mouth close to the side of my face. "That hurt."

I lashed out with a hand, cuffing him over the side of his head.

Ashton growled and got to his feet, hauling me along with him. He snaked an arm around me, holding my back tight against his chest. "Who gave you the right to decide? Why do you get to intervene with free will and what humans choose to do? It's their choice!"

"Dude." I coughed once, trying to work through the pain in my sternum. "Personal space."

"You think you're clever?"

"Funny, Anna asked me the same thing. You should ask her for the answer. Oh, that's right, you can't. I stuck the bitch in the proverbial looking glass."

Ashton's fingers dug into my chest before he let loose a snarl. He shoved me towards Ortiz, staying close to my stumbling body as he advanced.

Ortiz shifted, trying to catch me with her free arm and fire on Ashton at the same time.

It didn't work out that way.

I staggered a step before falling.

Ortiz sank her weight and reached out to grab me under one of my arms. Her balance was off, and the submachine gun lowered in her grip.

Ashton saw the opportunity and took it. He moved out from behind me, stepping gracefully around Ortiz and driving the bottom of his fist down on her wrist.

Ortiz's face flashed through a series of expressions. Her eyes snapped shut, and she winced as her grip on the weapon broke. It clattered to the floor as she shook her wrist. Her hold on me faltered, and I followed the gun, crashing to the ground.

Ashton didn't let up. His fingers dug into Ortiz's hair,

and he pulled hard.

She screamed, grabbing his wrist with her good hand and wrenching.

He struggled to hold her, leaning back to use the added leverage to haul her.

I panted for a two-count before scrambling to my feet. My fingers dragged along the floor as I snatched up the automatic weapon and lashed out with it. I drove its barrel into Ashton's ribs, breaking his grip on Ortiz's hair.

She found her footing and lashed out with a kick to the inside of his thigh before launching a knee into the underside of his chin.

Ashton's head snapped back, throwing him off balance as he staggered back.

I leveled the machine gun at him and loosed a micro-burst of several rounds.

The Faust shook and toppled to the floor. A fresh torrent of red coated his recently healed chest.

Blood-red was definitely his color. Shame it wouldn't last. The good things never do.

I pointed the weapon at his prone form and squeezed the trigger. A five-round staccato cracked out before the weapon clicked.

Crap. It'd been a stretch to believe there must've been a decent amount of ammunition left in the weapon after the Night Runners had tried to gun us down.

I tossed the weapon aside, falling to my knees over Ashton.

He wasn't breathing. His eyes showed no sign of movement.

I knew better. I balled a fist and drove it into his face. A wet slap filled my ears as my hand impacted Ashton's cheek. I clawed at what remained of his teal, collared shirt, and pulled him close. "You wanted to know what gives me the right to intervene with free will." I punctuated the statement with another blow to his face as I kept my hold on his shirt. "What gave you the right to lure them into temptation? To prey on them at their weakest?" I sank my fist into his nose. Cartilage folded and gave way with a sickening crunch.

The hollowness in Ashton's eyes vanished. A maniacal light filled them. His chest shook, the bullet holes gone, and he laughed. Blood and saliva frothed at one corner of his mouth as a violent cough took over. He laughed through it. "To be tempted is to be human. It's part of you. Your kind always wants something, and you're all too willing to pay the price. Even at the cost of others."

"Shut up." I socked him in the mouth. His lips split, and tendrils of his blood hung between his mouth and my fist as I pulled it away. I shook the fluid clean from my hand.

He sputtered, small bubbles of the saliva-blood mixture formed between his lips. "Feel…better?"

I decked him again. "Getting there."

His chest shook with a deep cough that sounded like it racked his lungs. "I bet." Ashton inhaled a long breath that was more of a wheeze. "You know, it's true though. People are always going to want things, sometimes terrible desires. And your kind has a long history of paying horrible prices for equally horrible wants. Don't believe me, ask Caroline."

My hand froze, and I glanced at her.

Caroline watched us in silence. Her mouth moved like she couldn't find the right words.

"What do you mean?" I kept my gaze on her.

"You never figured out what she asked for, why she's here. Her art career is still in the dumps. I know you know that much. So, what was it?"

Oh, hell.

I thought back to the memory from earlier and the swell of feelings that accompanied it.

Caroline and Daniel were in the hall. Close contact quickly led to a touch of intimacy. A touch that passed as quickly as it'd come.

Her letters came to mind. She'd laid her feelings bare in them. Caroline had also told me that she pulled her art from Daniel's gallery, a place that was successful. There was no financial reason to do that. It must've been personal.

Like having your feelings spurned.

She thought she had something with Daniel. She didn't. Nothing real, at least.

And that's what she had wished for. When it didn't pan out, she pulled her work from his gallery in anger. It wasn't long before her rage won out and she wished for something else.

My face must've shown some signs for Ashton to notice.

"Put it together yet?" He gave me a bloody, macabre smile.

"Caroline, is it true?"

She looked away from me.

Ortiz reached out, placing a hand on my shoulder. "Is what true? What did she do?"

Ashton squirmed in my grip. It was an act. He could've gotten free of my hold if he wanted. "Go ahead, Dan. Tell her."

"Tell me what?" Ortiz's stare bored holes into the side of my head.

I didn't want to answer that question.

But contrary to the Faust's promises, we don't always get what we want. Not without paying a hefty price.

I cleared my throat and looked Caroline in the eyes. "Did you kill Daniel Kim?"

R.R. Virdi

Chapter Forty-One

Caroline's mouth opened and hung in silence.

Ortiz's hand gripped my shoulder tighter than before.

"Caroline, hey, look at me." I shifted my head, trying to get her attention.

She did as I asked, but looked out of sorts. The question had rocked her hard.

"Go on. Tell them. It's all on you." Ashton let his head loll back, glancing at Caroline upside down and flashing her a bloodstained grin.

Ashton's comment prompted Caroline to return to reality, sort of. She blinked several times before speaking. "I... It's not like that."

I let some of the heat and metal out of my voice, hoping the softened tone would encourage her. "Then what's it like? Tell me?"

"Yeah, tell them." Ashton's smile grew.

I released my hold on him, letting him fall flat as I plunged a fist into his gut. "Shut up."

Ortiz squeezed harder.

I faced her and caught her look.

She held my stare before nodding towards Caroline.

The young woman was in shock. The added violence wasn't helping, not with what she'd already been through. Not with what weighed on her conscience, her soul. The extra aggression would drive her back into the shell I'd pulled her out of.

I lifted both of my hands into the air in a gesture of peace. "Caroline, just tell me what happened, please? What did you do? What did you ask for?"

She licked her lips, looking to the fallen Ashton before meeting my eyes again. "Yes."

One word. One helluva damning weight behind it.

"I did. I wanted you dead. I thought you were. When

you came back, I—"

"She seized up is what." Ashton leaned up and slammed an open palm into my sternum.

I gasped and fell back onto my ass, clutching my chest.

Ashton got to his feet and booked it towards Caroline with unnatural speed.

Ortiz moved to follow, but the Faust outpaced her by a ridiculous measure.

He was by Caroline's side before I'd gotten to my feet. Ashton knelt by her, putting a hand on her shoulder that drew a slight shiver from the woman. "She lost her mind when she saw you again." He looked directly at me. "She wasn't too clear on how she wanted you dead. I took creative liberty. It's Queens. Swimming with the fishes seemed poetic for an artist, no?"

I glared.

The look on Ashton's face told me he was enjoying this. "At first, Caroline thought I didn't hold up my end of the bargain. Then she thought I'd killed you and brought you back so she'd have a second chance."

Caroline flinched at the comment.

"It's funny, isn't it? The things humans tell themselves to feel better, to rationalize things. The little lies."

I felt Ortiz stare at the back of my head when he said that. My lies had caused her a lot of pain, confusion, and sleepless nights. Ashton had a point on that, and I had the feeling he knew it. I wasn't going to let it sit though. "Maybe, but we're not the ones using them to pervert people's desires. You take the things they're willing to do and give people a push into doing them. After all, what's the invisible, theoretical soul worth, right?"

Ashton put a hand to his chest in mock indignation. "You're forgetting who asked for my power—twice, in fact." He held up two fingers. "Caroline wanted you. She wasn't content with a little flirt session."

"What?" Ortiz's voice was like a hammer coming down on marble. It cracked through the room and drew our attention.

Ashton took a second to compose himself. "You didn't know." He smiled like he'd come across a juicy secret. "Oh yeah, Caroline traded her soul for something as simple as a roll around the hay with Daniel."

Ortiz winced for a split second that might have gone unnoticed had I not been watching her intently. Ashton's revelation had stung her. I didn't know just how far Daniel and Caroline had taken their relationship, but that was the kind of thing that'd leave a mark.

Ashton caught that and would likely exploit it. "Caroline." He turned his attention to her and stroked her cheek with the back of one of his fingers. "Did it ever get that far? You ever sleep with Daniel?"

Ortiz's hands blurred, and she drew her handgun. She sighted it on Ashton.

I didn't know what went through her mind, but I could guess. "Ortiz, he's too close to Caroline. Don't."

"I don't care." She quivered in place, practically radiating fury.

What?

I gawked at her. "You can't be serious."

Her face twisted in pain before she clenched her jaw. "They killed him, together. She's not any better than him. They're both monsters." Her hands shook, and the gun looked like it wavered more towards Caroline.

Maybe they were both monsters. Sometimes people make the best of those. We've got a nasty history. But we've also got one of compassion, of doing the hard things, even when something easier is an option. Especially when that might bring a whole lot more satisfaction.

I reached out towards the gun. My hand shook as much as Ortiz's grip on the weapon. "Hey, hey." I inched my hand forwards to get her attention.

She took her eyes off the pair against the wall. Ortiz said nothing though.

"Look, I know hearing that hurt."

Her eyes hardened, and she gave me a look that asked the silent question, "Do you?"

"I know it doesn't help that I look like this." I touched a hand to my chest. "But believe me, whatever happened between Daniel and her, it wasn't real."

Ortiz jerked like she'd been shocked.

I followed a hunch and put my hand on the barrel of the gun, brushing it aside. "That's what Fausts like him do.

They mess with your brain. Get you angry so you can't think straight. He wants you to make a mistake like shooting them both. He'll shrug it off. Caroline won't. Then what?"

Ortiz froze. "What?"

"You'll have killed an innocent person. What was her crime? Killing Daniel, sure. Can you prove it to the law? How about to your job?"

She stiffened, and her color paled a shade.

"You'd be killing her in cold blood. I know you don't want to hear it. Hell, I don't want to say it, Ortiz, but she's a victim too. She had her buttons pushed by a freak that's got untold years of experience at this. It's what they do. Didn't you hear him? She sold her soul for one bit of affection—attention—from Daniel."

Ortiz's shoulders sank a fraction. The anger, the stress, and everything that came with it was leaving her.

"It wasn't love. It sure as hell wasn't even real. It just...was. That doesn't make it hurt any less. But don't let him take something else away from you. Something you can't get back. You won't be able to sleep at night if you do this. I know you."

Ortiz cleared her throat and sniffed once. "Yeah, you do." Her eyes glistened.

I convinced myself I didn't see a thing. As far as I was concerned, she'd been stone-faced through all of it.

"Did you hear all that, Caroline?" Ashton cooed. "You're right. It wasn't real. Nothing more than intense infatuation. When she realized it wasn't enough and she couldn't have what she wanted, she came back and wanted to renegotiate." His laugh echoed through the exhibit.

I dropped my voice to a whisper. "If I can get him away from Caroline, can you nail him?"

Ortiz flashed me a look that made me regret asking the question.

Of course. I was an idiot for asking.

"And let me guess, that renegotiation ended up in Daniel biting the big one, huh?"

Ashton inclined his head. "Yeah. Anger is a great thing. Impulse-driven desire to hurt someone, to do something rash. People will give up anything unconditionally."

Oh crap.

I took a step towards the pair. "Caroline...please tell me you didn't sign over your soul just like that?"

Ashton snapped his finger. "That's exactly what she did. It's mine whenever I choose."

Tears marred Caroline's face. Her cheeks were reddened and swollen. "I didn't think it mattered."

People never do.

"I just wanted to be with someone who I thought got me."

Doesn't everyone?

"All I had was my art and you." She sniffed harder.

Sometimes that's all people have. It's not easy, but it's not something to make you want to hurt someone else.

Then again, maybe it was.

"I just wanted something to matter in my life."

Damn, who doesn't?

"Well it doesn't matter now, does it?" Ashton cradled her jaw in one hand.

I blinked, taking a moment too long to figure it out. "No!" I rushed towards him. "Ortiz, shoot!"

She didn't hesitate and fired.

Ashton's head snapped to the side, but not before his hand twisted.

Caroline's head snapped to the left, staring at Kelly. Her eyes almost looked like they shook in their sockets from the violent snap. A hollow look filled them seconds later.

Kelly stared into Caroline's eyes, unflinching.

Horrible things have a way of grabbing hold of you and not letting go.

This wasn't the first time she'd seen something die. But it was the first she'd seen a woman, a human, be killed while defenseless. Cold-blooded murder is never easy to witness.

Instinct told me to not let up on Ashton and drive him into the Neravene any way I could. My humanity, whatever amount of that I actually had, told me to make sure Kelly was okay. And not just physically.

Ashton shook his head clear. Spent lead fell from above his right eye, hitting the floor with enough weight to be heard across the room. He blinked several times before placing his hands against the wall and pushing himself up.

Ortiz timed it perfectly, dropping him with another

round to the skull the instant he came to his feet.

Ashton flopped to the ground.

It wasn't much, but if she kept up the cycle, it'd buy me just enough time. I rushed to Kelly.

She sat unnaturally still.

I came to her side and fell to a knee. "Hey." My hands went to her shoulders, giving her a gentle shake. "Hey, come on. Right here. Focus on me, Kelly."

She came back to reality, squinting hard.

"You're good." I bowed my head, giving her a small smile.

Kelly licked her lips and shook her head. "No, I'm not."

"Yes, you are. Perspective. You're alive. Rattled, yes, but alive. I'm here. Ortiz is here."

Another gunshot drummed behind us.

Speak of the devil hitting the floor.

"See? You're good. I don't need you to be perfect. I need you to tell me you're good and that you're ready to listen, okay?"

"I don't…" She bit her lower lip and stopped talking.

This wasn't working.

I grabbed her hands and brought the bands of duct tape binding them to my mouth. I bit down, using my canines to puncture a hole near the top. My thumbs went to the top of the tape and I tore. It took more effort than I'd thought, leaving me to twist and jerk at the tape. Her hands came free.

"Okay, Kelly, I need you to do something for me. You're stressed. You're overthinking. You need to do something. Your hands are clear; free your legs on your own."

She gave a slight bob of her head and proceeded doing as I'd instructed. Kelly pinched the remaining tape with her nails. She ground them against the material, loosening it enough for her to tear.

Bang.

Ortiz had dropped Ashton again.

I don't know how much longer she could keep it up.

Unless he was allowing it.

Ashton had been putting up nowhere near the fight Anna did. He hadn't even ditched his Skin Sheath.

He was stringing us along.

I turned my attention back to Kelly. "Okay, good. Now you're present. You just freed yourself."

She opened her mouth to argue.

"Nah-uh. Look. You're alive. You're free. You've got friends here. Focus on that. You'll have time to process everything else later. Where are you?"

"What?"

"Where are you?"

She frowned for a moment. "In an art gallery."

"Good. Work through a set of facts you know to be real. They'll help settle your mind."

"Then what?" She peeled away the tape clinging to her skin, wincing through the process.

"Then get yourself the hell out of here!"

Twin percussive beats rang out. Ortiz had unloaded two shots into Ashton.

"I can't."

What?

I stared at Kelly. "Like hell you can't. It's easy. Get up, move them legs, and hustle your ass out of here."

Another shot.

Ashton was recovering quicker.

Another bang.

Dammit.

I gripped Kelly's shoulders. "Look, you don't have to prove anything. Not to me. Not to Ortiz. And most certainly not to yourself."

Her hands came to fall on my wrists. She held me as tightly as I did her. "I do though. To me. I can't explain it."

She didn't have to. I knew where it'd go. I'd been through it myself many times.

"I know all these things are out there. And...I have to know more. I can't let this go. But—"

"But you're scared. You don't know how to process it all yet. Doesn't matter that you did it back in the Neravene. It's new each time. It's over your head. Your body is acting out of control. Your mind's going crazy. And, if you don't get something to hold on to, you feel like you'll drown in all the crazy. That about right?"

"Yes."

Thunder reverberated through the room five times.

Crap. Ortiz was really unloading into Ashton now.

"Fair enough. I don't know what to say, but I've got to say it fast, and I'm pulling things out of the air here." I cast a nervous glance over my shoulder.

Ashton leaned against the wall for support, but he didn't seem too bothered about the bullet burying into him.

"I want you to leave, yes. In part, so I feel better knowing you're safe and can't be hurt. Part of it is that I don't think you should deal with this. It's selfish, not my call, and whatever. I've seen this life do bad things to people. I don't want that for you." My words fell with more weight than I intended.

Kelly froze.

I could see her mulling through it all.

"I know, but I don't know what else to do. So, I have to do something—anything."

That settled it.

Sometimes people reach a point in their lives where they know they're stuck. No amount of self-talk can change that. Something's changed in them. They can't go back to the way things have been. And they sure as hell can't sit on the sidelines. They have to find a way to move on.

This was Kelly's moment.

And I hated myself for it coming to that. But I was going to help her through it.

Another gunshot ripped me from my reverie.

I looked around in panic. The shotgun was half a dozen yards from me. I scrambled for it, grabbing it by the strap and yanking it towards me.

The smart move would have been for me to hold on to it.

Sometimes the smart moves aren't the ones that need to be made.

I reversed my hold on the weapon, handing it to Kelly. "You ever use one of these?"

She looked at me like I was crazy. "Does it come with built-in Wi-Fi?"

I snorted. "No."

"Then, no. I've never used one." She took the weapon from me anyway, holding it like it was far more cumbersome than it actually was.

"Quick and simple then. Don't point it at anything you don't mean to shoot. Point, squeeze, be ready for the kick. Ashton, bad. Me, good. No shoot me." I gave her a goofy grin.

She swallowed and got to her feet. "Okay, I can do this."

I put a hand on her shoulder, reassuring her. "You can do this."

"Shit!" Ortiz's curse prompted me to turn.

Ashton cricked his neck to the side, slapping the side of his head with a hand. Drying blood marred his face.

Ortiz ejected the magazine, pulling out the replacement.

Ashton dragged his hand against his face to remove much of the blood. "I don't think I'm in the mood for any more of that." He charged Ortiz.

I rushed to meet him.

He closed the distance faster than I could move to intercept.

The magazine slammed home, and Ortiz trained the weapon on Ashton with practiced precision. A twin report echoed.

Ashton staggered. The left side of his body was driven back by the shots. The Faust collapsed to his knees but retained consciousness.

Good. This was going to hurt.

I increased my pace, lifting my knee as I came close. Momentum carried me forwards as I drove the bony joint across the side of his face.

He toppled from the blow. Blood pooled from his mouth and once again split lips.

Healing can work wonders. It's also a good way to suffer if you keep getting hurt.

Ashton groaned but managed to get to his side. "You can stop now. Things stop aching and screaming after a while. Eventually, the pain is more like parts of your body going numb. Besides, you know you can't actually kill me?"

Technically. Although I had a theory about that bit, one I had good reason to believe I was right about. It just needed testing.

I was looking at the dummy for it.

Ashton brushed off what remained of his clothing, more for effect than anything else. He got to his feet, eying us. "So, now that you've worked that out of your system, are you ready to hear my offer?"

Ortiz and I exchanged looks.

"There's a reason I haven't killed you yet. There's no doubting I can." Ashton's smile stretched the skin of his damaged lips further than should have been possible. The tissue ripped under the strain, and crimson gushed over his teeth.

Ortiz suppressed a shiver.

"I don't know. I'm pretty sure I can kill the bat." I winked at him.

He tilted his head like he didn't know what to make of that.

I sighed.

"Look, no one here is good to me dead."

I glanced at Caroline, then shifted my gaze to Ariel. I raised my brows.

"I got what I needed out of Caroline. Ariel wasn't one of mine. I just finished her."

Ah. I was right.

"You two made deals then ganked each other's humans. That way, neither of you broke your own word because, hey, accidents happen, right?" I clenched my jaw.

"Anna got careless though. She's new in this business. The girl rushed for souls, trying to make a good impression."

Impression. Meaning there was someone to please. Someone who had a name. One I intended to get out of him.

But this wasn't the place for that.

"Ortiz, what do you think? Should we trade up our souls for one itty bitty wish?"

She rolled her eyes, but a hand went to the chain around her throat and the cross that hung from it. "Only costs me my soul. But I'm kind of using that right now."

Ashton grimaced. "You're joking."

"No shit. I mean, you and Anna have great track records at keeping deals, right? But I'm sure they're swell monsters. I mean, you might just be walking about your business one day, Ortiz, and then bam, a piano lands on you."

Ortiz eyed me and smiled. "I'm more of a drums girl."

"Enough!" Ashton blurred into motion. He reached out, brushing past me and taking hold of the gun. It barked into his hand. The Faust didn't seem perturbed by the bullet in his palm. He ripped the weapon free and sent a furious backhand across Ortiz's face.

I moved to catch her. My shirt went tight around my body. Ashton pulled me close. My ribs screamed as his fist collided with them. His foot caught the back of one my ankles, pulling it out from underneath me. My back met the floor, and air fled my lungs.

Ashton stood over me, bloody lips peeled back in a gruesome snarl. "I'm giving you a chance at something. But if you can't see that, then maybe I should take something from you that will make you want to deal."

Oh shit.

He drove a heel into my gut, causing me to gasp for air I already had an issue inhaling. The Faust planted his foot there before stepping over me and towards Ortiz.

She struggled from the strike, clearly rung.

He moved with serpentine speed, sinking his weight and grabbing the back of her neck. Ashton hauled her up and swung an open hand at her face.

I heard a resounding smack.

Ortiz fell to the ground in silence.

I wheezed in protest, clawing at the ground behind him.

He snapped out with a short kick that drove his boot into her stomach.

She coughed and fell flat. Flecks of blood peppered her lips.

"Now, tell me. What would you give up for her? What's someone else's life worth to you?" Ashton planted his foot against her body and shoved.

Ortiz rolled to her side, a hand falling to her stomach and clutching it in agony.

"Stop it." The words strained my chest, but I had to say something.

"Make me. This is on you. It's all on you. Daniel, or whoever you are now. It's your fault. Give me a reason to make it stop. Give me something worth a damn. Otherwise, she's just another dead human. The world is full of them. Without their souls, they're worthless to me."

But not to the rest of them.

People always have worth. Always.

The Faust pushed Ortiz onto her back with his heel before placing his foot down on her throat. "Make me an offer. Make me a deal—a good one."

Thunder, amplified by a megaphone, filled my ears. Ashton's back exploded, and he was thrown to the ground like a truck had hit him. A grapefruit-sized chunk of his body was missing.

Holy shit!

Kelly stood several feet to our side, the shotgun hanging from one of her hands. She pressed her free hand to her shoulder and rubbed it. "Ow."

What little air I'd managed to suck in left me as I broke into laughter. "Famous last words. 'Ow.'"

"I'm sorry." Kelly shook the weapon like she was terrified of it.

"Don't apologize." I chuckled harder, causing my stomach to tighten. I sobered as I remembered Ortiz and clawed my way over to her.

Ashton didn't like that idea. The Faust had recovered to his feet, still nursing a hole in his body.

Kelly fumbled in her panic, struggling to work the forearm of the weapon to clear the spent shell.

Ashton screamed and leapt towards her. He ripped the weapon from her grasp, causing her to stumble in his direction. With a quick snap of his hand, he batted her to the ground.

She yelped as she hit the floor.

The Faust pumped the shotgun, ejecting the shell and priming a new one. He trained it on Kelly. "No more games. One of you is going to give me what I want."

He was right. And it was going to be me. I couldn't watch Kelly or Ortiz bite it.

"You win. Let's deal."

Chapter Forty-Two

Ashton's mouth pressed tight. He shut his eyes and inhaled deeply. "You're not lying."

"No." I didn't know how his sniff test led him to that conclusion, but I was glad it did. The last thing I wanted for was for him not to buy my words and take it out on Kelly.

"You care about them." His face twisted like he'd smelled wet garbage on a hot day in the city.

"I do."

Ashton scoffed and flipped the weapon in his grip. His arms blurred, pumping the butt of the weapon into Kelly's back.

"Stop, you asshole! You got what you wanted. Leave her alone." I clawed at the ground as I dragged myself towards the pair. Warning bells went off in my head as I pushed myself up. Ortiz was in rough shape, Kelly too. I needed to get Ashton out of here without making things more complicated for either of my friends.

Not as easy as it sounds.

"That makes you weak. Look at yourself. You're beaten. You're angry. And you just sold out. It's all because of them." He gestured to Kelly with a thrust of his chin before pointing to Ortiz.

I folded my fingers, making a fist and pushing against the ground with it. My body felt like it was made of cheap plastic. Anymore effort and I'd crumple in on myself. "You're wrong."

"What?" Ashton looked at me like I'd said something in another language.

Maybe I did as far as he was concerned.

Monsters don't always get the little things about being human. Things like friendship. Things like putting yourself on the line for someone else. It's not rational. It sure as hell isn't safe. But nothing about being human is. Guess that's what separates us from them.

I got to my feet and rolled my shoulders. "People aren't a weakness. Giving a damn about someone—something—isn't a weakness. It's strength. It's why people get up time after time of being knocked down. That's why I'm going to win." I gave him a toothy smile.

The Faust's eyes widened like he thought I was insane, and it was contagious. He recoiled a step, glancing over his shoulder to the mirror against the wall.

That's right. Just play Alice and hopscotch your butt out of here.

Ashton sobered, his jaw hardening. "Win?" He shook his head. "No, it's over. You've already lost." He pointed the weapon back at Kelly. "Unless you'd like to do what Caroline did—renegotiate? It won't end well."

I stretched my smile wider. "No, I'm good. Let's deal."

His eyes narrowed, and he gave me a look of suspicion. "Good enough for me." He bent at the waist, grabbing Kelly by her wrist and yanking her to her feet."

"The hell is this?" I took a step towards him before catching the look in his eyes. It was a silent warning.

"Insurance. I don't like my clients welching on deals." He gave me dirty smile.

"Yeah, because you're such squeaky-clean deal makers." I glared.

Ashton shrugged it off, backpedaling as he pulled Kelly along.

Kelly's face was a worried mask. She shot me a silent plea, asking for help.

She was going to get it.

I followed Ashton step-by-step, taking care not to advance too quickly and spook him into something rash.

He neared the mirror.

I wasn't going let him drag Kelly into the Neravene. Not with what she'd already endured, and certainly not under his terms. Not when that place was his seat of power.

Ashton looked over his shoulder to the mirror and stopped in place.

Kelly stared past me, her face going through a mixture of emotions before a hint of a smile touched her face.

I followed her look, finding myself smiling.

Ortiz shook her head, pressing a hand to it and wincing. Her free hand smacked against the ground, feeling blindly for her gun. She found it, pulling it close.

I turned back, giving Kelly a wink before I moved to the side to obscure Ortiz's line of sight.

Good thing that worked both ways.

Ashton fumbled with his one-handed grip on the weapon and his hold on Kelly. He let the gun go slack, hanging from its strap, before cutting through the air with his hand.

The surface of the mirror shivered like the glass was made of gelatin. The movement ceased as quickly as it'd happened. A prismatic rush of color rippled through the newly made Way, like watching a rainbow pass through glass.

Ashton had a finer touch with opening passages into the Neravene.

The manner in which creatures opened a Way spoke volumes about them. Open one smooth and controlled, it was a fair bet the monster was the same. That meant some things.

Ashton was definitely the one in charge of their operation. He had mentioned that Anna had been impatient. He was the Faust who likely chose to operate in the hospital. Heck, it was likely a moving gig. Pick out an apartment in a busy city or close enough to one, enough people would pass through any local hospital. Prey on the weak.

Easy targets.

He was the freak with the eye on the finer details.

The thing about that is, when you're eyeing things too closely, you miss the bigger picture.

Ashton tugged Kelly, forcing her to come along. His focus remained behind him.

Of course, why bother with the humans who pose no physical threat?

Ortiz was about to remind him why.

The Faust hauled Kelly up to the mirror. He tossed the weapon aside and turned to face us.

"Kelly, now!" I waved a hand to my side, motioning for her to move away.

She screamed in defiance and swiped a hand towards

Ashton's face. Her nails raked his face, drawing a series of angry gashes beneath his eyes and over his nose.

He winced, more in reaction than pain, but his grip weakened.

Kelly shoved him hard and slipped free.

I stepped to the side, turning back and gesturing to Ortiz with a thumb pointed in Ashton's direction.

"My pleasure." She loosed shot after shot into the Faust.

His torso jerked with each bullet. He stumbled back from the impact as she hammered rounds into him.

Ortiz performed a solo percussion beat. A staccato made solely of the sound bang drove the Faust up to the mirror. Another trio of bullets hit home before one found his forehead.

He tumbled through the glass.

Ortiz and I wasted no time catching up to Kelly.

I placed a hand on her shoulder, but my attention was fixed on the still open Way. "Are you good?" I caught a silent nod out of the corner of my eyes. "Good."

Ortiz stepped in front of me, her gun pointed at the mirror like she anticipated Ashton returning. "Kelly, go home. He and I will take care of this."

"No, we won't." I pushed gently against Kelly's shoulder, making it clear Ortiz should step away.

Ortiz raised a brow. "What?"

I matched her expression, quirking a brow of my own. "How do you feel?"

She squinted, unsure of what to make of my random question. "Like I was the piñata at my quinceañera—wrecked by a bat. I feel sorry for the piñata now." Ortiz gave me a thin, lopsided grin and pressed a hand to her sides.

"Exactly. Look, I don't want to say it, mostly for personal health reasons, but you look like crap."

She glared.

"See what I mean? In all seriousness though, you don't bounce back like I do. I'm made to take a beating, and this is one you don't have to take any more of."

She opened her mouth to protest, but I waved her off.

"I need you to do something more important. Wait

here."

"That's it?" She gave me an oblique look. "You want me to sit here and do nothing while you go finish this?"

I shook my head. "No, I want you to make sure Kelly's safe and stays that way. Once I go through there"—I pointed to the Way—"I want you to watch it carefully. If it looks like I'm not coming out after a reasonable amount of time, I want you to shoot it into as many pieces as you can. If you see anything in it, anything freaky or monstrous-looking, blow it."

"But…" she trailed off.

"Yeah, I could end up stuck in there. I'm not a fan of it, but it makes sure Ashton's not coming back that way. You and Kelly will be in the clear for a while. That matters." I gave her a knowing look. "Make it happen, please."

She bit her lower lip and nodded. "Yeah, I can do that."

"Thank you." I didn't look back as I stepped through the mirror. In truth, I don't know if I could've handled that.

The mirror clung to me like an army of small, liquid hands pulling me close.

I didn't fight it.

The world faded, replaced by a familiar scene painted from a palette consisting of brown and gray.

I touched down against soft ground and looked ahead.

Ashton stared back at me from a dozen yards away.

He had recovered while Ortiz and I had our conversation and felt it necessary to put some space between us. He could have lingered next to the Way and ambushed me as soon as I'd stepped through.

Which meant he didn't want me dead.

"What gives?" I turned to my side, eyeing him and positioning myself to guard the Way. If he wanted to get past me and have a shot at Ortiz and Kelly, I was going to make him work for it.

"I take it you're no longer interested in honoring that deal you made?" He gave me a weak smile. The prospect of me backing out on my word didn't seem to bother him much.

"What's in it for me?" I grinned. "You lost your leverage."

He waggled a hand. "Some of it, not all."

Say what?

Ashton cracked the knuckles of one fist in the palm of his other. "I'm patient. I once traded a man eternal life for his soul. Bound his age into a portrait. So long as he lived, I couldn't claim his soul. He thought he was getting the deal of a lifetime. I knew better. The vain guy eventually peeked at the picture and bit it. I got paid."

I blinked. "That was real? That was you?"

He grinned. "All stories come from somewhere. And I know the one you want to hear most."

"Yeah, and what's that?" I took a couple of steps in Ashton's direction. A whip crack sounded behind me. I turned my head without moving my body. The Way had shut behind me. A mirror, much like the ones floating around the rest of the place, hung behind me.

My way out.

Ashton moved a few feet towards me. "You want to know your past. I would too, in your shoes. Now, as you are, you're nothing more than a soul—currency, as far as I'm concerned."

The little shit trumpet.

"What, don't tell me you've convinced yourself that you're something more? Oh, I got it." He pressed a hand to his stomach as if to keep himself from laughing. "You think you're some sort of protector, helping people. Great job you did with Ariel, with Caroline, with the others."

My jaw clenched tight enough that the pressure spread through my gums.

"Or do you think of yourself as something else? Maybe a spirit of vengeance, righting those who've been wronged? Sorry, they haven't been. They've gotten what they asked for. Humans bring about their own suffering. No one does it better." He smiled like he was pleased with himself.

"Maybe so, but we don't need you helping us. So, go fuck yourself."

He puckered his lips together in an O. "Oh, riled up, aren't you? Maybe the problem isn't what you think you are; it's what you don't know what to think. Let me help you by asking the simple question." He cleared his throat. "Do you even know what you are? What or who you'll be tomorrow?" His grin widened. He was taking pleasure in the mental gymnastics he was sending me through.

I'll still be Vincent Graves. I'm not my body. I'm something more.

My fingers flexed. "You're right. My body—my face— will change tomorrow, but I know who I am today. And I'll still be that man tomorrow. Let me show you." I charged him, pulling my fist back. His face seemed like a good as place as any to bury my knuckles.

Ashton stood in place, undisturbed by my rush. "You know what the problem with this form is?" He pinched his forearm and gave a gentle tug.

Uh-oh.

"It's fast, familiar, and easy to move around in. But it's so limiting." The rest of his fingers dug into his forearm. He pulled like he was tearing wrapping paper.

Flesh and gore went into the air. Sinew and deeper tissue followed.

I didn't slow my pace despite wanting to retch.

Ashton tore his Skin Sheath, tossing it aside. The Faust's bat form blurred to the side as I came within reach.

I slowed down and pivoted so not to waste any of my momentum. My fist lashed out in a wide arc, clipping the moving Faust's shoulder.

Ashton grunted and took the blow without pause. He snapped a hand out.

I stepped back as the talons raked the air near me. Rows of heat danced over my chest. "Gyah." I pressed a hand to the area below my collarbone. Strands of crimson acted like weak glue, holding my hand to the sticky mess on my chest. I staggered a step away from the Faust.

He didn't let up, bringing a hand overhead as he attempted to sink his talons into my skull.

I peeled my hand away from my chest and stepped into his strike. Both of my arms went up and interlocked them at the wrists. I caught his blow against the long bones of my forearms. A shock rolled through my limbs, settling in my shoulder joints. I grimaced and pushed back against the devil.

"What are you hoping to accomplish?" His tongue lolled out of his mouth, threatening to touch my face.

I recoiled from it, still fighting against his hand.

The anatomy of a bat isn't that strong. They're built for flight and a select group of things. Combat wasn't one of them. They may be paranormal freaks with monstrous strength, but their body wasn't built to take hits. And in the Neravene, they were vulnerable.

I snapped my foot at the side of his knee.

Ashton growled and twisted away from me, breaking off his attack.

I followed up with a fist into the spot behind his left ear.

A guttural grunt left his mouth, and he fell to a knee.

"It hurts here, doesn't it? Haven't figured out why, but it's not bothering me a whole lot either." I took a step forwards and kicked. The flat of my foot met his face, driving him onto his back. "I'll take kicking your ass however I can."

Ashton's hands raked the ground, ripping loose sediment free. He flicked his wrists. Plumes of debris shot towards my eyes.

I raised an arm to shield me from any of the filth.

A dark shape darted through the cloud.

I raced towards it, but it was gone. Movement at the edge of my vision prompted me to turn in time to catch Ashton vanishing into one of the nearby mirrors. I wasn't going through that again.

I sprinted to it, making no effort to slow as I drew closer. I lifted a foot as I came a few feet from it. My foot crashed into the glass. It shattered the first time.

One down. A zillion to go.

If the freak had nowhere to run, he'd have to stay and fight. That was good news, and bad.

"Bastard!"

I turned towards the direction the curse had come from.

Ashton stood outside another mirror several dozen yards from me.

I raised the index finger and pinky of one hand, putting it behind my head to mimic a pair of horns. I dragged my foot along the ground, kicking up dirt behind me and letting out a sound a bull would make. "Bull. China shop. And you're about to get wrecked."

His eyes went flat, and his lips pressed together. "I

wanted your soul. I really did. It would have been like bottled power—leverage. The things old gods and nameless ones would have traded for you."

"And now?" I quirked a brow.

"I want to kill you." Heat filled his eyes.

"Was...my joke that bad?"

He screamed, crossing the distance between us with blinding speed.

I waited till he was more than halfway towards me before I rushed at him. I leapt into the air and spread my arms wide, hitting him with my shoulder in a tackle that took us both to the ground. "Whoa." I fought to pin his flailing hands. "You're like a bat out of hell. Get it?"

He lunged, snapping his jaws into the meat above my right wrist.

I screamed, lashing out with my left fist and smashing it into his face repeatedly. I kept it up like my hand was a piston of flesh and bone, driving it against his skull. A dull sound echoed like I was smacking a rolling pin into the meat of my palm. "How long can you keep this up?" The last punch forced him to break his clamp on my arm.

"How long can you?" He wriggled a hand free, swiping at me.

"Fwhaa!" I fell back as the claws grazed my left triceps. Ashton would have carved out a mini steak from my arm if I hadn't moved. The muscle burned and quivered, but the wound was superficial. It'd heal.

Most of the previous injuries from Anna had patched up just fine. The ones from Ashton would go the same way, provided I survived my encounter.

I squeezed my injured arm to stem some of the blood loss. It wasn't fatal, but I couldn't afford even that small of drain to my body.

Ashton snapped his jaws at the air like he was testing them out.

"How were the sandwiches?" I flexed my fingers, holding up a fist for him to get the message.

"Funny." His eyes narrowed into slits.

"I can be."

"Let's see how funny you are when I'm tearing your entrails out through your stomach. It'll be a real gut buster of a joke."

I blinked. That was decently clever and all kinds of hellishly disgusting on the visuals.

I pressed a hand to my stomach. "No thanks, just hearing about that is giving me indigestion."

Ashton gnashed his teeth. "Shut up. Just shut up!"

I brushed my thumb along my nose before extending an arm. I opened my palm and flexed my fingers, beckoning him to me. "Come make me."

Ashton inched towards me before turning around and running at full speed.

"Wait, what?" I lunged after him.

It was too late. He'd passed through another mirror.

The back of my neck felt like someone had pressed an ice cube to it. I turned on instinct.

Ashton hurtled through a mirror floating twenty feet above me and dove down towards me.

Primal fear galvanized me into action. I bound away from the impact spot and kept sprinting, trying to put as much distance between us.

Ashton hit the ground, landing on his haunches much like a cat.

I didn't think the Faust's body would handle a landing like that. But then, what the hell did I know about paranormal physiology?

Ashton sprung from the ground like his legs were coiled bands of steel. He tore into a sprint that shamed my own, gaining on me too fast for comfort.

I changed my game plan and adjusted my path. I hurtled towards the nearest mirror and drew my fist back. My knuckles met glass, breaking the sheet without a shard slicing through my skin.

Ashton stopped in his tracks. "What are you doing?"

"I've seen this movie before. Break the mirror, no more dickery from you." I raised a fist and let out a war cry that would have made Bruce Lee proud. Another mirror floated several feet from me, and I felt it could benefit from the same treatment. So I gave it to it.

Ashton roared, breaking back into a sprint in the hopes of catching up to me before I wrecked another piece of his domain.

I stepped to the side, bringing the back of my foot into the mirror. My heel struck and cracked the glass. It remained whole, refusing to give in. I screeched and slammed the back of my fist into it. Glass cried back, falling to the ground. "How many of these do I have to break before you've got no place to run?"

Ashton leapt and slashed the air in front of me, hoping to take away a good portion of my face.

I resented that and sank to the ground. He followed me, clawing at my heels as I kicked against the ground to backpedal away. "How are you still keeping this up? Heck, why can't you take a beating here, but you're shrugging off bullets in the mortal world?"

He didn't relent, swiping at the ends of my feet. "This is where we feed. This is where we open ourselves up. And soon, I'm going to open you up as well."

Ah. Like what had happened with Anna when she'd ingested a soul. They could eat and likely exchange power here. That meant they were open to harm as well. Whatever magic held them together, protected them in the mortal world, didn't do squat in the Neravene.

Curiosity sated, I felt it was a good idea to put the kibosh on the bat. I rolled over and put the front of my feet against the ground. I pushed off like an Olympic sprinter, heading for something that had just come into view.

A broken mirror about forty feet away. Something I hadn't broken in my battle with Ashton.

I wondered if the Faust was up for a little reunion.

Steel wrapped around my arms in the form of Ashton's hands. He had caught up fast and gripped me tight.

My arms felt like they were going to burst from the pressure. I lowered my head before rocketing it back, striking what I believed was the front of his snout with the back of my skull. The blow rocked me, sending my vision into a flash of black that took its sweet time recovering.

Ashton groaned, loosening his hold on me.

I wriggled free and took a set of awkward and unbalanced steps. Nausea racked my gut. I'd rattled my noggin harder than I thought. Cold instinct pushed me to break into wobbly jog that steadied as I ran.

I was too close to screw this up now.

Bits of mirror lay scattered on the ground. Some pieces sat in front of another mirror.

I doubled my pace, casting a wary look over my shoulder.

The Faust had vanished.

Great.

I came to the closest piece, smiling when I noticed another of the same size nearby. "Hey, Anna, long time. Miss me?" I scooped up the piece nearest me and flashed a smile to the piece a foot away.

The glass harboring Anna flashed like it contained a weak light. "I'm going to get out of here—"

"Yeah, yeah, and when you do, I'm dead. Heard it before." I touched a finger to my bleeding muscle and scrawled along the backside of the glass. The memory of the symbol eluded me, but I did my best. I'd find out soon if it was good enough.

A bone-rattling scream came from my side.

I gripped the glass in my palm like a makeshift dagger and turned.

Ashton hurtled out of the intact mirror hanging beside me. His hands wrapped around my throat and he took me to the ground.

Too soon. Too soon!

I bucked, shifting my hips and sending a knee up. It struck him where one of his kidneys would be. I threw my arms around the back of his head, clinching him tight and close. The move kept the mirror shard to his back and away from any unnecessary risks. Breaking it wasn't an option.

Ashton's hands scrabbled against my sides. Box cutters ran down my ribs as he raked his talons along them.

I screamed and dug deep into my dirty fighting playbook. My arms squeezed tighter, pulling Ashton close. I leaned forwards, opening my mouth and sinking my teeth into his shoulder.

He screamed so loud I thought it'd carry out of the Neravene and spook dogs. Ashton slammed his palms into the side of my ribs, heating up the already burning cuts.

I gasped, letting go with my mouth and falling to my back.

He broke contact and rushed past me.

I had an idea where he was going.

Anna still needed some time in solitary to think about what she had done.

I rolled onto my stomach and reached out with a hand. My fingers closed around his ankle, and I pulled hard.

He stumbled, falling to his knees and casting an angry look at me.

I gave him a goofy smile and waved with the mirror piece.

The Faust spat at me and turned towards Anna. He lunged, threatening to drag me with him. His claws tore into the ground, and he worked to rake his way forwards.

I used him like an anchor, hauling on his leg to pull him back as I brought myself forwards.

Ashton howled in defiance, rolling onto his back and kicking at me with his free leg.

I moved to my feet, scrambling over him. I trod over one of his wings, making a point of stomping on the thin bone connecting the membrane to the limb. Something cracked underfoot.

A pained wheeze left his lungs. Moisture lined the Faust's eyes.

There's a level of pain so hard to process that you can't make a noise when it happens. And I'd just introduced Ashton to it.

Live and learn, pal.

I moved over to Anna's fallen and trapped form, scooping her up with my other hand. I spun on a heel, facing Ashton.

He glared at me, tears matting the fur around his face. His chest expanded noticeably like he was seething. "Give her to me!"

I waggled the piece of glass containing Anna. "Uh, gonna have to go with no on that one. You two can have your playdate after I'm done."

His lips peeled back, and surgically sharp teeth welcomed me.

I licked my lips. I just had to get him a bit angrier so he'd be off his game enough to fall for it. My hand clenched the newly symbol-covered piece of glass. "Quick question."

Ashton glowered and snarled incoherently.

"I'll take that as a 'Shoot'"

His look intensified.

"The Night Runners, what'd you offer them to come after me? What good's a soul to them?"

"Nothing," said Anna. "But favors are. We have all sorts of credit built up among humans and other creatures. People desperate for an extension, willing to do anything to get it. Creatures that feed on souls gain power from them like old gods—those favors carry weight."

I bet they did.

Anna went on. "And everyone that has half a brain is looking to curry favor with the Peddler and—"

"Shut up!" Ashton's bark drowned out whatever else Anna had to say. "You talk too much, you greedy pig. You're the reason we're in this mess."

The shard holding Anna quivered in my head like it was angry. Anna puffed up inside the glass. "What did you call me?"

I buried their conversation. I so didn't need to be playing paranormal couple's counselor. "Both of you, shut the hell up, or I'll break Anna into so many pieces that not even Humpty Dumpty will be able to put this bitch back together again." I held up the backside of a mirror piece to Ashton, making sure he couldn't see the side harboring his Faust friend.

Ashton bristled. Anna did the same respectively, vibrating the mirror shard in my right hand.

I walked over to Ashton, kicking up under his chin. The tip of my shoe connected, snapping his head back. It wouldn't do much in the long run. I didn't need it to. I just needed to keep him down and weak for as long as I could.

Anna swore at me.

I ignored her. "Next question. The Night Runners didn't set Milo up to die, did they? That was you." I stared at Ashton. "You two were each other's proxies."

Ashton gave me a look that said it was obvious.

That's what I thought. The Night Runners were there to throw me off my game. Truth be told, the move had worked.

Ashton shuddered, coughing up blood and bile.

I had to say, with everything the Fausts had been

responsible for, it felt damn good seeing him hack up his insides.

It didn't last as long as I would have liked.

He clawed at the ground, getting to his feet with a running start.

I backpedaled but wasn't fast enough.

His palm rocketed into my chest.

I hit the ground like I'd been bowled over by a pro football player. The back of my right shoulder cried like it'd been wrenched from its socket. I rolled over and onto my back, breathing hard.

Ashton sauntered towards me, savoring my predicament. "Give me Anna."

"Sure." I tossed him the mirror fragment from my left hand.

He caught it mirror side up, not bothering to look at it.

"One last question, Ashton."

The Faust cocked his head.

"Mirror, mirror, on the wall, who's the douchiest of them all?" I smiled, waving the mirror piece with Anna in my hand.

Ashton looked down at the piece he held.

Anna screamed a warning.

Too late.

Ashton's fingers fixed to the broken mirror, refusing to let go. He outstretched his arms like he could push the glass away. It held firm, pulling his thumbs into the reflective lens. He screamed in protest. "I'm going to—"

"Kill me, I know. Your girlfriend threatened me with the same." I got up to a sitting position and leaned a forearm against one of my knees. "I'd tell the two of you to get a room, but I think I just gave you one for eternity. Sounds like you two have a lot to work out anyhow." I tossed the mirror containing Anna at Ashton's feet.

He looked to her in panic, falling to the ground and trying to pick her up.

It's hard to do that when your hands are being sucked into a mirror.

Take my word for it.

Ashton's arms sank into the glass up to the elbows. The process continued much like before but with an added twist.

The smaller piece forced the Faust's body to contort and press tight without regard for his mass and bone structure.

Joints screamed and cracked as he was crushed by an invisible compactor and forced to fit into the confines of the small mirror.

I winced and turned away.

By the time I looked back, Ashton had gone the way of his friend. I breathed a sigh of relief and went over to them.

Both of them unleashed a torrent of profanity that garbled into an unintelligible mess.

I bent at the waist and retrieved both mirror pieces. Every inch of my body flared in heated agony and dull throbs. Now that the fighting was done, every bang and dent called out loud. I stood still, just breathing and trying to will away the pain.

Anna and Ashton bickered all the while.

The lovebirds and their arguing went to the back of my mind as I trudged towards the mirror I had entered from. A silent prayer went through my mind in the hopes that Ortiz hadn't blasted the other end of the Way to smithereens.

I wasn't fond of the idea of being trapped in the Neravene with the blathering bats for all eternity.

The mirror drew closer, and Ashton grew loud enough to drown out Anna. "How did you know I was the other Faust?"

I exhaled as fatigue threatened to overtake me, but I didn't stop moving. "Anna slipped up."

The piece of glass housing her shook in silent rage.

"She let me know she wasn't alone. After that, it was simple. I put together what I'd learned about Fausts. You do the mortal thing really well, but your eyes are a shade off normal. Too much orange in that brown. You both smell the same, and I caught that same scent in all the places you two had been. Then in your apartment you had the candle. Good way to drown out your own stink."

Ashton's mirror shook harder than Anna's.

I imagined him glaring at her. "Not to mention she was in the hospital when Renee died, but I saw her in the Neravene. That means she held her contract and that you ganked her. I saw the mirror on your cell phone. You two also both vanished near instantly when I first met you. Anna used her makeup mirror, and you used your phone, didn't you?"

Both went quiet.

I took it as a yes.

"You know, I am pretty good at this investigator stuff. For all the rumors you've heard, you should have put more stock in that one. I—" My voice died out when I saw the figure lingering near my way out.

A young boy, one I'd seen not too long ago in a hospital bed.

Timothy.

Except he should have been alive.

Chapter Forty-Three

Fatigue fled my body, washed away in a sea of bone-deep anger and adrenaline. Glass cut into the soft tissue of my palms as I squeezed harder than necessary. "Which one of you?"

Ashton and Anna stayed quiet.

Timothy looked around as if he were lost.

I guess he was.

He didn't seem to notice us, even when he looked right through me.

I felt like the shattered bits of glass lying around. "Which one of you killed the boy?"

Silence.

It was a stupid question. Ashton had claimed his soul, meaning he had dealt with the kid. A kid!

I dropped both pieces of glass to the ground.

The Fausts yelped in surprise.

"What are you doing?" they asked in unison.

"What did you promise him?" I kept my eyes on Timothy, using him to fuel my rage.

Ashton sputtered before coming clean. "How do you think he got that joy ride? It was an easy mark."

Easy...

A kid.

"I set it up for him. He sold his soul for a drive. What does it—"

Glass crunched under my heel as my foot ground Ashton into nothingness.

Anna screamed.

It didn't last. I buried my heel into her piece as well.

I walked by Timothy and reached out to put a hand on his shoulder.

He looked right into my eyes.

I froze and couldn't meet his gaze. I looked away. "I'm

sorry, kid. I am so...so sorry." I concentrated on the mirror, staring deep into it in the hopes that it'd open before I would have to look at Timothy again.

It didn't.

The Neravene had a cruel sense of humor.

I held my gaze, desiring to be away from where I was. To be with Ortiz and Kelly. To make sure they were safe. Hell, a part of me wanted to see old Goldilocks after this and have him utter some pseudo-philosophical bullshit to me.

The mirror shimmered and flared into life. A Way opened.

Son of a bitch.

I gave Timothy one last look. "I wish I could take you back."

My words fell on deaf ears. The kid looked at his surroundings, unsure of everything.

I licked my lips, unable to bring myself to utter another apology. Looking away was easier. So I stepped through the mirror.

* * *

The art gallery welcomed me. I wish I could have said it was a warm one.

Ortiz sat cross-legged on the ground beside Kelly. Their gazes were fixed to the mirror almost like they hadn't registered my appearance from it. The shotgun lay across Kelly's lap. One of her hands rested on it.

I flashed them a lopsided grin and waved.

It took them a moment and a quick exchange of looks before they pushed themselves up.

My forearm tingled, prompting me to give it attention. Two hours had passed, but it was over. I held my stare for a five-count. The tattoo faded.

That warranted a sigh of relief.

Ortiz approached first, throwing her arms around me and squeezing hard enough to make me worry about my battered body.

"Okay, okay." I winced and eased out of her grip.

"Good to see you too."

She grinned and jabbed me with a fist.

I winced harder.

"Baby." Her grin widened.

"Pfft. I just kicked Ashton's ass. That's Monster-Slaying Baby to you." I matched her smile.

"So, it's over?"

I nodded.

Ortiz's shoulders sank. She looked as relieved as I felt.

Kelly slipped by her, eyeing the mirror behind, then me. "Really?"

"Really. It's done." I licked my lips, wondering how much to pry into the young girl's thoughts. She'd been through hell.

But sometimes, that's when you need someone to stick their hand in and pull you out.

"How are you holding up?"

She shuddered and glanced at Ariel. Her gaze shifted to Caroline before I could say anything to reassure her. "I'm..." She trailed off.

"Hey." I gripped her shoulders like I had done earlier. "Congrats."

She blinked. Her mouth moved without sound as she tried to dig up words she didn't have.

"You did it. You made it through your first monster shit-fest. You did good, kid. Now this is where things get complicated."

Her mouth twitched. "Now they get complicated? What about the ninja assassin cats, and the ball, and"—she flailed her arms at our surroundings—"and this?"

"The easy stuff." I gave her a knowing look.

Her eyes and mouth went flat.

"It's the truth. The hard part is remembering." I touched a finger to my temple. "This stuff will stay with you. But here's the thing. You can walk away now. It's over. And for you, that can be permanent. The choice now is, is that what you want?"

She looked to Ortiz as if asking for help.

Ortiz met her stare but said nothing. She understood the importance of the matter, especially with everything we'd just been through. It came down to one thing: choice.

This was Kelly's call. And whatever that was, it'd carry consequences. Good or bad. Likely both.

"I...I don't know." Kelly looked between the both of us for an answer.

I gave her a gentle shake. "Right answer."

"What?" She looked taken aback.

"Yeah. That's about the smartest thing you could have said. You were curious and jumped in feet first. Rookie move. But you did your best. You made it through, and you helped when you could. Heck, you saved Ortiz and me by putting a hole in Ashton when you did."

She beamed. "I did, didn't I? Total badass."

I squinted and eyed her sideways. "Don't let it go to your head."

She rolled her eyes.

Kids.

"In all seriousness, you showed that you're a lot stronger than you give yourself credit for. Heck, most people are and never know it. Now you do. There's a power in that, Kelly. Just keep that in mind and use it right, okay?"

She nodded and turned to Ortiz, giving her a self-satisfied smirk.

What the hell; she'd earned it.

I turned to my side, pushing the women from my mind for a moment. There was one other person who deserved my attention. Well, Daniel's at least.

Ortiz saw what I was up to and stepped towards me.

I held up a hand. "It's okay, I just...I have to."

She paused, then took a step back. Ortiz understood.

I knelt by Caroline's side and placed a hand over one of hers. I'd seen all manner of new things in the Neravene, and some of them had got me thinking. Maybe there was a way Caroline, or a piece of her, was out there somewhere—watching. It wasn't out of the realm of possibility as far as I was concerned. She needed to hear what I had to say.

"I don't know if you can hear me, but I sure as hell hope you can." I kept my voice to a whisper only Caroline could have heard had she still been alive. "I'm sorry. You didn't do right by the people in your life, but you didn't deserve this." I squeezed her hand. "Wherever you are, just remember this. Don't make deals with the devil. They're better at them than you, and they never play fair." I lifted my hand, brushing my fingers across her eyelids to shut them.

Getting to my feet was harder than it should have been, like I was carrying a backpack full of bricks.

Ortiz slipped a hand under one of my arms, helping me up.

"Thanks." My voice came out like grated stone.

"Sure." She nodded towards the hall we'd entered the gallery from. "We should go."

I looked back to Ariel and Caroline. "Yeah. How are you going to explain them?"

Ortiz swallowed, then bit her lip. "I'm not. I can't."

I stared at her.

"This world, this whole mess"—she released her hold on me and ran a hand through her hair—"it's not something I know how to fit into my world yet."

I stayed quiet.

"How do I explain this? How do I make sure justice is done?" She stressed that word. "Everyone who made a deal is dead or won't talk." Ortiz meant Eddie, the sole survivor. "The Fausts are trapped—"

"Dead. They're dead."

Ortiz stopped, giving me a hard look. "You killed them?"

I told her about Timothy.

Her gaze fell to the ground. "Oh. I can't blame you for what you did. I wanted to do the same to Ashton when he said those things about Dan and Caroline. Hearing what she did to him and what she wanted from him." Ortiz shook.

"Yeah, look how that turned out for her." I cast the dead woman a final look. "I suppose the only thing more tragic than selling your soul is the moment you realized you gave it away for nothing."

Ortiz turned on a heel and walked towards the exit. She'd heard all she needed and wasn't keen on hearing any more.

Kelly glanced at me as she set after Ortiz. She walked away with the shotgun hanging from her shoulder. Kelly's posture was straighter, her back tighter, and her shoulders pulled back.

She'd come out of this more confident than she'd come in.

It wasn't much, but I took the small blessing.

I followed both women out of the gallery and to the sidewalk.

Ortiz popped her trunk, ushering Kelly over. She took the shotgun from the young woman and put in the trunk.

Kelly stood in place, shifting her weight awkwardly like she was waiting for something.

I eyed her, then Ortiz. "Something up?"

"Will I see you two again?" She looked to both of us.

I gave her a goofy smile. "Do you really want to? You know what that would mean? Monsters, magic, mayhem."

She snorted. "Yeah, it's like a roleplaying game with a lot more danger. But I think I'd like to."

This case had taught me something. Don't push your friends away. I'd done that, kept them in the dark, and it'd come back to bite me. Kelly didn't need to get involved in this world, but keeping in touch wouldn't hurt. Because if you ever need them, your friends can't do much to help if you don't let them near.

"Yeah, Kelly, I think I'd like that too."

She gave me a wide smile and bobbed in place like she was torn between giving me a handshake and a hug. The awkwardness won out and she turned without giving us either, hustling to her car parked further down the street.

I placed a palm against my face, shaking my head. "She's not much of a people person, is she?"

Ortiz laughed. "She's a stay-at-home hacker. I think she takes online classes. People aren't her thing."

I guffawed and made my way to Ortiz's passenger side, getting in.

She hopped into the driver's seat and gave me a long look. "What next?" Ortiz started the car and put it into drive before I could answer. She pulled away from the curb, fighting the wheel before leveling it out.

"Take me to church."

Ortiz stared at me. "I'm not a fan of that song."

I snorted. "No, an actual one." I gave her the address of the church I'd officially started my case at.

Her mouth twitched, but she didn't question my

request. "You know, I remember the first time I met you. You brought me to a church then too. There was someone there." Ortiz pressed her lips together and frowned. Her eyes narrowed like she was fighting to recall something. "That's weird. I know there was someone else there. I can't picture him though."

I kept my mouth shut.

Ortiz muttered to herself, trying to make sense of what she'd seen that first time. Something about it was comforting.

I let her voice and musings pull me to the sleep I needed.

Fighting monsters is tiring work.

Chapter Forty-Four

An ungodly horn sounded, ripping me out of the blissful black.

I jerked awake, the seatbelt snapping back and holding me in place as I thrashed. "Who the what now?"

Ortiz broke into uncontrollable laughter, doubling over and shaking against the steering wheel.

I glowered at her and thumbed the release of my seatbelt. The high road would've been ignoring her childish prank.

Sometimes the high road's the one that's less traveled. Taking it easy for once was appealing.

I leaned over while she remained hunched over the wheel. My hand went out, slipping carefully through her open arms, and I pressed my fingers to the horn.

It sounded again, causing her to snap back like she'd been punched square on the nose.

She scowled at me but didn't say a word. Ortiz unbuckled her belt and moved to exit the car.

I reached out and grabbed hold of her shoulder. "Don't. Please."

She froze. "Why not?"

I arched a brow. "Truth?"

"It wouldn't hurt." Ortiz tilted her head, eyeing me.

"Because I'm going in there to die, Ortiz."

She looked away.

"You knew that was going to happen eventually, right? Look, I know you want in on all of this. You want to keep helping, and hell, I want your help."

Ortiz glanced at me, a light smile touching her lip. "Good. About time you realized that. You need it."

I tried not to laugh. "Yeah, I do. But the thing is, this job's done. That means I have to move on." I pressed my lips together and swallowed. "That means Daniel's not coming along. A part of you knew that when I came clean back in his apartment. You'd been looking into this for a while now. You know how the bodies I borrow end up."

Ortiz nodded, her gaze flitting away before returning to focus on me.

"If you come with me, it's going to rub salt in a wound that I'm not so sure has healed. Ortiz, you'll be coming to watch your friend's body die for the last time."

Her lower lip folded back and she chewed on it. "I know, and I know you're still holding out on something." Ortiz's eyes narrowed a shade.

Gulp. That was uncanny.

I waggled my hand in a gesture she'd recognize. "Maybe, but it's a secret."

Her eyes narrowed further. "You're lucky you're hurting, and that you're in Daniel's body."

I raised my brow higher. "Or else?"

"Or else I'd break that hand." A wolfish smile spread over her face.

I stopped waggling the hand. "Uh, right. In all seriousness, Ortiz, you've been through a lot recently."

"I can handle it." A familiar fire returned to her eyes, and her jaw hardened.

"I'm not saying you can't. I'm saying that I don't want you to have to. Got it? Look, let me spare you this. Maybe it's not so much about you as it is me?"

Ortiz caught onto what I was getting at. She blinked twice. "Oh, God. You still feel guilty, don't you? You think it's your fault for my being in the asylum, for everything I went through here. You blame yourself for me finding you in Daniel's body?"

I didn't want to answer that.

"Vincent, I forgive you." She reached out and placed a hand on mine, giving it a gentle squeeze. "I forgive you."

A lot of the weight in the world, some of the worst of it, can be lifted by those three words. Believe that.

Forgiveness is a power all its own. It isn't easy to accept, and it's endlessly hard to give. But it's powerful. No question about it.

Learn to take it when given and to give it when, and if, you can. Life's easier that way.

I cleared my throat of the imaginary blockage. "Thank you. I needed that. Doesn't change my answer though. I don't want you to see this. Sue me for not wanting to put you through watching your friend leave you again."

Her smile stretched wider, coming across like it was forced. "Like you could pay me if I did sue." The fake smile was definitely for my sake, but a hint of light reached her eyes, adding a bit of warmth to it. "And I'll be losing two friends if you think about it."

She was right.

"But I have a feeling you'll be back?" She gave me a hopeful look.

I answered with a goofy grin and a thumbs up. "Count on it."

She nodded more to herself than me. "In that case, here." Ortiz twisted in her seat, reaching around and behind her. Something crinkled. Ortiz lifted a brown paper bag, smaller than the sort kids used to carry lunches. She had her index finger hooked under the twin twine-like handles and gave it a jiggle. Something rustled within it.

"Oh, you shouldn't have." I threw a hand to my chest in a mock dainty gesture.

She rolled her eyes, passing it to me.

"What is it?" I took it from her and moved to open it.

"Not here. Wait till you're inside."

I gave her a look but didn't argue. "Okay." I fetched my journals from where I'd left them in her car and opened the door. Part of me wanted to stay there and talk with her. I heeded the other part and stepped out, not wanting to delay this any longer.

"Vincent."

I stopped and looked over my shoulder. "Yeah?"

"I know what you're doing. He's in there, isn't he?"

I let my face slip into a neutral and innocent mask. "He?"

"That's why you don't want me to come in there. It's the person I met the first time. You have someone else working with you on these. Fine. I can live with that. But you know I'm going to figure it out, right?" She gave me one heck of a grin and the look to match it.

I found myself smiling. Church had said something

about that. "Yeah, you ever think that maybe you're supposed to?"

Her expression faltered, replaced by a puzzled look.

I turned back and left her to it, walking towards the cathedral doors. "See ya!" I waved my bag hand without looking back.

A horn honked twice in reply.

I reached the doors and pulled one open with my free hand. A soft warmth, the kind you get from opening an oven or sleeping in freshly-laundered blankets, rolled over me. I embraced it, letting it ease my aches.

I put a hand to my mouth. "Yoo-hoo, Blondielocks, I'm home."

No reply.

Maybe the blonde jokes were getting to him?

I released the door, letting it drift shut on its own as I walked through the place. My journal-filled hand tapped against the pews, and I went as far as drumming the books gently against the wood. "I hear they're having a two-for-one glasses sale at—"

"Hello, Vincent."

"Screw me silly six ways to Sunday, and it's only Tuesday!" I spun around. The paper bag cut through the air, sailing an inch from Church's nose.

He remained icily calm. "It's not Tuesday. Tell me more about the glasses sale."

I opened my mouth to speak before realizing what he had asked. There wasn't really a comeback for that.

"It was a joke, Vincent." He gave me one of his thoughtful smiles.

"Leave the jokes to me; they're funnier that way."

"If you say so." His smile didn't falter, but a mischievous twinkle made its way into his eyes.

Jerk.

He moved past me to the next pew, sitting down and gesturing for me to do the same. "Please, sit."

Polite jerk.

But I plopped down beside him, letting the bag and journals come to rest beside me. "So, what's up?"

Church looked ahead, his mouth turning up at the corners. "I suppose I should be asking you that."

Fair enough.

"Uh, well, Ortiz dropped me off. I have a feeling she's still out there—"

"Yes."

I took a breath, trying to calm myself after being interrupted. I opened my mouth to speak.

"Calmness is like a body of water, Vincent. Something disturbs it, it ripples. Give it time, and it will settle."

I clenched my fists and my jaw. "Yuh-huh. Calm, that's me. I'm calm."

"If you say so."

Must not punch blonde and geeky in the face. Hitting people is wrong. But it feels good.

"Vincent, I was under the impression that you spent a great deal of your time hitting things and people." Church's face stayed neutral, but the upturned edges of his mouth twitched just enough for me to notice.

I ignored the part where he acted as if he could read my mind. I was learning to accept it.

"Acceptance is good in many things. It eases some of life's struggles."

A bit. I was learning to accept it a bit.

I exhaled, counting silently to myself before I was able to go on. "I'm pretty sure Ortiz means what she says. She's going to work on figuring you out, Church." I leaned forwards, resting my chin on my hands and giving him a look.

"I'm certain she will do her best. It may well be she figures me out, as you say, before you do." His mouth twitched a fraction again.

I ground my teeth. "Why do I have the feeling you're planning a lot of this?"

Church leaned back and blinked.

He blinked… I'd caught him off guard?

"Vincent, I in no way have planned much of this. We all work within a larger plan. Sometimes we can see parts of it. Sometimes we can't. Most of the time, in my experience, we see just enough of it to influence things on a small scale. We see enough to choose and make decisions. After all, isn't that what much of life is about?" His tone was soft and level, but something was off.

"Yeah, life and my case." I glared hard at him. "You sent me after a pair of Fausts. You know that, right?"

He tensed at the word. His shoulders stiffened, and his back followed. Church's posture became more proper, if that was even possible for someone like him. "I'm aware." The words came out clipped, devoid of his usual light tone.

If I didn't know any better, Church sounded pissed. Or as close to it as someone like him could sound.

"They were taking souls."

"That's what they do, Vincent. That's why you were sent to stop them." Church's voice softened a tad, but it was still off.

"Yeah, but they weren't playing fair. Not that monsters really do. Church, they were double-crossing people. These freaks were making deals then nixing them as fast as they could. It's like they were just trying to rack up a soul count, like—"

Wood shattered like it'd been struck with a sledgehammer.

I looked to the source of the sound.

Bits of former pew fell from between Church's fingers. He flexed them, looking at his digits like he was confused about what had just happened.

I wasn't. He had freaking pulped solid wood with nothing but his grip. Blondie had done it so casually that he wasn't even aware he'd done it.

I scooted away, putting some distance between us. "You okay?"

"Yes. Thank you." Clipped speech again. Church shook his hand free of the remaining particulate wood. He reached up and pulled his glasses free, plucking a handkerchief with his other hand. My blonde, and momentarily erratic, friend, polished his glasses before putting them back on. "I'm sorry about that."

Yeah, so was I. Whatever that was.

"I believe I should explain myself." Church exhaled like the last thing he wanted to do was give me answers.

"I mean, it'd be nice. But then again, you haven't always been an open book. Why break a streak and start now?" I gave a little chuckle hoping it'd lighten the mood.

"They shouldn't have been doing that, Vincent. Taking

souls is a crime as it is."

I started at him. "You do know that monsters do all manner of things they shouldn't, right? And crime, by whose rule? Come on, you know damn well vanilla mortals don't have any way of enforcing any rule over these freaks. Is it wrong? Hell yes. A crime? I don't know."

Church looked at me as if I were speaking gibberish. "It's a crime, Vincent. Take my word for it." His voice felt like it was accompanied by the weight of the world. It bore down on me, feeling like it'd force me through the pew if it kept up.

"Okay." It was all I could say after that.

"The human soul is not a plaything. It is most certainly not cheap currency to curry favors among the paranormal. But that is, however sad, what happens to it as you've seen."

"Yeah. Why?"

He looked at me as if not understanding. "Why what?"

"Why's it even, I don't know, allowed? Why are people allowed to sell it, trade it, whatever?"

"Free will." Church made it sound like it was supposed to answer everything.

It didn't.

"That's it? Because people are allowed to, they're allowed to? That's not an answer. That's just bullshit."

Church held his stare. "It is exactly what it is. People have free will, Vincent. The will to do good. To do and cause harm. To hurt. To live. To learn. To love. They cause others to suffer. Some help others prosper. But in the end, they have the right to live as they see fit and to influence the lives of others. That means for better or worse. It is what comes with freedom. That applies to their soul as well." His lips went tight like he wished that weren't the case.

"Yeah, and look what comes of it. You ever think that maybe free will was a mistake? I mean, there are a lot of good people out there. But there's a helluva lot of bad too."

"No." Church was a resolute as steel on that. There wasn't a question in his mind. He believed in free will, that was the end. "Free will is what drives much of the world, Vincent. One day you'll see that."

Whatever that meant.

"Doesn't mean a lot doesn't go wrong with it. People

make mistakes all the time." I thought of my own.

"They do. They can also use their free will to fix them. To do things to improve the lives of others or to reconcile." He gave me a knowing look.

"This is about me and Ortiz, huh?"

He nodded.

"I don't have the kind of money to pay for that kind of talk, Church."

He smiled. "Consider it on the house."

I snorted. "Thanks. It's a lot to unload."

Church leaned against the back of the pew like he was getting comfortable. The silent message was clear. He had all the time in the world for me.

I appreciated it. Especially since I didn't have much time at all. "I haven't made a lot of good choices recently."

"Who has, Vincent?"

I ignored the innocent question. It was meant to deflect from me, but the truth was, I didn't want to do that. I needed to get this out. "Mine have put people in trouble, danger, worse."

"So have the choices of others." He wasn't letting it go.

"I put Ortiz through a messed-up ringer. Dragged Kelly through the same."

"And you pulled them out of it as well. Stronger, if you hadn't noticed. They will carry scars, yes. What pain doesn't scar? But, with time, scars fade. That is, if you let them." Church sounded like his old self again.

I went on like he hadn't said a word. I'd heard him. Not sure if I wanted to believe him though. He was making it too easy.

In my experience, easy never paid off.

"And sometimes, Vincent, easy is just easy because. That is it. Life isn't always trials and tribulations. You don't always need to suffer. Sometimes the path is smooth. Learn to accept it, and, if you can, enjoy it." He gave me a bit wider of a smile.

Charming jerk.

"Everyone makes bad decisions, Vincent. Everyone. You are part of that no matter how removed you may feel. I know your life and the circumstances aren't easy. I know you feel out of place and not like one of them." He gestured to the cathedral, using the simple motion to imply greater meaning. "You may not have their lives, but you matter in them. You affect them. Change them. You save them, Vincent."

I opened my mouth but shut it as Church gave me a look saying he wasn't done.

"Everyone makes decisions. That is life. You cannot move forwards without choosing to do something. They will have costs. They always do. Everyone will make bad ones that come back to haunt them. How badly they trouble you is in part up to you."

I mouthed something unintelligible below my breath.

Church managed to catch it all somehow. "You opened yourself up and allowed someone in. After so many cases where you have been alone, that was hard for you. You trusted, and you wanted to be able to return that. You feel as if you've failed."

I nodded.

"Vincent, understand this. The people closest to us have the ability to hurt us, whether by intent or not. That is not a bad thing. It's a sign of a good thing. You opened up, let someone in where she can hurt you, and you, her. But that is also where trust is built. The place friendship is built. It goes back to choice. You have a choice, Vincent. You both do."

I licked my lips, not sure of where he was going.

"She forgave you, did she not?"

I inclined my head. "Yeah."

"And now you have to choose whether to accept that, truly. Are you going to move on and do something to earn her trust from now on? Will you move past a mistake that's holding you back so you can continue to be her friend and help her when needed?"

"I think I can do that." My voice was rougher than the shards of crushed wood Church had brushed to the floor.

"Good, because the people who can hurt you are the ones close enough to do it. The ones who can break you down can also build you up. They are the ones that matter, Vincent. They're close for a reason. Love them. Cherish them. Protect them. Hold onto them and don't push them away."

Every word hit a bit harder and deeper than the one

before it. I had the feeling Church had heard and seen a lot more than he'd let on.

I needed to start checking my pockets for a mini blonde and geekily dressed spy.

"Thanks."

"Of course. Now, are you going to ask what you've been holding back?" He smiled like he was in on a joke that I wasn't.

"Well, since you asked." I glowered at him. "One of the Fausts said something I couldn't make sense of. She mentioned a name—the Peddler?"

Church tilted his head like he hadn't heard me correctly. "I'm sorry?"

I repeated the name. "I don't know. But, based on the name and what Fausts do, it sounded like they were working for this Peddler. Maybe something to do with how they've been dirty dealing with souls? The name implies something like a seller. Why not? A middleman? Maybe the boss?"

Church rose from his seat, staring off into the distance.

"Church?"

"You're implying that someone or something, in addition to a pair of Fausts, has been facilitating in acquiring souls fast and for the purpose of pawning them off. Something treating this like a commercial enterprise, whereas Fausts traditionally claim souls for their own power."

I didn't know that last bit. "Uh, yeah."

Church's skin looked like it'd paled a bit too far, coming across like polished marble. When he turned to look at me, his eyes carried too much steel and cobalt to be his normal peepers. It was like looking at frozen lightning.

I shied away from the look.

"This bears further looking into." His face and eyes softened, looking like they'd never changed.

It had been a trick of the cathedral lighting that had led to Church's appearance coming off as so weird. At least that's what I told myself.

"Sure, I'll look into it when I can."

"Thank you." He sounded as if he weren't speaking to me. "Caroline's death bothers you."

I blinked. "Yes."

"Free will."

"So, I was supposed to let her die?" My fingers dug into the pew.

"No, you were supposed to let her live and act by her choices. To do what you could to save her. In the end, her choices decided her fate. And what a poor one it was."

I couldn't argue that. "She wanted the love of someone who'd given his affection to someone else. When she couldn't have that, she'd wanted him dead. In the end, she still ended up alone and without either want satisfied. What was the point?"

"Sometimes taking a shortcut to what you want carries a cost that isn't worth the price. Remember that, Vincent. In all your desire for answers, quick ones at that, don't do anything to jeopardize your future for scraps of knowledge about your past."

"Is that your way of telling me to stop digging?" I stared daggers at him, waiting for him to give the answer I knew he wanted to. But it never came.

"It's my way of warning you to be careful. You wanted to ask me about the Watcher of the Ways, didn't you?"

I had. A simple title Lyshae had mentioned during my case at the asylum. She'd told me that he'd have the answers. "Yes, I did."

"I can't tell you about that, Vincent. I'm sorry."

An edge crept into my voice. "Can't, or won't?"

"Yes."

Fair enough. I was used to that sort of treatment from Church. I changed the subject. "Mind telling me why I've been running around of late with monsters being able to smell that I'm a soul?" I arched a brow, waiting for his answer.

Church's mouth pulled to one corner in a micro-twitch. "Wear deodorant."

Ass.

He pointed to the bag Ortiz had given me. "Besides, you need to focus on something else."

I followed his point, staring at the bag. "Yeah, and what's that?"

"Killing demons today so you can face the devil tomorrow."

"The hell does that mean?" I turned back to face him.

He'd ghosted.

I sighed, looking around the cathedral more on instinct than anything else. It was useless. When Church pulled a Copperfield, he was gone.

Bastard.

I grumbled to myself and sunk a hand into Ortiz's bag. Something crumpled under my grip, and I pulled it free.

A letter.

I scanned over it. The note informed me that the gift inside was from both Kelly and Ortiz. It'd make my life a bit easier from now on and was a way to say thank you.

I frowned and reached back into the bag. My fingers brushed against cool aluminum as I pulled out the slender object.

It was a flip phone. The kind used and sold in bodegas and street carts as disposable burners. They were untraceable, topped up with minutes, and great for guys like me on the go. I flipped it open and thumbed through the contacts. Ortiz's number was there.

I had my own phone.

And it was pink with rhinestones glued to it.

I placed it next to my journals, knowing it'd be taken care of by Church. My soul would leave Daniel's body in the coming moments, but one thing weighed on my mind.

I didn't know what was coming next, but Fausts, trading souls, and the Peddler? Something big was going on with the paranormal in New York.

And if this case was a peek into it, I'd be dealing with darker things to come.

I needed a break.

ABOUT THE AUTHOR

R.R Virdi is the two-time Dragon Award-nominated author of *The Grave Report* series, *The Books of Winter,* and many short stories. He has worked as a mechanic, in retail, and now spends his weekends helping others build gaming PCs, all while continuing to write. An avid mythology buff, he keeps a journal following the fictional accounts of his character, Vincent Graves, and all the horrible monsters he comes across. He lives in Falls Church, Virginia, tinkering with cars, gaming computers, and chasing after his dog.

Thank you for taking the time to read this novel. If you would like to know more about the author, please visit:

http://www.rrvirdi.com/

Follow me on Twitter: **https://twitter.com/rrvirdi**

Follow me on Facebook:
https://www.facebook.com/rrvirdi

If you enjoyed this book, please consider leaving a review!